"Y" city

"Y" city

a novel

By Wade Rivers

"Y" City

Copyright © 2009 by Wade Rivers

Cover Design by Jessica Kinkel.
A special thanks and gratitude to Rachel Felts for her hard work and editing.

Manufactured in the United States of America.

For information, please contact:

The P3 Press
16200 North Dallas Parkway, Suite 170
Dallas, Texas 75248

www.thep3press.com

972-248-9500

A New Era in Publishing™

ISBN-13, Hardbound: 978-1-933651-39-2
ISBN-10, Hardbound:1-933651-39-3
ISBN-13, Paperback: 978-1-933651-40-8
ISBN-10, Paperback: 1-933651-40-7
LCCN: 2009900090

1 2 3 4 5 6 7 8 9 10

Author contact information:
Wade Rivers
www.waderivers.com

For my mother Lorene who I can't thank enough.
As a librarian and a mother, she shared with me her wonderful
enthusiasm and love for truly great stories.

Prologue

There are a lot of stories and folklore in these parts, some true, some a far fetch from the truth. But in these hills, stories are what people live on, the fuel for their lives, their subsistence to get from one day to the next. Nevertheless, there's no story quite like the one I must tell, because it greatly affected my life, as it did so many others around here.

Unless you live here, chances are you don't know about what happened at "Y" City, because we are very remote. "Removed" would be a better word, because it's as if everything outside our area of the planet doesn't even exist. Somewhere in time we departed from the rest of the country, philosophically and otherwise, and there is not any inclination that that will change, at least not in my lifetime.

This part of the country, western Arkansas and eastern Oklahoma, is primarily regarded as the Ouachitas. Time virtually skipped over these hills. For the most part, these are just quiet little towns, beautifully landscaped with the Ouachita Mountains and lots of rivers, ranches, and farmhouses cradled in the valleys. "Y" City is such a town. The mountains come together, forming a narrows with barely enough room for the two-lane highway to squeeze through the shoulders of the hills. Not much is there, a couple of gas stations and a motel, but you'd be surprised how many people stop and sit at a picnic table or toss a blanket on the ground to watch the river cascade across the boulders in the gorge.

"Y" City is aptly named; it's just a fork in the road, and they say everyone is going to go through there at one time or another. People from all over pull over and stop. You see them and their kids parked beside the river. They got their map pulled out and laid across the hood of the car to take a gander. They either go north to Fort Smith, south to Texarkana, or east to Hot Springs. I've seen them toting every bit of baggage they could possibly strap down to the top of a station wagon. I've even seen some in trucks so loaded down, the axle buckled, and yet others seem to have left everything behind. Perhaps what was or what had been was no longer important to them. They took off for some unknown destination, and fate seemed to have grabbed a hold of the wheel and steered them to "Y" City, which is where it just so happens that this story begins, and for some people, it is where their world will end. For the people in these parts, it is place where everyone's life was changed; for no one's life was unaffected by the chain of tragic events that began here on June 22, 2008.

I remember it was hot. Oh, God, was it ever hot! It was eighty degrees at six o'clock that morning, and it was a blazing 103 by mid-afternoon. Word spread like a raging wildfire that something had happened out at the Heaven Falls Ranch, something bad happened that shocked the whole town. Heck, for that matter, everyone from the Texas state line to Fort Smith heard about it. The Heaven Falls Ranch, you see, is pretty well known in these parts. Everyone around here has heard of the Taylor family. They've all driven by the Taylor's massive farm, extending for miles along the highway going into "Y" City. Everyone has heard of Rip Taylor, his fortune, and his beautiful wife. Lots of people have said it is the most beautiful, privately owned piece of property in the whole country. Two rivers join on the property, and on the back mountain a waterfall plunges down a crystal-laden ravine. And though several artists have been commissioned to paint it, other than a handful of workers, few, if any, were ever allowed on the Taylor estate.

And that's pretty much where this story begins, at "Y" City. If you haven't ever been there, chances are you will sometime. People now come from all over to take a look at the place; they drive by and see for themselves. And lots of folks ask me to tell them the story, because I was there that day at the Polk County Jail and was privy to all of the goings-on. I don't want to divulge the circumstances of my presence, but I assure you, I was there. From the moment the news broke till its unfortunate end, I saw or heard everything that happened. And in all my life, I've never seen people so worked up as the day they caught Harley Wright and the Texas Rangers brought him back to town.

Part 1

Chapter One

The folks who arrived early that morning at the jail were probably expecting sirens and much fanfare; instead the cop cars crept into town like a procession of nuns. The city of Mena was still half asleep, except for the two or three hundred people on the courthouse lawn. Their cars and trucks had, even at even that hour, taken every available place around the square.

Turning off Highway 71, the police cars crossed the railroad tracks and turned onto the main street just a few blocks south of the square, still in the shadows of Rich Mountain. There were four cars in all; one Texas Ranger squad car, a Polk County Sheriff's car, and two Arkansas State Police vehicles which had been escorts from the moment the Texas Rangers crossed the Arkansas state line.

A touch of daylight began to break over the city as they drove past the local businesses, heading up to the Polk County Jail. A small group of regulars stood out in front of the Skyline Café, sipping coffee from their Styrofoam cups and leaning against their pickups.

"Here they are," said one.

"There's Harley. That's him!" said another, pointing to the back seat of the Texas Ranger squad car as it passed.

The crowd that had been gathering around that morning was anxious. Folks pointed down the block to the four vehicles as they passed the businesses en route to the jail. Some scrambled to get the best view, pulling out their cameras — most just gawked. A few in the crowd hoisted signs in the air. "Hang Harley!" seemed to be the most predominate theme on the makeshift placards.

It was 6:13. It was going to be a long day, and it was already hot. The night had lent a little reprieve from the sunshine, but not from the heat. It was sweltering; muggy is what we call it. It was not the dripping-down-your-face kind of sweat that you get when the sun is beating down on you in the thick of the day; no, it's just that boggy kind of heat, draining you like a sauna would. Your clothes feel like they do when they come out of the dryer way too soon. They are hot and damp. They stick to your skin, and your body feels like it can't breathe. It is just uncomfortable, and that's how the crowd felt that morning. They were all uncomfortable, restless, and irritable, and the looks on their faces were morose, angry, and sullen — sullen as a cranky old maid on Valentine's Day.

The Arkansas State Troopers got out first, and people from across the street started moving closer. Others raised their kids to sit on their shoulders, and some jumped up onto the beds of pickup trucks to get themselves a better view. And then the shouts began.

"There he is!"

"Look at him. They got him. That's him all right!"

Lucian, the town's notorious idiot deputy, leaped out of the sheriff's car, holding a shotgun. He yelled something, and the crowd started backing off. He pushed his rifle against the chest of Ollie Waites, trying to shove him back across the street — not a good idea. Ollie could snatch that thing away from Lucian and beat him like a snot-nosed kid. Lucky for him, Ollie's wife grabbed her husband's shirt and started tugging on him to get back across the street.

4

Four state troopers cleared a pathway from the street to the jail, coaxing the crowd. "Ya'll get back. Come on. Move along. Ya'll get to see him."

Then, when it had settled down a little bit, the two Texas Rangers got out. They looked around, scanning the crowd. They stood there with the doors wide open, surveying very slowly all the surrounding buildings. Word was out that Harley wouldn't make it to trial, not in this county. With a good scope at a hundred yards, his head would be as easy to hit as a billboard from across the street; that's why they had taken all the precautions. Harley was a marked man.

After a few moments, the driver gave the other Ranger an affirmative nod and they opened the back door. Harley stepped out. He was tall, lanky, and everybody recognized his jet-black hair. His hands were handcuffed behind him, and chains were on his feet.

"You'll pay Harley Wright!" a woman shouted. "You'll rot in hell." Then they all started shouting and commenced to hurling insults and agitations. The Texas Ranger had a hold of him by the arm, and Harley's feet shuffled awkwardly underneath him in a series of miniature steps, as they scurried up the sidewalk to the jail.

One of the state troopers held open the front door, and there was a sigh of relief as soon as they brought him into the main hall. As the door shut behind him, he took a deep breath, and you could see the trace of fret across his brow — the look a deer has when it gets tangled up in barbed wire, like all it's ever feared has come true. It sure didn't make him feel any more comfortable, looking around the room, with six, maybe seven police officers with guns strapped to their belts.

Phones were ringing off the wall that morning as the two burly looking Rangers escorted him down the hall to the booking desk. His chains skidded underneath his long, lanky legs dragging across the linoleum floor, and his head slumbered down on his chest. The phones kept ringing, and it was loud. When they reached the front desk, Lucian jerked Harley's arm from behind. He spoke in halting nonsense, with inaudible mumblings interspersed. "I gonna . . . tak da prisona now."

The Rangers looked at Lucian, bewildered, not quite understanding what he was saying, with the side of his mouth so packed full of tobacco it looked like he had lodged a baseball between his cheek and gum. "Huh?"

Lucian tugged on Harley's arm again ". . . I'm da one in charge . . . bookin' tha prisona."

Harley looked at the Rangers. Then he looked down at Lucian, who barely came up to his chin. Lucian had a bit of tobacco juice oozing out the side of mouth, and he maintained this peculiar look on his face. Harley couldn't help but noticing he was tapping on his billy club.

Harley cleared his voice, "Sheriff."

Hollis Brown, who was sitting on the edge of a desk, turned around. He wasn't the biggest man in the room, but for a guy in his late forties, he was packed. Hollis was solid. You wouldn't ever know that he was the sheriff, because he never wore a uniform, just the badge. He hung up the phone. They looked at one another for a second or two, and then he nodded. Hollis's voice always had a little gravel to it. Some might call it a whiskey voice 'cept he didn't drink the stuff, not in a long time. He cleared his throat, "You've had a long ride haven't you?" Sheriff Brown stood up and walked over to the check-in counter, and the phone rang again. You could tell he was annoyed by all the hubbub in the room.

Teresa, the dispatcher, spun around in her swivel chair and looked at a couple of the deputies standing there. She huffed, "For heavens' sake, I'll get it." Then she put on a healthy-looking smile, "Sheriff's Office, can we help you?"

"Hey, Harley."

"Hey, Hollis."

"He any trouble, fellas?"

"Nope, not a bit. He slept most the way back." Then they chuckled, "He snored from El Paso all the way to Dallas."

"He confess to anything?"

"Nope . . . well, only to being a fool."

The sheriff pulled a pack of smokes out of his pocket and lit up a cigarette. They couldn't help but notice the No Smoking sign hanging on the wall right behind him. He grinned, "Doggone it. I was hoping ya'll would at least beat a confession out of him before you got him here. It would make my job a whole lot easier."

Harley's eyes widened, and the sheriff grinned. Harley couldn't tell whether he was kidding or not, but the Rangers laughed; they thought it was funny. Hollis then kind of waved him on with his hand, motioning down the hall, "Duke, why don't you take our suspect to the interrogation room, and make sure that he gets comfortable before we begin."

Lucian started to say something, but the sheriff interrupted, "And, Lucian, why don't you run down to the Skyline and fetch a breakfast for these two Texans. Ya'll 'er hungry right?"

"Oh, yeah!"

"Thought so."

The one not holding the shotgun stepped forward and handed the sheriff some papers, "We need you to sign these, and we'll bring in his belongings for the inventory."

The sheriff looked at the papers and pulled out his pen. His ashes fell off his cigarette onto the front page, and he flipped it to the floor. He mumbled under his breath, "Take him down. I'll be down in a bit." He looked around at all the deputies standing there with their backs squared and their arms crossed in front of their chests. "Okay, fellas, you've all got a look. You can tell your girlfriends and wives that you've seen him. So let's get back to your stations or go on home. I appreciate your help."

They all began to grumble, but they grabbed their hats and headed for the door. Duke took hold of Harley by the arm, and they started down the hall. Duke looked down at Harley's feet and stopped, "Hole' up." The big deputy turned back around to the sheriff, "Say, Hollis. Does he still need these?"

Hollis peered around the Rangers in front of the desk, inspecting the kiddie walkers chained around his ankles. "I don't know, Duke; he might decide to run again."

Teresa looked up at him and shook her head, "Hollis Brown!"

"Okay, okay, but leave his handcuffs on." He scratched his head and rubbed his chin, "Ah, what was that gal's name?"

"Sadie." She knew what he was thinking. Teresa was like an extension of the sheriff's brain. She filled in all the gaps in his thoughts, completed his sentences for him, and recalled names he had long forgotten. She was like his memory bank. She knew what he was thinking before he even knew what he was thinking, which the sheriff liked, because, with Teresa around, he had to do a whole lot less thinking and remembering. Teresa smiled, cute she was and pregnant. She started snickering, "We had this little ole lady here one time for a check in, and she had those ankle bracelets on. She wasn't but maybe five feet tall, and she was standing right there. We looked away for just a sec, and swoosh, she was gone."

Amused, the Ranger laughed, "We've had a few of them."

"Oh, I bet. We have too, but this lady you wouldn't believe. She was like a jackrabbit hoping all the way down the street." Teresa continued, laughing, "She was four blocks away before they could catch up to her. We had three deputies running after her, but that little thing could skedaddle now. Boing! Boing! Boing!"

They were all laughing, "She was a wildcat, I tell ya."

Duke unlocked the ankle bracelets and tossed the keys back to the Texas Rangers, "And she could bite too."

Hollis Brown handed the papers back to the Rangers, "Yeah, we've got a lot of those jackrabbits around here, and you know why?"

They shrugged. "Why?"

"Because our meth is better than your meth."

They laughed, "I dunno. They cook a lot down in South Texas."

"But, you see, we got the addicts to prove it. Some can run like jackrabbits. Some can fly. One guy was almost as fast as a train."

"Almost."

"Yeah, not quite, but almost. Try making that phone call, 'Hey, Mrs. Roberts, your son, Jess, the local hero and track star four years ago, well we've got him down here at the front desk if you want to come pick him up. Ah, no ma'am, you won't need bail money this time, you can just take him home. He's in a five-gallon bucket with his name on top.'"

The sheriff's face had turned serious, and he took a drag off his cigarette, "Yeah, and I lost two deputies, two good deputies over that one."

Curious, the Rangers asked, "Did they do something wrong?"

"Nope, there are just some things a man sees he can't ever get out of his mind." The sheriff looked around the room and then looked down the hall to Duke, who was still standing there with Harley. His face looked like a piece of stone. There wasn't much expression to it. Hollis then took a drag off his cigarette, "Say, Duke, tell Harley what our new policy is."

Harley shook his legs, as if to get the circulation back in them, "What's that?"

"We don't chase runners no more." His face was stone cold, "We just shoot them."

The two men stared at each other. Hollis Brown had an unnerving effect on people. He was hard to read. He could laugh with you one minute and say something that could cut your heart out the next. Hollis kept people off balance. Sometimes you thought he was joking and he wasn't, and other times you'd think he was serious and he was playing.

These two had known each other for a long time. Hollis had known Harley since the day he was born. They had a few run-ins but not much. You couldn't say that one man hated the other or vice versa, but there was something there. Just as Duke unlocked the big metal door to the interrogation room, Hollis called out, "Hey, Harley."

Harley didn't turn around. He just looked straight ahead. He had a blank expression on his face. Duke, who stood about six foot seven and was pushing three hundred pounds, squeezed Harley's arm in his big hand, "You look around when the sheriff calls your name."

Harley looked over his shoulder grudgingly. You could tell he was pissed, "What is it?"

"Just wanted to know what you thought of your fan club outside."

Teresa reached over the counter and poked the sheriff with her pencil. Her eyebrows furred up, and her lips tightened. Hollis could hear her saying unpleasantries under her breath. Harley pulled away from Duke and started into the room, when the sheriff called back out again. "Oh, Harley, you know another name for those people standing outside?"

Harley rolled his eyes and looked back at the sheriff with a smart-alecky sneer on his face. "No. What?"

"Jury pool."

Duke shut the door. The clang of the metal always had the haunting sound of finality. It was only 6:29. It was going to be a long, tense day. And it was just starting.

Chapter Two

The room showed no signs of enlightenment. Harley sat down at an old oak table, like you'd find in a library, surrounded by four pretty worn out, rickety chairs in the middle of the tiny room. Cinder block walls with about a half-inch layer of semi-gloss off-white paint made up the décor of the small cell. The floor was laid with the standard gray-and-white checkered linoleum tiles that you see in a lot of government buildings, and the metal door was painted gray to match. The ceiling consisted of industrial acoustic tiles with a four-foot, double-bulb florescent lamp. The décor served well its purpose in ferreting out the truth.

Harley looked around the room. He had been there before, but not for anything serious, just kid stuff. He had mostly stayed out of trouble; he tried to avoid it, but trouble always did have a way of following him. He hated the room. He always hated being closed up, but especially there in that room. There was only one window, and that was a small Plexiglas window in the door, which looked out on the wall on the other side of the hall and the curious eyes of the deputies that would peep in to check on him.

Harley was exhausted. He sat down uncomfortably in the chair, with his arms still handcuffed behind him. He sat there alone in silence for at least half an hour before anybody came in. His thoughts kept racing back over the last couple of days, and depression just seemed to swallow him.

How did it come to this? he wondered. *How did I get here?* He would rather be dead than where he was, the interrogation room, better known as the "lying and crying room." Some call it the "I want my lawyer room." Deputies have referred to it as the "I want my mamma room." Hollis Brown always referred to it as the "let's make a deal room." Some deal—ya make a mistake, you're at the wrong place at the wrong time and do the wrong thing, and you pay for it with years of your life. They'll take away twenty and give ya back five. They'll take away your family, your home, your job, and years down the road, when you're all wrinkled up and beat up, they'll kick you back out on the street.

There is no feeling like being there, shoved into that little place, and so a man starts to calculate, wondering how will he get himself out of the mess he's in, but he's got no cards. He's got nothing to deal with, nothing to give back. He's got nothing to offer, except what comes out of his mouth. A man barters for the very years of his life with a little truth, a confession. That's all they want, because with a confession they don't have to have any facts really. They don't really need any evidence; as long as they have a confession, they have a conviction. But in Harley's case, nothing would probably save him. And he knew it.

Harley closed his eyes and said something he had never said before. In a very quiet whisper, he said, "Oh, God, help me." His lips moved, but with all the commotion going on outside, he couldn't hear his own words, it was more like a breath. His body slumped down in his chair. He had that awful pain that so many get when they reach this point. It's indescribable really; it's just a sickness that oozes through your stomach. It feels like there is a hole in your gut and someone or something is pulling your intestines out slowly. It feels like a knotted rope being pulled through your gut. You start to shake. You want to scream. You want to cry, but there is nothing you can do to stop it.

It's called fear.

Harley noticed his hands twitching. He felt cold, but he felt hot. He squinted his eyes and moaned. Outside, he could hear the crowd. Inside, he could see their faces. They were faces he had known all his life, and now suddenly every face he had ever known hated him. There was no one, absolutely no one, in the whole world who would be on his side. He groaned again, and then there was someone at the door. It was Lucian, the half-wit. He was looking in the room. He must have come back with the Rangers' breakfast. Lucian smacked on a piece of bacon and grinned at Harley, and Harley thought to himself, *What is that dimwit looking at? It's just me.*

He could hear him mumbling something, but nothing Lucian said ever made sense, he was practically incomprehensible. As he watched Lucian smack his lips and pick his teeth, he noticed tobacco juice drip from the side of his mouth.

A thought raced through Harley's mind: Maybe . . . just maybe . . . this was hell. This was it. Maybe he'd been shot in the back, down at the Mexican border, didn't even know it. Just died and came to on that long ride back across Texas. It was, after all, a journey through darkness, stopping every couple hundred miles or so to drive through another late-night Taco Bell. Maybe this is where he'd spend eternity — in this little cell, looking at Lucian, the only blibbering idiot who would eat food and chew tobacco at the same time. Makes sense. This could be hell all right; no sane person could dispute that. He marveled at his epiphany-like revelation. "This," he concluded, "is hell, and hell is the Polk County Jail." And to add to the torture, Harley visualized that every day he would be taken into a courtroom where all the people who hate him could make false accusations and slander him all day long. That too would surely be hell. And a group of his peers, neighbors, and acquaintances, could look on with disgust and contempt, or worse yet, apathy, and then judge him for everything he ever did, real or concocted. Didn't matter, he was there to be judged, to be found guilty.

And, yes, his grandmother would be right. She had always been right. She said long ago that this is where people end up when they didn't follow the straight and narrow. Maybe his prayer was too late. Maybe God couldn't help him now. It was all over, the sentence pronounced, only the inflammatory accusations were left to be hurled. "Womanizer!" "Thief" "Adulterer!" "Lazy, no good riffraff." He had heard it all before.

Harley looked at Lucian with absolute repulsion. *This is just too much,* he thought, *way too much for anyone to handle.* Harley leaned forward in his chair and pulled his hands around to the side. "Watch this." He wiggled his fingers as Lucian watched through the window. He wiggled his fingers again, and Lucian pressed his face against the glass to get a better look at the demonstration. Then Harley dropped his thumb, then he dropped his index finger, then he dropped his pinky and ring fingers, and then Harley burst out laughing.

Lucian started ranting and raving and took off down the hall, and Harley just kept laughing. *If this is hell,* he thought, *I might as well have some fun with hell's resident idiot.* He couldn't believe he laughed; he hadn't laughed at anything in days, maybe it had been weeks. He couldn't remember when his life seemed normal.

Just then, he heard the sound of the deadbolt being unlocked. The sheriff walked in. He held a tape recorder in his hand and had a couple of legal pads with him. And Duke, who had to bend his head down just to get through the door, followed close behind.

The sheriff sat down and put the stuff on the desk. He had a humorless expression on his face. "Enjoying yourself?"

Harley had kind of a smirk on his face.

"You know, you'd be a whole lot smarter, Harley, if you didn't think that everyone else was an idiot."

"I didn't say that you was an idiot."

"It wouldn't matter whether you did or not, because your opinion is not something that I have much regard for anyways, but that fella you just flipped off, that fella you call an idiot, just happens to be related to half the county, and if you ever had a shot of getting a decent jury, you just blew it. So who's the idiot?"

"But he is. Why do you even have him around Hollis? Everybody knows what he is. Hell, he is the laughing stock of the whole county."

"If he was, you just happened to snatch first place from him."

Duke laughed. He looked like Hoss Cartwright without the little patent leather vest and ten-gallon hat.

"But Hollis, haven't you ever seen him out on the highway, leaning against the patrol car? He has singlehandedly destroyed tourism. No family in their right mind is gonna stay here with him out there on that highway, gawking and grabbing his crotch, especially if they have a teenage daughter. They gonna pull out the map and find them another town real quick."

All the time Harley was talking, the sheriff was setting up the recorder and putting in the tape. He laid his legal pad out. "Testing. Testing." He put the microphone on a little stand between them. "You through yet?"

Harley slumped back down in his chair, "Yeah. I guess."

"Good, because if you're through, we've got some mighty important business to attend to. You're involved in a high priority case, Harley; in fact you are the only person in the history of Arkansas who received immediate extradition papers from the state of Texas. Did you know that?"

"They told me."

"Good, so I hope you don't mind if I get right to what we need to talk about, and it is a little bit more important than whether a man picks his teeth or scratches his crotch, wouldn't you say?"

"Yeeessss."

Duke leaned over across the table to Harley, "You need to say 'yes sir.'"

Harley sighed, "Yes . . . sir."

Sheriff Brown had his glasses on; he lowered them and looked at Harley. "Look at me."

Harley glanced at the sheriff, and the sheriff snapped, "No, look at me!" The tone in his voice was serious, and he had a way of looking at you that just chopped through the bull. It is hard to explain to a person who hasn't seen him firsthand, but his eyes kind of penetrated people. Even if you started to tell him a lie, you knew that he already knew it. There wasn't any place to run, his eyes just kind of stared you down.

Sheriff Brown picked up his pencil and tapped it. He leaned across the desk to Harley. "I don't personally care whether you call me 'sir' or 'yes, ma'am.' I just want the truth. Understand?"

Harley nodded.

"A lot of people have got questions about the circumstances prior to your hasty departure from 'Y' City the other day and, in particular, from Heaven Falls, and I imagine by now you understand why, don't you?"

Duke sat at the end of the table with his hands folded in front of him. They were massive. Sheriff Brown sat directly across from Harley, sliding the recorder closer to Harley, he began writing some notes. He didn't look up, he just wrote.

"Yes, sir, I know why, and that's why I've come back."

Hollis looked across the brim of his glasses, "Your coming back wasn't exactly voluntary was it?" Duke let out a hearty laugh. Until then, Harley could never quite figure out what Duke reminded him of. He realized Duke reminded him of Jabba the Hutt in *Star Wars*. Imagine Jabba with a trooper hat on, and that is what Duke looked like.

The sheriff gave his deputy a stiff glance. The meaning was obvious, and Duke quickly squelched his laughter. "Okay, I believe we can start. Son, I think you know the gravity of the situation here. While you were in playing games this morning with one of my deputies, I was on the phone with the governor, and I can tell you he doesn't make phone calls at seven a.m. on a Saturday morning unless it is real important to him. He asked me himself when I was going to charge you."

"Why should I say anything to you then? Ya'll already made up your mind. I'm already convicted."

"You're not convicted yet, but if you did those things up there at 'Y' City, you will die. Right now every bit of evidence I've got shows you did it. You've only got one hope if you're innocent; I need to know everything you can tell me. Right now there are just a whole lot of questions about you, and your only chance, Harley, is that you can tell me something that would prove you're innocent. Are you ready?"

"Yeah, but I'd feel a lot more comfortable talking, if I didn't have my arms bent behind me in these cuffs."

The sheriff motioned to Duke, "Take 'em off."

Duke took his handcuffs off, and Harley sighed in relief. He shook the circulation back into his arms and rotated his shoulders back and forth. His arms were long and tanned. With every movement he made, muscles rippled up and down his forearms. He was lean, but his arms were large for his size. Harley hardly ever wore anything but a white cotton T-shirt and jeans, and his T-shirt was a little on the dingy side, which was to be expected since he probably hadn't changed clothes or slept now in two days. His hair was thick, and he immediately began to scratch his scalp like mad.

"Feel better?"

"Man, do I! Thanks, Sheriff. After twelve hours in cuffs, I was beginning to feel numb, like my arms weren't there no more." He stretched his arms out across the table and folded his hands. He had big, boney hands with scars all across the knuckles, probably from fights or from barbed wire. Most cowhands get cut a lot from bailing wire or barbed wire, and their hands are usually chapped. He didn't have any tattoos like most of the people coming into the jail nowadays, and he didn't have any tracks or needle marks. Harley never was a druggie. He never did associate with those kinds of people and had pretty much kept to himself as long as the sheriff had known him. The only trouble Harley had ever been in before were fights, and they were usually over a girl—someone else's girl—and then it was usually two or three of the local boys against him.

The sheriff tapped his pencil on the desk. "You ready to get started now?"

"I'm ready as I'll ever be."

"Good." The sheriff hit the record button, and the tape began rolling. "Are you going to tell the whole truth and nothing but the truth?"

"All that I know."

"Good." Hollis looked over at Duke, "I think I can handle this."

Duke just sat there.

"Alone."

"But . . ."

"Go finish up those morning logs and get started on that inventory report." He turned up the volume on the recorder and Duke left. "Okay now, we are taping an interview with Harley Wright on June 24, 2008, at the Polk County Jail in Mena, Arkansas. Harley, give me your birth date please."

"January 12, 1983."

How old are you?"

"Twenty-three."

"Do you understand that you have a right to have an attorney present and that you have the right to remain silent and that anything you say can be used against you in a court of law?"

"Yes, sir."

"Harley, let's start with the beginning. I want to know everything from the first time you were ever out there at Heaven Falls Ranch."

"That was two years ago."

"Fine, start there." The sheriff leaned back in his chair. "I want you to tell me everything that has gone on from the first time you went to the ranch till the last time you left, do you understand?"

Harley sighed, "Well, that's a lot of time. A lot has happened in two years."

"That's all right, we've got time. We ain't leaving till we get it, but, Harley, you've only got one chance here to tell it straight. I don't do a take and retake. If you start lying you're gonna mess yourself up real bad. Have you got that?"

Harley nodded understandingly and then took a deep breath. There were people walking back and forth outside the room that created a distraction, but Harley looked down at the tape recorder and watched as the wheels turned. It was like he was seeing his life going back in time, rewinding. He wished he could go back. Things would turn out a whole lot different; for one thing he wouldn't be sitting here now. Harley told the sheriff how he had driven out to the ranch that first day.

Leah Taylor was the one who did the hiring; her husband Rip owned maybe fifty businesses and didn't get involved with the affairs of the ranch. He owned a slew of gas stations across western Arkansas, Texas, and Oklahoma. They were called Get-N-Run. He also owned a bunch of pawnshops and Pronto Peso Check Cashing. Rip was a rich man, but Harley was just glad to have his measly ole job. He told Hollis how he had worked at the tire shop in Mt. Ida, fixing flats and changing oil, until Leah's daughter came by one day and told him about her mom needing a mechanic on the ranch; that's how he found out. Hollis kept writing notes on his pad while Harley told how she kept coming by in her little red BMW to get this done and that done. He told how all the guys got worked up when she came by, but to Harley she was just another high schooler.

Sheriff Brown pulled his glasses down to the tip of his nose and peered at Harley, studying his face, "Did she flirt with you?"

"Yes and no. I didn't really know her . . . I mean, everyone knew who she was because she was Rip Taylor's daughter, but that's about it."

"Was there anything going on between you?"

"No." Harley could see Duke's shoulder outside the window. He was obviously trying to listen in. Harley glanced at the sheriff and kind of pointed to the door with his eyes. "She flirted with me, that's all, but not much. They all do."

A deep, muffled voice came from the other side of the door, "Teresa did my report. I'm finished."

The sheriff got up and unlocked the door. "Geez, will you get in here and sit down?"

Duke sat down and grinned. Sheriff Brown locked the door again. The crowd could be heard outside, but nothing audible could be discerned. Harley thought he heard clapping, but he wasn't sure. The sheriff looked back over his notes. He rubbed his forehead like he was trying to concentrate, "Okay, um, you were talking about how the girls flirted with you, right?"

"At that age they all do. If they've got a car and a radio, they are always trying to get someone's attention."

Duke looked at Harley, confused, "What's he talking about?"

"Oh, Duke, he's talking about how all the high school girls flirt with him."

Duke's big forearm came down on the table. "Whadda ya mean? Not Tater!"

By Tater, he meant the pride of his life, the huge apple in his eye— his 220-pound daughter and the high school mascot—lovely Tater who fell in love with every boy mascot who came to town. Only in America could you find a 220-pound, hairy Bearcat mascot chasing a scared, little 120-pound Swamp Rat across a football field on a Friday night. It is not necessarily what you might call great entertainment, but it was certainly amusing, and the love interests of Tater often captivated the halftime crowd a lot more than the marching band.

Harley skidded back in his chair, he thought Duke was about to come across the table for him. "No, not Tater! I promise!" The image of her sitting in the car next to his at the Cruisers drive-in suddenly flashed in his mind. One time she parked next to Harley, and he looked over at her smiling with a triple thick shake in her hand and a French fry dangling out of her mouth. Harley shook his head as if coming out of a bad nightmare, "No, Duke, I never flirted with Tater. Believe me."

The sheriff seemed amused, "By the way, how is Tater?"

"Fine. She's gotta a job at the Burger Joint."

Hollis glanced at Harley. His eyes sparkled, and the edges of his lips curled into a grin. Harley was trying hard not to laugh and thought the sheriff was too. The last thing he wanted to do at that point was offend Duke. The sheriff realized he had better move it along, "Well, that's good to know. Okay, where were we?"

"You were asking about girls who flirt . . . I think?"

Hollis cleared his throat, "What about Leah Taylor? She flirt with you too?"

"No. She wasn't like that. She was just nice. She was a lady."

"Okay, so what happened? Go back to the ranch. Tell me what happened when you first got hired."

"I drove out there that June. It was hot, real hot, remember? I had never been there before, just heard about it like everybody else, and I sorta had a feeling long ago, when I was a kid, that one day I'd be there." Harley took a deep breath and continued, "And as far back as I can remember, I always wanted to work there. I guess I wanted to live there. I can remember driving to 'Y' City and passing by that big, long fence and looking across the ranch to Taylor Mountain. I even measured the fence one time on my truck odometer; it was two and a half miles. So when I drove out there for a job, I was pretty excited and a little nervous. When I turned into the ranch and drove through the big iron gates, I could see the hands out in the field with Mrs. Taylor, and she rode up on her horse as I was parking my truck up by the house. She asked me what I wanted."

"I bet she did."

Harley glared at Duke. "I told her I wanted a job. She asked me if I was good with a wrench, and I told her I was."

"Had you ever met Leah before?"

"No. I had seen her in town like everybody else, but that was the first time up close."

"And what did you think?"

"She was beautiful."

"That's it?"

"What do you want me to say? You now what she looks like. She was prettier than I thought because I had never really seen her up close, face to face, just passing down the road in that old truck of hers or at the feed store with her hands. But when she took off her hat and her hair fell down to her shoulders, I realized that she was drop-dead gorgeous, and I think anybody would say that."

"I'm not asking anybody, I'm asking you. So, were you excited about working at the ranch, or were you excited about working for Leah Taylor?"

"I was just happy to be making eight bucks an hour instead of seven at the tire shop!" Harley was a little incensed by the questioning, but he knew he wasn't in the best position to be getting in the sheriff's face about it. He didn't have the best education, but he wasn't stupid by a long shot. Being a suspect in a high priority case was one thing, but being a mouthy suspect in a twelve-by-fifteen-foot concrete room was quite another. Harley faced the reality of the situation, he was their dog right now, and he was probably going to get kicked around some before it was all over. He wasn't in the best position to fight back, and the only way he was going to get anything was to stay cool.

Harley didn't smoke, but he wanted one now to calm his nerves. Talking about Mrs. Taylor and the ranch had begun to unsettle him. He looked at the pack of Lucky Strikes in the sheriff's shirt pocket.

"Can I have one of those?"

"Haven't you seen the No Smoking signs? You know the rules. You ain't supposed to smoke in a government building, and if you hadn't guessed by now, we ain't letting you outside to have one."

Harley smiled, "Well then, can I have a beer?"

They both laughed. "Well, Harley, we can't do that either, but . . ." he pointed to the tape recorder and slid the pack of smokes across the table to Harley, "they haven't taken away our ability to imagine smoking a cigarette, have they?"

Hollis leaned over, lit Harley's cigarette, and continued talking, "Yes, one day we are going to be a smoke-free society. We'll all be crack heads, meth addicts, on Xanex or cough syrup, overweight, underweight, and unemployed, but we'll be smoke free." Hollis lit himself a smoke, leaned over, and spoke into the machine, "Can't wait, how 'bout you?"

Harley leaned over to the microphone. "Sounds good to me."

Teresa tapped on the door.

Hollis looked at her in the Plexiglas window. "Go see what she wants," he said to Duke.

She tapped again and pointed to the sheriff.

"Sh . . ." Hollis sighed, "I'll be back."

Teresa escorted him down to his office, and they closed the door.

He was glad they went into his office, away from all the phones ringing at the front desk. "What is it?"

She put her hands on her hips, "We're having a bit of a problem here."

"What is it?"

"We don't have anyone after this shift."

"Whadda you mean?"

"Roger called in sick. Thomas said his ex-wife dropped his kids off a day early, and he's got nobody to take them, so he can't come in. Goose just left to go on his vacation to Florida, and Henry was supposed to be back from Guard duty, but he's emailed me saying he's been detained down at Fort Benning." She handed Hollis the chart. "Take a look."

"Hummm." Hollis took a drag off his cigarette and flipped his ashes towards the can. He missed.

"I'd call Wendell at Mt. Ida, but with the way you totally have blown him off the last couple of days, I wouldn't count on a bunch of favors."

"We'll work it out."

She put her hand on her stomach and patted it like she was soothing her baby, "We'll? Are you saying 'we' but meaning me?"

"That's what you get paid for."

"Hollis Brown, don't you get me started. I get paid for being your dispatcher, not your secretary."

"Are we going back over that again?"

"Hollis, what I'm worried about is the crowd out there. It keeps getting bigger, and the people are getting kinda, ah, well they are getting pretty hostile."

"There is nothing to worry about. Geez, I know everyone of them, known 'em all my life. They're just blowing steam. They ain't gonna do nothing." Hollis hugged her, "You stop your worrying; it's not good for you."

She gently pushed him away and went and stood by the door, "This is different, Hollis. I'm getting phone calls, and they ain't saying nice things."

"What do you expect? Harley never was too popular in this town."

"They started about Harley, but now they are about you."

Hollis shook his head. "Me?"

Teresa nodded.

Hollis sat on his desk and flipped his ashes toward the can. He missed again. "Oh, this whole thing is gonna blow over. I've seen 'em get riled before."

She leaned her back against the door. She was pretty. Teresa had shoulder-length brown hair that always managed to get in front of her face, and all the guys thought it was sexy the way she was always having to blow a few strands to the side. She had gained a few pounds, of course, with the baby, but she still looked good, and on a bad day, like this day, just the sight of her made things go a whole lot better. But most importantly, she was the one person at the station who had always looked after him, and Hollis knew it, and he knew to listen to her. Teresa looked down at the floor. "I dunno, Hollis, there is something about this that I just don't like. I started getting these calls yesterday, and I've already had six or seven this morning. These people are mad. What are we going to do if we can't get any relief?"

Hollis shrugged, "Guess I'll lock down the jail, and I'll do it."

"You and who?"

"Just me."

"Are you hearing yourself?" she huffed. "If something isn't done, you're talking about you against the whole town."

Hollis stood up from the desk and handed her back the clipboard. "I've got to get back to the interview."

She stood with her arms folded in front of her, as if blocking the door. "That's it? You're not going to call anyone?"

"I can handle it."

"Why don't you call Sheriff Thompson up at Scott County? He's tried to call you, but you're always too busy."

"I can't call him and ask for help, not after this was put in my jurisdiction. I mean, after all, the reason why I got the case was that we had the bigger courthouse and more law enforcement. We were supposed to be able to handle this better, remember?"

"Hollis Brown," she snapped, "I can't believe you are so damn prideful you won't ask him for help. Have you lost your mind?"

He snuffed out his cigarette in the ash tray. The phones were ringing at the desk, and he looked up a Nehi-sign clock on his wall. It was 8:07. "It will be alright," he said reassuringly, "It always works out. I've been in jams before, and it always worked out."

Her lips were curled up tight, and he could see in her eyes she was mad. "This is different Hollis; I'm telling you this is different.

I've got a real bad feeling about this, and you're gonna need some help, a whole lot of help, before this is all over."

She blew the hair out of her face and stomped back to the dispatcher's desk, shaking her head.

Hollis picked up the Post-it note with Sheriff Thompson's number on it. He reached across his desk for the phone and started to dial, but then he looked at the clock again. He paused. *Later,* he thought, *I'll call him later on. I'll call him as soon as the interrogation is over. The crowd will go; the town will settle down. Everything will be alright.* Sheriff Brown hung up the phone and went back down the hall.

Chapter Three

As you might expect, many things raced through Harley's mind that morning. He felt like he was running lost in the woods and wished he had a compass to help him get his bearings on his predicament and figure out a way out. All he knew was he despised Lucian and he didn't trust Duke, or anyone with a badge for that matter, but in a weird sort of way, he felt comfortable around the sheriff. But then, a lot of people had said that.

He sat there listening to the discord outside; Duke was kinda nodding off in his chair. The noise reminded him of the low, hushed sound that emanates from a seashell. But like waves on the shore, some can be soothing and some can be angry. These were angry waves and, like a tide coming in every few minutes, they seem to crush against the building. That knotted feeling twisted inside every time he heard the roar outside, but as he sat there alone he thought about the sheriff, and for some reason he felt a bit of security being where he was. Had he gone mad? Only a fool would trust a man with a badge.

He didn't know Hollis Brown all that well, but he knew he didn't want to be on his bad side. He heard stories about how he brought in suspects who were mighty beat up, but no one could say that they didn't deserve it. From all accounts, Sheriff Brown did have his days, and if someone got mouthy he'd pin 'im, cuff 'im, and haul 'im in. But on the other hand, he'd be the first to help you fix a flat tire. Every kid who ever drank a beer in Polk County probably had Sheriff Brown confiscate it and pour it out on the ground before he drove them home.

In the very brief visitations that Harley had in the jail — what you might call "overnighters" — he'd heard the lowdown that the biggest mistake people ever made about Hollis was to underestimate him. Fellas told him how he got most of them to laugh their way into a confession, and some got to liking Hollis so much they wanted to brag about what they had done. When he had enough on them, he hit the stop button on the recorder and thanked them for their cooperation. Then he booked them, and to their stunned surprise, he had the last laugh.

Nevertheless, most people in town, and that includes the criminals, generally liked and respected him. Harley never really had any beef with the sheriff that he was aware of, at least not like some of the guys did who occupied the cells on a more frequent basis. There weren't but maybe twenty or thirty guys in the whole Polk County Jail at any one time, and as far as Harley could tell, crime wasn't what you'd call rampant. There were a lot of reasons for that though; in western Arkansas and eastern Oklahoma, nearly everyone packs a gun. Armed robberies were completely unheard of because every store owner had one. And by freak accident, if a store owner shot and missed, there'd probably be ten other barrels drawn on the guy before he made it to his car. He'd become what you might call a complimentary target, courtesy the citizens of Mena, Arkansas.

Lately though, there had been a string of burglaries. They started a couple years back, but were pretty spread out so no one thought they were connected at first. They were random thefts, sometimes it was jewels, sometimes electronics. But after a while, they started to get more regular, and no matter what the store owners did, the burglar never got caught. Some people in the town thought Sheriff Hollis was losing his edge.

Harley sat there and listened to that crowd. The town was in an uproar, and the sheriff was on the hot seat. He was puzzled by how it had turned so ugly so quick, because as far as he knew, the sheriff had always been pretty popular. All it would take to get them to shut up and go home would be for the sheriff to charge him. He didn't stand a chance. He knew how politics worked; Hollis was elected, and they were voters. The only thing that gave Harley some comfort was that Hollis was one man who didn't seem to give a hoot about what other people thought. In fact, he was kind of famous for that.

He heard the key rattle in the door. It was Hollis. He had a thermos of coffee and some cups. As he closed the door behind him, Duke woke up, and by the look on the sheriff's face, he wasn't too happy. He put the thermos on the table and looked at Duke.

"Want me to go and get ya a cot?"

Rubbing the sleep off his face, Duke said, "No, no. I'm fine."

The sheriff poured him a cup of coffee and slid it over to Duke. "It was about ten years ago when a deputy fell asleep over at Broken Bow. When he woke up, the prisoner had his gun pointed to his head. The guy splattered his brains on the wall." Hollis paused. "Shame, huh?"

Duke didn't say anything. Harley gestured with his hands and shrugged his shoulders as he looked at Duke as if saying, "It wasn't me." Both could sense the sheriff's mood was a little on edge.

Sheriff Brown hit the record button and pointed to the mike. "Start." That's all he said.

Harley leaned back in his chair and began talking about the first couple of weeks out at the Heaven Falls Ranch. He told how Mrs. Taylor didn't ask for any references or anything when she hired him but told him up front that if he wasn't any good she'd fire him. In her words it was "Easy come, easy go," and she laughed when she said it. He knew real quick she was a lady he couldn't b.s., and it was obvious that she had the respect of every man on the ranch. Right away, he commenced to fixing things. The hay bailer was broke, tractors sputtered, and all the equipment was in bad need of repair. The old hand, Ezra, had let things go for a while. Harley found little half-pint bottles hidden everywhere, so he figured that's what the real problem was. "They say he used to be a pretty good mechanic, but not from what I'd seen."

"What happened to him?"

"She ran him off, and not under good terms, from what I understand. The hands told me that she leveled that Remington .30-30, that she always had strapped on her saddle, at him and told him that if he didn't get in his truck and leave, he was gonna be missing some parts he didn't want to lose."

"And?"

Harley laughed, "I guess he wanted to keep his parts."

"You think she'd have done it?"

"Oh yeah. No doubt. But she wouldn't really have needed to do nothing with those Mexicans around. They'd do anything for her. They wouldn't let nobody mess with her. Every one of them woulda laid his life down for her in a sec."

Hollis poured himself a cup of coffee and refilled Duke's, "Serious?"

"She was a lot more than just a boss to them, they loved her. She was the only person in this whole county who treated them decently, like they weren't some second-class citizen or something, and when she told them to do something, they did it . . . pronto."

The sheriff wrote some notes down on his pad and flipped the page, "Did Ezra ever come back, that you know about?"

"I never saw him, and I never heard about him coming back after that day."

Hollis looked at the clock and took another sip of coffee, "All right, let's go on. Now, what about Dallas? Did you see her much around there?"

Harley eased back in his chair and changed his posture. "I didn't see her at all that first month or so. I didn't do nothing but stay in the shop and work on that equipment, but after a while, she started coming by every now and then just to say hi. She came and went as she pleased. She slept until late in the morning and would take off in her little razorback, red BMW, peeling down the road with her music blaring."

The sheriff glanced at him with his eyebrow raised, "She ever flirt with you?"

Harley crossed his arms and leaned back. "She'd just wave and stuff when she walked into the house or when she was leaving. Some afternoons, she'd swim in the pool, and I'd hear her music way over at the shop so I knew she was there, but she usually went to the club, that's where she hung out."

"Why would she drive twenty miles to the country club when she had a pool in her own backyard?"

Harley huffed, "She didn't go there for the swimming; it's 'bout the attention. She was sixteen and the richest girl around. She is spoiled rotten to the hilt, and she wants all the attention."

"Well, how much of your attention did she get? I'm sure she had to get some of it, right?"

"Well, Sheriff, whadda ya think? I mean, I'm a normal guy, and I don't think no different than any other guy around here . . . or you for that matter. I mean, what do you think when you see a little five foot seven sixteen-year-old running around in a bikini no bigger than a Band-Aid? Just the average girl cranks up the temperature a little bit, but she wasn't your average girl either — not in the looks department. I mean, she is Leah Taylor's daughter. I swear God didn't make a mistake when he made her mother, and when he made the daughter he just duplicated the mold."

"I'm not asking if she was good-looking. I'm asking if she was getting your attention, and besides, it's not what I think, it's what you were thinking. You better remember something real quick, it wasn't me they picked up down there at the Mexican border. So what I think doesn't have a damn thing to do with it . . . understand?"

Harley knew he had riled the sheriff. "I got it. I got it."

"I hope you do because it's your neck, not mine, and you better not forget that." He flipped back through his notes and took a long deep breath, "Ahhumm, okay so let's back up here and tell me what was going on out at the ranch. What were you thinking?"

According to Harley, he was real happy to be working at the ranch. It was good to be making eight bucks an hour, and the scenery was a whole lot better than the tire shop. He spent most of his time in the shop, working on equipment, and he could see Dallas whenever she was out by the pool. She was always talking on that razorback, red cell phone; it hardly ever left her hand. He recalled how he'd step outside sometimes and take a breather from the shop, and if she was out there, she'd do her "howdy" wave and then go right on talking. He admitted he was real tempted to go over to that nice, big pool and take a dip, and she even invited him a time or two, but he knew better. He was a work hand, and he wasn't gonna do nothing stupid to get fired over. Mrs. Taylor had told him that after three months she'd bump him up to ten bucks an hour, and that's what he kept thinking about. Harley wasn't the smartest guy, but he wasn't altogether stupid either. A lot of guys were getting laid off at the mill, men were losing their homes, and ten dollars an hour, at a ranch like that, was pretty darn good for a guy who had dropped out of school. He also said that if he did get fired, he wouldn't be able to go back to the tire shop. When he quit, his job was filled that day.

The sheriff asked him if he was sure he never took a dip in that pool, and Harley denied it. He poured another cup of coffee and scooted back in his chair. "But after a while of watching her lounge about half naked, it did get more difficult not to think about it. There were days when I probably didn't need no jack to lift a rig off the ground, if you know what I mean. I was like a human forklift, and every time I turned around, I was knocking something over. A man's gotta learn to keep his mind off certain things, but I figured out a little trick a long time ago."

"What was that?"

"I just think of my bank account." Harley laughed, "When your life savings is $43.75, it's like water on a hot fire, sizzzzzzzz." Duke and Harley chuckled.

Hollis shook his head, "Cool it off, would it?"

"Like a slap in the face! But there was something else I thought about too."

"What was that?"

Harley took a sip of coffee and stared at the sheriff, "Rip."

All three men looked at each other, and Duke nodded and chuckled out loud, "You ain't all dumb. He is what you would call a mighty big deterrent all right."

"He is more than a deterrent; that man is meaner than King Kong."

The sheriff lit a cigarette and slid the pack over to Harley, "You ever have a run-in with him out there?"

Harley shook his head and told how he hardly ever saw him. He was scared to death of him, as were all the hands. Every man there avoided him whenever possible. Fortunately, Rip left early every morning. Usually he was gone before Harley got there.

As Harley spoke, they could hear some commotion outside. It was hard to distinguish through the walls, but it sounded like clapping and applause. The sheriff and Duke seemed to ignore it, like it wasn't happening. Harley continued with his story. He told how he got everything up to snuff and in good working order around the ranch, and Leah Taylor finally got him a horse to ride. He had never done much riding and didn't know a darn thing about horses, but he had to if he was going to stay on at the ranch. The horse that Leah got him didn't particularly take to him and had some peculiarities that she didn't mention to him at first.

"He bucked, you mean."

"Oh yeah!" Harley smiled. It was obvious that he enjoyed working on the ranch, and he told how Mrs. Taylor used to tease him in those early months about his riding abilities. She even told him that she might end up getting him a bicycle to peddle around the ranch on, if he couldn't learn to stay in the saddle.

Hollis smiled, "She told you that?"

"All the time. She'd ride by when I was getting up off the ground and laugh. One time she said she was going to start letting me go home early in the afternoon so I could watch Roy Rogers on TV and see how real men ride. You see, my horse was named Loco, and I didn't catch on at first, but Loco had it out for me, and she thought that was funny. They could have named him Kicker or Spitter, because he did those things too. I mean that horse did everything to me. He bit holes in my pants, he'd turn his butt around to my face and fart, and . . ."

Hollis grinned, "And what about Mrs. Taylor?"

"She'd say stuff like 'I saw a right pretty Huffy bicycle the other day at the Wal-Mart. You want me to pick you up one next time I go in?' Another time she said that she saw one of those red flyers with the ribbons on the handle grips, but figured she'd ask me before she bought it, just to make sure that's what I wanted. God, did she laugh about that, her and those Mexicans! One time we was eating lunch, and she pulled an advertisement out of her saddlebag and started showing the fellas. She started laughing till tears ran down her face. It was some dude wearing those Speedo biker shorts with a banana-looking hat on his head. She said, 'This could be you, except you'd be wearing a cowboy hat and boots.' I don't think she could finish her meal, she was laughing so hard."

The sheriff grinned and shook his head. Then he chuckled. Then he laughed; his shoulders bobbed up and down. Finally, he smiled and took a puff off his cigarette, "I guess you liked her then?"

Harley nodded, "Yeah . . . I sure did."

Grinning, he asked, "She ever get you that bike?"

"Nah. I finally learned to ride him. See, he wasn't really mean; he was just jealous. He used to be her horse, and he didn't like the fact that she started riding another horse. They're kinda funny like that."

"So he took it out on you?"

Harley's chiseled face beamed wide, "Did he ever. Loco knew more tricks . . . it was like he musta laid up nights thinking of ways he was gonna ruin my day." Suddenly, Harley saw something in his peripheral vision. He looked to his right; it was Lucian, looking through the Plexiglas. His nose was smashed up against the glass, and Harley could see his nose hairs sticking out. He had never seen so many nose hairs in all his life, except they didn't look like hairs. They looked like quills, big black and gray quills—just like a porcupine. *My God!* Harley thought to himself, *How could air pass through his nasal passages? If you duct taped his hands and mouth, he'd suffocate, or his nose would collapse, trying to suck in some air.*

Lucian's mouth scrunched up into a tight little fist, and he commenced to jabbering something inarticulate about the cigarettes on the table. Harley smiled and waved his hands as if to say, "See, no cuffs," and Lucian went off on a tirade.

Sheriff Brown got up from the table and went to the door, saying as he went, "My God. What does he want now?"

He unlocked the door and stood there with his hand still on the door knob, signaling to Lucian that he wasn't going to let him in.

"Ain't supposed to be no smokin' here in dis building, specially no prisona."

Brown pointed outside. "You get your ass out there and take care of that crowd, and quit telling me how to do my job. You hear?"

Harley looked at Lucian and grinned. He took a puff on his cigarette and smiled and then pretended to be scratching the side of his head with one finger.

"But he'za ain't pose' ta smoke in dis building . . ."

"Lucian, get your ass . . ."

He left. Sheriff Brown slammed the door and locked it and sat back down. They could all hear the crowd outside. It was strange. Harley looked at Duke, Duke looked at the sheriff, and Sheriff Brown looked at Harley, all without anyone saying a word. They just listened. It reminded Harley how he used to stand on his grandmother's back porch when the sky turned dark and listen for a tornado. Together they would walk out in the backyard and stand by the clothesline, and her head would turn every which way, inspecting the swirling clouds overhead. She'd get this strange look in her eye, and he remembered how, on several occasions, she took him by the hand and ran for the house, saying, "Let's get inside and hunker down." There was always just this look about her, it was worrisome and still. Hollis had that look. And so did Duke.

No one said a word. Harley snuffed out his cigarette, and then it was like a wave of applause pushed in from outside the wall. "What do they want, Sheriff?"

Hollis sighed. He started to speak and then sighed again, as if carefully searching for the right words, "They think they want to avenge a tragedy. They think they want justice. But the truth of the matter is most of those people don't even really know the Taylors. So it's not really personal to them, but they want to think it is."

Hollis looked up at the clock. It was 9:20. He pulled out the tape from the recorder, labeled it, and put another one in. Sheriff Brown was mumbling some stuff to himself, "Let's get back to business, boys. We've got a long day ahead of us, and before long TV reporters are going to be here, and it ain't gonna get any better. Rip Taylor is bound to show up too."

"Television reporters? Rip?"

The sheriff picked up his pencil, "Uh huh, you're real popular, Harley. They were here yesterday, they for sure gonna be back today. Rip was here too and had to have five deputies escort him out, twice. And now that you're here, do you think he ain't gonna show up?"

That knot twisted another couple of times in Harley's gut. He felt sick inside, even a little faint. He leaned his head down to the table, reached over without looking, and pushed the record button. Harley moaned, "Oh God, let's get started."

The sheriff looked at Duke and pointed to Harley with his face down on the table, "You understand why we've got to get through this? People wantin' answers."

"Yeah, Sheriff. I've got the picture."

"Keep in mind, this is your first day back. It has been going on like this for three days. There is something else you need to know, Harley; I haven't been sitting around here picking my teeth. I've already interviewed about thirty people, and let's just say there are some discrepancies. Other people's impressions of you are not that favorable."

Harley looked up, "I never said I was an angel."

"Don't worry, that thought never crossed my mind. So let's go back to the ranch, and tell me about Dallas again cuz some people have said one thing and some have said another, and now I want your version."

Sitting back, Harley rubbed his face and then cleared his throat. He began describing how Dallas started flirting with him more and more. When he was way out in the fields, she'd come out and see him and talk. It was a big ranch, thirty-five hundred acres in all, and he'd be mending some fences or looking for a lost head when she'd come riding up to him on a four-wheeler. She hardly ever rode a horse; she didn't like them much, or maybe it was the other way around. Harley told how she would sometimes bring him a Coke or water. It was hot, even in September, so he certainly didn't turn it down.

Sheriff Brown began to grill him on what was happening between them, and reluctantly Harley admitted they started making out. The sheriff had a hard time believing that he didn't come on to her, but he flatly denied it. He said it was all her. She chased him. He said that Dallas was the kind of girl who had never really been told no. "It was like she didn't even understand the word and had no intent on ever learning it."

"You knew her age, right?"

"Heck yeah, I knew her age. I told you that, but her age didn't stop her. I'm telling ya it was a game to her, like it was some kind of human experiment, and I know from the talk in town that she did everybody the same way. That's the way Dallas was; it was like a game to her."

"Pretty dangerous game, wouldn't you say?"

"Yep, I could lose my job."

"Why didn't you just tell her 'No'?"

"If I told her no, I'd make her mad, and if she got mad, she could say I came on to her and make me lose my job. Understand? So I had to go along. I was caught in the game, her game . . . and . . . well, she was fine."

The sheriff observed his body movements, especially his eyes. He didn't blink at the questions; his eyes stayed focused, but he could tell Harley was still uneasy with talking about Dallas, and figured he wasn't getting all of the truth. "Are you telling me it was just making out? Is that what you want me to believe? I mean, it strains the imagination to think, here is this very pretty girl and she likes you, you're way out in the middle of nowhere, and you are all alone with her. I'm sure there had to be some nice, shady spots on that ranch and presumably some springs to cool off in. I mean, you've got Heavens Falls. You're supposed to be the town stud, so why stop at making out?"

Harley took a sip of coffee and put it down. "Man, I wanted to, but I didn't go no further, I swear. I'll be honest with you, Sheriff, I've been with girls who were under eighteen, and it didn't bother me none. I ain't Saint Harley, and you aren't going to be readin' 'bout me between Luke and John. But with Dallas, I was scared. All the time, I kept my eyes peeled out, looking to see if some one was coming, but I knew if someone did come, I couldn't hide it. I felt like Leah could look right through me."

"Why is that?"

"I don't know, I guess because she trusted me."

"You felt loyal to her?"

Harley confessed that Dallas was pretty hot, but that he felt obligated to Mrs. Taylor. She hired him, and he wanted to please her, and in his opinion, Mrs. Taylor was prettier than Dallas. Dallas was an absolute ten, but he said if a guy pulled up to a drive-thru on a Saturday night, he could find one almost like her. He could go to almost any high school game and he'd find a ten. Maybe she might not be wearing a cheerleading outfit, but she might be in the band or somebody's mother in the stands. Dallas was a definite ten, all right, but she wasn't the only one. One the other hand, there was only one Leah Taylor.

"So what you're saying is, there wasn't anything special about Dallas?"

Harley rolled his eyes, "You're outta practice, Sheriff. It's sorta like brim fishin'. You can catch a batch of brim in a stocked pond. At first, it's kinda fun, but as you get older, you know that you're no fisherman. And after awhile, you even feel kinda ashamed bringing them home. It's just too easy."

"I see. So what you're saying is, you'd had all the brim fishin' you wanted?"

"I'm saying that it ain't even really fishin' when they are jumpin' in yer boat, so why should I risk everything for just one more? But I'm telling ya the problem wasn't with me, the problem was with her. I had to fight her off, and let me tell ya, she didn't want to stop; her hands were all over it."

"Just a minute." Hollis turned his page and wrote some more, "Okay, go on. So how did you handle it?"

"I put her off. I told her, 'Hey don't tease the lion.' I had to get back to work or I'd get fired. I made up stuff I had to do so she'd leave."

"And then what would happen?"

"She'd go. She got satisfaction knowing that she got me all worked up. She liked that, and I'm not so sure that wasn't what it was all about anyway."

"You kinda surprise me, Harley, I didn't figure you'd be the kind to turn down a free meal, so to speak. The word a lot of people use to describe you is 'opportunistic.'"

"They may be right. But I had an opportunity to become something more than Harley Wright 'the grease monkey at the tire shop,' and Mrs. Taylor gave me the best shot I had in my whole life. She didn't ride my back. She treated me decent. I knew I had a good thing there, and I didn't want to blow it cuz some girl was horny."

"So if someone said you was after Dallas, they'd be lying? Is that right?"

Harley looked exasperated. His shoulders slumped down. He leaned back and kinda shoved the empty chair back with his foot. "How many times do I have to tell ya? She was after me! I couldn't get rid of her. There wasn't anyone happier in the whole world than me, when she went back to school that fall."

Unwrapping the cellophane from another tape, Hollis laid it on the table and labeled it without looking up, "Okay, okay, go on. What did school have to do with it?"

"She was gone . . . all day. I didn't have her bugging me like before. I could do my eight hours of work and go home. She wasn't preoccupied with me anymore; she had a whole school full of boys falling all over her. During that first summer I was the guy who entertained her ego when she got bored. She didn't need me once school started, she had a hundred of 'em at school."

"Did you know any of them? You got proof?"

Harley paused and gave the sheriff a you-sure-are-dumb-as-dirt look. "Whadda ya think I did, go around conducting interviews? I didn't care 'bout what she did. She didn't interest me, understand? But for your information, I heard she had one of the lifeguards on the hook that summer, and there was talk about some guys on the football team, but not the local boys, she wouldn't let them touch her."

"You got names?"

"Nope."

"What else you know? Why not the local boys? You're local."

"I can't read her mind, but I guess she didn't want anybody bragging about her in the locker room, at least around here." Harley explained how it worked with underage girls. They generally like older guys, because older guys couldn't talk. If he talked, it could cost him some jail time. Unless a guy was an idiot, he didn't go around broadcasting it, and that's one reason he figured she was so hot after him, same with the lifeguard. He was older, at least twenty, a college guy.

Hollis listened to everything Harley said. He nodded and rubbed his chin. As Harley talked, the sheriff just kept writing down notes and then flipped the page.

"Mind if I get up and stretch?"

Hollis didn't look up, he just kept writing, "Go ahead."

Harley stretched his long arms up to the ceiling. He could almost touch it, and it was at least nine feet high. He twisted side to side, popping his back, and rotated his neck from shoulder to shoulder. For a while now, he had hadn't heard the crowd. He listened. Nothing. It was finally quiet. "I wonder how come we can't hear them anymore. Think they've given up?"

"I doubt it. They probably went home to make some more 'Hang Harley' signs."

Duke leaned across the table, "Or to get some more rope."

Harley gave Duke an eat-shit grin, "You ought to be real nice to me, Duke. When the sheriff left 'while ago, and you were napping, I could have pulled your pistol out, and if I was a real bad guy, I could have splattered your brains across the wall. I mean, if I wasn't such a nice guy, there'd be someone in here right now, mopping your face up off the floor with a rag and bucket."

Hollis glanced over his glasses at Harley, "That would never happen here."

"It could have, if I were really a bad guy."

"You think so, smart ass? I've got a policy—no loaded guns in the building. You'da been standing there with an empty pistol going 'click,' 'click,' and then it'd been your face they'd be mopping up with a sponge and bucket."

Harley gulped, "I was just jokin', really, I was . . ."

The sheriff took off his glasses and tossed them on the table. He leaned over on his elbow and pointed his finger right at Harley's face, "You were being a dumbass is what you were doing. You've been like that all your life, smartin' off to people. That's why all these people are here, cuz you've said something or done something to just about everybody in this town, and that smart aleck mouth of yours just might get you shot or hung."

"I said I'm sorry."

"Grow up, Harley. 'I'm sorrys' don't cut it anymore." The sheriff told him how serious things had gotten around there. If he let him go, chances were ninety-nine in a hundred that he'd be shot before he made it to the city limits. He was like a marshmallow at a Boy Scouts campfire; he was about to get roasted. It was time he stopped his wise-cracking jokes. There wasn't anyone in his corner—no one. Not one buddy, not one girlfriend had come by to say they thought he was innocent. "Notta one. Zip."

Harley took a deep breath. It was all sinking in. He didn't want to hear it, he didn't want to hear any of it, but the sheriff was right, and he knew it. "You're right. You're right about everything. I have pissed off a lot of people, but I'm telling you, when I went to work out there, I looked at it like a chance to turn my whole life around. Honest, I did. I didn't want any trouble, I swear. I ain't lying, I did everything I could to avoid that girl. I don't care what people say, that's the truth. I know you don't believe me, Hollis, but all I wanted was just to do an honest day's work and get paid for it.

"That's admirable."

"It wasn't easy, cuz Dallas would come over to my house too, and I had to run her off from there. Shoot, I was scared to death of what would happen if Rip came driving up one night when she was there. I had dreams of him breaking down my door. I've heard of what that man could do. There were a lot of reasons for me not to mess with her, see."

Skeptical, Hollis asked, "How did you get rid of her?"

"I told her that someone else was coming, a buddy or friend."

"Friend? Buddy? That's a joke."

"It worked, cuz she didn't want no one to see her over there, but man she didn't leave without leaving me something to think about. That's what she was after."

"Harley, in case you're wondering, I've already talked to three girls who have told me you were with them when they were underage, so if you did something with Dallas you might as well tell me. One more ain't going to make any difference at this point."

He cleared his throat, "Please, believe me. I'm telling you the truth. We never went all the way! But I had to button back her blouse many a time before I kicked her out the door. She was hot, I'm telling ya. She could make a pan of water boil just by walking by it."

Hollis and Duke looked at each other. "I'll say this, you are lucky Rip never did show up, or we wouldn't be having this discussion."

"Tellin' ya. I was scared of him. I grew up hearing stories about that man, and I didn't wanna have no part of him."

"Shows you've some brains. I've seen Rip palm a watermelon with one hand and crush it without flinching. Duke knows his strength." The sheriff motioned to his deputy, "Show him."

Duke rolled back his sleeve over his massive arm and showed Harley the scar.

"They arm wrestled in a match about twenty years ago, and Rip broke Duke's arm in half like it was a chicken bone. Duke went into shock, and Rip grabbed the pile of cash and said, "See ya."

Harley's eyes widened, "Man, that was cold."

Duke rolled his sleeve back down, "Ya don't wanna mess with him."

Curious, Harley asked, "You ever wrestle with him Hollis?"

"Not after that."

"Did you before?"

The sheriff nodded, "Once."

"And?"

"It was a draw."

Smack! Harley slapped his hand down on the table. "Way to go, Sheriff! I heard something about you beating Rip Taylor, but I didn't know what it was about."

"That was a long time ago, and I guarantee ya, I wouldn't try it again. Sides, it was a draw. I didn't beat him. The sheriff looked down at the tape recorder and hit the stop button.

"Tell me about it, come on."

Hollis looked at his watch. "We don't have time." He put in a fresh tape and hit the record button and began the usual introductions. He looked back at his notes again and sighed, "My God, we've got a long way to go. Let's go back to what you were saying about Dallas. She came over to your place that first year, so what happened after that?"

Harley took a deep breath. You could tell he looked slightly more worried now. The talk about Rip didn't calm his nerves. He picked up the pack of smokes, pulled out a cigarette, and toyed with it in front of his face. "Eventually she just stopped coming by, especially in the winter, because she was real busy cheerleading with basketball and stuff. I saw her less and less. They play a lot of games, and she was gone a lot. There might have been times when she came by, and I didn't know it because I would have other people over. I know she wouldn't stop if someone else was there."

"By people, I gather you are talking about girls."

"Women."

"You dating anyone?"

"I never really dated, they just came over." Harley looked over at Duke. His face was a blank, expressionless, it was as if he became just another brick in the wall. Harley mused that if he sat there long enough, he might get a coat of latex across his face the next time the painters put on a fresh coat.

The sheriff kept writing notes without looking up, "That's convenient."

Harley had an itch in his crotch and started scratching it since neither on of them were paying attention anyway, "Ah, I don't make the money to go out and spend on steaks and stuff, besides when I'm off work, I'm bushed. I don't feel like getting up and driving all the way into Hot Springs to do something."

"Makes sense."

"Well, they know where they can find me. With me, there is no big scheduling problem, if I'm there, I'm there, and if I'm not, I'm not."

"You're not much for romance are ya?"

"Hey, I've lived on my own since I was fifteen, and I can tell ya they all like it that way. I feel sorry for the guys who go out there and put a ring on their finger, cuz then they come by and show me. Fifteen minutes later, they ain't wearing nothing but the ring. How's that for romance?"

"Pretty bad."

"They don't want romance. So the way I figure it, if you can get it delivered, why go out?"

"Your generation is something else."

Tap. Tap. Tap. It was Teresa. "Reporters."

Hollis hit the stop button and nudged Duke, "Wake up, the circus is back." He then waved his arms around, trying to disperse the cloud of smoke lingering in the air. "God forbid they see that."

Harley looked at them through the glass, three cameramen along with three reporters. One of them was pretty hot, a tanned brunette. "Where is she from?"

"Texarkana, I think." Hollis straightened up the table a bit. "I've got to go and talk to them. How about some fresh coffee? Need to go to the john?"

"I'm hungry, that's all."

"We'll get ya something." Hollis patted him on the shoulder as if to reassure him that it was going to be all right, but it was stiff, superficial.

"Thanks." Harley stood by the door and looked at the reporters up at the front desk. They were all sticking their microphones in Teresa's face. He could hear her telling them something about the "announcement." There was a lot of confusion. The sheriff was right, it was a circus. He remembered the big top when it came to town when he was a kid. He remembered how they turned off the lights in those dank, dingy canvas tents, and then the spotlight would come up on the sawdust floor. A clown would come out and everyone would clap. People would be spilling popcorn and Coke everywhere, and the makeshift bleachers were sticky from the people who'd sat there before. This was a circus all right, and he was in the center ring.

He was the clown, the idiot, the fool, the monkey—the grease monkey. As Hollis and Duke locked the door and walked down the hall, Harley thought to himself, "This is it. It's showtime."

Chapter Four

They came for the big story, and it made Harley sick. It reminded him of a birthday party once when he had eaten too much. Everyone was running around and hollering, and he couldn't wait till they went home so he could spill his guts. That's how he felt. There was so much chaos.

Leaning his shoulder against the door, as he looked down the hall at the ruckus, he had to crane his neck down a bit to see everything going on. What a mess. There were Hollis and Teresa, simultaneously talking to reporters. There was so much chaos, that he could hardly hear anything being said. He kept hearing the words "murder" and "charge," but it was impossible to decipher anything else.

The cameramen kept getting in the way, and the backs of all the reporters facing him, totally blocked out the whole front desk. Harley couldn't help but notice the brunette—she had great legs and a fine butt. Harley thought to himself, *What am I thinking? A butt like that ain't never done nothin' but get me in trouble,* but then he thought, *So what's wrong with thinkin' 'bout it? How much more trouble can I get in?*

Harley got to thinking that if he could just talk to her, maybe when he got out, if they didn't hang him, he might call her, and she might come by. He could toss a couple of Salisbury-steak dinners into the microwave, and she might pop a beer. He tried to get a view of her station logo on the camera and then he saw the microphone she was holding. Channel 5, he had to remember that.

Harley stood there gandering through the Plexiglas window. What was he thinking? He was crazy. Normal men didn't think like him. In jail, the crowd, a trial for his life, and he's thinking about playing rodeo in his bedroom with a reporter?

His high school counselor was right—he had behavioral issues and would have a hard time adjusting to society unless he had structure and discipline. Maybe he needed to write her a letter: "Boy, you were right."

Finally, he heard the sheriff say, "No more questions." Harley could tell by the looks on their faces that they were all upset the sheriff was kicking them out so soon. Harley stood back a bit as they were walking down the hall toward the exit, and then a cameraman shouted, "That's him!" In a flash, three huge television camera lenses were trying to get a shot of him through that little Plexiglas window, and they were banging something fierce against the door.

Harley didn't know what to do. He stood back and waved. Then he could hear the sheriff shouting, "Get out." All of a sudden, they were gone, and he could see the sheriff and Duke escorting them down the hall to the exit. As he looked back the other way, he saw the brunette reporter as she walked by. Harley smiled, but she gave him a grim expression. She walked about two more steps and stopped, like she froze. She turned her head back toward him. She had beautiful brown eyes. She smiled.

"Out," Hollis said.

She held her hand up and did a little bye-bye wave. And then she was gone.

Hollis walked down the hall to his office, and Duke stood guard at the front door.

It showed 10:10 on the Nehi Drink clock mounted on the wall next to an eight point buck Hollis had hanging behind his desk. Hollis's office was the only room in the building that wasn't coated in a half-inch layer of semi-gloss, off-white paint. He had his walls inlaid with rustic barn wood which gave it a comfortable country feel. And being wise to the assembly of town complainers, he paid for it out of his own pocket, every dime.

Hollis walked behind his desk and plopped down in his worn, roll-around, oak and leather chair, and, as was his custom, he tossed his legs up on the desk, shoving a stack a papers over with his boot. The little lights were blinking on his phone. Geez, he thought to himself as he looked over the half dozen Post-it notes that Teresa had pasted around, in front, and on top of his old phone. He rubbed his temples as the throbbing began. *If only the crowd would go away, it would be so much simpler,* he thought. *There wouldn't be any pressure.*

Teresa came barging in, "Aren't you going to return those phone calls?"

Opening one eye, Hollis said, "Yeah, gimme a minute." He closed his eyes again.

"Scott County Sheriff called again. Aren't you gonna tell him you're shorthanded? We need some help down here, you know? I don't know why you let those state troopers go. Take a look at that crowd out there, Hollis. We could sure use them now. And another thing . . ."

Opening one eye again, squinting in the glare of the light, Hollis said, "Why don't you go home and take one of those nice pills and come back?"

She put her hands on her hips.

"Sorry, I didn't mean it." He rubbed his face and groaned as he lifted his legs back off the desk. Teresa still stood at the doorway, glaring at him something awful. "Really, hon, I didn't mean it. But you don't need to get all worked up about things, this thing is about to come to a head. About another hour, and the boy will pop. I've been greasing him good. By lunch time he'll be confessing to everything all the way back to stealing his grandma's cookies when he was five."

"Oh yeah? What if he's innocent?"

"Innocent people don't go jumping in their trucks and hauling ass to Mexico."

"He would if he was scared."

"There ain't nothin' to be scared of. I told him the truth would set him free."

Teresa walked over to his desk and slapped a file down. "You remember that yourself before the day's out." She spun around and stormed out.

"Geez, I wish you'd hurry up and have that baby."

Teresa stopped suddenly at the door, "What did you say?"

"Nothing."

"You know, I was going to name this baby Hollis, after the man I have admired so much, but there are days when I wonder if that would be such a good decision."

He put his glasses on, "I'm sorr . . ."

SLAM! She was out the door.

Hollis looked at all the Post-it notes. He picked them up and looked at each one, and then, as was his habit, he put them all together in a little pile. He looked over at the clock and thought to himself, *Yeah, Harley was about to pop. Get him going some more, relax him, lead him to the scene. He'll get all emotional, and it'll all come out.* Hollis stood up and stretched and went to the little window in his office and looked out. It was partially covered up by some bushes, and he stood there looking at the crowd outside. He recognized every face. *Yeah, it won't be long, and all this will be over.*

Hollis looked at the clock and left his office. He popped a bag of popcorn and moseyed around the front desk, trying to find the right words to tell Teresa he really was sorry, but every time he started to say something, she turned the other way. He was sorry that he had said anything to hurt her feelings. She was almost like a daughter to him; he'd known her since she was a child. She'd stroll in to the police station when she was a little bitty girl, and he'd treat her to Honey Bun out of the vending machine. They went way back, but now she was sitting behind the dispatcher's desk, fuming. He walked over and stood beside her, "Ah, when's the baby due?"

She got up and brushed by him with some files, "Excuse me."

He tried again to talk to her but realized, as with a lot of women, it was not the time. He had to let her fume a little, let her fuss about it some more, and then he'd try later. The bell rang on the microwave, and she opened it and tossed him the bag none too lightly. "It's done."

Hollis stood there with the bag in his hand and motioned for Duke to come with him. "Let's go finish this," he said, and they headed back down the hall. He could see Lucian standing in front of the doors outside, scratching his butt. The thought crossed his mind, *Don't shake hands with Lucian today, whatever you do.*

Harley was sitting in the exact same position he was when the sheriff left. He looked at the bag of popcorn, "Geez, I was gonna see if I could get some hash browns and gravy, but popcorn?"

Hollis opened the bag and shoved it over to him, "I thought you'd be a little more grateful, but if you don't want it, I'm sure Duke would like some."

Harley started munching down on a big handful, "Dis is fine."

"Thought so." Hollis flipped over the tape in the recorder and poured himself a half cup of coffee from the thermos. "Let's get started." Hollis pushed the button on the recorder, and did the usual introductions. Harley started talking again with his mouth full of popcorn. The sheriff rolled his eyes, looking at him, knowing that it wasn't going to be the clearest-sounding tape he ever recorded. But Harley wasn't stalling. He was talking, and they were getting closer to the truth, even if it was garbled.

Harley described how Mrs. Taylor pretty much ran the ranch without Rip. Harley worked with the crew and the foreman, Santana. They had a heckuva winter that first year. The ponds froze, a well pump went out. They ran short on hay and had to bring in a lot of feed. The sheriff stopped him from going on. He didn't need to know about that, he just wanted to know about Mrs. Taylor.

Harley hesitated for a bit and then grabbed another handful of popcorn, "Okay, okay . . ." He started talking about how they used to ride together. He'd ride Loco, and she rode Sweets. They covered nearly all the ranch together at one time or another. She knew every cow, and could tell instantly if one was sick. She knew more about cattle than any man he'd known, and it amazed him that even with five hundred head, she'd know what calf went with what cow.

Even though he was alone with her sometimes, he usually was working under the eye of Santana or one of his men. He was what was called a "hand's helper" or "second hand." In other words, his job was to do whatever he was told to do, but he didn't mind it. According to Harley, Mrs. Taylor would meet with them all, early every morning and give out the instructions for the day—things like bail hay, mend fences, unclog a stream, anything. She'd ride around, inspecting everything, and sometimes she'd pull out that .30-30 and pick off a coyote hauling butt across the ranch with a neighbor's chicken in its mouth. She hated them, along with armadillos that dug holes in the ground. Those holes were dangerous to horses and their riders, so she would shoot them and throw them back in their holes, and one of the hands (usually Harley) would cover them up with a couple shovelfuls of dirt.

After the morning rounds, Leah would head back to the house to do paperwork in her office. Her prized bulls brought upwards of five to ten thousand dollars, some had even gone higher. People would pay good money just for the breeding, and she made some major money selling the "contents"—that's what she called it anyway—for fertilization. Harley explained to the sheriff and Duke that was one job he didn't do on the ranch

Everyday they were in the fields, she would bring them all lunch, unless it was raining real bad or a blizzard, then they'd come up to the house to eat. All she ever fixed them was Mexican food, nothing else. Harley said she'd sit right down there with them and eat rice and beans out of a big pot, wrapping some grilled venison in a tortilla. "She ate just like them, talked just like them." She spoke Spanish the entire time she was there, and he hardly ever knew what they were talking about, till they started laughing, and then he knew it was about him.

The sheriff turned his page, "Did she laugh at you a lot?"

"All the time. She got to laughing so hard sometimes she could hardly breathe. Tears would roll down her eyes and she be saying gringo-this or gringo-that. They'd point to him and all crack up. Harley told how he complained to her one time that all she brought was Mexican food, and so the next time out, she brought a big thing of tamales, but for him she brought a children's Lunchable with a little container of milk. They all cracked up when she handed him a paper bag that contained apple wedges and peaches in ziplock bags.

The sheriff smiled, "And you didn't get mad?"

"No, but I never asked for anything else again. I shut up and ate what they ate." Harley said he never did mind when she joked with him. He loved to see her laugh, and she had the finest smile he ever did see. She wasn't like any other woman he had ever known; she was just down to earth. She talked with the guys, worked with them, and joked with them, but she always was a lady. She let him know that he wasn't going to get preferential treatment because he was white; in fact, she seemed a little partial to the Mexicans. She told him once that they were her family.

The sheriff let Harley talk and talk. He just prodded him along every now and then with a question here and there, but all in all, Harley was pretty relaxed. He seemed to enjoy talking about the ranch, especially that first year, and from what the sheriff gathered, he must have been a pretty good hand. He enjoyed his work, even when it was pouring down rain and water dumped off his hat "like a gutter pouring off the side of a house." It was hard and cold, hot and smelly. His hands got torn up from all the barbed wire he strung, and he got kicked and butted and stomped on by both bulls and horses, but Harley didn't seem to mind it. The hazards of the job didn't bother him; in fact, he confessed that he loved being there more than anything in the world.

"Did everyone feel the same way?"

"Of course. How could a man not?"

"What about Dallas, how did ya'll feel about her?"

"It was different," he said. Dallas didn't treat people like her mom did, and people didn't respond to her in the same way. "You'll have to ask them, but I don't think they liked her at all, and I know she talked about them like they were dirt. She didn't really hang out at the ranch much, Sheriff, to be honest with ya."

The sheriff leaned over and checked the recorder. He flipped the page on his note pad. He looked over at Duke and raised his pencil, "Okay, now what about Leah? You were around the men. Did they ever say anything about Mrs. Taylor being . . . good-looking, like when she rode off, was there talk about her in a way that indicated that she was, a . . . uh . . . you know?"

Harley furled his dark eyebrows, "I'm not so sure what yer saying, Sheriff. What are you saying?"

"Did they comment on her in a sexual way? Is there any possibility that any of them might have wanted her in that way?"

Harley clinched his fist. "No!"

"Sorry, Harley, but I had to ask. I've talked to maybe thirty people, and there are some who have suggested things. We've got to check it out."

"It's our job," Duke said.

Harley looked over at Duke, he wanted to jump across the table and slap him. He couldn't understand why he was there in the first place, three hundred pounds of muscle, and a pumpkin for a head.

"You didn't know her, Sheriff, like we did. These people in this town always said stuff 'bout her. But there wasn't a finer woman anywhere. What pissed me off is they figure that since Dallas is a slut, her mother was, and that ain't right!"

"Then I need your help." Hollis paused for a moment and leaned back in his chair.

Harley didn't say anything. He adjusted his chair and leaned back.

The sheriff could tell he wanted to talk but was hesitant. He couldn't push Harley now, because he would clam up, maybe to protect himself, maybe to protect Mrs. Taylor. They were at a point when a lot of guys get lawyered up, and if Harley did, it would be difficult getting to the bottom of what happened. Harley was definitely the key. The sheriff sat there quietly and let Harley think. He poured him a cup of coffee and slid the cigarettes to the middle of the table.

After a long pause, Harley looked at the sheriff with the saddest eyes, "I would never want to hurt her."

"I know you wouldn't."

"It's not right the way they talk about her. There ain't a finer woman anywhere, I swear."

Hollis leaned over to Harley, "You see, I've got to separate the facts from the fiction here. I've got to pull the lies out from the truth and say 'here it is.' This is where you can help. You know the truth, don't you?"

Harley sat quietly and nodded.

"Okay then, let's just bring it out, all of it. I know she was a good woman, and I'd like the record to show that."

"You know what makes all this worse? She was a very religious woman, not religious like them, but religious in a good way. I've heard what some people have said about her, but they didn't know her. All of us had total respect for her. She didn't ask for no help to get up on her saddle cuz she wants you to grab her ass or nothing. She was decent sheriff, real decent. Did you know she always prayed before her meals? She helped people all over the county, and they didn't even know it was her doing it, and some of those same people are probably talking about her right now. It just pisses me off."

The sheriff sighed, "I know she was a woman of deep convictions, Harley, and you can say what you want to about those people, but they're not her judge. I'm not trying to be her judge either, or your judge, what I'm trying to do is get to the truth. That's all, do you understand?"

Harley looked over at Duke and shuffled his feet. He turned away from the table. "Does he hafta be here?"

The sheriff motioned to the door and handed him the coffee thermos, "Why don't you bring back some fresh coffee? And take your time."

As soon as Duke left, Harley spun back around, looked down at the recorder, and even pulled the mike a little closer. He started to say something, and then pushed himself away. Hollis was calm and patient. "I know at some point, your relationship with Leah changed, right?"

Harley nodded, his eyes off in a deep stare.

"Okay now, Harley, listen to me if you will. What I know is what other people have said, and she's not here, so I need to hear it from you. You have two choices, you can either leave the lies out there to trash this woman's name forever and ever, or you can free her from that. Whadda ya wanna do?"

Harley took a deep breath. His big shoulders exhaled slowly, his arms relaxed. "It was sometime in spring when we had what you would call personal conversations. It was still basketball season, maybe February or even March. It was the end of winter, after work, and I was in the Mount Ida Café on a Thursday night. It was raining and the high school was having a game. She walked in and sat down at a booth by the window, then she saw me from across the room. We were just about the only people in the restaurant; you know how it is on game night."

The sheriff nodded and Harley began depicting what happened next. She got her tea and came over to his booth and sat down. They started talking, and she told him that was where she first met Rip, when she was eighteen or so. Her mother worked in the shoe factory up the street, and her grandmother washed dishes there in back.

"Maime?"

Harley couldn't remember her name, only that Leah said she was about thirteen when she started waitressing there. He said she asked him about his family and where he was from. They had never talked about stuff like that at the ranch, didn't have time. Anyways, somehow it came up, and they discovered they were both from Story. She knew his mother and dad. She remembered hearing about his dad the day he died in a logging accident. Harley said he didn't know it, but her daddy died too when she was young, so they both had something in common. Harley told the sheriff that he figured out that Leah was the Reed girl, that his momma always used to talk about when he was just a kid. Her family lived in a house down by the lake, and the government ended up taking it.

"It was the Corps of Engineers."

"That's right, that's what she told me. Something about they took the land when Lake Ouachita was built and gave them a lease, but when the last child turned eighteen, it had to go back to the Corps."

Hollis knew the story well, most people did, so he knew Harley was telling the truth up to that point. "On the day after her eighteenth birthday, the Corps showed up on their property and bulldozed down her homestead. They were driven off."

"So she told you about that, huh?"

"Oh yeah, but there is a lot more. I had heard about the Reed family all my life but never did it dawn on me that it was her. All I ever had known her as was Mrs. Taylor. I didn't connect her with the Reed girl who had lived down the road when I was just a kid."

"So she was the same one?"

Harley nodded and started telling a story about when he was just a little boy swimming with his mom and dad over at Dragover, just past Lady Ghost road. The river was perfect, the water was crystal clear. Harley said he remembered seeing this beautiful woman come down the slopes to the water where they were all swimming. There was a man with her, but he just stayed up at the car and didn't come down. Harley thought he might have been only about four or five year old, but he was sure of one thing, the woman who came down and got in the water was the most beautiful thing he'd ever seen. He was in an inner tube, and she swam out to where he was and started pushing the tube through the water, gliding along. It was as vivid to him now as if it had just happened yesterday. Young Harley was mesmerized by this graceful woman. He leaned over the tube and watched her legs stroke like wings through the water below him. She moved effortlessly, graceful like a ballerina, but what he remembered most was her radiant smile and how the sun glistened on her skin. "Then," he said, "she crossed back over to the shore and came up out of the river, and the water poured down her body. It was the first time I ever thought of a woman like that, and it was a sight I've never forgotten."

"What happened next?"

"She waved good-bye to my family and walked back up the hill. I remember asking my mamma who she was, and she told me she was an angel.

"She called her an angel?"

"Yeah, you know how you say someone is an angel when they are just a really good person? But I thought she was a real angel, so growing up, I always believed I had met an angel from heaven. I never put the two together until that night in the restaurant."

"Did you tell her that?"

"Are you kidding? That was something I kept to myself. I'm sure she wouldn't have remembered something like that. It was a long time ago."

Hollis took a deep breath and sighed, "Man, that's quite a story."

"Yeah, think how I was feeling. I guarantee you I didn't pinch myself in that booth that night. As far as I was concerned, it could have just rained forever, wouldn't a bothered me if we never left."

"What else ya'll talk about?"

"Politics."

Hollis had a perturbed look on his face, "Politics?"

"Just shittin' ya," Harley chuckled, "You think I'm gonna waste a good evening like that talking politics? Or sports? Not me."

"Well, what did ya'll talk about? You talk about Rip?"

"No. We didn't have to, and I didn't want to. No point in ruining the evening. He never came up, and even though I was a ranch hand, I hardly saw him. Like I said before, it was like they weren't even married. Anyone who was around there knew there was nothing there. They pretty much lived separate lives. She ran the ranch, and he ran those Get-N-Runs. I heard he had a honey in pert near every town between Fort Smith and Texarkana."

"She talk about it?"

"Didn't have to. I could tell."

"All that experience come in handy, huh?"

"No, but you can tell a lot more about a woman by what she doesn't say than what she does."

"So she doesn't say anything about him at all?"

"Nope, not then. That whole first year I worked for her, he was never mentioned. Most women would talk about their husbands and what they did over the weekend, like if they fished all day or watched games on Sunday, blah, blah, blah. But she said nothing, and I never asked. She really was kinda a loner I think, a loner in her own house. And I guess she figured she could talk to me that night because I was alone too."

They talked for a while about her. Hollis was surprised that she was so isolated, he'd see her picture in the paper donating money to one cause or another, and he just figured she had it all. Harley said that after they talked that night in the café, it was back to business as usual the next day on the ranch.

Sheriff Brown looked at his watch and scratched his head. He still had a bewildered look on his face, "Okay, but somewhere along the way things changed, right?"

"Yeah, as we got closer to summer, everything changed. It got kinda crazy, but . . . say, is there anyway I can go to the can?"

"Can't you wait and let me get this part down before you go? How 'bout ten more minutes?" He looked at his watch again.

"Can't hold it." Harley smiled, "'Bout to go like a fire hydrant."

"Darn!" Sheriff Brown turned off the tape recorder, "I'll get Lucian to go with ya."

"Geez, Hollis, I'd just as soon pee down my leg as have Lucian go with me."

"You might just have to do that, cuz you ain't leaving this room without an escort and cuffs on." The sheriff unlocked the door and called out for his deputy. Lucian walked out of his office, "Whadda ya doin?"

"Makin' a phone call."

"Get down here and cuff Harley. He needs to hit the john."

Lucian walked down the hall to where they were standing. "Put your hands behind ya boy." He snickered, "Got a 'fession outa 'im yet?"

"I'm getting his story, is that all right?"

Harley was turned around, and Lucian was about to cuff his hands behind his back, when he said, "It's gonna be kinda hard for me to unzip my pants with my hands back here don't cha think? Or are you wanting to do that for me?"

Hollis laughed and Teresa giggled, "Yeah, Lucian, you should really think about that."

Hollis gave Lucian some leg irons and told his deputy to get going. Lucian cuffed Harley's legs and followed behind him into the men's bathroom down the hall. There was a tiny one-by-two-foot window above the urinal that Harley looked out. It looked like a tailgate party at a Razorback game—cars everywhere, trucks with tailgates down, people sitting in lawn chairs. Harley unzipped his pants and let it rip. He closed his eyes at the feeling of relief gushing from him.

After he was finished, he turned around and started to zip up. He noticed Lucian staring down at him. "What's the matter, you ain't ever seen the real thing?"

Lucian sucked in his gut and pointed to Harley's pants, "Wh're yer goin', dat pecker gonna be . . ."

"Shud up." Harley pulled back his fist, and Lucian bolted for the door. Harley grinned as he washed his hands and threw the paper towel in the trash.

As he was walking back down the hall to the front desk, the noise of the crowd swept into the building like a fiery wind. Everyone looked up. Sam Langston the local attorney slammed the door shut behind him. Now there were other attorneys in town, but Sam was by all accounts *the* man. If you had a problem, Sam took care of it. He was respected (as far as lawyers go) and well liked. The short attorney grinned as he strolled down the hall, "Holy Moses, I thought surely somebody musta seen Elvis again to get that many people here."

His gray mustache crawled across his face like a caterpillar when he talked. Not one to be called a trend setter, Sam wore a slightly faded, light blue seersucker suit and an old, white straw hat with a red-ribbon band. His southern drawl was as slow as his granddaddy's pocket watch that dangled from a chain.

Not from Arkansas originally, Sam migrated to western Arkansas from Auburn. Some say he had to leave Alabama after getting sideways with some senator's daughter. Whatever the reason, Sam came to Arkansas where he had no love grudges to contend with. He was a man whose ambition, by all accounts, never matched his intellect, but his wit was known far and wide. Sam knew something most attorneys didn't: if he could ever get the jury laughing, get them to snickering, he could get his man off. And he usually did, much to the chagrin of his fellow members of the bar.

"Howdy, Hollis." His mustache wiggled, "I thought the art of public servitude was nearly extinct, but not here in Polk County. We have the finest assembly of peace officers that can be bought . . . er did I say bought, I meant *paid for*." Sam slapped the sheriff on the shoulder and looked inquisitively into his eyes, "Hollis, you ain't lost yer sense of humor in all this have ya?"

"Just my sanity."

"Good, cuz a man's got to keep his sense of humor. Sanity is not a necessity, right, Harley?"

Harley looked over at the attorney who was a good seven or eight inches shorter, even with the hat, "Uh, right, Sam. I guess that's right. I'm just lookin' to get outta here. Can you help?"

"Well, that's why I've come by, to see if you've got any bruises or whip marks you can show me. Have they use the hose on ya yet, or hooked you up to Ready Freddie and turned on the juice, huh?"

Chuckling, Harley said, "Why, no."

"Sheriff, this ain't no interrogation goin' on here, this here's a picnic. Put ole Lucian in charge. He'll get some straight answers, even if he's got to make them up. Sure they haven't beatin' ya boy?"

Puzzled, Harley raised his eyebrows, "I don't think so."

"Doggone it, I was looking for a lawsuit." Sam looked over at Teresa behind the desk, "Got any wrecks I can go to? A fender bender? Give me something, it's been a slow month."

"No, Sam, you're too late again. That handsome lawyer from DeQueen who tips so well has already been here. He got your leads. You know, he drops a hundred here every now and then just to be friendly."

Hollis put his clipboard down on the desk, "Yeah, Sam you're cheap."

"Shoot, I ain't having any luck today. How about you, Harley, how's your day going? I hear you came in to answer some questions, is that right?"

Shuffling his leg irons around, he replied, "Well, yeah, I've come in to talk about tha . . ."

"His being here ain't voluntary, Sam. He was heading to tamale land when they caught up with him."

"It's a free country. He hadn't been charged with anything yet."

Hollis gave the little attorney *the look* — a look that said "don't go start nothing." He folded his arms and sighed, "What's yer point?"

Sam walked over next to Harley and nudged him, "No point, no point. Chief, you don't mind if I have a word or two with Harley alone, do you?"

Hollis looked at Harley and shrugged, "It's up to you."

Harley smiled a mouth full of relief, "Why, sure!"

"Good, we won't be long."

"Yeah, well, ya'll go ahead and talk. We're waiting on lunch from the Skyline right now. Sam, you want something?"

"No, thanks, just ate." Sam pointed to Harley's leg irons, "By the way, Sheriff, what's this?"

"Just a precaution, Sam."

"Now, Hollis, you can't go doing that until he's been charged. You know that."

Hollis gave Sam that look again. He didn't want the little attorney meddling in his affairs, "The code book also says that I have the right to restrain anyone who may do bodily injury to themselves. And if Harley decided to leave right now, I surmise that he would be jeopardizing his health, and if you have taken a good look at that crowd out there, I am sure you would agree. Until that threat is gone, he will remain restrained in my jail."

"Ah, Hollis, he ain't going nowhere."

"Nowhere but burritoville."

Sam pushed Harley into the room, "Now what did ya go and do that for Harley?"

"Well, I thought it was a good idea at the time. I wasn't thinking like I should, I was . . ."

"Sit down there, Harley." The door was shut and locked behind them. Sam looked over his shoulder and around the room. He scooted his chair back and looked underneath the table, then he stared up at the ceiling vent, squinting his eyes. He leaned over the table and spoke in a very quite voice. "Harley, I want you to look at me right now."

He pulled his chair closer, "What is it, Sam?"

Whispering, Sam said, "I want you to tell me the truth right here and now, this is your one shot, and don't give me any bull. Did you do it?"

A dead serious look came over Harley's face. His mouth was drawn, and his eyes piercing. He moved his head from side to side. "No, Sam, I didn't do it."

Sam studied Harley's face and hands, he was an expert at deception. He was acutely aware that Harley Wright was the most unpopular man in the county right now, but that didn't make a man guilty. Sam was certainly no fool either — guilty or not, there was an angry crowd surrounding the courthouse. It was a crowd of clients, a crowd of past clients, present clients, and (if he didn't piss them off) hopefully a crowd of future clients. Every one of them wanted Harley's butt to sizzle like a piece of fat jack on a hot grill. There were a whole lot of them, and only one of Harley, so Sam began listening to his story, while simultaneously weighing the balances of justice in his mind. A little here and a little there, but if he was guilty, all the weight would be on one side. Let him fry.

Sam looked at his watch — just a few minutes till eleven. Twitching his nose and pointing to his watch, Sam reminded Harley, "Hurry up, we don't have much time. Keep it to the facts, only the facts. Okay?"

Harley quickly went over everything that happened. He spoke in a low voice, a hair above a whisper, but Sam's hearing wasn't all that good, so he leaned over closer to Harley and turned his head sideways. He would stop Harley in the middle of a sentence from time to time to ask him to repeat what he said, "What was that? . . . okay, okay, now tell me what happened next." Sam didn't take any notes on paper, but he didn't miss a detail. A curious fellow he was; his eyes would blink, and he'd adjust his glasses that kept slipping down to the end of his nose. Sam kept asking him to go back to the morning it all happened and go through the details again of what happened, right up to the time Harley left town. Sam listened quietly to Harley's southern drawl, whispering on occasion, "Stop, repeat that. Okay, okay, go on."

They weren't in there but maybe six or seven minutes alone when Hollis unlocked the door; lunch had arrived. The smell of meat loaf entered the room before Hollis did—fresh-baked meat loaf and mashed potatoes. He slid the Styrofoam box over to Harley and tossed him a plastic spoon. "Have at it. Sandra gave ya the extra-heapin' portion there, Harley." The sheriff looked at the attorney and winked, "Sam, you shoulda got ya self some. You're missin' out."

Harley was tearing into his meal like a kid attacking the first present under the Christmas tree. With a mouthful of lunch bulging from his mouth, Harley concurred, "Sheriff's right, Sam, she makes the best." Cornbread and green beans were going down the hatch just as fast as his meatloaf. It didn't even look like they stopped in his mouth long enough to be chewed on.

Hollis sat down and started doing the same thing. "You gonna represent Harley there, Sam? I ain't railroading him if that's what yer thinking. He's been volunteering everything up to this point."

"I know that, he told me, and I told him that if he's innocent, his best chance is to tell you everything that happened, right, Harley?"

Harley nodded; he had a mouth full of lemon pie that was piling down his chin. Sam took one glance at the yellow mush churning between his teeth and held up his hand, "Don't say anything, please. Just eat your meal. I've gotta go and check on some things, but I'll be back later to see how things are going."

Neither man seemed too interested in anything but his meal, "So, you're going?"

"Like to."

Hollis got up from the table, wiping his mouth, and unlocked the door, "Say, I've got some reports coming back this afternoon from the state lab that I'll share with ya if ya want? We'll know a lot more when we get those in."

Sam picked his hat up off the table and patted Harley on the back, "Sounds fine to me. Harley, it was nice chatting with you. I'll see you later."

Harley reached over and picked up a slice of cornbread off the sheriff's box, "Yeah, yeah, good seeing you too, but ah . . . you will come back later, right?"

"Sure, sure." Sam tossed his hat on his head and walked to the door where the sheriff was standing. He hesitated for a moment, and then looked at Hollis, "Say, I know it's not the time, but how is Barbara. I mean, how's the chemo been going?"

A glint shown in Hollis's eye, and there was a trace of a faint smile, "She's making it. Only three more weeks of treatments, and then we'll just wait and see. But you know Barbara, ain't nothing stopping her. She's always took it better than I did."

"I need to go by and see her."

"Yeah, you do. You've always been one of her favorite people. Did you know that you have always been on top of her prayer list? Over ten years now."

Sam looked at Hollis, puzzled, and stroked his mustache, then raised his eyebrows and chuckled, "I don't know how to take that, is that a compliment or an insult?"

"I'd say it's a compliment. When a woman like Barbara loves a person like that, you better be thankful."

"Well, I'll be. I didn't know that. So, you're really serious, she really does pray for me? Why don't you have her pray for a wife number three?"

"After your first two, I didn't think you'd want any more trouble. Maybe her prayers are stopping you from taking a beating like you did last time."

Harley chuckled, "Yeah, who did she get for a lawyer? He musta been pretty good."

"I don't want to talk about it. But, I'll go by and see her sometime soon."

"You'd make her day."

"Will you tell her to put me on her list?" Harley asked. "I need all the prayers I can get right now."

Both the men looked at Harley and shook their heads. In less than a minute, he had devoured his whole lunch and was pilfering off the sheriff's plate. Nevertheless, Hollis smiled, "I'll be sure to pass that on to her."

"Tell Mrs. Barbara to sign me up."

"Got it. See ya, Sam." Hollis locked the door and sat down to what was left of his meal. Harley watched as he started to take a bite of his greens. The sheriff paused, he looked perturbed, "Will you stop lookin' at me?"

"Sorry, Sheriff, I'm still hungry."

Hollis slid his box across to Harley, "Gosh! Take it. You can have it all. I can't eat with you looking at me like that."

"Thanks, Sheriff." Harley wolfed down the remaining portion of Hollis's meal.

Sam walked through the mob outside of the police station, and was thinking to himself as he looked at all the faces in the crowd, *Bankruptcy, bankruptcy, bankruptcy. Divorce, divorce, divorce. Insurance fraud, assault.* He knew every one of them.

"Hi, Sam."

"Mornin', Sam."

"Did ya see him, Sam?"

Sam nodded politely as he walked out to his car. It was a mob, and he knew that Harley was as good as done. There was just a slim ray of hope, and Sam knew he needed to check it out fast. Harley hadn't provided much, but if what he said was true, it might be just enough to save his life.

Chapter Five

Hollis leaned back in his chair and tossed one leg up on the table, as the wheels of the recorder turned slowly, mechanically, round and round.

Listening to a man's story was like watching a movie in a theater. The white wall behind Harley was like a big screen; the events were in living color, and this suspect the narrator. But better than a movie, Hollis controlled the projector in this theater. He could rewind the projector and make Harley go back over sketchy details, or fast-forward over parts that were irrelevant. And with his keen eye for detail, he could zoom in on some of the most minute aspects.

Taking a statements gave him a rush better than any movie he had ever seen. He was fascinated with their stories. For Hollis, it was more thrilling to him than the movies he saw when he was a kid at the old downtown theater, though he would never admit that he actually enjoyed it. Hollis got comfortable in his seat, and told Harley to continue with his story.

Harley told Hollis all about the seductive tactics of Dallas, how she showed up at his house late one night when it had been raining, her T-shirt wet and dripping in the cold of the night. Other times, she cornered him in the stalls after he had just laid them with fresh hay. Hollis could picture her long, straight, silky blonde hair swishing from side to side as she tried to get Harley's attention. When Harley described how she held her Coke can between her legs as she drove around town, the beads of moisture from the can rolling down the inner thighs of her long Coppertone legs, he could see it. He could see Harley leaning against her convertible, talking to her as she widened her legs and reached down between them, rubbing her fingertips across the top of her can. He could view her just as plain as day as Harley described that Dallas took some big gulps, licked the rim, smiled, and put the can back between her legs, squeezing it till it crinkled. He could hear the can pop just like Harley had heard it, and then he could visualize her laughing just as Harley described. And when she handed Harley the can, smiling and cajoling him, saying that "It tastes good too," Hollis could see her just like Harley had as she drove off, tossing her hair back over her shoulder.

As Harley expounded on his story, it was easy to see that mother and daugher were polar opposites except for looks. Although the mother was twenty years older than her daughter, they could easily pass for sisters. Dallas was three to four inches taller than her mother; her hair was light blonde, while her mother's was honey blonde. Leah's hair was shoulder-length and wavy, but it was their personalities that made them extremely different.

From Harley's description of Mrs. Taylor, she was modest. She practically always wore jeans or corduroys around the ranch. The only exception was when she was up at the house; occasionally she'd wear some cutoffs with tennis shoes or sandals. During the extreme summer, she might ride the four-wheeler out, wearing shorts instead of riding her horse, but you could pretty much count on her being in her jeans.

Though it was obvious to any eye that she was well-endowed, Mrs. Taylor virtually always wore buttoned-up long or short sleeve shirts, either western or denim. She buttoned them to the top two or three buttons, even when it was a hundred plus degrees, that's just the way she was. She never flaunted her looks, according to Harley, and anytime they went any place and men made passes at her (which they always did), she never responded. Not a hint of flirtation. She would be friendly, not cold, but at the cattle auctions and such, it was all business. It was almost as if she didn't care that she was beautiful. That's what made the two women so different. One was doing everything she could to hook every guy, and the other didn't care.

Hollis looked at his watch occasionally and scribbled down a note or two, but he primarily just leaned back and listened. "Go on," he'd say. Once in a while he'd tap his cigarette pack on the desk, slide out another cigarette, and light it, and then he'd slide out another one for Harley and roll it across the table to him, tossing him the lighter. Mainly he just listened. Harley could tell he was fascinated by the story.

The Taylors were an odd lot, known by everyone, but known intimately by almost no one. Mrs. Taylor was not a social bug, and despite being the biggest rancher in the area, she didn't get involved in all the associations that are affiliated with ranchers. She was devoted only to the things closest to her, the ranch and her workers. Leah was almost reclusive in a way, or at least that's the way Harley was describing her. He said that sometimes she'd drive that ole pickup truck of hers out to one of the ponds and park underneath a shade tree to read. Sometimes she'd write. He didn't know what exactly, but she had this old, leather-bound type of journal that she'd write in. She kept it tucked under the front seat, along with her Bible, and sometimes they be working and she'd say, "I've got to go," and she would just ride off. They would watch her ride up to the stables on her horse, and then a few minutes later, that old truck would be creeping off to the far corners of the ranch.

"They were different, completely different," Harley explained. Dallas craved attention, but her mother practically craved being alone. But it wasn't like she did it all the time, just sometimes. And it wasn't like she didn't like people, she did, but there was something about her that Harley was trying to explain but couldn't find the words for.

"Deep?"

"Yeah, that's it. She was deep. There was just something inside of her, like this whole world she just kept to herself." He could see it in her eyes. He said that sometimes when he looked in them, they were like topaz peepholes into another place. He could get lost just looking at them because, as he said, he didn't look at them so much as look into them. Sometimes, lots of times, he would look at her and start looking into her eyes, and he'd totally forget what he was doing.

"They were captivating, and it was dangerous, especially being around horses and bulls and such. A man's got to pay attention, or he can get hurt quick."

Harley's narration was vivid; the sheriff could see her on her horse with her tan corduroys and snake boots — not snakeskin boots, but snake boots. "Copperhead stompers," is what she called them. They came up about eighteen inches high and laced up the front and had a rounded toe instead of the pointed toe of a cowboy boot. They looked a lot like English riding boots, but were designed specifically to guard against snakes. She wore those and her cowboy hat nearly all the time, and sometimes she wore a scarf or handkerchief around her neck. The sheriff rarely saw her, but in small towns you bump into people, and she was as Harley described to a T.

Finally, when it seemed like Harley was reaching a stopping point, the sheriff asked him the question he knew would be coming, "Did you have sex with Dallas?"

"You want the truth?"

The sheriff nodded, and Harley pointed to the recorder. They stared at each other for a moment, and then Hollis reached over and turned it off.

"It ain't right that a man has to go to jail for that. I didn't chase her, Hollis, she was all over me!"

"I've got to have it on tape. I've got to have the truth, all of it, and I know you're scared of telling me the truth, but if you're innocent, it is the only thing that is gonna get you outta' here, do you understand?"

Harley shook his head, "No, I don't, but I guess I trust ya. I know you're a good man, but I . . . I dunno."

Hollis sighed and rubbed his face, "I try to be." He was worried that Harley would clam up, and he didn't want that to happen now. They had made a lot of progress and an interrogator can blow it if he pushes too hard, or miss the opportunity by not pushing hard enough. Hollis searched for the right words to say, he paused, "I've already heard from the other side, so I'm just giving you the chance to tell me your side, that's all. But, if it goes to the prosecutor, your chance is over. He won't care what you have to say."

"I'll talk," Harley reached over and turned back on the recorder. He said that Dallas came by nearly every day, and she wasn't taking no for an answer. He'd be in the barn feeding and brushing the horses, and she'd walk in and shut the door behind her and just get wild. He didn't know how to say it other than she just went for it. She must have been with someone else already because she was begging for it.

"Who do you think?"

"Could have been anyone, or it could have been everyone. I think the lifeguard was one of the guys, cuz she got real pissed off when he got fired."

Harley told him how he heard that Leah got him fired because she was afraid that Dallas would get pregnant. That was her big fear—that Dallas would get knocked up by some guy who would then try to cash in on the deal.

"So after the lifeguard got fired, you figured you were her number one prize?"

"Right, maybe I wasn't even number one, maybe I was just the most handy."

"Did you go all the way?"

Harley claimed he couldn't stop her. "She knew exactly what she was doing, and she could use it against a guy because of her age and who her daddy is."

"What do you mean?"

Harley glanced over at the door; he could just feel Lucian on the other side. A shadow passed in front of the light coming underneath the door, so he lowered his voice and leaned closer to the sheriff, "She tried it with me."

"In what way? Like blackmail?"

"Kind of. She'd come and get what she wanted and then say afterwards stuff like, 'You don't hafta worry, cuz I won't tell. I'd never let them put you in jail.' She'd say something to make me think about it, you know, and it was sorta like a trap to begin with. She'd coax me into sex so she could use it against me."

Harley told how she started asking him for favors like buying her beer. He knew she could get anyone to buy her whatever she wanted, but she was testing him. The thing was, she didn't even really drink that much, and besides her dad had plenty stocked at the house. She wanted control and knew what to use to get it. One time, according to Harley, she asked him to beat up a guy who dissed her, but he talked her into changing her mind.

"Who was it?"

"It was the mayor's son. The little pissant took her to the school dance and told some guys around town that they did it, and it pissed her off real bad." Harley knew he had a problem on his hands because if he didn't do what she asked, then she be pissed at him, so he did everything he could to talk her out of it. He agreed to just talk to the kid. Harley told him that he'd "be a bigger hit at college if he showed up with all his teeth," and fortunately, he listened. If Harley had beat him up, he knew he would be going to jail, and if he pissed Dallas off real bad, he could be going to jail, so he was relieved it turned out the way that it did. But after that, he knew he couldn't trust her, she was vindictive. He knew what she was capable of doing and would do, and that was just the start of it. If she ever took it to her daddy, jail would have looked like a sweet alternative.

Sheriff Brown didn't say anything. He glanced at the little Plexiglas window out of the corner of his eye, like there was something there, but there wasn't anything. He was stalling, trying to think of what to say or ask next. The crowd could be heard outside, and something banged against the outside wall. They both heard what sounded like a loudspeaker blaring in the streets. It was near noon, the crowd was getting restless, and the sheriff knew he was going to have to make some kind of announcement that day. He looked at his watch and put a new tape in the recorder. He wiped the sweat from his brow. Hollis pushed down the red record button and leaned back, "Let's roll."

Harley watched him exhale, his body relaxed. Hollis tapped the note pad with his pencil like a secretary and nodded at the mike. The sheriff was ready.

Hollis flipped back to the previous page and adjusted his glasses. He gave the usual introductions and noted the time they began the tape and then asked Harley begin again with when and how Leah figured out that Dallas was sexually active, "Start there."

Harley began recalling the details of how it all came out. He said that Leah approached him one day at the shop and asked him about it.

"She wasn't what you'd call upset or irate, but she was straightforward like she always was."

Harley felt sorry for her because he knew the truth, but he couldn't bring himself to tell her. He felt really bad about it, but he was caught between a rock and a hard place. He wanted to be honest with Leah, but if he was, then he'd suffer retaliation by Dallas, so he lied. He denied any knowledge of anything, and afterwards he told Dallas that he couldn't have anything to do with her anymore. But she didn't give up; she kept coming by his place after-hours.

He wasn't seeing her at the ranch as much, because her mother was watching things a lot closer now. There was a feud going on between them, and it was starting to get a little tense.

"Okay, I've got that, but then it went to another level right? Something else happened?"

Harley lit a cigarette and popped his neck. He was feeling the tension but knew he couldn't avoid the subject any longer. According to him, it was one day about a year ago, last June, when everything changed. He said he had to go up to the house, to her office, and give her some samples of some heifer's blood that he took that morning. Something was ailing them, and Mrs. Taylor didn't know what. Everyone else was off; it might have been a Mexican holiday or something, he couldn't remember. Earlier that morning, Dallas and her mother had a big fight. He could hear them all the way out at the corral, but they had been fighting often anyway. Dallas stormed out of the house, jumped in her car, sped all the way down to the highway, and then tore off towards town. He thought to himself, *Uh oh, something bad has happened,* and he didn't look forward to going up there and giving Leah those samples. He was real nervous. He figured it might have had something to do with him, and he'd probably get fired. "I told myself, 'This is it.'"

"Was anyone else there? At all?"

"Nope, just me and Leah. I went into the house and to her office in the back. She asked me to shut the door behind me. I thought I was going to be fired; she didn't look right. She was upset, and I could tell she had been crying. She had her hair up in a French braid, and I was standing over by the door. She asked me to come closer and I did. She looked at me kinda funny and took the samples from my hand and put them on the desk behind her. She was standing there in those tan corduroys with her knee-high boots. She had on a long sleeve, silk shirt. And then she asked me what I thought of her. I didn't know what she meant at first; it was the strangest question."

"In what way? Like a boss?"

"That's what I wondered. I told her that she was a great boss and I liked working with her, and she said, 'Not like that.' She asked me what I thought of *her*. My mouth went dry. My heart started pounding so hard, I could hear it all the way up in my ears. I was scared to say anything, and she asked me again to tell her. She said, 'It's just you and me here, Harley. It's okay, I just need to know.' I felt like my knees were going to buckle. My hands even shook, but I told her that she was the best-looking woman I had ever laid eyes on, period. There just wasn't no second. The moment I told her, it seemed like the whole world just stood still. I thought, *Uh oh, I've blown it now, she's gonna fire me. I said the wrong thing, I shoulda' kept my big mouth shut.*"

"Go on," Hollis said.

"Then she said she'd 'make me a deal.' I thought it was some kind of trick question at first, like she'd let me work for two more weeks and then I'd hafta find another job, you know because of Dallas and all. But instead, she took off my hat and said that I could have all of her that I wanted, so long as I never touched Dallas again. Those were her exact words."

Hollis was somber, stunned more like it. He sat there gazing at Harley, with his pencil in his hand. In a raspy, barely audible whisper, he said, "Go on."

Harley told how she tossed his hat over onto a chair. She let down her hair and unbuttoned her blouse, button by button. Her hands looked feminine and womanly. He remembered there was a slight tremble to them. She stood there in front of him; her butt was against the desk. He couldn't believe what was happening. Her shirt hung open just a couple of inches as she unbuttoned her shirt from the top down. She was a wearing a black bra and breathing really heavy. He still hadn't touched her, he just stood there. And then she took her shirt by the collar and dropped it from her shoulders, and it fell to the floor. He couldn't believe what he was looking at, how beautiful she was, how perfect.

She looked at him, and in the softest voice he ever heard, she said, "Hold me." They just looked at each other, standing there, and then he put his hand on her waist and felt her skin for the first time. He said he had never felt a woman like that in his entire life, and he just squeezed her hips in his hand and they kissed.

Harley noticed that the sheriff was looking a little flushed, "What's the matter? Ya lookin' a little red in the gills, Hollis."

"Hold on." Hollis pulled out a prescription bottle and downed a pill real quick. He chased it with a cup of coffee, leaned back in his chair, and took a deep breath. His eyes looked like owl eyes after they've just spotted their prey. His big old fingers had trouble putting the lid back on the little tiny pill bottle.

"Need help?"

"No, I don't! I got it off; I can get it back on."

"Just askin'."

"Shewww," Hollis let out a deep breath. His hands fidgeted with the bottle cap, and then he just finally gave up and stuck it back in his pants pocket. "Then what?"

"I didn't waste no time." Harley looked over at the door to see if anyone might be eavesdropping. He lowered his voice, "It was the most incredible experience of my life. I tore it up. She hadn't been touched in a long time either, I can tell you that. I tell ya, Hollis, a man could go all over this entire world, every country there is, and see every darn thing God has made and never see anything as beautiful as that woman." He shook his head in a daze, "You just wouldn't believe how perfect she was."

The sheriff turned off the tape recorder. He was sweating. "I've got to get some water."

"Me too. It's been driving me crazy for the last year now. You can't imagine what this has done to me. Every time I ever think about her, something just runs through me. I get all jittery inside, and sometimes I shake and sweat just like ya are right now."

"I ain't sweatin'."

"Then there is a leak in your forehead, cuz ya got little beads of water all over yer face."

Hollis got up from the table and went over to the door, wiping his head, "It's summer; everybody sweats in the summer." Hollis unlocked the door and stepped out to the hall. "Get us some water!"

Harley grinned, "You might wanna get one pitcher justa pour it on ya, or else stick your head under a faucet." He chucked at the sheriff who was trying to ignore him, "Yeah, and ya shoulda tried working round her. It'd drive you nuts. It did me."

Teresa brought in two pitchers of water and looked at the sheriff, "Is something wrong?"

"Oh no, just a little thirsty, that's all."

"You want me to turn up the air conditioning, bring ya a fan?"

"No, no."

Harley laughed, "He'll be alright. He's just getting old, and he hasn't had his furnace cranked up in a while."

"Huh?"

Taking a drink, Hollis said, "Never mind about him. Any calls?"

"A zillion—everybody—newspapers from all over, radio, even the governor's office again."

Taking another big drink, Hollis asked, "What about the lab?"

"They're done; it's on its way."

"Thanks, hon." Sheriff Brown locked the door behind her and sat back down. He put his elbow on the table and rubbed his forehead. Harley didn't know what to think. He suddenly felt like he had just told someone he had been with his sister. The sheriff sighed, "My, my . . . I never would of known. I had no idea that's the way things were out there."

"You asked."

Perspiration was still beading up on his forehead. He wiped his sleeve across the sweat and leaned across the table, practically whispering, "You swear this is true?"

Harley nodded his head. He said that he usually has a clue what a woman is thinking, but he had no idea what was coming that day. But, from the time he first touched her, he knew he would never be the same. The touch of her skin rushed up his arms and through his whole body. He knew from that first moment that he could never get enough of it. It didn't really matter to him what happened from that point on, as long as he could have her, nothing else in the world mattered. He didn't even think about Rip. Harley admitted it sounded crazy; there he was in the man's house with his wife. But if Rip came in he coulda killed him and it wouldn't have mattered, because he would have died a happy man. Harley didn't know how long they were in her office that first time, "Maybe hours." It was like they lost touch with reality. Personally, he felt like she just broke down, life had overwhelmed her, and when she finally let it go, she let go completely. "Everyone has gotta have some release, and she had things that had been building up in her for a long time." Harley noticed the tape recorder wasn't running, "Don'tcha wanna know what happened?"

"Ahhhummm," Hollis cleared his throat. "We don't need to have everything in public record." He motioned with his head to the outside, "They don't need to know all the details. Just keep going."

"Okay," Harley leaned back in his chair and stared up at the ceiling. He began talking about driving back home after that first time. It was like coming out of a dream, he could barely drive straight or keep from swerving all over the road. He kept thinking to himself, *This can't be real,* but it was. He said he had sex with lots of women before, but this was totally different, totally, and he knew what it was. He had never had a woman who felt like she did, it was like all the rest were just girls; she was a woman, but it was more than that, he was in love. After he got home that afternoon, it hit him, he wasn't gonna be able to see her again till after the weekend. That's when he realized for sure that it was love, because he couldn't wait to see her. She did something to him that no one else ever did. He didn't know if it was the way she held him or the way she stroked his hair or maybe how she breathed in his ear, but she was all he could think about. He couldn't believe it all happened, and so fast.

The next morning he woke up and kinda checked himself mentally. He had to stop and think, *Did this really happen or was it a dream?* He fixed himself breakfast and sat down at his little kitchen table. On his chest was a long, blonde hair, her hair. It was real alright, and it hit him again. Crazy thoughts went through his head, here he was and she was out at the ranch, and he wanted her. He wanted her again, but it was insane to think about that, because she was out there with Rip.

As he described it, he felt like a man who needed a drink, but the liquor store was closed and he'd have to go all day Saturday and all day Sunday. The exhilaration turned to remorse, almost like a depression. He didn't know what he was going to do.

The sheriff raised his eyebrow and cleared his throat, "What did you do?"

Harley said he paced the floor, trying to think of how he could see her. Every thought he had was crazy. He thought about driving back out there and, saying he forgot some tools, see if she could meet him out at the barn or something, but that was crazy. He thought about calling her and seeing if she could come into town, but what if Rip answered? What would he say? "Hello, Rip, can I speak to your wife and see if she can come over and tear it up for a few hours?"

"I knew I was cracking up Hollis, I mean I honestly considered just driving out there and saying 'Okay, Rip, here's the deal. I've been with your wife, and I can't live without her, so I'm just taking her, and you're gonna hafta let her go or just kill me. Which is it?' I honestly thought about doing that, and for a while it seemed like the best thing to do, and then it would hit me that this kind of thinking was nuts!

"So . . ."

Harley said that he got to the point where he couldn't eat, he kept fretting about it so much. And then he didn't know why, but he ended up calling one of his old girlfriends, a real nice girl. He plumb wore her out that day. She had no idea what was going on, and he didn't have the heart to tell her. He knew it wasn't right to use her like that, but if he didn't, he was afraid he was going to do something even stupider, "Like show up at the ranch and get both of us killed." Harley paused, "You want the girl's name?"

Hollis shook his head, "No, it ain't important. Keep going."

Hollis watched Harley's hands and took notes. The tape recorder was still off. In interviews, the body language is sometimes more important than what people say. Harley gestured a lot when he talked about Leah, but on other subjects, he kept his hands in his pockets or doodled with his fingers like he was bored. He yawned a lot, but of course he was tired. Hollis knew he was getting to the hot spot; he had to keep him going. Just a little bit more and he'd get what he needed. He knew what went down at the ranch. "So tell me, what happened next? What happened that first day you came back? Did she blow you off?"

"No."

Harley said it wasn't like that. He said he showed up that Monday morning and she sent them all out into the fields. She asked how he was doing, and he told her he hadn't slept much. She looked at him with those blue eyes and told him that she hardly slept either. He went out with the hands and couldn't stop thinking of her, so he watched the house until Dallas drove off; it was about eleven o'clock, he thought. He went up to the house, and she was in the kitchen just starting to get lunch ready. She asked him what he wanted, and he told her he forgot something in her office. She stopped what she was doing, put down the bowl, and smiled, "Why don't you go and get it."

"That's what she said?"

"Uh hum, and I did. I don't think any two people stripped so fast in their entire lives. That door hardly shut before I had her in my mouth."

Another bead of sweat was bulging from Hollis's forehead, "Ahhumm, so did this become a daily thing or what?"

Pop! Harley cracked his neck to the side, "I wish . . . but no." Pop! "She regained her senses a little bit and got real careful. She wasn't a stupid woman. One day a week the house maid came out, usually Wednesday's, so we couldn't be together then. Lots of days Dallas hung out, and there were days when I couldn't get away. Santana had me doing something with him or the other guys. That second time was the only time that I'd say it was risky. No, everybody had to be gone or at least way out somewhere on the ranch."

"And Rip?"

He was always gone, according to Harley. He had his little honeys in various towns throughout the area, and that was his thing.

"Dallas musta got her a fella or two, because she was gone a lot also."

Harley knew she was doing some traveling, because he checked her mileage when he changed the oil — about three thousand a month — that's a lot of trips somewhere.

All in all, life couldn't have been better for Harley, or that's what he claimed. He said he felt like the luckiest man alive. He was twenty three, had a good job, was "making love to the most beautiful woman in the world," and got to be with her five days a week. And he was in love.

"What more could a guy ask for?"

He didn't call any ex-girlfriends over anymore. It was just that one time, and he figured that it had more to do with love than anything. It was, as Harley described, more of an "emotional deal." He was in love with her, and it wasn't like he had to compete against anyone else. The relationship was between the two of them, only they knew about it, and he had this strange peculiar comfort in that.

"Don't get me wrong now, but in a way, it was kinda like how you feel toward your first good lookin' teacher, know what I mean?"

Hollis nodded without looking up. He was writing some more notes, "Okay, go ahead. So you fell in love with her, but she didn't know it, right?"

"Of course not. She knew I liked her. I mean, we joked around together all the time. We had a good relationship, but there was nothing said like that."

Harley revealed more about the Taylors' marriage and how bizarre it was. He had heard from lots of people that Rip liked the cheap, trashy type. He liked the pick-me-ups and cheap motels. Everybody knew that he threw his money around, picking up waitresses or girls at the cash registers.

"That was his thing. He liked buying people. That's how he got Leah in the first place; he had money, and she was trying to support her family. When you're poor and someone has got money, they look like a godsend. Rip used that all his life, and it always worked for him."

"She told you that?"

"Yeah, not right away, but later she talked about it. She said that it wasn't really a marriage so much as 'purchase.' She was his trophy, just like the elk and bear that he had hanging in that big game room."

Harley depicted a fabricated marriage, the poor girl who married the rich man. She went from waitress to socialite, but she didn't fit in. She wasn't the country-club type who Rip liked to impress. When she got pregnant, she thought that might change things, but it didn't. Very rarely did they ever do the family thing; it was fragmented from the start. She stayed on the ranch with Dallas, and he'd come home with stuff for their daughter. She could smell other women on him as he gave Dallas dolls or jewelry. There was never anything for her, and she knew she couldn't say anything or do anything because she could be back on the streets, and she was still trying to help her mamma and grandma out.

Hollis pushed himself back from the table. He had a long, dejected look on his face, "My, my," he sighed, "I had no idea. What a waste of human life."

"I'm telling you. I never knew it was like that until she told me. You have no idea how lonely and hurt she had been . . . for years. Do you understand now, why she ended up doing maybe what she did?"

Hollis's eyes were shut. He just nodded. He didn't say anything.

Harley pointed outside, "They sure don't know what that woman went through. They have no idea."

"Okay, tell me about Dallas now." He pushed the red record button, "Tell me about her. Gotta be kinda hard keeping all this from her about her mother, right?"

"Well, yeah, I told her I started dating a lady down in DeQueen, and we were getting serious."

"Why did you tell her that?"

Harley leaned across the table, "Hell! Man, don'tcha understand nothin' 'bout women? Ya can't ever just break up with one; you hafta always tell 'em it's someone else, and you sure can't tell 'em you just don't want to see them no more or some nonsense."

"Like doing their mother."

"That too. So I made up someone else. See? I told her I was dating a woman who had two kids, and they were needing a daddy."

"Did it work?"

"It worked for a little while, but she was spoiled and selfish. 'No' is not in her vocabulary. I think that if she wasn't involved with someone else, I wouldn't have stood a chance."

"So there was someone else, you think?"

"I'm pretty sure, and if it's who I think it is, he's married and got kids. I'd sure hate to cause the man trouble cuz she is still underage."

"Okay, go on."

"To be perfectly honest, I didn't know if I could hold out. I was glad to see her go back to school again. I was scared to death that I was going to give in one day. I had this fear of doing it and breaking my promise to Leah, but it was hard to get rid of her sometimes. She said she was in love with my lips and that I was the best kisser."

"Geez Louise, like I really care about that! Gosh, Harley, we've been in here six hours and that's about all I've go to tell them. Hear those people out there? I don't think their interested in that. I'm not interested in that. And you know what? Nobody is telling me what yer saying either. Everybody's story is different from yours."

"All I know is what I told ya."

"Anybody ever see ya'll together?"

"No."

"Dallas?"

"No."

"Did ya ever check into a motel together, use another name, go shopping together? Did ya go to a park or a movie or any place where ya'll coulda been seen?"

"Nope."

The sheriff sighed, "That's where I have a problem." He tossed his pen on the desk. "You're the only one who is telling me the story this way. No one else in the whole county is giving me the story like you are. Some have said that they believe you might have been infatuated, even obsessed with Mrs. Taylor, but, I mean, no one has told me you guys were having an affair. No one."

"I swear, Hollis, it's true."

The sheriff shrugged and looked at his watch, it was just past twelve. "Well, I'm listening, but all I have is your word, and a lot of people will have a hard time believing just your word. A man carries on an affair for a year, there is usually some sort of evidence: love letters, pictures or a card, something, but you've got squat."

Harley reached into his back pocket for his wallet. It was gone, and then he remembered they had it. "There is something in my wallet."

"What, a picture?"

"No, a poem she wrote."

"Poem?"

"She used to write a lot, I told you that, and she gave me a poem one time that she wrote.

The sheriff got up. He hit the stop button and stretched. Cars were honking their horns outside. They could both hear the phones ringing down the hall. "You say it is in your wallet?"

Harley nodded, "I would never throw it away."

"You better hope it's there, cuz you need somethin' son. You need some help like nobody's business. I'll be right back."

Chapter Six

Harley sat alone. He was scared.

He tried to discern for himself the feeling of the crowd outside. It was an awful sound. He listened to the voices, the cheers; their muffled sounds permeated through the walls. It was the sound of judgment.

He thought back on the question the sheriff had asked earlier: "Where was his fan club?" Where were all those girls who told him that they loved him? They signed their notes with hearts and kisses. Where were his friends from growing up (all two of them)? Neighbors? Where were the people from Grandma Bass's church? Classmates? Work hands?

Harley thought to himself, *My uncles, they're still alive; where are they?* He must have had at least fifteen cousins spread here and about, where were they all?

His story was different from everyone else's, that's what the sheriff said. He wondered what were the others' stories, and who had told them? *What would they know anyway?* he thought. They weren't up at the house when he was there with Mrs. Taylor. No one else was at his home when Dallas showed up in the middle of the night. How could people say things that they don't know anything about?

He started thinking about what Hollis had said, "As many as thirty people were giving a different story?" Thirty? He couldn't imagine what thirty people could possibly know about him that would be of any significance. Who were they? Only the Mexicans had anything good to say about him. So who was it? It had to be his girlfriends, or ex-girlfriends, but what would they know about him out at the ranch? None of them knew anything; he never told anyone anything.

Harley mulled it over, tossed it around, and then he remembered the sheriff's words, "Some people say that you had an obsession with Mrs. Taylor."

Obsession? Was that what it was? Harley grabbed the locks of his hair and pulled. Was that a possibility? Could that be true? Was if feasible that everyone else was right and he was wrong?

If that were the case, he'd be insane. He'd be crazy, a raving lunatic. A man so out of his mind that he imagined things to the point that fantasies became reality, and if that was the case then probably nothing he said was true, it was some sort of twisted fabrication in his mind.

He could hear the voices ranting outside.

"No!" Harley shouted. "No, this can't be true!"

Harley got up and paced back and forth. He walked over to the door and looked out the Plexiglas window down the hall. Maybe that's what all the fuss was about—the state troopers, the rangers, the crowd, the TV people—they caught the lunatic, and it was him. Harley felt sick; he turned and slid his back down the wall, his long legs drawn up before him, his eyes closed, and his face buried to his knees.

His body riveted in convulsions, and a cry burst forth from deep down inside. His hands covered his head, and he sobbed. His diaphragm burst with massive, wailing heaps, and the only sound that he could hear were his own sobs. His tears poured like a stream through his knees, splattering on the linoleum.

Harley didn't care if anyone heard him. He didn't care anymore if Lucian had his ear pressed to the door, or if people in town knew, or even if the sheriff heard. Everything inside him just suddenly let go, and he couldn't stop it.

He hadn't cried like that since he was a child, since that cold winter day when his mother died. He remembered how his world ended when he got off the school bus with his satchel of books. The ambulance was there and men carried a draped body in a gurney down the slippery, wooden, porch steps. Standing in a puddle by the road, he dropped his books. Her arm fell off the gurney and blotches of blood soaked through the bed sheet draped over her body. He remembered their faces in the grizzly gray rain, how they shut the door and locked it. A neighbor asking, "Where do you want to go live?" That was it, that's all there was, it was over. Age eleven and his world ended.

And so he cried in that cell like he did long, long, long ago on that first night he slept alone. He had forgotten what it felt like . . . until now. The feelings were identical: loss, hopelessness, and fear. He was buried in grief.

Meanwhile, down the hall at the dispatcher's station, it was sheer chaos. Teresa was in a tiff trying to locate some deputies to fill in, but her efforts did little more than draw an apathetic response from her boss. Administration wasn't necessarily his strong suit, and for that matter it was becoming obvious to Teresa that public relations wasn't either.

"Hate calls," that's what she called them. They had lit up the switchboard that morning and were really getting ugly. She finally walked into his office and shut the door. "Is there something going on that I don't know about?"

Hollis shuffled around through the papers on his desk talking to himself which had recently become an annoying habit. He was only halfway listening to her, "Like what?"

"I dunno, Hollis, maybe like have you really pissed someone off here lately?"

He picked up an evidence bag that he hadn't yet labeled. He pulled out a billfold and fumbled through it.

"There it is." Hollis said, fishing a piece of paper out of the billfold before putting it back in the bag. He unlocked a safe and tossed it in, all the while mumbling to himself.

"Whadda ya mean 'pissed off?' I haven't done anything. Why ya askin'?"

She could tell he was clueless. He really didn't know. She could tell he was totally preoccupied and wondered if it would do any good to tell him anyway. He looked at her, totally befuddled, like he had no earthly idea what she was talking about, and as was his habit, he switched topics, "Heard from Barbara? She all right?"

Teresa knew it was useless trying to talk to him now. He would just brush off the threats, downplay them. He wasn't the kind of man who got all shook up over things like this. Besides that, the phones kept ringing, and if he didn't care about people threatening his life, why should she get all bent out of joint? Flustered, she put her hands on her hips and sighed, "She's fine, Hollis. I just got a call from her while ago."

"Did you tell her I would probably be home late?"

"Hollis, she knows better than anyone else just what kinda day yer having. I think she knows by now you'll get there when you get there. Besides, some folks are keeping her up to date."

"That's good."

Teresa didn't say anything she wanted to. She wanted to tell him that Barbara had told her she was getting angry calls. People would say the cruelest things and hang up. Barbara was worried about her husband too, but with Hollis, it didn't do any good to bring it up. He wasn't listening.

Teresa returned to the dispatcher's desk, ever the more frustrated, and began answering the phones. Duke was milling around doing a lot of nothing, answering a phone every now and then. He mainly raided the snack machine and patrolled the hallway leading to the front door, eating Cheetos and sipping on a Pepsi. It was pushing 102 degrees outside, and tempers were flaring. A fistfight broke out earlier in the street, and people's language was beginning to get awful out there. The only levity was when the Johnson boys drove around downtown in their truck with an effigy of Harley tied to the back, bouncing and rolling along. A stream of hisses and boos commenced when Duke stopped them and untied the mangled overalls and boots and tossed them in the dumpster out back of the police station. Personally, he didn't see any harm in it, but the folks were getting a little out of hand, and he knew that. The next thing would be to start torching it, and with it being hot like what it was, that would have been a big mistake.

Just then, the door opened down the hall; it was Sam again. Hollis came out of his office, holding something in his hand, "Glad you're back; I got something I want to share with you."

"Fine, fine. Be glad to, Sheriff, and I got a question for Harley, if you would much oblige me?"

The two walked over to the interrogation room, and Hollis unlocked the door. Harley was sitting on the floor when they walked in. He didn't say a word, he just sat real quiet.

"Want to join us?" The sheriff was puzzled by his suspect.

Harley stood up but kept his head down; he didn't even acknowledge Sam. He wiped his face with his sleeve and grumbled under his breath, "I guess so."

Hollis had hoped he'd break and sensed that he was ready to. He knew not to push a suspect; just let them come out with it. He sat down and pulled out the note, unfolding it on the table, "I found it, Harley; I found the poem."

Hollis slid the paper over to Sam, "I'd like Sam to take a look at it and tell me what he thinks." Hollis handed the poem to the attorney and then kidded Harley, "By the way, you might want to clean that wallet out sometime when you get the chance."

"Well I like to save stuff."

"No, museums save stuff, but candy wrappers with phone numbers, rubbers, and ticket stubs from rodeos three years ago, that's trash. Geez, Harley, that thing was as heavy as a brick."

"I know, but . . ."

"Save it. We don't have time." The sheriff motioned to Sam, "So whadda ya think?"

His mustache moved from side to side. A grim look came across his face and he shrugged his shoulders, "It's pretty sad, it really is."

"But it says what I told you, Sheriff. She wasn't no happily married woman, I don't care what they say! That proves it. Doesn't it, Sam? I mean, it shows that she's unhappy and she's thinking about running off and all."

Sheriff Brown hit the tape recorder, "Now wait a minute, before we go to jumping to some wild conclusions, let's just let Sam read it for the record and see what it says." He motioned to Sam.

Sam adjusted his glasses and held the paper out in front of him. A deep, penetrating look fell across his face. They watched as his eyes studied her words, and then he cleared his throat and began to read out loud.

Running from Tomorrow Today

I'm running from tomorrow
today.
Running from the past,
like a deer through bramble brush.
I am running for higher ground.
I am running in the heat of the day.
I am running in the dark of the night.
I am forever being chased
by all my tragic mistakes.
I've been running all my life
from the fear of every tomorrow,
all the faults of all my yesterdays.

I'm caught in between the two,
no place to hide, no place to stay.
I'm running in fear of the future.
I'm running from tomorrow
today.
— Leah Taylor

All the men were silent for a moment after he read the poem. They just looked at one another. Each man had heard her voice and seen her face in those few words.

Harley put his head down. The sheriff took the poem from Sam. He held it for a moment, and then he started to tuck it away in a file. Pausing, he looked at the note again and left the room, saying he was going to deposit it back in his safe "where it can't get lost."

"Do you think that proves I'm innocent, Sam?"

"Not by a long shot. A good attorney can twist it and make people believe that she was running from you."

"But you know that's not what she meant; she didn't have anything to fear from me. Come on, Sam. You know that."

Sam leaned over and grabbed Harley by the arm. Almost whispering, he said, "The most important thing is not what I think." He pointed at the door, "It's what that man thinks down the hall. That's the only thing of any importance to you right now." He patted him on the arm reassuringly, "Now, that poem was a good start, it got him to thinking, but yer gonna hafta have a lot more. Now tell me quick, where is the key to your house? I went out there and couldn't get in."

Harley leaned over to Sam and whispered to him where he stashed his extra key, just as the sheriff was unlocking the door. He could hear the sounds of the phones ringing and the fax printing as soon as Hollis opened the door.

"Damn madhouse out there." The sheriff stood in the doorway and looked at Sam. The day had already been a drain on the sheriff; you could see the exhaustion in his eyes. The jovial attitude he had earlier had long since disappeared from his face. He looked anxious, and Sam knew he need not wait around for a hint. He grabbed his hat and got up from the table.

"I'll be seeing you, Harley."

"Coming back?"

"Oh yeah, the sheriff and I'll have a chance to talk then, right, Hollis?"

Hollis didn't acknowledge his comment. "Hate to hafta run you off, but I've got a lot of work cut out for me here." Sam had known Hollis for a long time. He had never seen the man shudder at anything; nothing seemed to bother him, ever. But something wasn't quite right, something was very much bothering him. He didn't know if it was the crowd, or if he had gotten a disturbing phone call, or if maybe it was the poem. But something was bothering the sheriff all right, and Sam knew better than to push it.

"Thanks for letting me see him again, Hollis."

Hollis didn't even look him in the eye, he just shut the door. He sat down quietly at the table and shuffled some papers back and forth. He exhaled several times long and slow. Harley sat quietly, not saying a word. He could tell something was bothering him too.

"Dallas is coming down here." His voice sounded almost monotone, flat and without emotion.

"When?"

"In just a bit." Hollis sounded remorseful, but he said, "We've got to get going, Harley." He popped open the door to the recorder and slid in another cassette tape. "Tell me more about Mrs. Taylor. Whadda ya think went wrong out there with her marriage?

Harley sighed. He stood up and went to the window and looked out. He stared far off, as if looking back over the years. "Well, from what she said, it never was good. She realized from the start that it was a mistake."

He began describing how she explained it to him. According to Harley, Rip treated her bad from the get-go. "A month into their marriage, he called her a two-bit dishwasher. If she cleaned the house real good, he'd toss a ten down on the floor and say 'There's your tip.' Leah said she didn't know why he was cruel, but he was."

Hollis interrupted, "I thought you said she never talked about him?"

"I said she never talked about him at first, never said a word, but later on she did. She told me everything. She told me the sex was horrible; he wanted her to do all kinds of stuff she didn't want to."

Hollis turned off the tape recorder, "Go on." He wanted to ask what but then he didn't want to know either. He felt dirty even hearing about it. "Why didn't she do something about it, she tell ya that?"

Harley said that she was stunned at first. She thought maybe she might have been at fault, because she wasn't exactly sure what she should expect. She got pregnant so quickly that she had to stay in it up to a point, or that's at least she told herself. Harley sat back down. He looked depressed, and it was obvious he didn't like talking about it. "Ya know, she was a religious person, so she prayed about it, and she said it did get better. There would be times when he treated her normally, and she'd think, 'Well, it's all over. It's in the past.' And then he come home one day and start in again with his insults. Then it would stop again, and she'd think it was all over, things would be fine, but they never really were."

"Did he beat her, she ever say anything about that."

"Nope. He never did. She told me he never touched her, and I never saw anything either like a black eye or a bruise. Everything he did was verbal, he just put her down."

"He was degrading, but no physical violence."

Harley paused, "Ummm, he never touched her, but he did tell her that if she ever left him he'd 'take care of her.'"

"Whadda ya mean, 'take care of her'?"

"He told her there would be an accident. Her car would miss a turn, or a piece of heavy equipment would fall on her. One time, he put his hands around her neck and told her how easy it would be for him to snap it. Then he said he could slip her foot into the stirrup on her saddle and give her horse a good whack and he'd run half a mile before he'd ever stop."

"He told her that?"

"Yeah, and then he asked her how she thought her face would look in the casket after it had been dragged around the ranch a couple of times?"

Hollis wasn't sure whether to believe him or not. He had a tendency not to believe, except that he knew Rip and knew how intimidating and belligerent he was to people. Harley said that he never did things in front of people like the country-club crowd, he'd act like the perfect charmer, and then when everyone was gone, he call her some degrading name. It was like he had to put her into her place, inside a little box. He had total control over her, but he did it all with words . . . and fear.

"So she feared for her life is what you're saying?"

Harley leaned across the table and gave the sheriff a dirty look, "Wouldn't you?"

"Well, she could've gone to the police."

"You're joking, right? Who do you have who would have stood up to him? Lucian? Duke? You? You want to tell me you had the balls to go out to his ranch and tell him to quit . . . ah, never mind. She was scared, so scared she told me that if she ever left, she would have to change her identity or stage her death."

"You can't be serious."

"Serious as a heart attack. She thought about a boating accident, maybe, on Lake Ouachita. They don't always recover the body, you know. And she thought about a fire, maybe in the barn. Of course she didn't ever do it, but she thought about it."

Harley went on, describing other things she told him. There was one thing that the sheriff thought rang true, because he had known Leah since she was a girl. The thing that actually scared Leah the most was being poor again. Rip had told her that she'd never get a dime and wouldn't live long enough to spend it if she ever tried to divorce him. According to Harley, being poor like what she had been messed her up. She was scared to death of being so poor again that she'd have to beg from neighbors.

Hollis knew the story, almost everyone did. Her life had been a series of tragedies. First the Corps took their farm and then leased it back to them, and her family got screwed on the deal. Her brother and sister then got run over by a drunk driver while they were waiting for the school bus. A year later, her daddy got killed in a logging accident, and her mother never was right after that. Depression almost killed her. Leah often had to walk to the neighbor's house to borrow some flower to make some pancakes, or meal to baste a chicken she'd caught (or stolen).

The worse thing, the absolutely worse thing, was that day she turned eighteen and the government drove them off their land. The lease was up. Her family's home was bulldozed, and all they had was a couple of suitcases and a truck packed down with furniture, junk really. She, her grandmother, and her mom had nowhere to go. They were homeless, actually homeless, and Harley was right, it did mess her up. It was one of those things in people's lives that causes them to say, "No matter what, absolutely no matter what, I will never be like that again." And that was Leah, no matter what, she wasn't going back to sleeping on neighbors' couches again or living out of the truck, having to park it at camping sites where they could use the restrooms for a day or two before the park rangers ran them off for squatting.

Hollis listened and knew at least that part of story was true. He knew of the family's hard times and the humiliation they endured, and he suspected that's why she married Rip to begin with. It may have been hard, but at least she wasn't poor.

The sheriff pondered and scratched his head. He scribbled down some notes and leaned back, "You think that's why she wouldn't ask for help? It seemed to her like begging?"

"Geez, I dunno. I just know she was very strong-willed. She wasn't gonna ask for no help from no body. You should know that much about her."

Hollis closed his eyes and shook his head, "What a shame. What a damn shame." He turned the page and hit the record button, "Okay, let me ask you another question. What about Dallas, or anyone, even Rip — did anyone ever suspect what was going on between you two?"

"No, not ever. Dallas didn't have a clue. Are you serious? She'd blow a gasket and go straight to her Dad. No one knew anything."

"What about the housekeeper, could she have known?

"Marie? Nah, she only came like once a week. She didn't know squat. My God, we weren't stupid, Sheriff; it wasn't like we were in one room getting it on while she was in the next mopping floors."

"But could she have heard something? Maybe ya'll talking, her on the phone?"

"Nope. Listen to me, she came in once a week and did clothes and vacuumed and mainly picked up Dallas's room. I was always way out in the fields anyway, so why are you asking?"

"Sometimes when someone has information that is damaging to another there is blackmail."

"Blackmail?"

"Listen, number one, she's rich. Number two, she's having an affair. And number three, she must keep it a secret. Add it up and you've got a perfect candidate for extortion. Quite frankly, Harley, your best chance of getting out of here is if someone blackmailed her. Someone may have known about you and used it to profit, but maybe something went wrong. That's why I'm asking, so you're saying that there is no chance that Marie or the Mexicans knew anything, is that right?"

Hollis waited for the answer. Most guilty people jump at the chance to pin it on someone else, to deflect attention away from themselves. Harley sat there thinking, "Ummm, no there's no chance they knew. Like I said, we were real careful; it wasn't like I was out there running around grabbing her butt in front of people. Heck, I didn't even do that when people where gone. To be perfectly honest, I'd have given anything to be with her more, but it wasn't all that often, sometimes we'd go two weeks. She was careful, very, very careful. And besides, Leah would have told me if someone were blackmailing her."

Tap. Tap. Tap. It was Teresa. She held up her hand like she had a phone. They watched her lips move, "The captain."

Hollis shook his head no and mouth the words "not now." He didn't have time for the state police, at least not then. Teresa gave him a disappointed look and left.

Harley continued talking about Leah and the disturbing relationship she had with Rip and with Dallas. He said that Rip hardly ever touched her; their relationship was about nonexistent. It was the loneliest house in the whole world. He would be there the entire weekend, and they would hardly ever speak. He would walk right by her and not say a word. The sheriff chewed on his pencil and listened, wondering if that was possible. Would a jury believe that? Then he thought about the poem. It certainly looked like her handwriting. It spoke volumes about her life, how trapped she felt, and how she apparently carried on a façade, but for what? He listened and wondered to himself, *Was it possible that the woman was terrified of being killed if she left, or was it like Harley said, that her horrible experiences as child, the shame she endured from poverty, scared her so much emotionally that she was held prisoner to fear?* Hollis patiently listened, totally intrigued by the saga that was being unveiled.

He rambled on back and forth from Rip to Dallas and back again. But Dallas was the part the sheriff couldn't understand, why they didn't get along. From all appearances, Leah seemed like the doting mother, driving her daughter to all the events when she was a child, attending all her games. Dallas had nothing but the finest of everything, including a mother, so he couldn't understand the problem. But, according to Harley, Dallas was jealous of her mother, which she shouldn't be, because she almost looked just like her.

The sheriff already knew a lot of the details. Like everyone, he knew the background about Leah and her legendary looks. She was a waitress there at the Mt. Ida Café all the way through high school, and someone suggested she enter the local beauty pageant. Reluctantly she did, and of course she won. That automatically put her in the Miss Arkansas pageant. A poor girl from a poor county, she had to borrow dresses and the money to make the trip. She didn't want to go because she had no talent, didn't sing or play piano or dance. She had been a dishwasher and raised on a farm, but that was about it. But they say when she came out in her evening gown, there was a hush that fell across the crowd. She was absolutely the most stunning woman to have ever walked across the stage. They say if she could have played "Chopsticks" on the piano, she would have won it all, but without the talent they could only award her first runner-up.

That's what drew the attention of Rip Taylor, the rich, thirty-four-year-old bachelor from "Y" City. But even without that notoriety, Leah was always stunning. She didn't need a title, she didn't ever want it, but it was something that Dallas resented, because people still talked about how beautiful her mother was. Harley related how whenever they were together, Leah garnered nearly all the attention, even from the young guys. It infuriated Dallas to no end. What she didn't understand was that it was her mother's personality that made her so attractive; she was genuine and funny. She had a way of making people feel relaxed, and Dallas couldn't even fake it; she was too self-centered and spoiled, and it showed. Dallas was gorgeous, but she still couldn't compete with her mom, and the thing that pissed her off the most is that her mother never wanted the attention. That killed her.

What Hollis still had a hard time accepting is how Rip could not want her. Why did he prefer the cheap, sleazy types to Leah? To him it didn't make sense. He knew from the scuttlebutt growing up that was also the way Rip's dad was. He was a well-known womanizer, as well as a cheat and a gambler. Cougar Taylor was hardly a father figure and certainly not the type of husband anyone would want to emulate, but it sure seemed as though Rip turned out to be a lot like him. Harley talked about that too. Leah told him stories about Rip's father, stories Rip told her.

Hollis listened, almost mesmerized, by the account Harley related. Hollis sat up in his chair when out of nowhere Harley blurted out that Mr. Taylor, Cougar that is, got his money from the mob back in the early days. That sounded unbelievable; there wasn't a mob in "Y" City—that was ludicrous. Then Hollis remembered the mob used to be in Hot Springs; they used to own a lot of gambling houses back in the fifties, actually, they used to run the city there. Lots of books had been written about the Mafia and it's infiltration into Arkansas. Before Vegas, Hot Springs was their favorite hangout. It was where they came to relax, take hot baths in the spas, and gamble. They gambled a lot there.

There were a lot of missing pieces still. Hollis looked at his watch, it was almost one o'clock, and he seemed to be getting further away from the answer rather than closer to it. As he listened to his story, he almost found himself believing Harley. But if it was true, that meant a whole lot of other people were lying. It meant maybe he had only scratched the surface. He listened to the crowd and wondered what on earth he was going to be able to tell them now.

Tap. Tap. Tap. They both looked over at the window. Teresa was there. Hollis shook his head sideways, "Not now."

Tap. Tap. She pointed him to come. "I have to talk to you," she mouthed.

Hollis grabbed a couple of tapes that he had recorded and went to the door and opened it up, "What is it?"

"I need to talk to you. Now."

He looked over his shoulder at Harley, "Stay put. Act normal."

They shut the door and went down the hall. Harley could see them go in the sheriff's office. A few minutes later, Hollis came back out. He didn't look too happy. Harley could see Hollis and Teresa talking; there wasn't anyone else that he could see.

Hollis walked back into his office. He never sat down; he just paced back and forth with the phone in his hand.

After he came back out, Harley saw Hollis grab a clipboard off the wall and study it with Teresa. Teresa stood sideways, and Harley could see how big she was. She was one of those people who, no matter what happened, had a smile on her face, big dimples that just never went away. He imagined she must be a very good mom, the type that makes every child feel better, just by her disposition.

He heard the crowd again; their noise came down the hall like a wave. He watched Hollis through the Plexiglas as he turned his head toward the end of the hall. Hollis pulled his glasses down to the end of his nose and stared, motionless.

Harley heard the click, click, click sound of high heels, and then she walked by. It was Dallas. Her long blonde hair draped across the back of her red, silk dress. He watched as she passed by smoothly. Hollis stood there, he didn't move. He seemed hypnotized. Hollis looked at her coming down the hall, as if he had seen a ghost. She was spellbinding in her beauty, exactly like her mother. Harley thought to himself, *This is the end.* She was going to seal his fate right now. He knew if she put her razzle-dazzle on the sheriff, he was toast. Harley closed his eyes for a brief moment. He knew what she might say. *Oh, God,* he said to himself, *oh, please help me.*

Part 2

Chapter Seven

Dallas walked right by him, not even casting an eye in his direction. She sauntered down to the dispatcher's desk as smoothly as he had ever seen a woman walk. He hadn't seen her in maybe a month, it might have been two, and it seemed to him she had grown some more since then. With her high heels, she was nearly six foot, much taller than her mother was. Her skin was Coppertone golden, and her dress, which stopped just above the knees, revealed the same shapely legs as her mother, just longer.

He couldn't hear what she was saying; her voice was always soft. She had the kind of voice that made men just give in. Harley watched as she wiggled her ankles in her white-satin, high-heel shoes. The muscles in her calves gyrated, reflecting her tone like gold flashing in a pan. Harley had never seen her in anything other than her bathing suit, cutoffs, or jeans, but she looked super fine in her red silk dress, especially the way it was tapered at the waist with a gold, looped chain. The silk clung to her butt, and her ass shimmered every time she shifted her stance.

Harley could see Hollis nodding as she talked to him, and then he pointed to his office; they went in and he shut the door. Harley leaned back against the wall; he knew exactly what was going on. He knew Dallas wanted his hide. He looked back down the hall again and could see Teresa with the phone in her hand; she looked frantic. He got that sick feeling again and sensed it was all going to be over for him. What the sheriff and Sam told him was true; if he went on trial he was doomed. He wouldn't have a snowball's chance in hell — didn't matter who his lawyer would be. If she went before a jury and pointed the finger at him, it would all be over. That would be it. He remembered an old joke they used to say in school, "What does a worm in a chicken house say? . . . Why is everyone pecking on me?"

Harley slumped down the wall. He was the worm in a town full of chickens alright, and the queen of all hens was there to get a piece of him.

Meanwhile, Hollis listened politely as Dallas lamented what a tragedy this had been to her own life. Though she didn't cry, she stated how she had grieved and been depressed. Then she said she felt hot and lifted the thin spaghetti straps of her dress and blew some air down her front, like she was trying to circulate some air to her buxom breast. Hollis didn't conduct the interview with Dallas that past Thursday at the ranch, he had let one of his deputies do that while he collected evidence. So he hadn't personally seen her recently; in fact, he couldn't recall seeing her since she was in junior high. He was stunned actually, for the last time Hollis could recall seeing Dallas, she was just a skinny teenager, very pretty but with a mouth full of braces and kind of a gangly figure. My, how she had changed; she was gorgeous. Just like her mother.

Dallas had the same high, round cheekbones that her mother had, but her eyes were bigger though just as blue. Her chin was like porcelain that was smooth to perfection. As she spoke, Hollis listened, but he couldn't take his eyes off her mouth. She had perfect, white teeth and full, red lips. Her whole mouth glistened, and her teeth sparkled like freshly polished opals, and while she talked, he realized that he wasn't really hearing her, he was just watching. Hollis rubbed his face several times and squinted his eyes, as if trying to wake himself up from a dream. It was as if he knew it was Dallas, but he was seeing Leah.

Occasionally he muttered the words, "I understand," "I know how you feel," or "We're doing all that we can." Much to the sheriff's surprise, she didn't call Harley names or cuss. They were no overt displays of histrionics. He had expected someone much more childlike, but she was anything but a child. He realized that she was far more dangerous with her beauty than Rip was by his brute force. She struck him as a person who could truly get anything she wanted from a man. As she gazed into his eyes, he felt like a mere bug being swept down a rain-soaked creek. He had seldom felt powerless in his life, but he did now.

"What are you going to do?"

Hollis looked at her surprised, "What?"

"Hollis," her voice was smooth as honey, "what are you going to do? I can't sleep at nights. You don't know how this feels, and I'm confused because he hasn't been charged yet." She took a deep breath, and her eyes roamed across Hollis as if they were hands.

"You don't know how lonely I feel," she said. Then her voice dropped to a whisper, "I've lost my mother. I have no grandparents left. And I'm afraid of what this man might do to me if he walks out of here. You've got to help me . . . please."

Hollis watched her figure as she stood up from her chair. He thought she was going to walk to the door, but instead she leaned across his desk. She put her hands down on his papers. He thought for a moment she was about to crawl across the desk to him. Her long blonde hair swayed in front of him, and the top of her dress plunged lower from the weight of her breasts, showing him the fullness of her cleavage. He looked away.

"Hollis?"

He opened the bottom drawer of his desk and acted like he was looking for something.

"Hollis, look at me." She reached her hand over to his chin and turned his head toward her, "Won't you promise me I can count on you?"

Sheriff Brown took a deep breath and stood up, trying to ignore her, "Well, it's not there." He shut the drawer to his desk, "Let's go out here and talk. I need some coffee. Want some coffee?"

Dallas walked around to the edge of his desk and stood before him. She kind of twitched her hips and gave him a sad little girl look and pouted her lips, "Don't you care what happens to me? Aren't you going to help me, Hollis?"

He tried to get around her. She was standing right in front of him, and so he put his hand on her side, trying to nudge her body gently away from him, but she didn't move, she was firm. Her waist was in his hand, and it felt good to his touch. It felt so good, he wanted to squeeze it, but he jerked it back on impulse the moment the thought entered his mind. Hollis looked at her, bit his lip, and tried to say something like "Move, please," but for the life of him, he couldn't say anything. His mind was totally blank.

Practically cooing, she said, "You're avoiding my question." She took her finger and scratched at a button on his chest. He looked at her hands; her nails were perfectly manicured, long and polished. "I just need a man right now I can count on. It's you isn't it? I can count on you."

Ding-a-ling–a-ding-dong!

Dallas smiled and opened up her tiny, white-satin purse. "Oh, darn," she said politely. The phone rang again. "Sorry, but I have to get that."

She finally stepped aside and let Hollis pass.

"Hello."

Hollis walked straight to the door and quickly opened it as she talked on her phone. He stepped inside the dispatcher's area and lowered the thermostat. "Teresa, aren't you hot? It's burning up in here."

Nonchalantly, she answered, "Nope, I'm fine."

"Well, I'm not." She could see the perspiration on his forehead and the look of a lost goose on his face. Teresa shook her head; she wasn't quite sure of what to make of Hollis. Sometimes her boss acted like a man in total control, and other times he acted like a total goober. Hollis poured himself a glass of water while Dallas was still talking on the phone. He went back to the doorway of his office and watched her. She clicked her heels when she talked and smiled at him as she slung her hair over her shoulder. She definitely wasn't like most girls right out of high school; she was in a league all by herself. It didn't appear to him to be anything but meaningless conversation, but obviously she was engrossed in whatever she was talking about. He looked at her with her tiny phone in her hand. It was an itty-bitty thing, silver and black.

"I've got to go." Dallas closed her phone, put it back in her purse, and walked to the doorway where Hollis was. He stepped aside.

"Can I have a pen and piece of paper?" She wrote down her number and handed it to him, "I want you to call me and let me know when you're going to press charges." She sighed, "Then I'll be able to sleep . . . please."

Hollis took the number and put it in the pocket of his shirt, "I'll let you know." He paused and pointed to her purse, "Say, where can I get a phone like yours? Where did you get that one?"

"At the Phone Shoppe." She pulled it back out and stood next to him. He could feel her hips brush up against his side and wiggle. She held the phone up, showing him the gadgetry, "Smile." Dallas leaned her head over next to his, and he felt her hair on his face as she tossed it to the side.

Click. She snapped their picture. "See, I can save your picture and store it as a screen saver. Cool, huh?"

"That's pretty neat. Teresa, did you see that?"

"That's just, like, so cool!" she said with mock enthusiasm. But the look on her face clearly showed she was perturbed and disgusted, "I have to go to the ladies room. Hollis get the phones will ya?"

Dallas smiled, "Well, I have to go. Call me." Hollis eyes followed her every stride down the hallway and out the door. He could see the TV camera crews approaching her from across the street and the crowd surround around her.

"Hollis Brown. You ought to be ashamed of yourself."

"What?"

Teresa walked off in a huff, "You know what."

A few minutes later she came back out. She flicked water in his face and pointed her finger at him, "You had better watch out. That's all I'm saying." She looked at him and shook her head, "And just so you know, she has already been over at the prosecutor's office. She was seen over there several times yesterday. So don't go thinking you're something so hot."

Hollis kind of ignored her. Teresa followed him back to the interrogation room, and he pulled some tapes from his pocket. "Oh yeah, I forgot. Put these back on my desk, and something else . . ." Hollis opened the door to the interrogation room, grabbed his note pad and flipped it to a blank page, and tore it out.

Teresa looked at Harley, he looked tired, "How's it going, Harley?"

He rolled his eyes, "Rough, I never thought I'd be here."

"Me neither, Harley, me neither."

Sheriff Brown finished scribbling down some notes, "Here, I want you to make a phone call and ask them these questions. If they have it, I will be down later today to pick it up. Tell them not to touch it."

She looked puzzled.

"Don't ask," he said commandingly. "Just do it."

"Geez." She gave him a salute, tossed him a bag of freshly popped popcorn, and walked away grumbling something about his personality. He wasn't sure what she said, but he knew it wasn't spoken in her usual, loving manner.

Hollis scratched his head and locked the door. "What a day," he said. He sat down, opened the bag, and let the steam pour out before pouring the popcorn into a bowl and leaning over to sniff it. Harley watched him out of the corner of his eye as the sheriff turned back through the pages in his notebook.

Harley folded his long arms on the table and laid his head down. Hollis gave him a quick glance.

Almost mumbling, Harley said, "It's getting to me, Sheriff. There is no way I can win. It's gonna be me against her. You saw her, Hollis. Nobody's gonna believe a guy like me, if she comes strutting into some courtroom. I'm dead."

"What are you telling me? Are you wanting to change your story?"

"No, what I told you is the truth." He stood up and went and looked down the hall. "But I don't think anybody wants to hear the truth. There is not a person in this town who will side with me, and who can blame 'em?"

"Well, why don't you sit down and tell me the rest of the story. I'm still listening."

"Really. I seen the look in your eyes when she walked down the hall. She's got you wrapped up too."

Hollis rolled a pencil between his hands, "I must admit she wasn't quite what I expected. The last time I saw her, she was just a teenybopper. If you turned her down, I have underestimated you."

"How's that?"

"You're more of a man than all the men I know."

"It wasn't that hard. You don't realize how much I loved her mother."

Hollis thought about that and wrote some notes. He put in a tape and pushed the record button. Harley strolled back over to the table, swung his long leg over his chair, and sat down. "Say, what is going on out there. Is it just you and Teresa here? Where is everybody else?"

Hollis looked like he was lost in thought, "Oh . . . yeah. I . . . um . . . I've got manpower problems. Two deputies aren't showing up for work. The state troopers who were here for backup are getting off work, and we don't have any replacements yet. No big deal."

Harley leaned back in his chair and grabbed a handful of popcorn, "Aren't ya worried about that crowd out there?" He was dropping some on the floor as he talked, "Sounds like it's getting bigger to me."

Hollis shrugged, "Things will be all right. I'm not worried." He didn't sound too convincing to Harley. His face revealed a deep anxiety. Hollis squinted his eyes and poured another cup of coffee. He slid the thermos over to Harley.

Harley poured himself a cup and slid the thermos back across the table, "Who you gonna have on duty tonight?"

"That's a good question. Right now it looks like me."

"You? You and who?"

Looking annoyed, Hollis answered, "Me. Just me."

"Are you serious?"

"Yeah, I'm serious. This doesn't look like a comedy club, does it? You don't see Jerry Seinfeld around here, do you? Hey, I'll get some relief in here tonight; Teresa is working on it. Don't you worry about that."

Harley looked at the sheriff, but Hollis didn't look back, and he knew that wasn't all there was to it. He could hear the noise outside. It sounded more like revelry before a football game. Cars were honking horns, and occasionally it sounded as if someone was shouting on a bullhorn. Harley could never distinguish the words they were saying, but he figured it wasn't flattery that they were articulating. Harley cleared his voice, "There is something you're not telling me, isn't there, Hollis?"

He didn't look up. "No, not really. We are just shorthanded, that's all, it happens in law enforcement all the time. Everything is under control though."

Hollis leaned back in his chair and folded his arms across his chest. "But you know, my life would be a whole lot easier right now if I would just go ahead and book you. That's what they want. But I don't run things the way they want, I run them the way they should be, and folks around here are getting a little nasty about it."

"What do you mean 'nasty'?"

Hollis told him not to worry about it. There were a lot of things that went with the job that weren't pleasant. He explained that there had been some nasty phone calls, but that went with the territory. Hollis lit a smoke and slid the pack over to Harley. He mentioned that he didn't care if he was popular or not, but they had started calling Barbara, and that pissed him off.

"Are they threatening you?"

Hollis shrugged, "I'm the sheriff; I live with threats, but I also have faith that God will protect me, even when my badge and my gun won't."

Harley was silent and so was the sheriff. Harley was digesting what the sheriff had told him. Finally the sheriff looked at his watch, "Well, we still have a long way to go. Do you remember what we were talking about?"

"I think we were talking about Rip's dad."

"That's right, you said something about how he liked cheap women and something about the Mafia. What's that all about?"

Cougar Taylor was a notorious character in these parts, always had been. In fact, he was legendary, just like Rooster Cogburn. Rooster Cogburn was the sheriff in the late 1800s who John Wayne made famous in the movie *True Grit.* John Wayne won his only Academy Award for Best Actor for his role in that movie. What most people don't realize is that there really was a Rooster Cogburn, and still is. His nephew carries the same name and lives in Polk County to this day. He is almost as notorious as his famous uncle. Rooster lives up on Shady Mountain and still drinks moonshine, at a hundred years old. So when Harley started mentioning stories about Cougar, Hollis was curious, because he knew Cougar and Rooster had been two peas in a pod.

"You want me to tell you about the mob?"

"I want you to tell me what Leah told you."

"Well, she just told me how Cougar and Rip came into their money."

Hollis grabbed some more popcorn and leaned back. He put his feet up on another chair. He looked at the wheels turning in the recorder and motioned for Harley to continue. Popcorn fell into Hollis's lap, and he picked it up and popped it back in his mouth. "Go on."

Harley grabbed some popcorn as well and popped open a can of coke that Teresa had brought in earlier. He too leaned back in his chair and began recanting the story that Leah told him. Cougar Taylor was a notorious gambler and bad with money. It was as if he had holes in his pockets. Cougar had inherited the ranch from his grandpa Seldon Taylor, but was always on the verge of losing it. One night, as the story goes, Cougar went up to Sock City, which is now called Pencil Bluff. Sock City was called Sock City because gamblers came there from all over with their money tucked away in their socks. The old general store stills stands where gamblers used to roll the dice and toss cards.

The likes of Al Capone and Lucky Luciano, as well as hundreds of other mobsters, used to vacation in Hot Springs. They'd come to gamble, bet on the horses, and chase women. The Hot Springs spas were where they'd relax, far away from the Feds, and it was the one place in the whole country where they felt safe. You see, Hot Springs was neutral ground. Arch enemies in Chicago and New York would lounge together in the same spa. They'd even play cards together, but when they went back to their towns, the turf wars were back on.

Sock City was one of the places that they gambled. It was forty miles away from Hot Springs and twenty miles from "Y" City. No one ever recalled Capone being there, but his couriers stopped there.

They'd often go there on the way to catch the train out of Mena to take the loot back to Chicago. Most of the time, two couriers would travel together, and being mobsters, they were always packing heat. People knew not to mess with them, but they hadn't run into the likes of Cougar Taylor.

According to Harley, Leah told him that sometime during the 1960s, two mobsters showed up at the general store there in Sock City, and they committed the cardinal sin of all mobsters—they touched the boss's stash. They had twenty-five thousand dollars in a suitcase and figured they could take a few old hicks from the sticks. Well, old Cougar acted retarded; he acted as if he'd never been in a card game before. He stumbled into the room with a fifth of rock gut and plopped himself down at the table. Cougar acted like he did most of the time, but this time he was stone-cold sober.

He slurred his words, money was falling out his pocket, and he leaned back in his chair, holding up his cards up, and squinting his good eye at them before tossing down his bet. What they didn't know was that the fifth was 99 percent water. It only had a taint of whiskey in it, just enough to give him a smell. And, well, before they knew it, they had lost five hundred dollars. It was the boss's money, so they gambled more, trying to get it back. That was a big mistake. They figured a drunk's luck had got to run out. They even had to prop him up a couple of times to keep him from falling facedown on the table. They just knew he'd mess up, so the game went all night and into the next day. They kept opening that suitcase to pull out some more. Finally, they were at a point where they were so desperate, they started doing double or nothing, and in the end, Cougar was sitting there with twenty-five thousand dollars of the mob's money.

When it was gone, all gone, they realized that all the other fellas around the room had guns. Cougar grinned at the two men, and they heard him click back his revolver under the table. "I think we're done. You best be going now." That's all he said, and they were escorted out to their sedan and pointed in the right direction.

Everyone knew they'd be back. They couldn't show up in Chicago empty-handed; that would be a death sentence. So they spent the night in Mena and tried to figure out what to do.

Now Cougar was anything but an idiot. He knew they'd be coming back, so he hightailed it, but the last place he'd go under those circumstances was back to his own home.

The very next night they showed up at "Y" City, looking for Cougar. "Guess they figured they'd catch him at his house, stick a gun in his face, and get their money back, but they figured wrong. Rip answered the door, and he was telling the truth when he said he hadn't seen 'hide nor hair of his daddy.' But then when he heard them mention the twenty-five thousand, Rip came up with a little game plan of his own. He wasn't but twelve or so at the time, but he had been doing a man's share of the work around the ranch since he was knee high to a grass hopper. He had personally grabbed more than one creditor by the collar and thrown him back in his car, and he had bloodied up a few others pretty good when they came to the Taylor ranch and started harassing his mother. But these guys, he knew they weren't going away so easily. So on the night they came a knocking at the door, Rip acted skeered and confessed to knowing where his daddy stashed the loot; it was out by the lake. And so, as the story goes, on that moonlit night, the two mobsters, sitting on each side of the kid, went riding out to Lake Ouachita with a shovel in the back."

Rip pointed to an old logging trail that went down to the lake's edge. With headlights piercing the darkness through the trees, they crept down to the shoreline.

Well, according to Harley, Rip started digging while the two thugs leaned against the old Lincoln, smoking away on their cigarettes. After digging down about three feet, Rip's shovel hit a rock. "That's it," he said, "It's in this metal box." Those two mobsters practically knocked each other down, jumping for that hole. Their hands dug down through the dirt, trying to grab the box. They made the mistake of taking their eyes off Rip. Neither one of them probably saw it coming, but he finished them both of right then and there.

Leah had told him that fifteen years later, they discovered the old Lincoln at the bottom of the lake during the summer of 1980, the hottest year on record. The lake was way down, and they found lots of things that had been missing, but that old Lincoln with Illinois plates had two skeletons in the trunk, and one of them had its head completely chopped off.

"I remember that; I was a rookie that year. So that's what happened?"

Harley nodded, "That's what she told me. That's where he got the money to start buying up gas stations, that twenty-five thousand dollars." Harley took a sip of coke and continued on with the story. He explained that Rip caught up with his old man after "taking care of business down at the lake" and took the money away from him before he could spend it or lose it gambling. Rip made his dad a deal, and he bought that first gas station in Mena. He ran the station himself and doled out a stipend to Cougar every week. Cougar went for it because, number one, he didn't have to work, and number two, he got enough cash every week to go drinking and playing. To a man of such little ambition and morality, it was a dream come true.

For all Rip's flaws, business savvy was not one of them, nor was his drive. He awoke early every morning and saw to it that the cattle were taken care of, then he'd go by the station on the way to school. He'd go there after school and run the place till closing time. He'd do the books and study, fix flats, pump gas, change oil, everything. After running the first gas station a while, he realized that the real money was in the merchandise, not in the labor, and so he just figured out ways to market the merchandise better. After two years, he was able to buy another station, and by the time he graduated from high school he owned three. He was making more money that the superintendent of the Mena schools, and he learned quickly what money could buy.

Rip became the charge of everything. Cougar was always laid up in some motel. Some say Rip provided him with just enough cash to drink himself to death, which he eventually did. They say it was a heart attack, because he'd been with a young girl when his heart finally gave out, but it was the drinking. When Cougar Taylor finally died, he owned nothing; he had signed it all away for a bottle of booze. Rip's financial dealings were always suspect, but who was going to question it? Leah had said that Cougar died penniless, Rip had purchased Heaven Falls from his dad for a paltry sum, and given his mother a lifelong estate, meaning she could stay there for the remainder of her natural life, but she did not own it, Rip did. By purchasing the ranch from his dad, when Cougar died, he had nothing to leave Rip's younger brother and sister. They got nothing — zip. And when Maw Taylor died, he kicked them off the land. He wasn't even subtle about it. She was buried at two o'clock, and by three, a moving van was in front of the Taylor house, taking all their belongings to storage.

Hollis sighed, "That's the most cold-blooded thing I think I've heard in my life." He looked at Harley in disbelief, "Now, you're sure she told you all this?"

Harley shrugged, "How else would I know about it, Sheriff? You think Rip would tell me? Come on now, of course it was Leah who told me." Harley reached over for a smoke, "Now don't you see why she was so scared of him? I mean, if he would do that to his own family, he wouldn't have no problem doing that to her. Heck, Sheriff, he figured out a way to legally steal the whole ranch away from his own brother and sister. You think he'd ever let Leah get a hold of it? No way."

Hollis jotted down some notes. He could see why Leah would be terrified of him. Rip might have actually told her what all had happened just to keep her scared. If she was scared, she wouldn't try for a divorce. He wouldn't ever have to worry about her getting part of the ranch in a settlement. Fear paralyzed her into staying right there, and yet he did everything he wanted. He became a lot like Cougar, just showing up at the house to get some rest before going back out, and Leah was too scared to do anything about it. The thought almost made Hollis sick, and the poem she wrote began to make a lot more sense.

Hollis looked at the cigarette pack on the table. They were getting near empty. He looked at his watch and couldn't believe it was almost two o'clock. He was trying to piece it all together, but the more that was revealed, the more complex it was becoming. Hollis pulled out the third to last smoke in the pack and lit it. His cigarette hung from his lip as he quickly wrote some notes. Rip would have had motive to murder her if he knew about Leah's affair. He wasn't a man who would have stood by and let some cowhand do the polka with his wife. And Rip was smart enough that he'd figure out a way to get rid of the problem and get away with it. He had an air-tight alibi, or did he? There were witnesses who placed him down in DeQueen when Leah was found, but Hollis began to wonder, what if the witnesses were lying or intimidated?

Then there was the old drunk, Ezra. Maybe he did come back and got revenge. He said he would. He had motive, and he knew the ranch. Hollis had a handful of witnesses who said Ezra told them that "someday he'd get even."

Hollis took a drag and thought some more. Blackmail always seemed like a viable option; she was the perfect candidate. From his experience, it was nearly impossible to keep a secret; someone is always going to know. And with her being as rich as she was, knowledge of an affair would be like money in the bank to the right person, or wrong one, depending on how you looked at it. She'd have to pay; she wouldn't have any other choice. There was just no way in the world she could ever let her husband know, not Rip. If there was a blackmailer, and if he was a man, he might have wanted more than just money from her. In fact, he probably would. If she resisted, then it could have become dangerous.

Hollis rubbed his head; he didn't know what to make of it. He wanted to just get up from the table and go home to think about it, but he couldn't. There was a mob outside; they were pushing for answers, or better yet, a villain. Finally, Hollis just leaned back. He shoved his notepad away from him. He really didn't have enough of anything to go on. His only chance to get to the bottom of it all sat in the chair on the other side of the table. It was Harley. Somewhere in his statements were the answers he was looking for. The evidence was there, somewhere. He just had to find it.

Hollis rubbed his face and chin. He thought for a moment and then asked, "Do you think the Mafia could have ever figured out that Rip had their money and come after it?"

"Forty years later? Nah, I don't think so. Geez, it was in the sixties when all that happened; I wouldn't think so."

"Yeah, you're right, but she never mentioned anything else to you about it?"

"Nope. As a matter of fact, I was kinda surprised she mentioned it to me at all. Leah was not real talkative to people in that way, she just didn't say nothin' 'bout her private life, 'cept I think she just got lonely."

"What else did ya'll talk about?"

"I asked about how Rip got his name. See, I heard it was in a football game cuz he ripped off some guy's face mask, but she said that wasn't so. When he purchased the gas stations, he didn't have time for no football, he had work. Anyway, one day this man comes in there complaining about the work done on his car, and he starts arguing with Rip and calls him some names. The guy was big and used to pushing people around, but what that guy didn't know was that at sixteen Rip could already whoop any man in Polk County. When the guy pushed Rip, that was it. Rip knocked the man down, straddled him with his legs, shoved his hands into the guy's mouth, and yanked liked the dickens until he ripped his jawbone completely out of socket. It just hung off the side of his face like a piece of bone in a bag of skin."

Hollis shook his head, "I can't imagine the pain that guy went through."

"She said that's what he would do. He liked to break people's bones in ways they could never repair. Like Duke."

"Why do you figure she'd ever marry a man like that? She say?"

"She didn't know until it was too late. She was a waitress and nineteen. Marrying Rip solved the money problems; at least, that's what her mamma told her."

Hollis remembered, "Yeah, it shocked some people, shocked me. I didn't figure he was her type."

"She didn't know until it was too late. And since she is the type who is always gonna try to do the right thing, she tried for years. After eighteen years, she finally just gave up. She gave it up with me for nearly a year. Leah knew having an affair was wrong, it might have helped for awhile . . . you know, to feel loved and all, but it was still wrong, so she did the right thing again and ended it."

"She ended it." Hollis looked at the recorder to make sure it was getting it. It was.

"Oh, it was her all right," Harley chuckled, "you think I'd end it? No way! But there never was a fight between us, never was. This last year had been the best year of my life. I was in love with her; I had never been so happy. I enjoyed every minute I ever had with her, but I could tell the weight of the world was bearing down on her shoulders. She'd get this far-off look in her eyes, and some days she'd just be real quiet. She'd drive off in that truck and park it and spend the whole day alone, just thinking."

"About what?"

"It was worry and guilt. She thought about the shame that it would cause Dallas if we got caught. She didn't want to hurt her. It seemed as though about once a month she say, 'I'm sorry, but I just can't do this anymore,' but then after a couple of days she'd see how I looked and feel sorry for me. She knew I was dying, and then the next thing we'd know, we'd be together again."

"So it was like no matter what she did, someone was going to get hurt?"

"Yeah, but what bothered her most was this God thing. She talked about God like he was a person. It wasn't so much that she was being unfaithful to Rip, she was being unfaithful to God, and she couldn't handle that. And I tried to argue with her about it, because you know how Rip was, but what was I gonna say about God? I couldn't say anything. How ya gonna argue with that?"

"You can't." Hollis looked down over at his notes, "Okay I think I got it. So tell me, what happened with you? Ya'll broke up, right? When was that?"

"Last month."

"May?"

"Right before Memorial Day weekend. Dallas was still in school. She was a day or two from graduation, and the hands were off, Pancho Villa holiday or something. So we decided to ride our horses up to the falls because it was such a beautiful day. The sun was out, the sky was blue; it was perfect. We rode up the mountain, going higher and higher until we could see past Poteau Mountain over in Oklahoma. I remember thinking, 'This is the best day in my life, it can't get any better than this. It was one of those days I knew I'd never forget, so even while it was happening, I was thinking, 'Save it, save it, cuz it will only last for a little while, then it'll be gone.' You know what I'm talking 'bout?"

"I know the feeling," Hollis said as he leaned back and put down the pen. He folded his arms. The lights were dim, the projector was on. "Go ahead." He glanced at his watch again.

Harley told how they rode up to the falls, and they were bigger than he had seen before. There had been lots of rain, so they were really roaring. He saw the huge crystals jutting out from the rocks, and he could see the bottom of the pool clearly. It must have been ten feet deep, and the water was as clear as champagne. They got off the horses and walked around the pool. He held her hand as they walked over the rocks and found a nice, big, round rock in the sun where they took off their jeans and laid out. She was wearing a bathing suit underneath, but he didn't have nothing but his jockeys on when he jumped in.

"Was it cold?" Hollis asked.

"You got that right! She laughed at me as I was swimming around trying to get warm. She kept making excuses for why she wouldn't get in, but finally, when the sun was right overhead, she jumped in too. The water warmed in the sun, and there was a spring over to one side of the boulders where the water was warm, so we swam over there and sat on these big boulders just a few feet under the surface. She sat in my lap, and we watched the falls together, and then all of a sudden, the whole area just lit up with colors. When the sun hit those crystals, every kind of color you can think of just shot up through the water. I couldn't believe it. I knew then why it was called Heaven Falls, because it was the closest thing to Heaven you're probably gonna find on earth. And then she took me by the hand and we went into the deep. Leah put her arms around my shoulders and wrapped her legs around my butt and squeezed me real slow, over and over. I took off everything she had and tossed it to shore, and it was like the first time." Harley stopped and just closed his eyes.

Hollis looked at his watch, it was ten after two now. "Can we get to the breakup?"

"Shhh. I'm not done yet! You see, when it was time to go, I was on the bank, so I tossed her bathing suit, which she put on underwater. When she came up out of the falls, I saw the way the water poured off her body, and I knew for sure that it was her I'd seen a long, long time ago, way back when I was a kid!"

Harley looked over at the sheriff, "Don't you see? She was the angel I used to pray to, to dream about. It was so weird when something that was a dream my whole life suddenly became real. And not only was it real but I'd tasted it, loved it, and made love to it. It was indescribable . . . it was . . ."

Looking annoyed, Hollis responded, "I think you've described it very well, but you're not the only one to have that experience. Maybe it's not exactly like that with everyone, but whenever a man loves a woman, it is like that."

Harley shook his head and gazed at the floor, "Well, right after that, I had that feeling that I lost her. It was like I knew she was leaving again. It was the exact same feeling. What do you call that?"

"Déjà vu."

"That's it! I just knew that she was going away. I knew that was going to be it, that she was going to leave, and I'd be stuck all over again with just my dream. I knew that I knew it was gonna be gone because I'd felt it before."

"So what happened next?"

"She got dressed back into dry clothes, and then she took my hand and told me to sit down. She had something to tell me, and I knew what it was. I just knew. She put her head on my shoulder and she cried. The tears just poured, then she wiped them away, and I knew what was next."

Hollis found himself actually feeling sorry for him. He hated having to dig for information that was so personal, but it was his job. Harley looked like a puppy that was just abandoned in an alley somewhere. He had that lost look in his eyes. His head kind of stooped down, and his eyes barely lifted to the table. His voice dropped off to barely a decibel above a whisper, and so Hollis was reaching over to turn up the recording volume when a tap came on the window. It was Teresa.

Hollis rolled his eyes and shook his head, "Not now," he mouthed.

She nodded up and down, and then held up her index finger. He could hear her through the door, saying, "One minute, just one minute."

Hollis reached over and patted Harley on the shoulder, "Stay put. I'll be right back."

Harley didn't know why they even bothered to close the door. He could understand both of their muffled, whispering voices, and he heard all he needed to hear. The prosecutor was coming; he was ready to file charges.

Chapter Eight

The word "prosecutor" sends shivers down anyone's back who has ever worn jailhouse orange. Not that Harley was wearing that yet, but he had the feeling they had a jumpsuit for him ready-made.

He had heard of Rick Snively, the only man in the county who regularly got manicures, shaves, and forty-dollar haircuts. His suits came from Bowman's in Little Rock or the Galleria in Dallas, and his shoes cost more than most people's paychecks. He was making a name for himself in western Arkansas as an up-and-coming ball buster, and the word was, he was eyeing the Arkansas attorney general's office.

Sometimes, the most dangerous person you'll ever find is a prosecutor, especially in an election year. Such was Rick Snively — self-centered, egotistical, and power hungry. People should tremble at the thought of men in office who possess far more ambition than morality. Unfortunately for Harley, Mr. Snively fit the prototype of the modern-era politician completely.

But Mr. Snively had a problem, which now became Harley's problem. The problem had to do with public perception. See, in all of Polk County, there weren't more than twenty or twenty-five guys in jail. The meth labs had been shut down, and the smart criminals took their occupations elsewhere, where it was be a lot more profitable and a lot less risky. In essence, there just wasn't enough crime for an ambitious prosecutor like Rick Snively to make a name for himself. Putting people away in the slammer for stealing the tires off a tractor doesn't garner the headlines that attract statewide publicity.

That all changed with Harley Wright. Now Snively had his villain, and with his villain, he had what he so desperately needed — statewide recognition. Since everything went down in "Y" City, Rick Snively had been at the forefront of all the attention. He held press conferences at the jail, at his office, and at the ranch. He even did a TV interview with a reporter from Amarillo. They must have been looking for something juicy. Rick Snively even got a picture on the front page of the Fort Smith paper, which showed him calling the Texas governor about getting Harley extradited back to Arkansas. The caption hinted that he was having to do the job that the Arkansas attorney general should have done. In reality, it was Hollis Brown who had already taken care of business. Snively's call was only a publicity stunt.

To say the two men didn't get along is a world-class under-statement. Two men couldn't be more opposite. Snively was jealous of the sheriff. It was Sheriff Brown who kept crime to a minimum in Polk County, not him. People in the know, knew Snively was a hypocrite because, although he talked about wanting to get tough on criminals, he actually wanted some real criminal activity so he could make himself look good in front of the public.

What Hollis didn't like about him was that he overcharged people. He was successful in getting big-time sentences on pretty minor crimes. He put one man away for twenty years for possession of twenty dollars in drugs. It destroyed the guy's family and kids, and Hollis wondered, *What good did it do?*

There were countless cases where the sheriff and Snively knocked heads, and it was all the sheriff could do not to give him just a real good ass-kickin'. Snively totally abused the law; he was not a good public servant.

What Hollis did not like above all else was Snively meddling in his business. Hollis was the one who was supposed to conduct the investigations, not Rick Snively. Snively bullied people and intimidated them. He'd tell a guy that he was going to slap thirty years on him unless he confessed to a lesser crime and maybe do only five years. So if a guy was twenty years old, he'd probably confess to the lesser crime. The problem was, what if he was innocent? Snively was proud of the way he got confessions out of innocent people, and more than one young man signed away years of his life, rather than risk losing it all in a courtroom.

Hollis didn't like that at all, but his ways were starting to lose out to the more flamboyant Rick Snivelys of the world. Snively sounded good, he looked good in front of the camera, and he joked with reporters. To hear him talk about law and order, you would want to vote for him, unless, of course, you knew the truth.

Truth be told, old Hollis Brown had hung around in office a few years longer than he wanted, to protect the people from Rick Snively. The last few days with the crowd made him wonder if he had made the right decision. If the people were that upset with the way he conducted business, maybe he should step down and let the likes of Rick Snively run the county for awhile. Maybe they deserved one another.

Harley looked through the Plexiglas window at the sheriff talking with Teresa. He had never been real religious, and he didn't understand things like faith, but he closed his eyes and said a quick thank-you to God for the man standing outside that door. It was a scary feeling to be sitting where Harley Wright was. He could be thrown to the wolves, and probably everybody in town would be happy. The prosecutor would get what he wanted, the public would get what they wanted, and the community's perception would be that Polk County would be a safer place.

There was only one person who stood between him and that eventuality, and it was the man who had been hammering him with questions for the last eight hours. Harley stood up and went to the window, "Can I pee?"

Hollis reached back with one hand and opened the door without looking. "Take five minutes."

Harley looked at the sheriff, bewildered, "Aren't ya gonna cuff me?"

"No."

"Escort me?"

He pointed to the crowd, "You ain't going anywhere."

Harley went on down the hall to the bathroom. Strange, he felt safer inside. It was odd how a few short hours had changed how he viewed everything. Polk County Jail was the last place he had wanted to be, but now he was glad he was there and not outside.

When Harley returned, Hollis handed him a couple of bills, "Why don'tcha get some snacks and come on back?" He pointed to the vending machine down the hall.

Hollis and Teresa kept whispering like he wasn't there, and he didn't know why. He picked up just bits and pieces of their conversation. He overhead something about phone records and Ezra—they had him locked up in Oklahoma for questioning. It felt really odd to be standing there at the vending machine. There was no one at the front desk; the place was empty. Normally there was a jailer and a few deputies hanging around, but today there was no one.

Harley looked outside the glass-plated door by the machine. There was a short walkway between the jail and the courthouse. The door was chained shut, and he wondered whether that was to keep him in or them out. Harley smooth out the creases in the bill, slid it into the machine, and picked out a few items—a Snickers and some chips. Next he got a Coke. He peered outside at the crowd but was careful not to let them see him. He was amazed at all the people; they were standing all the way down DeQueen Street. He could see people he immediately recognized from school and people from stores he had shopped in. *Why*, he wondered, *were they so quick to judge?*

Harley took a bite out of his Snickers and headed down the hall where the sheriff and Teresa where just finishing up. "When's Snively coming?" he asked.

Teresa poked him with her pen and grinned, "As soon as he gets his nails done, I reckon."

"Nails?"

Hollis tugged on Harley's shirt, "You don't wanna hear about it. Come on, we've got to get going here."

Teresa said, "Now, Hollis, don't you go getting all jealous you didn't get yours done."

Hollis didn't say anything. He just growled and shut the door behind them. Harley commenced to munching on the chips. He was thankful to have them; he knew the sheriff didn't have to do that. Hollis glanced over his glasses at Harley while he took a tape out of the recorder and put in a new one, "Guess you heard Rick Snively is gonna hold a press conference here this afternoon. He's ready to charge you."

Harely popped open his can of Coke, "Whadda you think?"

"Honestly? You know what I think?"

"What?"

"I think he needs to keep his butt in the courtroom and outta my jail." Harley could tell the sheriff was pissed. He scooted his chair around and took a deep breath, "Let's get going." He looked back over his notes and said, "Umm, you were just telling me about déjà vu or something, remember?"

"Do we have to talk about that?"

"'fraid so."

"She started cryin', and then she told me it was going to be the last time we were together. I knew it was coming, I just knew. She told me that she had reached a decision and it was final. She was going to try to make her marriage work. She was going to give it all she had . . . and, if it still didn't work out, she would at least know she had done everything in her power. But mostly, she told me, she had to get things right with God. She told me she really had never totally trusted Him, she had trusted money and material things, but never did really trust Him a hundred percent because of stuff that had happened when she was a kid."

"Like her daddy and her brother and sister dying?"

"Yeah, and losing the farm like that and all. Life had been pretty tough on her, and she told me that deep down inside she had always blamed God, but she just got tired of blaming Him."

"So, what was your reaction? Didn't you get mad? I mean, it had to get old, you know, break it off, start it back, break it off again. Weren't you getting a little tired of it?"

"I couldn't be mad at her, Hollis, I loved her. I watched her day after day, living with the guilt, and I knew how it was all killing her. It was strange, but I couldn't blame her. I wanted to, but I couldn't. So we left the mountain, and it was a long, long ride back down. Everything felt strange and out of place. The mountains didn't look the same anymore; the clouds and sky were different too. The world didn't look the same as it did when we were going up. I felt kinda sick, and when we got back, we unsaddled the horses, and neither one of us hardly said a word. It was just so weird. I got back in my truck and drove home, and it was like the whole thing never even happened."

"You mean the Heaven Falls thing, the swimming and stuff?"

"It was like the whole last year never happened. It was over. I was back to being just an ordinary ranch hand. She told me before I left that she'd see me Monday, and that hurt, but it's kinda hard to explain."

Hollis poured some coffee and looked at his suspect, "So you're saying that you didn't feel angry? You didn't feel at that moment that you might have been used?" He watched for Harley's response carefully, to see if there was any hint of a lie.

Harley nodded, "Well, yeah, I did feel kinda like that. But it wasn't so much being mad as it was just sick. I honestly felt like I had the flu. I went home and just plopped down on my bed and didn't wake up till the next day. I lost my appetite, didn't do nothing that whole weekend. I was just sick; it's hard to describe, it really is. You ain't ever been through anything like that. It sucks, just really sucks."

"What happened next?"

"I went back to work Monday, and I stayed out there I guess about another week or so, but she had to let me go cuz I just couldn't work worth a flip. I was messing up and Carlos and Santana knew something was wrong with me. I guess she figured she had to let me go before I did something stupid like run after her or something saying, 'I love you.'"

"You think 'bout doing that?"

"I thought about dropping to my knees and begging her. I thought about it every time I saw her."

"So what happened?"

"She came up to me one day after work, after everyone else had left, and handed me an envelope with a check in it. It was my pay plus two weeks. She was real nice about it; I guess you'd say she was kind. She told me that no one was as sorry to see me leave as she was, but I couldn't be there anymore. It was too hard on her, and she could tell it was too hard on me. She said that someday I'd make some woman a 'damn good husband,' but that I needed to get on with my life and go out there and find her. She started to cry again, and I did too, mainly because it always hurt me to see her hurt."

"So you left. That was it?"

"Yep. I was depressed like you wouldn't believe. I went home and could hardly sleep. I felt like I'd been dropped from a plane without a chute. The next morning was a monster to roll out of bed, but I did; I knew I had to. The next week I went back to town and started to look for work, and everywhere I went, people would ask me the same stupid question, 'What happened at Heaven Falls? I thought you liked it out there.'"

Hollis prodded him with questions, trying to find a trigger. He wondered if maybe there might be more pent up anger than what Harley was revealing. Surely there had to be. Harley had to have felt like a fool to be used for a whole year like that and then just let go. But the more questions Hollis asked, the more he realized, Harley never did get angry. Like he said, Harley just loved her. The following weekend, Harley said, he tried to get himself back into the scene, so he went out to Mountain Harbor. The place was crawling with babes out for the summer, and if you're young and looking for girls, it is the place to be. But, according to Harley, he couldn't even strike up a decent conversation with them. He'd lost his touch, 'the Harley magic.'

"I felt like some kind of idiot from outer space, standing around the docks. There were chicks there, but every time I started to try and talk with them, it was like I was throwing bricks. It was going nowhere. After I asked them their names and where they were from, I just kept drawing blanks. I was totally not scoring. I had nothing. I just didn't have it. It was gone. I had nothing left, Hollis. She took it when she left."

"She ruined you? Left a hole in you big enough to put your fist through?"

"Exactly! I'd been walloped. And I knew I wasn't gonna get over this thing quick. See, I thought I'd just head out to the lake, pick me up a little honey, take her back to my place, and forget all about Leah, but then I couldn't. I was kinda shocked you know, I mean, when it wasn't happening. I thought to myself after I left Mountain Harbor, *Not only am I going to have to go without Leah, but I'm gonna hafta do it cold turkey.* I didn't know if I could handle that."

"No relief in sight is what you're saying."

"None, and no second place lined up either. I struck out, and darn it if I didn't strike out a couple of more times in town. It totally sucked man. You wouldn't believe it, but guess who the only girl in town was would give me the nod?"

"Fresh outta of guesses. Who?"

"Tater, if you can you believe it."

"You didn't."

"Of course not, but what's scary is, I thought about it. That's how low down I was feeling. I was saying to myself, *Alright, here you go, boy, from the best to the worst.* After two weeks I was ready for anything. Man, I tell you, when I couldn't see her no more, it was like my whole world came to an end. I had been living my dream for a whole year, and then it was like, *Bam, wake up! It's all over, back to your stinkin' ole life that you had before. Back to nothing.*" Harley leaned over the table. His blue eyes were piercing, and he said matter-of-factly, "It was like death, just like death. When she said it was over, it was over. My dream died, and I died with it."

"After she dumped you . . ." the sheriff paused, "after she broke it off. You milled around depressed for a few weeks, and then what happened?"

"Well, uh, after a couple of weeks, I came to realize she was right; I accepted it. I understood why and all that. I just had a hard time not being able to see her again, and so I thought if I could just see her once a month, then I'd have something to look forward to each month. That's the idea I had."

"Are you talking about meeting at some motel or something? What did you have in mind?"

"No, no. I'm talking 'bout just seeing her. I mean, arranging for us to bump into one another at the drive-in and talk. You know, like, 'Hey, how are you doin'?' and stuff. We could talk from one car to the next. Just meet and talk, that's all."

As the sheriff looked at his suspect, he envisioned a big, flashing sign over Harley's head, blinking on and off the words STUPID . . . STUPID . . . STUPID. Curious, he asked, "What did Leah say to that?"

"She didn't like the idea. I called her at the house, and she told me it was over. She was sorry and asked me not to call her at the house anymore. She was that way; Leah was straightforward. She told me straight in the beginning, and she told me straight in the end. She didn't cut no corners. She didn't try to shambozal me . . ."

"Shambozal? Harley, that's not a word."

"Yeah, it is. I think it's French."

"I think you're thinking of 'bamboozled,' and it ain't French."

"Whatever. Don'tcha wanna know what happened?"

"One of these years, sure."

"Anyway, I thought about what she said and decided to try one last time. I knew she would hang up on me, so I wrote a little letter and took it out there that morning real early."

"To the ranch? How early?"

"Yes, to the ranch, it was about four a.m. I couldn't go to sleep anyways, and I sure didn't want to show up after sunrise."

"Didn't you worry about Rip seeing you?"

"I figured he'd be gone; he was most nights. But his truck was there, so I eased up the drive with my lights off and put the note in the visor of her truck."

"You must have been out of your mind; that sure was risky."

"I had to do something. I couldn't go on like I was, so I put the letter in her visor because that's where she kept her keys. I drove back home and went to sleep. I knew she'd call me later that day."

"So what did this note say?"

"That I loved her and missed her. I wasn't gonna bother her no more, but there was something I needed to talk to her about."

"That's it?"

"Well, I said I was going nuts not seeing her and all."

"You said 'nuts'?"

"I dunno. I might have said 'crazy.'"

"Did you say anything about sex or making love to her?"

Harley scratched his head, "Gosh, I . . . I don't think so. It wasn't graphic or nothin'. It wasn't no porno letter; it was just, 'Hey I miss ya; can we talk?'"

"And you thought she'd call you?"

"Of course. Listen, she wasn't no coldhearted lady. She was sorry for what she'd done to me."

"You don't think that maybe she just used you and then dumped you when the heat was on? That perhaps she'd planned on firing you from the start when she was done with you, and that it was annoying her that you kept coming back? Ever think about that?"

Harley folded his arms, and he looked away. His eyes glanced back at the sheriff, and Hollis could tell he was riled. "You want to know the truth? Yeah I thought about it. Sure I thought about it. There was a whole big part of me that said I just got suckered, but I know something about women, something that you don't. She might not have ever said she loved me, but she cared about me. She didn't ever just jump up and have a cigarette afterwards, saying, 'Well, back to work.' She wasn't like that, but I don't guess you'd understand."

"Maybe I wouldn't."

"And I'll tell you something else . . . she did call. She called me that morning and told me to get outta there. Dallas had found the note and was taking it to Rip. Yeah, she did care. She cared a lot."

"What? Say that again. You're telling me she called you that morning? You talked to her?"

"No, I didn't actually talk to her. I was outside piddling in the yard. I got the lawnmower started and was doing some work that I had let go for about three weeks. I went in to get me a bite and saw the recorder blinking."

"So she left you a message?"

"Uh-huh."

"When was that?"

"Right about twelve, I reckon."

"Do you know what time she called? She say?"

"I ain't real sure, but I came in at about eleven for some water, and she hadn't called then."

Hollis was scribbling down notes just as fast as his pen could move, "Okay, she called sometime between eleven and twelve. So what did she say? What was her message?"

"She said that Dallas had found the note and that she was real, real mad. She told me to get out of town 'now,' to pack and go right then, cuz she was taking the note to Rip. Leah had been crying, I could tell, but she was also calm, almost whispering."

"Humm, she wasn't hysterical?"

"No, she was just very matter-of-fact. It was quick, like bam, bam, bam. She said what she had to and got off the phone. She wasn't loud; as a matter of fact, I could hardly hear her."

"Was Dallas still there?"

"I think so, but she didn't exactly say. Somebody was there, because she was whispering don'tcha think?"

"Where was Rip?"

"Ask him. How would I know?"

"What about the hands?"

"Man, I couldn't tell ya. I wasn't there, but they were probably out in the fields, I guess."

"But you think Dallas might have been there?"

"I don't know for sure, but she said Dallas was going to take the note to Rip, so I guess that means she hadn't already gone."

"Okay, Harley, what did you do next?"

"Hell, I started packin'. I was in shock, ya know. It wasn't what I expected. I was expecting, well, never mind, I wasn't expecting this to happen. It was all my fault, and my mind was squirming like a toad on a jigging stick. I just threw some clothes in a bag, grabbed my shaving kit and threw my saddle in the back of the truck."

"Saddle? You thought 'bout a saddle at a time like that?"

"Hey, she gave it to me. It was the most valuable thing I had."

"Okay, okay. Did you take anything else? A gun?"

"Don't own one."

"What else?"

"Nothing. I was outta there in ten minutes. Got some gas, and I was gone."

"Anyone see ya?"

"Everyone saw me. I was at the station with two of your deputies."

"They see you?"

"I hope so. I stood in line with 'em."

"Who were they?"

"Jefferson and that midget-looking cop."

"Crandel? The short guy with a flattop?"

"Yeah, people call him 'Nightstand' because he's so short."

"All right, Harley, then what. You went to the bank, right?"

"Yep, I withdrew everything but five bucks."

Harley told him how he had about fourteen hundred bucks saved up. It was about twelve thirty, maybe twelve forty when he left the bank. He started heading out of town when he thought about Leah having to face Rip alone, and he couldn't let that happen. He was worried she'd end up being dragged across Heaven Falls Ranch with her foot in the stirrup and her head banging along the ground. The thought of it repulsed him, and he pulled his truck over to a screeching halt. He whipped the truck around and barreled out to the ranch. It was a thirty-mile drive from where he was, but he floored it and blew over the mountains, passing everyone and everything. He said he smoked it all the way to "Y" City. Finally, when he reached Heaven Falls, he tore down the long front drive to the house and came skidding to stop in front of the house. Leah's truck was outside where it was usually parked, but no one else was around.

The sheriff interrupted, "No sign of Dallas?"

"Nope. Gone."

"And Rip? Did you see his truck?"

Harley shook his head.

"Okay, tell me what happened." Hollis said as he looked at the tape, to make sure it was going, and turned up the volume.

Harley took a sip from his Coke and tossed the empty can underneath the table into the trash. He laid his hands flat on the table in front of him, and Hollis noticed his thumb had a nervous twitch to it. Harley sighed deeply and looked at the recorder; the reels were slowly turning.

"I drove up to where her truck was parked. I got out and looked around, and, to tell you the truth, I was relieved when I saw that her horse grazing out in the field and no one was around. I looked in her truck and was hoping to find the note still there, but it was gone. I walked around to the side of the house and could hear an engine running inside the garage, and I knew it was the T-Bird by its sound. It's gotta a real quiet hum, but it was never used 'cept for in car shows, and I was thinking, *This is weird. Why would she be going to a car show on a day like this, when all this is happening?*"

"You couldn't see the car?"

"No, the garage door didn't have windows, but I was thinking that something wasn't right. I thought a hundred different things at the same time, ya know, but it didn't make sense. I thought, maybe one of the guys was getting it ready for her, or maybe Rip was home and he was using it. I didn't know, so I walked around back to where the kitchen was, because that's where you can enter from that side of the house. Suddenly, I thought of the only thing that made sense. I thought she was taking it. She was packing her bags and leaving."

"What happened when you went in?"

"I went through the kitchen, cuz that leads to the garage, and I . . ."

"Did you touch anything in the kitchen? Did you stop and look around?"

"No, cuz I figured she was in the garage, but when I opened the door to the garage, the fumes hit me."

"Were they strong?"

"They about choked me. My eyes burned, but I could see Leah in the front seat, and I yelled at her to turn the engine off. I hadn't realized what happened. I put my shirt up over my mouth and opened the garage door so the fumes would get out, and then I ran over to where Leah was in the car. I opened the door, and her head was turned to the right and looking down at the floorboard. I thought, *What is she looking for? Doesn't she realize what is happening?* So I yelled 'Leah! What are you doing?' At that moment, I reached in and turned the key off, and I looked at her face."

Harley stopped and dropped his head in his hands, "It was horrible."

Hollis sat there quietly. Neither man said anything. Harley ran his fingers through his hair, like he was massaging his scalp, and the sheriff could hear him taking deep breaths. Harley didn't look up, he just breathed for a least a minute until finally the sheriff said, "Harley, I know this is tough but you've got to talk about it."

"I know . . ." he paused, ". . . I know. And I'm to blame."

"What happened?"

"I yelled at her again. I yelled 'Leah, what are you doing!' I turned her face to mine, and that's when I knew she was dead."

Hollis picked up a smoke and rolled it around his fingers, thinking. He shoved the pack over to Harley. "Tell me exactly everything you did next and every thought you were thinking. Can you do that?"

Harley nodded. He looked away.

"Do you remember everything?"

Harley nodded again and still didn't say anything.

"How did you know she was dead?"

"I think I'm gonna get sick."

He bent over with his elbows on his knees and started to gag. He pulled the wastepaper basket in front of him. He did a couple of dry heaves, but nothing came out besides a bunch of phlegm and saliva. After a little bit, he slid the trashcan back up underneath the table. His eyes were watery and red.

"You gonna be alright?"

Harley nodded and belched, "Just got to me that's all, I'll be fine. Let me catch my breath and I'll be okay." Harley leaned back in his chair and took a couple of deep breaths. He sighed, "You can't forget something like that. It's been going over and over in my mind. Why? It didn't make sense. Why would she start the car in her garage on that day? I thought she had just messed up, that it was an accident. I didn't know how it happened; I just knew she was dead. I mean, when I turned her face to mine, I could see she was gone. There was nothing there, no life at all." Harley shook his head back and forth, "Her eyes were barely open; her pupils weren't showing. The color was gone from her face, and when I touched her, her skin was sticky."

"Sticky?"

"Yeah, and cold, not refrigerator-cold, but cold and rubbery like chicken feet. I touched her cheek and jerked my hand back. I pulled my head out of the car and stood there looking at her through the windshield, and got I sick."

"Did you throw up?"

"All over. I ran outside and puked. I was sick from it all and probably poisoned by the fumes. I was gasping for air and got real dizzy. My head felt like it was going to split in two, and I could hardly stand up, so I just leaned against the outside of the house and puked some more. I was sitting there, throwing up, and I kept thinking of something else that just made me sicker. Her lips were blue. They looked like some cheap, powder-blue lipstick that teenage girls wear. It just didn't seem right, you know, because she was always so beautiful, and there she was with blue lips and this awful expression on her face."

"Ohhh, geez," Hollis said, fiddling with his cigarette and looking away. He rubbed his head and then leaned across the table and patted Harley on the arm, "I know this is going to be tough, but I have just got a few more questions for you. I don't like having to ask you this, but it's my job. Understand?"

Harley nodded, "Go on. Ask."

"At anytime during all this, did you think it could have been a suicide?"

Shaking his head, Harley answered, "Never."

"Harley, an hour or so before, she called you and told you that her husband was going to find out that ya'll had an affair, and then you find her in her car with the garage door shut and the engine running. I would think it might be suicide."

"You might think that, but that's because you don't know her. I do, and she would never do that. Never."

"Okay, did you think it might be murder?"

"Honestly, I didn't think about that. I just thought it was an accident. She started her car and went out and got in it. Maybe she wasn't thinking about the door being closed, and before she knew it the fumes got to her. I'll tell you what I thought, though, I thought it was my fault. She was dead because of me. If I had listened and left her alone, none of this woulda happened. I remembered that she said, if I loved her, I would leave her alone, but I didn't do that. I wrote that stupid note, and that's why all this happened. When I was catching my breath, that's what I was thinking. She was dead, and it was all my fault.

"I can't get those words outta my mind. If I'd just listened, we wouldn't be here, none of this would be happening. I'd probably be working around my house, and she'd be out riding Sweets across her pastures right now, or maybe she'd be swimming . . . or . . ."

"You'll drive yourself crazy wondering about all the what-ifs. We've all got some what-ifs in our lives, but we have to go on."

"I'd give anything to be able to go back to that morning and do it all over." Harley looked off. "I should have listened."

"So what did you do next?"

"After my head cleared and my eyes dried up, I thought maybe I'd been mistaken, maybe she was just passed out. So I went back to her car and looked at her again. I picked up her wrist, but there wasn't no pulse. Her face was sort of turning gray-looking. She was gone, and I remembered what she said. She told me to go, and so I pushed the garage-door button and left."

"Did you ever think about CPR?"

"No, I never did. Not until the much later when I was thinking back over everything. But it wouldn't have done no good. She was dead for a long time before I got there. If you felt her, you would know what I'm talking about."

"Okay, did you see any blood on her forehead? Do you remember that?"

Harley scratched his head, "Nope, I don't recall seeing nothing but her eyes. They were rolled back in her head. And her lips, I told you about that."

"Leah had an abrasion on her forehead, a pretty good-sized cut, and she had another on the back of her head. But you're saying you didn't see either?"

"Nope."

"Okay, let me ask you another question. Did you see anything unusual in the car or in back of it?"

Harley thought for a minute and shook his head, "No, it was just a car. I . . . I really wasn't looking around for nothing. I just saw her and ran to the car. She was all I really saw."

"So you didn't see a hose?"

Harley had a bizarre look on his face, "Nah, what kind of hose?"

"Did you see a hose going from the tail pipe to the passenger-side window?"

"No way! The only thing I saw was Leah."

"Harley, when they found her, a hose was taped to the exhaust pipe and put into the passenger-side window. It would be real hard to miss. If you did as you said, Harley, and walked outside for a few moments and then walked right back into the garage, it would be pretty hard not to see the tail pipe, wouldn't it?"

"I agree, but I don't know. I didn't see it! I swear."

"Harley, it strains the imagination to think you didn't see a gash on her forehead and didn't see a hose going from the tail pipe to the car window."

"I don't know what to tell you, Hollis. I didn't see nothing but her. That's all."

"Okay, I've got one final question for you. You find the woman who you say you love, in her own home, suffering from carbon monoxide poisoning, and you don't call 911. Did you not think she might need help?"

"She was dead."

"And what if she wasn't?"

"I couldn't have saved her."

"You say you couldn't have saved her, but, let's see, you didn't use CPR, and you didn't call 911. The question that is going to be asked is, 'Did you really care to save her?' And then they are going to ask, 'If you really cared so much about her, why did you take off for Mexico?'"

"Doesn't look good, does it?" Harley asked.

"No, it doesn't."

Hollis took out the tape and grabbed his notes together. He looked out the window. Rick Snively was there.

"It looks like the prosecutor has arrived."

Chapter Nine

As soon as he walked in, Teresa started sneezing from his thick cologne. When he walked crisply down the hall, she wondered to herself why in the world a man wanted to wear a suit on a Saturday when it was 102 degrees outside.

Rick was his polished self in his expensive patent leather shoes and double-breasted blazer with a lace handkerchief sticking out of its pocket, starched white shirt, and silk tie. Everything about him looked perfect; he even looked like he had ordered the light–brown, Jamaican tan from the tanning salon to match his primed, spike hairdo with a touch of mousse.

"Nice 'do, Rick."

"I get a better cut in Dallas, but I wouldn't want to tell Reba that."

Teresa sneezed again. "The sheriff's been expecting ya."

Rick looked in the mirror behind the dispatcher's desk and adjusted the knot in his tie, trying to get it perfectly centered, "That's good. I'm about to hold a press conference, and I just wanted to go over a few things."

Teresa put on a fresh pot of coffee, "Oh, really? What about?"

"Filing charges. WKYB in Texarkana is going to be here, Channel 5 from Fort Smith, and if they make it in time, KATV–Little Rock. Saturday is usually slow for news, so we should be the lead tonight. Gonna watch?"

"I think I know what is going on here, don't you?"

"Yeah, but you get to see the town on the news, and me."

Teresa took some deep breaths and sat back down. She blew her nose long and loud, "I know what you look like. I see enough of you already."

They heard Hollis come out of the interrogation room and lock it behind him. Teresa was relieved he was there; she always felt uncomfortable around Rick but didn't know why. Hollis had a grim look on his face. He walked right by Rick, holding his files and tapes, and went into his office, "I'll be right with you."

Hollis put the material down and leaned across his desk to check the messages. Another half dozen Post-its littered his phone. Coming back out, Hollis poured himself some coffee, "Want some?

"What kind is it?"

"I dunno; it's coffee."

"No thanks. I'm just here to clarify a few things with you. I am going to file charges against Harley today. Got a press conference scheduled at four, and I just wanted to see if you had anything you'd like to share."

Hollis cleared his throat. Teresa knew the look, and so did Rick. Hollis Brown was good at a lot of things, but concealing his anger was definitely not one of them. "Ahem. You're doing what?"

"I'm filing first-degree murder charges against Harley."

"Based on what?"

Rick sarcastically responded, "Well, Sheriff, you should know. I have motive—a disgruntled former employee who was obsessed with Leah Taylor. I have opportunity—he knew the ranch, and he has told the Texas Rangers he was there. And most importantly, I have forensic evidence. The state crime lab sent me their preliminary report, and his fingerprints are all over the place. And if that is not enough, I practically have everything but a videotape of him savagely knocking her unconscious and stuffing her in the car. His fleeing to Mexico establishes guilt."

"How did you get a hold of the fingerprint reports? We haven't got them yet."

"I have contacts."

"They are supposed to come to me first, and then you get to see them."

Teresa held up a fax report, "Ahem. We just got them."

Hollis went over and grabbed them out of her hand. He looked at the first page and then the next and the next, "These are inconclusive. Fingerprints alone don't establish guilt, and there are other prints on this report. You going to ignore that?"

"He was there; that's all I need to know. Harley Wright is known to be a skilled liar. Maybe he has got you fooled, but not me. If I walk into a house and find a woman dead, I'm calling 911. I'm not jumping in my truck and taking off for Mexico. Twelve men and women on a jury would agree. If they are innocent, they call for help; if they are guilty, they flee. Oh, I'll get a conviction, and it will be for first-degree murder because it was premeditated. He took his money out of the bank and packed his bags before he ever went out there. That proves he went there to kill her and leave." Snively looked at Hollis and smirked, "The boy's toast."

Hollis rotated his head back and forth across his shoulders. Just the presence of Rick Snively gave him headaches. He studied the lab reports some more, still seething that Snively had actually gotten them before he did. Hollis reached for a smoke from his pocket and fired it up while pacing back and forth.

Teresa sat at her desk between the two men, turning down the squelch on the radio so she could listen but not interrupt the men. She pulled out another Kleenex and sneezed. "Oochu."

"Is his smoke bothering you?" Rick asked.

"No, just allergies."

While Hollis studied the report, Rick elaborated on his claims, "I will state that this was a deliberate, callous act of cold-blooded murder. The facts will substantiate that he was infatuated with her; he left her a note, which I have here, and set the stage to meet her alone later in the day, and then, when he knew no one was there, he went out and killed. He attempted to cover it up by staging a suicide and left. Hollis, the evidence leads us to draw no other conclusion, can't you see?"

"You haven't been in there with him for the last eight hours. I have, and I am not about to put a man's life on the line unless I am absolutely sure it is the right thing. There are other possibilities, things you haven't even looked at. You are jumping way too soon."

"Hollis, you've gone soft. You let me in there with him and I'll have a signed confession in thirty minutes. I don't know what your problem is."

"Look, he's in my custody, Rick, and I'm going to do things my way. Do you hear me?"

"I told the crowd out there that if he gets off, every thug in three states will come here, because if a man can get away with murder here, they can get away with anything. That's why we must get a conviction. I am holding my press conference, and you can be part of it. I let you speak some, don't worry, but it would be great for public image if we were together on this, Hollis. I mean, I don't have any problem sharing some of the glory."

Hollis rolled his eyes and tossed his cup in the trash, "Glory? You see glory in this?"

"There is if we do our job and protect the public."

Hollis was growling under his breath, and Teresa knew he was about to come unglued, "Hollis. Hollis, settle down."

Hollis walked around to where the young prosecutor was standing and pointed his finger at him, "No, you're not holding a press conference here. Because if they show up with their cameras, and you're on this property, what they are going to is film me throwing your ass in jail for interfering with a criminal investigation. You better listen to me, pup, and listen to me good. You threaten me, and you better be ready to back it up, because . . ."

Teresa stood up and put one hand out and her other one on her baby, "Hollis, settle down! Look, Rick, you don't need to be coming in here, trying to push buttons. We have him here in custody; he's not going anywhere; why don't you just wait?"

Hollis blew some smoke in his face, and Rick turned away. Teresa sneezed again, and Rick looked at her, "Is his smoke bothering you?"

She waved her hand and pointed to Hollis's cigarette, "That? Nah, I sneeze all the time. I'm all right."

Snively looked at the sheriff, "That's a Class D misdemeanor, smoking in a public building. You could have charges filed against you for that. You ought to put that out."

Hollis walked over to him like he was about to punch his lights out and flicked his ashes in his direction, "Really? You want me to put it out? Huh?" Hollis held it up, "Because I'll stick it up your ass right now if you want me to!"

"Hollis Brown! Get a hold of yourself, both of you, please."

The sheriff took a long drag off his cigarette and grinned, "If you hold a press conference on my property here, I'm going to arrest you for interfering with an ongoing investigation. And just to let you know, hot shot, there are about twenty guys back there in that jail who would love to share their cell with you tonight. So you think about that when you put on your big smile in front of the cameras."

Snively adjusted his tie and patted back his hair. He didn't look that worried; in fact, he smiled, "Oh yeah, well let me tell you what I'm going to do. When I walk out of here, I'm going to file motions to move investigative jurisdiction back to Scott County, where it should have been in the first place, and to relieve you of all investigative authority and responsibilities on this case. Upon which time, I surmise that the people of Polk County will subsequently remove you from your duties and terminate your employment. Harley Wright will then be transported to the Waldron jail in Scott County, where he will be formally charged."

Hollis shook his head and snuffed out his cigarette on the bottom of his shoe, "Get outta here. You got ten seconds to hit the door."

"I'll see you, Hollis. You better go ahead and start cleaning out your desk right now."

The sheriff watched as the brash young prosecutor walked outside to the swarm of town folk. He thought to himself, *There probably goes the next attorney general, perhaps the future governor, who knows.* But he just couldn't stand him. Hollis walked back around to where Teresa was, plopped down in the swivel chair, and threw his leg up on the table.

Teresa looked over at him, "You didn't handle that too well, Hollis Brown."

Agreeing with her, he said, "No, I didn't, did I?"

"You know, you could use some work on your diplomatic skills."

"Why bother now; it looks like my career is about over. The nerve of that pissant."

"Hollis, I don't know what to tell you, but you only thought you had trouble before. You've got real trouble now."

Hollis picked up a clipboard, "Did you ever talk to the Scott County Sheriff?"

"No, you kept saying you would."

"Well, I got busy. I should have."

"He was going to send you some deputies to help out, but I doubt he will now. He probably doesn't want to get in the middle of a situation between you and Rick, especially if he knows that Harley may end up being transported up to him."

"What about the state police?"

"We've got two coming from K unit over in Hot Springs, but they have to patrol the roads. We can't use them here at the jail, if that's what you mean."

"I've still got Duke and Lucian."

Teresa looked worried. "Hollis, can he do what he says? Can he take Harley out of here and charge him in Scott County?"

"Afraid so. It would take the judge's signature, but yes, he can definitely do it, all right."

"Oh brother. Poor Harley."

Hollis stood up and stretched, "There's probably only one way that won't happen, if I somehow find out who did it and file charges against them in the meantime. They won't have two different jurisdictions filing charges against two different people for the same crime."

"You think he's innocent then?"

"I'm leaning that way, but I don't have the evidence yet. I'm just now getting down to the bottom of things here, and then Rick the Prick shows up. But there is a good chance he may be right too. There are just so many things about Harley's story that don't add up, and Snively is right, there is enough evidence right now to get a conviction."

"So what are you going to do?"

"When I go in there, I'm gonna hafta try to bust him again, see if something shakes out, see if he starts changing his story. If he does, then he did it."

"And if he didn't?"

"That means that there is a murderer out there, and I've got to find out who it is." Hollis hung the clipboard back up on the wall and walked into his office, "I'm going to call Barbara; don't disturb me for awhile, okay?"

Teresa nodded and picked up the phone that was ringing, and Hollis called his wife. It was pushing 2:35. He had missed lunch with her, and he knew he was going to miss supper. They had a TTY machine hooked up at their house, which meant that when Hollis spoke, she was able to read his words on a little machine similar to a caller-ID screen, and then she could speak into the phone back to him. There was a little delay in between the time he spoke and she talked back, but it was sure a lot better than nothing. He rarely had to call her, though, because their house was not more than four blocks from the station; it was just on the other side of Janssen Park, and Hollis was accustomed to going home a couple of times a day to check on her. There were lots of times when he'd go home and take a nap, but he hadn't been able to do that in months.

"When are you coming home?" Barbara's voice was soft and quiet.

Hollis didn't want to disappoint her, but he figured he might as well tell her now, "Honey, I might have to be down here all night."

"Can I come down and help you? You want me to bring you supper?"

Hollis did. He loved her cooking more than anyone else's, but he didn't want her to have to walk through the angry crowd. He didn't want her to know how bad it had gotten. "No, babe, we're probably gonna order pizza. I've got some coupons down here."

"I guess that means no date tonight."

He picked up her picture on his desk and held it. "Sorry, stood up again."

"That's alright, I can get another, there's always the Internet," she giggled.

That's one of the things they did together. They surfed the Internet, looking for people who were dating in the community. They always got a kick out of the things that people said about themselves. It was funny—they nearly all said they liked horseback riding and the outdoors, but most of them stayed home, watched TV, and drank beer all night. Half the men didn't work, but they all sounded like entrepreneurs. "Self-employed" usually meant, in reality, "broke and unemployed."

Hollis looked at the pile of papers and notes on his desk and then looked up at the clock, "Honey, don't worry. I've got enough troubles already. I've got to go."

"I'm going to miss you tonight. I wish you were here."

Hollis told his wife he loved her and that he missed her too. In all the years he had been a cop, she never complained about his work or his hours. In fact, she never complained to him about anything. Barbara was just always there for him, which is probably why he loved her so much. She was like a bright flower for every gray day he had. She brought him laughter and joy and . . . she was loyal.

When Hollis got off the phone, he studied the lab reports some more. There were some discrepancies, but there was no doubt that Harley's prints were on the T-Bird. He was there, all right. Snively had also left Hollis a photocopy of the letter Harley wrote. Hollis was pissed that Snively had not turned over the original, but that didn't matter for now; the note was pretty incriminating . . . for Harley.

The sheriff could hear the phone ringing and couldn't believe that, of all days, he couldn't get any more help down at the station. He quickly called some people who had always come down to the station to fill in before, but he couldn't get anyone. It was like everyone was gone. Finally, he called the Scott County Sheriff and talked to the deputy in charge.

"He's out," the deputy said.

"Can you have him call me? This is Hollis Brown. I could use some help down here tonight."

"I'll leave him your message."

"Can't you call him?"

"He's out, that's all I can say."

"Will you tell him it's urgent?"

"If I see him, I'll let him know."

Hollis realized he had messed up big time. The Scott County sheriff had called three times that morning, but Hollis had ignored him, and now the tables were turned. Hollis took a deep breath and sighed. Teresa was right; he could use some polish on his diplomatic skills. He had rubbed a lot of people the wrong way, and now it was coming back at him. Hollis got up and walked down the hall to the interrogation room, realizing that his life would be a whole lot easier if he just sided with Snively. Maybe Snively was right; maybe he should just charge Harley. The crowd would get what they wanted, and he'd look like a hero. He would even get his picture in the paper and be on TV. . . . He could be home tonight in his easy chair, watching himself on the evening news, and Barbara could be rubbing his neck and shoulders while he delighted in her homemade pie and ice cream.

Hollis looked at his watch, it was ten till three. The press conference was going to be in one hour. If he could get Harley to change his story one iota, he'd be home for supper tonight.

Chapter Ten

Harley could tell by the sheriff's demeanor that things were not good. He sat down with a grim expression on his face. It seemed like the noise outside had picked up again. Maybe there had been lull around lunchtime when everybody went to get a bite to eat.

"Something wrong?" Harley asked.

Hollis lowered his glasses to the end of his nose, "Does something look like it's wrong?" He said it like he had a chip on his shoulder, like he was ready to pick a fight.

"You just look kind of funny, that's all."

"Believe me, nothing is funny. Not a doggone thing." He put a tape in, opened a file and studied it, and then closed the file. " I've got some more questions about last Thursday out at the ranch." Hollis folded his arms and leaned back. He looked Harley squarely in the eye, "Now, you said you were in love with her, right?"

"Yes."

"Would you give your life for her?"

"Of course."

"Okay, so here is a woman you love and would give your life for, but you don't give her CPR or call 911. Can you explain that?"

Harley repeated what he had said already—that he knew she was dead. Her color was all wrong, her skin was cold, and she wasn't breathing. He was absolutely sure of it. The sheriff listened for a little bit and then decided to jerk on Harley's emotions to get more out of him.

"You're not a medical expert though. Did you know that's why they call a doctor to give a medical opinion?"

"Yes, Hollis, I know that."

"But when it came to the most important person in your life, you just didn't think it was necessary?" Hollis doodled on his pad, waiting for a response.

Harley was getting a little steamed. He didn't like the questions or what they were inferring, "Hell, Hollis, I'm not Jesus Christ! I can't bring her back from the dead."

"No, you're right about that, you're definitely not Jesus Christ, but what I can't get is why you didn't think it was important enough to consult someone else. I would have. Don't you think she at least deserved that, or was she not that important to you?"

Harley lowered his voice and spoke slowly. He leaned across the table with both of his big hands doubled up into fists. "I don't care if someone calls me stupid, and I don't care if someone says she didn't love me, but don't ever say I didn't love her, because I did."

"Really? So you just left her there for someone else to find, someone else to deal with her body? Come on, Harley, it wasn't like she was a sack of potatoes brought home from the grocery store or a bag of trash you were going to take to the dump. She is a human being, for crying out loud, and that's how you'd going to leave her, just sitting there, waiting for rigor mortis to set in? Don't you feel at all guilty about that?"

Harley jumped up and kicked over his chair and then smashed his fist down on the table, "Hell yes, I feel guilty! I am as guilty as I can be, because I screwed up and cost Leah her life, but once she was dead, she was dead, and there wasn't nothing I could do about it. I shoulda listened. I should have just stayed away, taken my lumps, and gone on, but I didn't." Harley sat back down in his chair, "I just couldn't let go. I was an idiot."

Hollis sat quietly. He was unmoved by Harley, and at that moment he didn't have any sympathy for him either. Hollis pulled out the coroner's report and shoved it over to him. "You want to see something that will make you sick? Take a look at this. The coroner arrived out there that afternoon. Coroners can use a variety of tests to determine cause of death and time of death. Without going into a lot of details, they can pretty much determine time of death by body temperature. Do you see what time he says she died?" Hollis pointed to it.

"One o'clock."

"That's right. So if she was dead when you got there, it wasn't by very long. What your conscience has got to live with is the what-if. What if she wasn't dead? What if she was near dead and just passed out? What if you carried her with you when you went outside to get fresh air? What if she could have come to when she got some fresh air? Or what if she could have been revived if you had rushed her to the hospital?"

Harley didn't say a word. He just looked at the report, stunned. He handed it back to the sheriff and looked down at the floor. "If you want me to confess, I will. Let's just get it over. I don't want to go through this anymore."

"What are you going to confess to, killing her or being responsible for her death?"

Harley shrugged, "Does it matter? I mean, it doesn't really matter, does it? She's dead. Leah is dead, and it's my fault. Anyway you want to look at it, I deserve to die, right?"

Hollis looked at his watch and thought about it. He looked back through his notes and stood up and paced back and forth. He stopped and scratched his head and sat back down. "I take confessions on videotape and have to get a witness in here when I do, but before I go bring all the equipment in here, I've got just a few more questions for you, all right?"

"Sure, whatever, but I'm ready to get this over. I'm ready to be done with it."

"When you left Heaven Falls Ranch that day, you went and got a motel room in Texarkana. Why did you stop there? That's not that far. It's only two hours away."

"I drove down to Texarkana because it just seemed like the best place to go, that's all. I had no plans, none."

"So you weren't planning on going to Mexico? They found some brochures in your truck; did you know that?"

"Lemme tell ya what happened. I took off from Heaven Falls, and it was like two little voices were speaking to me, one on my right side and one on my left. I kept asking, *What should I do? What should I do?* One was saying turn here, and the other was saying turn there. Honestly, I didn't know which way to turn, and the next thing I knew, I was all the way down in Glenwood, and I figured I need to go a little further, and so that is when I decided on Texarkana. I was just going there to get away and think. I mean, I wanted to get my mind to aim straight. Hollis, it's hard to explain, but you know how it is when you're looking through your sights on a gun and you can't get a bead on your target, so just just keep moving? You know what I'm talking about?"

"Yep, go on."

"Well, that's the way my mind was. I just couldn't get a clear thought."

"You couldn't get focused."

"That's it, and so I decided to just stop and spend the night, hoping my head would clear the next day, and I could come on back here to answer questions and tell the police what happened."

"So you were thinking about coming back at that point?"

"Right. See, if I was going to Mexico, why would I stop at Texarkana? I would have blown right through and not looked back.

See, I figured I had better tell ya'll everything I knew. But that night, when I was watching the news, and I knew right then I'd better keep on truckin'."

"So you saw the news that night?"

"The ten o'clock news. I was lying in bed, watchin' the tube, when I saw my picture flash up there on that TV with the words 'Murder Suspect' all across the screen. I figured I'd better hightail it quick."

"So what did you do?"

"I grabbed my gear and left."

"Right then?"

"I don't think they hit a commercial break before I was across the Texas state line. When I saw my picture on that TV, I could just imagine that toothless old woman downstairs in the office on the phone to the police saying, 'He's here, he's here! He's in 211!' So I split like the dickens. I wasn't thinkin' 'bout Mexico, at first, I was just thinking 'bout just goin' west. I drove and drove and drove all that night, and the next morning, when I was sittin' in a truck stop in Abilene eatin' breakfast, I start looking at the map and there's ole Mexico. I didn't see nothin' else on that map; it was like every arrow was pointing that way."

"So what about wanting to come back and get things straight, you gave up on that idea?"

"When I saw 'Murder Suspect' plastered on that TV, all I wanted was to get away from Arkansas, as far away as I could get."

Hollis reached into the ashtray, pulled out a half-smoked cigarette, and flicked the ashes off the end as he relit it. "So Mexico wasn't planned. You didn't leave Heaven Falls planning on going to Mexico?"

"Look, if I was really planning on doing that, don't ya think I would have taken a whole lot more with me. I didn't have a duffle bag full of clothes. I left nearly all my shirts, bunches of jeans, and my TV and stereo. I didn't take my coffee pot, nothing."

They could hear some crackling outside; it sounded like fireworks going off. Hollis started to get up, but then settled himself back down. "Oh, well," he said. He rolled his pencil between his hands and looked at Harley, "So, tell me about Mexico."

"I picked up these brochures and, man, it sure looked pretty. I figured I could speak a little Spanish and might fit in. I might find me a ranch to work on. So I headed to El Paso, that's where I'd cross. But when I pulled up there to the border crossing, they stared at me like I had blinking lights on the top of my truck flashing, 'Wanted: Murder Suspect,' cuz they sure gave me a strange look."

Harley shook his head, "There must have been ten cars ahead of me. Then it was nine, and then eight. Each time a car went through, I got ten feet closer to freedom, and I could almost taste it. I swear I could smell fresh tacos cooking on the other side, but when I pulled up, this Mexican reached in my truck and pulled out my keys, and another one stuck a gun through the passenger-side window. I thought, *Oh shit!* Just ten more feet and I'd have been free, ten feet."

"Not much of a welcome was it?"

"Not like they advertise in those brochures. I never saw no pictures of someone spread-eagle on that hot pavement with a shotgun halfway up his rear."

Hollis laughed and coughed out some smoke, "Spread-eagle wasn't in your travel plans, I take it?"

Hollis looked at his watch and stood up and stretched. "I'm going to step outside for a little bit, and while I'm gone, I want you to think back over everything you saw at the Taylor ranch that day, okay?"

"Okay."

"I want you to think about everything you touched, everything you saw. If you picked a booger, I want to know about it, understand?"

"All right, but I told you everything. When you come back, are you going to be taking my confession?"

Hollis walked over to the door and looked down the hall to the crowd outside. His face was turned away from Harley, "If you killed her, I am."

"She's dead because of me."

Hollis squinted his eyes, as if he was looking at something outside, "That may be true, but it's not my job to punish people for things that their conscience should be doing."

Harley looked confused, "Huh?"

"Let me put it another way. I once knew a man, knew him well, as a matter of fact, who lost two of his children in a fire. They say the fire started because the chimney flue had not been cleaned out. Now he knew he was supposed to do that, but he didn't. There is no doubt that his actions, or lack of actions, resulted in that fire that cost two of his four children to die. But he didn't murder them. Every night when he sits down at the dinner table, there are two empty chairs. In every family photo, there are two missing faces. He has got to endure every day of his life, knowing two people won't be able to enjoy that same day. So what is that man's punishment?"

"Himself."

"That's right. Now, if you murdered her, I am going to punish you to the greatest extent of the law. But if you didn't, I don't have a thing to do with your punishment, only you do."

Hollis opened the door and told Harley to stay put. A minute later he opened the door again and tossed him a magazine. It was a detective magazine. "Read this for awhile; I'll be back."

Harley looked at the magazine and flipped through the pages. Cops were weird, he thought. They seemed to get off on busting people; they all had this attitude. Hollis had it too sometimes.

Harley got up and went to the door and looked out the little window down to the front desk. He looked at a picture in the magazine and then looked back down the hall. He flipped to the next page and did the same.

All the time the sheriff was gone, the phone was ringing. Harley could see Teresa down at the dispatcher's desk with the phone in one hand and the radio mic in the other. About that time, Duke and Lucian came in; both were soaking in sweat. The back of Duke's starched shirt looked like it had been dropped in a puddle; his armpits were big, round, wet rings. Lucian didn't sweat as much, but Harley knew from other encounters with him that he stunk. He stunk even when it wasn't hot and humid; it was just the smell of his skin. Harley watched as Duke grabbed the keys off the wall and went into the jail in the back. Harley watched as Lucian walked into the sheriff's office and closed the door. He didn't know where Hollis was; he couldn't see him from the angle he had, but a few minutes later, Lucian came back out. He never bothered to help Teresa answer the phones or do anything else.

Harley flipped through the pages some more. There were lots of ads for police equipment: bulletproof vests and Tasers and stuff like that. He reckoned it was pretty dangerous work. He knew he'd never want to do it. Harley figured the sheriff was getting the video equipment, and he and Lucian would be lugging it down the hall any second to set it up. He really didn't care; he had decided to give them what they wanted. He'd put on a big show for them. He'd tell 'em how he beat her and choked her and how she screamed before he knocked her out. He'd give them a a real story, and he'd even turn around to make faces at the people in the courtroom and snarl in front of the cameras. Screw it, he didn't care.

Harley was gazing at the pictures in the magazine when Hollis came back down the hallway. He wasn't carrying anything. Harley thought to himself, *Hollis is so absentminded, he can't even find the video machine; he probably can't remember where he put it last.*

Teresa held up the phone in her hand, and Hollis grabbed it as he walked by. He sat on the dispatcher's desk with his back to Harley, and then they heard a loud bang at the other end of the hall and a voice that everyone recognized — it was Rip Taylor.

A chill went down Harley's spine. He eased back away from the window as the big man passed. Rip was cussing all the way down the hall, and his voice shook the building the same way a megaphone vibrates bleachers at a game. Rip was tall, at least two inches taller than Harley, and a good fifty pounds heavier. But with his Stetson hat on, and his black and silver, spiked-toe cowboy boots, Rip looked like a giant. He was almost as big as Duke, but he was leaner and meaner, with no fat, just muscle.

Oh my God, thought Harley, *hell is here now*. Rip was cussing at the sheriff like he was a punk kid. His voice was deep and reminded Harley of a chain being dragged across gravel.

Harley had darted back the moment he saw Rip stomp down the hall. He caught just a glimpse of his face, he looked nasty like he had drunk all night and just left a barroom fight. He was wearing his big, copper, rodeo belt buckle that nearly blinded people when he walked past and had a black coat on with silver fringe tapered down the inseams of the arms and across the front of the chest. For a man his size, it must have been tailored-made.

Hollis stood up from the desk, came around to the front, and stood there with his hands on his hips as Rip marched down the hall. He was saying something, but Harley couldn't tell what it was. Rip yanked off his hat and swatted the air in front of Hollis's face, but Hollis didn't so much as blink. Rip's long, reddish hair flew everywhere, and he brushed it back out of his face with a big swoop of his hand. Harley always thought Rip looked like a Roman soldier the way his sideburns came down the side of his jawbone, like they were part of a helmet. He had a Fu Manchu mustache that rose from his chin and crossed his lip. And while his hair might have been a little scraggily, his mustache was trimmed to perfection and appeared to be chiseled on his face.

Hollis took off his glasses and handed them back across the desk to Teresa. He didn't look unnerved. Harley strained to hear what Rip was saying, but for the life of him, he couldn't hardly make out the words because Rip's voice was so low it didn't carry very far, it just shook everything within a short distance. Harley did hear him say something about "Snively" and "filing charges." They talked back and forth until Rip stuck his finger in the sheriff's face. Hollis slapped his hand away and pointed to the door. "Get Out!" he shouted.

Rip stomped his foot and cussed some more, and Harley was surprised when Rip turned to leave. When Harley saw him coming, he slid down to his knees with his back to the door. He felt as if toxic waste was floating in his stomach, as Rip's heavy boots stomped past. There were two inches of solid metal separating him from Rip, and yet he felt scared to death. Harley heard Rip slam the door as he went outside, and he stood up again and looked down the hall. He couldn't believe that Rip had never seen him. He was more surprised that he had even gone.

As soon as Rip left, Hollis sent Teresa on an errand. "Where is your car parked?" he asked.

"Out back where it's supposed to be."

Hollis took Teresa into his office and closed the door. Lucian milled around outside while the phones rang. Teresa came back out and grabbed her purse, and as she was leaving, Hollis yelled, "Oh yeah, get me two packs of smokes."

Duke came back out from the jail cells with a clipboard in his hand, and Hollis went down the hall to take another pee. Lucian was at the doorway to the sheriff's office when the phone rang, and Lucian slipped into the office again. Hollis returned just as Lucian was walking out.

"What are you doing in there?"

"Thought I'za heard da phone ring."

Something struck the sheriff as odd about Lucian. "Stay out there, you hear?"

When Duke got off the phone, the sheriff told them that he needed to talk to them both. The phone rang again. "Don't answer it," he said.

Lucian smiled, "Gonna announce charges? You sure don't wanna piss off Rip." He laughed.

"Yeah, Sheriff, people been here all day waitin' for the announcement. I've been telling 'em it'd probably be three or four o'clock before you filed charges. Things take awhile."

Hollis leaned back against the wall, "Oh you did, and what if I don't file charges? What if he's innocent? You guys ever think of that?"

Lucian laughed, "Da whole town knows he did it, they just waitin' fer yer do yer job."

"And how do you think I'm doing my job?"

"Kinda slow."

The sheriff looked quizzically at Duke. "And how about you, Duke? You got an opinion on how I am doing?"

"Come on, Hollis, it's hotter 'n dickens out there. You said the other day that you were gonna fry him when you got him back here, so why don'tcha just charge him and let them go home. What's the harm in that?"

Lucian walked around, picking his teeth, "Yeah, get it over with."

Duke was the sheriff's best friend in law enforcement, and Hollis had listened to him in the past. He used Duke for a second opinion sometimes, just to see how another officer felt, and gave him the chance to express himself now. Duke walked over to the sheriff, "Let the jury decide, Hollis. If he ain't guilty, he'll go free. Come on."

"Am I the only friggin' one around here who cares?" Hollis kicked a wastepaper basket across the room, "What's gotten into you two? Don't you ever think that the guy down there in that cell could be you?"

Neither man responded; they just had blank, empty looks on their faces. It was as if they were oblivious to what Hollis was talking about.

"Think whatch yer want, Sheriff, but Rick Snively's gettin' ready fer a press conference. He's gonna put Harley away, whither ya like it or not. And Rip says . . ."

"Who?"

"Rip."

Hollis was ready to grab Lucian by the collar and throw him out the door. "Rip Taylor doesn't run this jail, I do."

"He pretty much runs everything else, and he don't put up with no procrastinatin'."

"I'm not procrastinating, Lucian, I'm doing my job. Speaking of doing your job, I want both of you to go out there and move that crowd back. I want them backed up at least a hundred feet from this building."

"You can't do that. This is public property. They gotta right to . . ."

Hollis pointed his finger at him. "Lucian, you do what I say, or I'm gonna take that badge off you right now. I've heard about enough out of you for one day."

Duke grabbed Lucian by the shoulder and pushed him toward the door. "Let's get going and do what the sheriff says."

Hollis was really upset. On top of everything else, he had to deal with insubordination and ignorance. Lucian was becoming more and more of a pain in his rear, but being as shorthanded as he was, he had to keep him around just to have another body with a badge. He sat down at the dispatcher's desk and looked at the clock. It was 3:35, time was running short. The phone rang.

"Sheriff's office."

"You tell that sheriff that it's time for him to retire. If he can't do his job, he should . . ."

Hollis looked at the caller ID. It was Melvin Tannehill. "Why hello, Melvin, this is Hollis. I didn't get that last part. I should do what?"

Melvin hung up with a click.

Hollis slammed down the phone and grumbled some unkindly words. The phone rang again, and he answered rather rudely, "Hello. What do you want?"

A timid voice on the other end replied, "Ah, is this the sheriff's office?"

"Yes it is. What do you want?"

"It's Riley Jones from Pizza Go. It's Saturday, and ya'll always order pizza ahead of time."

"Oh, hello, Riley. This is Hollis. Sorry about that."

Hollis looked around the desk for some paper or notes. He wasn't sure how to order or what to get, "Ah, hey, I'll have Teresa call you back. She knows what to do."

Hollis hung up the phone. It was one of the privileges Hollis granted the inmates. If they were good all week and there were no fights, they would get pizza on Saturday night. Jailhouse food was awfully bland and consisted of lots of sandwiches and cereal, anything you can eat without a fork or knife, and pizza was something that everyone liked. You wouldn't think that a few slices of pizza could motivate good behavior, but Hollis found it did. Very few fights broke out in his jail, and when they did, the others jumped in to stop it. They didn't want two guys' squaring off to cost them a half dozen slices of supreme pizza from the Pizza Go.

Hollis wrote down a note for Teresa to order pizza when she got back. He rubbed his eyes. He didn't know what was taking her so long. Then he noticed a legal pad on her desk that had a bunch of names and numbers on it and the time they called. At the top of the page it had the word "AGAINST" written in big letters. Hollis didn't know what that meant. He looked down the page again. Thirty-seven names had been listed since eight o'clock that morning. He flipped through the pages until he found a nearly empty page that had one name on it. At the top of the page was written "FOR." Hollis thought for a moment, then he figured it out and remembered what he had asked Harley that morning, "Where's your fan club?"

They had all turned on him like they did with Harley, except for Mrs. Dietermier, who counted on Hollis to take her to the beauty parlor once a week.

Hollis looked at the list of names. He wasn't really surprised. At about that time, Teresa came through the backdoor, and Hollis jumped up to meet her.

"What took you so long?" he asked

She tossed his cigarettes to him, "Here," she said it in a huff. "Traffic. You ought to see it. It's backed up clear down to the tracks." She gave him the eye, "So, don't you go giving me a hard time."

"Where is it? You got it?"

"Yeah . . . I didn't, like, drive over there and forget. It's right here."

"Let's go in my office." They both stepped into Hollis's office, and he left it open by a couple of inches so he could see down the hall if anyone came in. She handed Hollis a manila envelope, and he pulled out a dozen printed pages. "Come here and look at this."

Hollis and Teresa looked over the pages of numbers, thousands of numbers.

"Geez, Harley was right. She talks on the phone all the time. Look at this, the last call she made was at 11:21. The calls stop till the next day," Hollis said.

Teresa gasped, "Is that when she got the new phone, the one she showed you?"

"Yep, did you get the phone?"

Teresa pulled out a plastic baggie with a red-and-white cell phone in it and handed it to Hollis. The sheriff looked down the hall to make sure no one was there. He held the baggie up, looking at the phone inside it.

Hollis pulled on a pair of surgical gloves, opened the bag, and pulled the phone out. He inspected it with a magnifying glass, holding it gently between his index finger and thumb. "Teresa, look at this. I can't see too good."

Hollis switched on the lamp on his desk, and they inspected the phone under the light. Hollis turned the phone over to its back side, and they could see a fracture in the outer cover. It wasn't much, just a crack. The back plate of the phone cover didn't fit squarely, and the battery compartment was loose. Hollis looked at it through the magnifying glass and then handed it to Teresa, "See anything?"

She smiled, "Well, Sherlock, you might have something here. Let's look inside." Teresa took a letter opener off the desk and pried the back cover off, "Look here, Hollis. Look down in those little grooves."

Hollis took the magnifying glass and studied the back casing. There was something dried in the cracks — it looked like blood. "You think that's blood?"

Teresa smiled, "It certainly looks like blood, but look here." Teresa opened Hollis's drawer again and fumbled around for some tweezers. Very gently she pulled something off the phone and held it up.

Hollis squinted, trying to see what she had. "What is it?"

Teresa grinned, "It's a hair."

Chapter Eleven

"Showtime" is what they call it. It's theater, every ambitious politician's dream. The stage was set; the cameras were positioned just right. The reporters had scripted their lines, and the people were ready to applaud every word that was to be announced.

By some people's estimation, the crowd had surpassed five thousand, which was extraordinary, considering the town's total population, according to the 2000 census, was not much more than that. Folks were angling to get themselves choice views, and it was decided that Prosecutor Snively would do two different takes: one up on the back of a pickup truck so the folks down the block could see, and the other one would be on the ground with his back towards the courthouse.

The sweaty people in the crowd dabbed their foreheads and necks with handkerchiefs, waiting the final moments before the press conference began. There was a lot of last-minute jostling to get the best angle for the announcement. People were there from as far away as Poteau and Murphesboro. Lots of folks were there from

Waldron and Mt. Ida and just about every little town from here and yonder. Everyone was complaining of the nearly unbearable heat and humidity, and the lower the sun dropped in the western sky, the more blinding it became in everyone's eyes.

Rick Snively took one last look at his notes before he jumped up on the back of the pickup truck. He straightened his tie and wiped some perspiration off his forehead. It was almost time.

Hollis had walked to the end of the hallway and looked out the window. Rick apparently had decided not to do the press conference on public property after all; the camera jocks were all across the street in a parking lot. He looked at his watch, it was 3:56.

"Call Snively. We can still get him."

Teresa called the phone number she had written down. It rang and rang some more; Hollis could see Snively easily from where he was. Finally, the prosecutor looked down at the phone clipped to his belt.

He answered, "What do you want, Hollis?"

"Hold on, Rick, the sheriff has something urgent to tell you. Don't hang up."

Hollis came running down the hall and grabbed the phone from her. "Rick, this is Hollis Brown. I wouldn't start that news conference if I were you."

"You threatening me again?"

"Rick, please listen. I just got something that you need to see right now. Please don't do that news conference till you see this."

"I've seen enough, Hollis. I'm ready to announce charges."

Hollis paced back and forth, trying to think of the right words to say. He wasn't in the habit of pleading with anyone, and he didn't want to have to go out in front of that crowd and create a scene. "Think about this, Rick, what if you file charges, and the next day I hold a press conference that totally refutes everything you claim? You'll be the laughing stock of the whole state. You couldn't buy a vote in this fall's election."

Smugly, Rick responded, "I don't think I have to worry about that."

"Listen, all I'm asking for is five minutes. Five minutes—that's all. You come in here for five minutes and let me show you what I've got, and then if you want to hold your press conference after that, do it."

Hollis waited; all he heard was the crowd. Snively didn't say anything, and Hollis figured he would just hang up the phone. He looked at the clock, it read 3:59. He figured it was too late.

"I'll be there, but this had better be good."

The swarm of citizens pushed in closer to the prosecutor and the TV crews, where Rick Snively stood on the bed of a truck. He held up his hands and got everyone's attention. "We have some evidence that has just been brought to my attention. There will be a very short delay, and I thank you for your patience, but I will be right back."

The citizens grumbled as Rick made his way through the assembly of folks in the street. He heard their complaints all the way up to the jail, "What's going on?" "What happened?" "What now?"

Snively burst through the door. "Okay, Hollis, what is it? This had better not be some publicity stunt."

Hollis motioned for the prosecutor to come into his office. "Shut the door," he said.

"Make it quick, I don't have time."

"I'll show you this on one condition."

"What's that?"

"You don't reveal anything to anyone about this yet—no one. Do you understand?"

"Okay, okay, what is it?"

Hollis tossed him the phone records, and Snively looked them over, "So, I don't get it, what does this prove?"

"Dallas's last phone call was at 11:21. We believe that was to her friend Cassandra Jennings. It was a four-minute-and-thirty-second call. No other calls were made by Dallas on her phone until 9:30 the next morning."

Getting impatient, Rick interrupted, "Enlighten me, Hollis. What does this mean?"

"No other phone calls were made because her phone quit working. According to the clerk at the Phone Shoppe, she said that she dropped it and it broke. So she received a new phone yesterday morning, and her phone calls resumed."

"I've had three phones in the last year. So what's your point?"

"Did you return you old ones?"

"Of course. They were insured."

"Did they have blood and hair on them?"

The light Jamaican tan seemed to drain from his face. Snively's total expression changed. He looked like he was struggling to comprehend just what Hollis said, "Did you say blood and hair?"

"That's right, and it's all getting ready to go to the state lab. I'm sending it down tomorrow to get it tested."

Rick looked shell-shocked, "But where . . . how did you get this information? How did you get those phone records that quick? You couldn't have already gotten a subpoena, Hollis, I know that. How did you do it?"

Sheriff Brown smiled and walked over and took the phone records out of the prosecutor's hands, "I have my contacts."

Snively didn't look too happy. He stood there with his hand on his chin, rubbing it slowly in deep thought. "So, where is the phone now? Can I see it?"

"Nope. I'm going to keep it in a secure place until I can get it to the lab, but I wanted you to know about it. If you go out there right now and file charges against Harley Wright knowing what I have just told you, the election will be the last thing you have to worry about. You could be disbarred."

"You can't do that to me."

"Filing charges against someone when you know there is evidence that might exonerate them is, well . . . it's a criminal offense, isn't it?"

Rick's face dropped. He rolled his eyes up into his head, and they kind of quivered there. "Oh, crap! You did this to make me look like an idiot, didn't you?"

Hollis went to the door and opened it. The phones were ringing off the wall. "I just got this information, and you can think what you whatever you want of me, but I didn't have to make that phone call to you. I could have let you go ahead with your news conference, and maybe I should have, because I think you're a little too quick with other people's lives. You can go ahead a do your little news conference now, but if you file charges after seeing this evidence, your career is over."

Rick looked sick. He had his whole speech planned out, and now he was going to look so stupid going back out there to that restless, irritable mob to tell them he was not prepared to file charges after all.

"What do I tell them?

"Tell them the truth."

"What is the truth?"

"The truth is we don't know yet."

Rick started down the hallway and turned around, "You're sure that's her cell phone and not someone else's?"

"It's hers, and guess what? I'm getting all her text messages sent to me. Everything she's texted and everything she's received in the last thirty days. I should have that by tomorrow."

Snively looked as though he had seen a ghost. His complexion was pale, his face look was deflated, and even the little spikes in his hairdo appeared wilted. Hollis watched as Snively walked back across the street and couldn't help but be a little amused at his audience's display of disappointment.

He could see the mob outside and Snively standing on the back of that pickup truck, waving his arms around, trying to quiet them down. A few people tossed their empty lemonade cups in his direction as he made his announcement, and the reporters turned off their cameras and began packing up their equipment. To say the least, they were peeved. They had driven hundreds of miles for the big announcement, and now nothing. Hollis knew something else, too. There was one man more than anyone else who was not going to be taking the news well, and that was Rip.

As the crowd dispersed, a red BMW drove slowly by Rick Snively and the reporters. Everyone knew who it was. Hollis saw only her car; he couldn't see her face, but she was the first to leave, and after making it through the crowd, she turned onto Mena Street, and her tires were heard squealing for what must have been two blocks. There was no doubt where she was going and who she would be telling.

Hollis almost felt sorry for him because he knew that Rick Snively was going to have to answer to Rip. Rip Taylor was his biggest backer; he had supported him financially in every election, and Rip didn't throw his money at anything without expecting something in return. But Rick had nothing to give now. In five short minutes, his whole career had taken a nosedive, and the worst was yet to come because he still had to hear from Rip. The crowd might boo and hiss, and reporters might walk away disappointed, but Mr. Taylor did things that changed people's lives forever. Snively had to face the man. So much for his political grandstanding.

Hollis wondered if maybe there wasn't even more to it than that. He had never seen a man take news so hard in his whole life. When Rick looked at those phone records, his whole face turned pale white. Hollis wondered if maybe Rick had known something he hadn't shared, if there was more evidence that Snively knew but hadn't been forthcoming about. He wondered if maybe there wasn't something Snively was hiding.

Chapter Twelve

Hollis took the information that he had gathered — the finger-prints and phone records, Dallas's cell phone, and the report from the state crime lab — and sealed it in a manila envelope. He instructed Teresa to take it to his house and give it to Barbara; she would know where to put it. In twenty years, there was only one other occasion that he took extra precaution with evidence. What he had was too explosive to just leave it lying around for anyone to see or get their hands on.

Teresa put the envelope in her purse, "You want me to get you something while I'm out?"

Hollis rubbed his chin, which was now beginning to show signs of stubble. He scratched his head, "Ah, you know what, why don't you bring me a couple of shirts? I might want a fresh one, and Harley's been in that same T-shirt for a couple of days. It's getting awful hard to stay in the same room with him."

"That's a good idea, and so if anyone asks . . ."

Just then they looked outside and saw Sam coming. He had his hat pulled down to just above his glasses, and they could see him nodding to the folks in the crowd as he walked up to the jail. "Here comes Mr. Excitement."

Sam burst through the door, "Darn, Hollis, I'd expected you to start firing tear gas on them by now. Just how big ya gonna let that crowd get?"

Hollis stood up from his chair, "I thought they'd all go home by now. Rick's big press conference got cancelled, or didn't you hear?"

"I heard. I heard." Sam strolled over to the water fountain and got a drink. "You must have something good because I heard he looked like he swallowed a turd after he left your office."

Hollis laughed, "Yeah, he did look a little on the pukey side."

The phone rang and Teresa picked it up. The voice on the other end had an angry snarl to it, "Whadda ya'll operatin' down there? A bed and breakfast for criminals? Why, I ain't . . ."

Teresa slapped down the phone, "Jerk."

Sam raised his eyebrow, "I take it the public relations department is officially closed for the weekend. Is that right, sweetcakes?"

"Hey, Sam, she's a little touchy. You might want to tiptoe around her for awhile."

Teresa grabbed her purse, stuffed the envelope inside, and blew her hair away from her mouth. Teresa was one of those women who looked even cuter when she got angry. There was a certain glint that would flare up in her eyes. It brought out the passion in her, the fire, and then she could smile right afterwards and just melt you.

She walked around to where Sam was standing and raised her eyebrow at him. "Sam," she said, taking a deep breath and stopping. She started to say something again but just walked out the door, shaking her head.

"I've got some evidence that may just blow this town apart," Hollis said

"This is pertaining to Harley?"

"Some of it, but it all pertains to the case." Hollis lit a cigarette and sat on the edge of the desk, "The folks out there aren't going to like what they hear."

"So what you're saying is: they are already mad, and if this comes out, they are going to get a whole lot madder, and possibly at you?"

"They ain't gonna be happy. Teresa's about had it with 'em too. She's a little on edge." Hollis showed him the clipboard of all the calls. "This is just about half a day. Can you imagine what will happen if I announce that he's not going to be charged?"

"How's it looking?"

"It could go either way." Hollis lowered his glasses and looked at Sam. "I have a couple of strong suspects."

"Well, I've got something you need to take a look at."

"What is it? Let's have it."

"I want to play it for Harley; it's a tape."

Hollis took a deep puff off his cigarette and then coughed repeatedly. He choked on his own smoke, and tears welled up in his eyes. He motioned to Sam, "Water."

The little attorney poured a cup and handed it to him, looking at the sheriff with concern. "You might wanna think about quitting there, Hollis. Smoking is gonna kill you one of these days."

"Whadda ya talking about? That's why I do smoke." Coughing, he continued, "I figure if I can shave twenty years off my life, Barbara won't have to push me around in a wheelchair at some nursing home wiping the drool off my chin." Hollis coughed some more and took another drag, "This way I'm just making it easier on her."

Sam shook his head and rubbed his mustache. "If you really want to make it easy on her, why don't you just go stand in front of a train at six o'clock some morning. She wouldn't even have to buy you a casket. She could just put your remains in a shoe box."

Hollis coughed again and snuffed out his cigarette with the bottom of his shoe. "You know, that is a thought. Wouldn't even need a cemetery plot; she could just bury me by the azalea bushes or under the weeping willow."

"You know, I don't know who is sicker, you or me."

"Me."

"I think you're right." Sam pulled the tape out of his pocket, "You ready to listen to it now?"

Hollis radioed Duke from across the street, asking him to watch the phones while they went into the interrogation room.

Harley had been taking a good nap. The detective magazine still lay in his lap, and his head was down to his chin. Sam walked in, sat down, and looked at the young man. He was amazed that he could fall asleep in a chair like that.

"Harley," Sam said.

He was sound asleep and snoring away.

"Harley."

He still didn't wake up.

"Here, let me do it," Hollis said as he whacked the table. "Wake up!"

Harley jerked his head up and looked around, "Huh? What?" He looked at Sam sitting next to him, "When did you get here?"

"Just a second ago, and I've got the tape. It was still there in your recorder. This is just a copy; I've got the original at my office." Sam then explained that the tape was the one that had been in Harley's answering machine.

"I thought my men went over there looking for evidence. I can't believe they didn't find that."

Sam shook his head, "Hollis, they have gotten pretty sloppy if you want to know the truth. I don't know what they were doing over there, but they left the place pretty torn up."

Harley sat up. He wasn't happy, "Torn up? What do you mean 'torn up'?"

"Ransacked." Sam took off his hat and laid it on the table. "They tore it up but didn't find this. Now that's sloppy! What were they looking for, anyway?"

Hollis looked surprised, "Well, ah, they were supposed to look for a . . ." He reached over and snatched the tape out of Sam's hand, ". . . stuff like this. I'll have a talk with 'em."

Harley started to say something, but Sam interrupted, "Shh, let's listen."

Hollis put the cassette in the machine and hit play. They all waited. Harley's voice came out loud and crackly, "This is Harley. I'm out right now. Leave yer name and number, and I'll call you back. Bye."

They all knew the voice that followed the beep. Leah's voice matched her face; it was pretty and soft. "Harley. Harley? If you're there, pick up the phone! Harley, please pick up the phone. Dallas has found your note. Why did you write it? She is going to take it to Rip, and they know everything now. Harley, get out of town, darling. Just Go! Go anywhere as fast as you can. I'm sorry I ever got you . . ." the tape crackled, and what she said was inaudible, ". . . involved, but just go. Listen to me. Please, don't come here!" There was silence on the tape and then the sound of a door slamming and then Leah whispered, "I've got to go, Dallas is . . ." The rest of what she said was garbled, and then the phone was disconnected.

They sat there and watched the wheels turn. Sam reached over and hit the stop button. All three men looked at each other. It was an odd feeling for all of them, listening to the last words she said. Sam had his head down in deep thought, and Hollis cleared his voice, "Very interesting, but it still doesn't prove Harley is innocent."

"It doesn't? I think it does. It makes absolutely no sense to kill a woman you're madly in love with, especially if she's trying to save your life. I think it proves a whole lot. For one, you don't have motive."

"It's just one phone call. We still have Harley's fingerprints, and we know he was there. They could still have had an argument."

Sam lowered his glasses and looked at the sheriff. They had known each other for a long time and had always been honest with each other. Each man had respect for the other, but Sam wasn't liking what he was hearing from Sheriff Brown. They argued back and forth, and all the while, Harley just sat there with a somber look on his face. He was oblivious to what they were saying. Hearing her voice brought her back to him for just a second. It was as if she had entered the room and talked to him, but he knew it really wasn't so. It was just a piece of plastic wrapped around two spools in a casing. It was just a tape, and that was all he had left of her, that little tape.

"Can I play it again?"

"Huh?" The sheriff looked at him and shrugged, "Sure, why not."

The two men continued arguing back and forth as Harley played the tape again.

They heard Leah's voice telling Harley to leave, and they listened for the silent part on the tape again. They heard the door slam. Hollis reached over and stopped the cassette.

He took a deep breath, "What door is that? Can you tell?"

Harley face was long and drawn. His eyes were misty. "The garage."

"From the kitchen to the garage?"

Harley nodded.

Hollis sighed, "I don't think I can listen anymore." He took out the tape, "Sorry, Harley."

Hollis scratched his head with his pencil and then pulled out a file that he had buried under a stack of papers.

Harley looked puzzled, "What is it?"

Hollis scratched his head again with his pencil and then tapped it on his teeth for a second, "Ah, Harley, where would they keep the duct tape in the garage?"

"Third drawer in the far left cabinet."

"And where do they keep the box cutter?"

"The same drawer."

"And where do they keep the scissors?"

"Gosh, I don't know. I guess inside. I don't ever use the scissors; if I want to cut something, I just use my pocket knife."

"What would you use to cut duct tape?"

"You don't cut duct tape; you just tear it in half." Harley was wondering what the sheriff was after. "What is it?"

Sam interrupted; he had the file in his hand and was reading through it. "Your fingerprints are on the kitchen door. They are on the garage door, the driver's-side door of the T-Bird. They are on the dashboard and the keys, but they are not on the duct tape or on the . . ." He turned the file around for Harley to see, "the vacuum hose."

"That means I didn't do it, right?"

Sam raised his eyebrow and looked over at the sheriff, "It means that they would have to play leapfrog with the facts to say you did it. The evidence here is inconclusive at best. For a conviction, it must be beyond a reasonable doubt. That's a lot of doubt."

They heard shouts through the cinder blocks and could hear firework explosions outside. Loud, high-pitched rockets burst in the air. Sheriff Brown shook his head, "Well we aren't through here yet. I've still got a whole lot of questions to answer, but this report presents a lot of doubt. Why would someone leave fingerprints all over and then put on gloves to cut the duct tape and wrap it around the vacuum hose?"

"So, you know I didn't do it, right?"

"Most people don't stop halfway through a crime and put on gloves to finish it, but, you see, there is a prosecutor and he is good at what he does. He'll take some information like this and tell a jury that in anger you lost your head, knocked her down, and then decided to kill her. Maybe the car was already running, who knows? 'Does it matter?' he'll ask. And then he'll say you started to think about covering your tracks and that's when you put the gloves on. You put them on and finished the job."

"But that's a lie."

Sam interjected, "But the question is, can the evidence support that? That's what the sheriff is saying. He has to look at everything."

"Well, what about the tape? Come on, Sheriff, you just listened to it."

"I listened to a woman begging you not to go there, and you did."

Harley slid back from the table. He was getting angry. "Is that what you heard?" Harley raised his voice, "I heard a woman scared to death, that's what I heard, and I tell ya what, I . . . I . . . " He slammed his fist down on the table and rattled the recorder. "This is crap! That's what this is." Harley reached across the table and grabbed the fingerprint file, "Whose fingerprints are on there anyway?"

Whoosh! Hollis snatched the file back from Harley, "You had better sit your butt down right now, son, before you get yourself in more trouble than you can deal with. It ain't any of your business what's in here, and if you start getting all prissy on me, I'll just go ahead and lock you up in back right now."

Hollis pointed his pencil at Harley, "Right now you're still our number one suspect, if for no other reason than innocent people don't try to run across the border. You hadn't been out of the Ouachita Mountains your entire life, and then suddenly you're fleeing for Central America. I mean, ding, ding, ding . . . the bells are going off. Whether you like it or not, that gets you first place in the suspect category."

Harley's shoulders just slumped. He let out a deep breath. "Just go get that video thing. It don't matter. No matter what comes out, ya'll are gonna say I did it."

Harley put his head down on the table. He was completely exhausted. One minute it looked like he was going to go free, and the next minute it looked like he was going to fry. Hollis looked over at Sam, "What do you think, Counselor?"

"You're right, but where's the motive. It's hard to convict without a motive."

Hollis stood back up and grabbed all the material together. He made sure he secured the cassette, "That's why they are called crimes of passion. They'll point to Harley and say, 'Here is a man who was dumped by a beautiful woman. She used him for a year and tossed him away. She not only dumped him, but took his job away. He couldn't find any other employment, and he begged her to take him back. He was obsessed with her, and when she wouldn't take him back, he came up with a scheme to kill her.'"

Harley's face was down on the table. He moaned, "Just get it over with."

"Harley," Hollis said, quietly.

With his head still down on the table, he responded, "What?"

The sheriff called his name again, and Harley looked up. "What do you want?"

Hollis motioned for Sam to come with him. "That's what they may say, but they don't run this place. I do. And I don't think you did it, but I have to be sure who did before I can let you go."

Harley looked stunned, "Why don't you think I did it?"

The sheriff looked away down the hall, "Because the most important fact is the simplest one — you loved her. And I know what that means."

"You do?"

"Yeah, Harley. And when a man loves a woman, I mean, when he really loves her, sometimes he'll do some pretty stupid things."

Harley started to get up, but the sheriff motioned for him to sit down. "Here he comes."

"Who is it?"

"Rip." Hollis looked at his watch, "I'm just surprised it took him this long." Hollis's throat went dry. "I'm afraid your trouble has just begun."

"He wants me locked up? Charged?"

"Not this time. I suspect he wants me to release you so he can deal with you." Hollis turned around to Harley, "And you had better hide; he's got 'Welcome to hell' written all over him."

Part 3

Chapter Thirteen

What began as an affair between two people had set into motion a chain of events that led to a crisis, and the repercussions continued expanding. It was like a set of dominoes, human dominoes that started splitting at "Y" City and just kept tumbling down every road and through every town. But what we often see, as in the case of "Y" City, is that these events didn't just happen overnight. The right conditions had long been in place. All "Y" City needed was a little shove for everything to come crashing down.

Hollis felt like a man who could see the dominoes smashing toward him. He couldn't run; he didn't want to run. However, it all came down to whether he was going to stand his ground. And if that meant he was going to be crushed, it meant he was going to be crushed.

Hollis looked outside to the crowd that had turned against him and shut the door to the interrogation room quickly and locked it. Behind his back, he handed Sam the keys and muttered out of the side of his mouth, "Hold these." Sam tucked them into his trousers as Rip stomped up the steps to the jail in the blazing sun. A crowd of people followed behind him.

Lucian was right at his side when he opened the door. Hollis had already walked over to the front desk and turned around when Rip burst in, slamming the door against the wall. The sheriff felt the deepest sense of dread in having to face Rip, and deep down inside he knew that it was only his badge that had protected him in the past when they had come close to confrontation. But now that badge was nothing more than a thin piece of tin, and it wouldn't be enough to keep the two men from going at it.

As Rip came down the hall with his shoulder-length, red hair pulled back behind his ears, his hair resembled feathers of a rooster leaping into a cockfight. Hollis immediately noticed his huge fist, knuckled down to the bone. Rip's eyes were red, an angry, bloodshot red. He had seen him before like that and figured he'd been drinking.

Hollis had hoped this day would never come, but it was here. As Rip stomped down the hall towards him, Hollis pushed back all other thoughts in his mind. Rip's eyes were cold and steely, piercing like a snake. They were glassy and red, full of hate. He looked around the room and Lucian laughed. Rip walked right up to Hollis and stood in front of him. He stood there, breathing heavily, and then very slowly the words came out one by one, "Where . . . is . . . he?"

Lucian pointed back to the interrogation room, "Back der, he'za in der."

The sheriff looked at the huge man. Behind him he saw the faces of the crowd pressing against the plate glass window outside.

Rip snarled, "If you ain't gonna charge him, let him out."

Hollis pulled his shoulders back determinedly and took a deep, slow breath. Hollis was a man who didn't stutter. His voice was calm and firm. Not a muscle in his face twitched, "He's not going anywhere right now, Rip. I'm not done with the investigation."

The two men stood toe to toe. They were built quite differently. Rip Taylor was tall and broad across the shoulders, while Hollis was shorter and more compact. Rip's arms were long, his fists massive. Hollis was stocky and had powerful forearms. He had a pudge around the middle, but his back was thick like a fullback's. Rip's Fu Manchu mustache bristled around his gritty mouth. Hollis could smell the bourbon.

"Oh, you're done with it alright," he sneered down at Hollis. "You're finished." He nodded to Lucian, "Go unlock the door."

Hollis barked back at his deputy, "Lucian! You stay put!"

Rip motioned with his head toward the wall behind the dispatcher's desk, "Get the keys."

Hollis pointed to his deputy, "YOU take orders from ME!"

Rip turned around and looked at the crowd outside and extended his arm out to them, "Take a look around, Hollis. Ain't nobody gonna listen to you. No one. Not a soul in this town."

Trying to interject some sensibility into the situation, Sam interrupted, "Rip, why don't you just let the investigation takes its course? I mean, if Harley's guilty, why don't you give Hollis here time to gather all the evidence?"

Rip spun around with his hat in his hand and pointed it at the little attorney, "You little shit! You're finished too. You think you are going to come in here and help out that cowpoke?" Rip walked over to Sam and bent down like he was talking to a kid. Sam's nose twitched from the overwhelming smell of whiskey. It was rolling down Rip's neck in sweat. It was raw and nasty, and the musk Rip used couldn't cover up the odor. His lip was raised above his teeth as he snarled at the attorney, "I shoulda fired your little, incompetent butt a long time ago, you little weasel."

Lucian laughed, "Yeah, he'za been talkin' to . . ."

Hollis cut him off, "Shut up, Lucian."

Lucian kept jabbering about Sam seeing Harley, so Hollis walked over to him and grabbed him by the arm, "You get outta here. You're fired. Period."

Rip turned around, laughing, "Fired? You really are an idiot, aren't you? You don't even know what's going on, do you? There are petitions all over town. You are going to be removed from office. Hollis, you're finished."

He looked over at Duke and then at Sam. The attorney sheepishly looked back at his dear friend, "The quorum court is meeting tomorrow, Hollis. I . . . I just couldn't bring myself to tell you."

Sam had seen the petitions at the gas stations around town; he had even seen them being passed around outside in the crowd. He had wanted to say something, but every time he started, he just couldn't get out the words. Plus he figured the case would be resolved by now and things would go back to being normal again.

Hollis then looked at his big deputy, his closest law-enforcement friend, the man he had trained since the day he pinned on his badge, "You know about this, Duke?"

Duke nodded quietly and Lucian snickered, "Whaddaya gonna do, fire me? I'll just be rehired tomorrow." Lucian's jaw was packed full of tobacco, and he did a long, dribbley spit into the trash can. "Iza probably be de sheriff," he laughed.

That was more than Hollis could stand. He started for Lucian, but Rip stepped in front of him and squared his shoulders. Rip cocked his head to the side and looked down at him. Then he pushed the sheriff, "Pack up your gear and get, boy." Rip snapped his fingers at Lucian and pointed to the keys on the wall.

Hollis looked over at Lucian. The room was completely still; even the crowd outside was totally quiet as they looked on at the scene in the jailhouse. Hollis glanced up at Rip and then back at Lucian. "You make one move for those keys, and I'll kick your butt right here and now."

Rip laughed and pushed Hollis again, "I'll take care of this. Old Hollis ain't gonna do nothing. He's a coward, just like his old man."

Hollis's hand started shaking. He felt flashes of heat across his face and cold adrenaline rushed through his veins. His stomach turned inside out. He could feel his muscles twitching throughout his whole body, and his knees began to shake. There was a visible quivering to his legs. Sweat beads bubbled above his brow, and sweat began to drip down the bridge of his nose and slide to the side of his face. Hollis clinched his fist. He strained to get out the words, "Rip, you . . . need . . . to leave."

They stood toe to toe, and Rip Taylor towered over Hollis. His jaw was wide and full of muscle; his neck bulged with veins. Hollis had never known a man who wasn't just scared to death of Rip, and Hollis was no different. He was an old cop and tough as nails, but he was just an ordinary man

Rip laughed in Hollis's face. It was a deep, taunting, mocking laugh, loud and slow. He was enjoying it. He held out his big hands, "Well," he said, "why don't you just make me?"

Hollis stared straight at him. He didn't take his eyes off of him. Hollis called to his deputy, "Duke."

Duke didn't say anything. He started to walk over to where the men were, but then he turned and walked the other way.

Hollis called out again, "Duke!"

Rip laughed, "Duke knows better. It's just you and me." Rip stroked his Fu Manchu and grinned, "So, if you want me to leave, I guess you're gonna hafta do it yourself. That badge ain't gonna help you this time."

Sam couldn't stand watching the sheriff being challenged like that right there in his own jail, with the town folks looking on, with his own deputies betraying him. Sam slapped his hat down on the table. He was angered and agitated, "Dog gone it, Rip, be sensible! You're messing with the law here. Hollis Brown is still the sheriff, Rip. If you want him removed, fine, but until that happens, he's still the law here."

Lucian snickered again, "Not fer long."

Rip took off his hat and pulled his hair back. Then he squared his hat back down and smiled, "The law is who I put in office. Ain't that right, Hollis?"

Hollis didn't say anything. He just stood there with his arms folded and his teeth clinched. Sam could see the muscles trembling in his forearms.

"You see, Counselor? The sheriff here ain't half the man he pretends to be, are you?"

Hollis still didn't say anything.

"There are things about Hollis here that he doesn't want people to know. Is that why you married a deaf woman? So she couldn't hear what kind of man you really are?"

Hollis's eyes flittered for a second. He shook his head and struggled to get the words out. It was almost a whisper, but everyone in the room heard it. Hollis's face grimaced with strain, "Get out."

A wicked grin spread over Rip's face, and he pointed to his own chest, "You going to tell me to get out? No, you ain't telling me nothin'. You're just a measly little public servant who can't even afford to pay his own wife's hospital bills."

Rip looked around at Lucian and Sam, "You want to know who he came to when he couldn't pay her bills? Huh? It was me." Then Rip looked at Hollis and shoved him with his finger, "Don't you think it's odd there, Hollis, that your wife is walking around today because I paid for her care, and yet my wife is killed and yer gonna let her murderer go free?" Rip put his hands on his hips and snarled, "You're a double-crossing, no good punk, Hollis Brown. You ain't worth a damn. I think I need to teach you a little gratitude."

Duke turned and left the room. He unlocked the door to the jail cells in back and disappeared with clipboard in hand.

Hollis heard the heavy door slam as Duke left, and then he heard the people outside laughing. He heard his name over and over. With a quick glance outside, he saw their faces. Just the day before, he would have called them friends.

Rip stepped even closer to the sheriff. They were right in front of Hollis's office. Rip's eyes looked like a big cat's right before he pounces on his prey — they were hungry and mean. The grinding of his clinched teeth could be heard across the room. The sheriff suddenly looked puny next to Rip. Hollis reached for his handcuffs and pulled them out. "You are gonna hafta go, or I'll have no choice but to lock you up."

Both Lucian and Rip laughed. Rip looked over at Sam and Lucian, "Did you hear that? He's threatening me. Doesn't a man have the right to air some grievances about shoddy police work? What's this country coming to?"

Swish! Rip snatched the handcuffs from Hollis's hand and held them up. "These things ain't big enough to put around my wrists anyway." Rip held up the cuffs and smiled, "Watch this." He twisted the cuffs and pulled them taut. Rip gritted his teeth and growled.

With a snap, he broke them in two, as if there were made of dime-store plastic. A piece of the broken chain flung across the floor, and Hollis looked at the broken set of handcuffs dangling from Rip's hands. He remembered that he had no gun, no pepper spray, and no club.

Hollis grabbed Rip by the arm. It was as if he had grabbed a hold of piece of iron. With all the courage he could muster, he said, "You're going to leave and leave now. Or I am going to arrest you."

Rip didn't budge. Hollis tried to push him, as if he was going to take him to the back, but Rip stood as firm as a brick wall. "Get your hands off me, Hollis."

Hollis pushed him again, and Rip growled, "Get your hands off me!"

In a split second, Rip took Hollis and swung him around, lifting him completely off the ground and smashing him into the wall. The impact shook the building, and not more than twenty feet away, Harley was watching the whole thing from the Plexiglas window.

Rip grabbed Hollis by the throat with one hand. Hollis struggled to stay on his feet, and Rip pressed his large frame against Hollis's neck with his arm stuck straight out. His fingers dug into Hollis's skin like cat claws and blood was rolling down the sides of Hollis's neck. Hollis struggled to get air; Sam could see his diaphragm expand, trying to catch his breath.

Rip had him pinned with both hands in a chokehold around the sheriff's neck. Rip lifted him off the floor and smashed him to the wall again. Hollis grasped for breath but couldn't get air, and his feet kicked wildly, trying to touch ground. His hands were twisting and turning as he tried to break Rip's grip, but Rip was too strong. Grunting and grinning, Rip pressed all his weight against Hollis's neck, and then he held his neck with one hand and taking the other, grabbed Hollis's head and smashed it against the wall. Blood was coming down everywhere. It was dripping down the cinder block walls and splattering on the linoleum tile. Hollis's blood was oozing through Rip's fingers when suddenly Sam lunged for Rip's back. He wadded up his fist and hit him in the shoulder. Just as quickly, Rip swatted him with a backhand, sending him sprawling across the length of the floor to the dispatcher's desk, his glasses shattered on his face.

The sheriff was now beet red. His mouth gaped open, and his eyes were transfixed in a wild gaze. Rip snorted and pounded him again and again. He was uttering profanities and cursing the sheriff. Hollis's eyes begin to close. He looked as if he had passed out. Then Harley heard a scream.

"STOP IT, FOR GOD'S SAKE!" It was Teresa.

Everyone turned around and looked at her coming down the hall. She had her hand on her stomach as if she was just about to have the baby, and Rip's satanic-looking eyes glared across his shoulder at her. Sam struggled to his feet, and then Harley yelled out. They could all hear him from inside the interrogation room, "You want me? Take me! Just let him go!"

Rip looked like a madman coming out of a trance when he heard Harley's voice. His eyes glared back over his left shoulder though he still had the sheriff held to the wall. Harley could see the sheriff's eyes were almost shut, and his feet weren't kicking anymore, they just dangled limply a few inches above the floor.

Teresa came rushing toward them, then she stopped, there was so much blood. She held her stomach and gasped in horror, realizing that the shock might hurt her baby. She didn't know what she was going to do, and then suddenly Hollis seemed to regain his breath. He took his two hands and began rotating Rip's wrist. The fire came back in his eyes, and they could see him prying Rip's hands from his neck. They struggled hand to hand, their fingers clinching the other's, down to the bone. Rip leaned over Hollis, trying to force him down to the floor, and then he started trying to smash the sheriff's foot with his boot. Rip kicked and stomped, but kept missing. Then Hollis lunged from the wall, throwing his body through the air with his fist catching Rip with a left hook across the jaw.

Rip's head snapped backwards; his hat flew off his head. His long legs buckled under his big frame from the jarring blow. Rip staggered backwards across the linoleum floor with his hands still clinched in a fighting position. Hollis bent over, finally freed from Rip's death grip and gasped for air. His hands were on his knees as he struggled desperately to rapidly get air back in his lungs. The whole front of his neck looked like the skin had been peeled off. He had been mauled by Rip's hands, and the wall behind him was splattered in red.

Hollis panted and wheezed; his blood dripped from his chin down to the floor. He turned to Teresa, his voice hoarse and hardly above a whisper, "Call . . . the . . . state police, now!"

No sooner had the words came out of his mouth than Rip charged Hollis again. Right at the moment Rip reached for him, Hollis ducked and spun around, catching Rip with a sharp right to the side of his jaw and knocking him into the wall headfirst. The impact sounded like a bulldozer crashing into the building. Hollis held his hands up, poised to fight, and when Rip turned around, a deep gash had split open the top of his skull at the hairline. Blood streamed down between his eyes.

Teresa screamed again and held her hand protectively over her baby, "STOP IT! JUST STOP IT! RIP TAYLOR, THIS IS CRAZY!"

Rip stood there panting. His lip curled back, and he took a few more breaths. Both men stood there, Hollis's hands were up, ready to fight, and Rip's were at his sides. Finally, Rip pointed at the sheriff, walked over, and picked his hat up off the floor. He swatted his knee like he was swatting off dust. Rip walked over to Hollis and smiled, "I ain't done with you yet." Rip pulled back his hair and put on his hat. He looked almost happy, satisfied somehow. There was something about beating a man till the blood ran through his hands that thrilled him.

"You're through, Hollis. I'll make damn sure you're through in this town."

Sheriff Brown didn't shout, he just pointed to the door, "Get out."

Rip stood there. No one knew whether he was going to leave or whether he was going to plow back into Hollis again. His huge blood-covered hands were at his sides, and blood streamed down his face. The foul smell of sweat, whiskey, and musk reeked from his pores. He enjoyed it. It was what he had always done best. A smile crawled up the side of his face, and a daunting glint came into his eye. Rip Taylor gave the sheriff an affirmative nod, "You're mine, Hollis. You're all mine."

"Get out."

As Rip turned and walked down the hall, he stopped at the interrogation room. He and Harley looked at one another. Rip walked up to the door. He had to stoop to be at eye level with Harley, and they stared at each other with only about two inches of steel separating them. Harley looked at the gash in Rip's forehead. It looked as if it had been split open with an axe. He stood back. It was a face that Harley never wanted to see again, not in all his life. He was terrified of the man.

BAM! Rip kicked the door and laughed. He stomped down the hall towards the exit. When he got to the door, he stopped and turned around. He looked at the sheriff and nodded matter-of-factly, "You know . . . all hell is going break loose now."

Rip's macabre face revealed that he took an evil pleasure in what he did. The words seemed to echo in the hall and then he heaved the door open and left.

More than anyone else, Hollis knew exactly what that meant. They weren't idle words or a mere threat. All hell was indeed going to be unleashed. Hollis glanced at his watch; in a few more hours, it would be sundown, and he knew that the man would be back.

Chapter Fourteen

Duke walked back in with his clipboard in hand, just as Lucian started to slip down the hall to the exit. Hollis reached over and quickly grabbed him by the collar and jerked him back around. The cowardly deputy tried to pull away, but Hollis stopped him cold and threw him back down the hall, past the dispatcher's desk.

"Ya . . . ya . . . better not touch me, Hollis." Lucian held up his hands up, protecting his face, as if he was scared he was going to get smacked.

Hollis was was livid. He shoved Lucian further down the hall towards where Duke was. Duke's eyes widened like a screech owl's as he fumbled with the keys. The sight of all the blood down the front of Hollis's shirt shocked him into a stunned silence. He could see the blood dripping down the wall and running all over the floor. Duke realized that Rip was gone. He didn't know what happened; he just knew that he had deserted his sheriff.

With his big hands trembling, Duke fumbled, trying to lock the door. Lucian was backing up and jabbering nonstop about Hollis hurting him. His hands were up by his face, and Hollis pulled back his fist. Finally, Teresa yelled out, "Lucian! Shut the hell up."

Hollis had Lucian backed into a corner. "Don't hit me. Don't hit me, Hollis. I . . . I . . ."

"You aren't ever going to where this again," Hollis said, ripping the badge off Lucian's shirt. "Now take off your belt." Lucian unbuckled his belt which held his gun and Mace, and Hollis snatched it from him and tossed it back over to the desk.

"Keys."

Lucian pulled out the keys to his squad car, and Hollis snatched them from his hands, "Now, get out!"

Lucian had to walk around him, and as he headed down toward the exit, Hollis spun and gave him a kick in the seat of his pants, "GET!"

Lucian bolted for the exit, and then the sheriff looked over at his other deputy. Duke clumsily put the keys to the jail cells back in his pocket. "My God, what happened?"

Hollis turned and walked away from him. He was so mad, he was afraid he'd hit him; he sure wanted to. He went back around the corner to the dispatcher's desk, and Duke followed. The deputy knew from experience that when the sheriff got real quiet, it was best not to say anything. Hollis then picked up a pack of cigarettes from the table and lit a smoke. His cigarette hung down from his lip as he began to slowly unbutton his shirt. The phones were ringing. He didn't bother to pick them up, and Sam came over to the sheriff, trying to mend his wire-rimmed glasses so that they could fit back on his face. He adjusted them and set them down on the bridge of his nose and examined Hollis's neck.

"My God! You need to go to the hospital."

Hollis mumbled something. His voice was hoarse and barely audible. Duke came in behind Sam. "Wha . . . wha . . . what happened? Where did Rip go?"

Hollis took a long drag off his cigarette and then blew the smoke up toward the ceiling where the fan dispersed the smoke around the room. He winced as he took off his shirt. "You deserted me, that's what happened."

"I'm sorry, Hollis. I just froze. I . . . I . . ."

"I could have been killed."

Hollis had never been so disappointed in anyone in his whole life. He wanted to just lean over and slap Duke. He wanted to get in his face and scream at him, but he just hurt to darn much all over. Most of all, he didn't even want to look his friend in the face anymore. Hollis took off his shirt and wiped his hands with it. Then he wadded it up and threw it in the trash can. Hollis picked up one of the shirts that Teresa had brought from his house. He turned away from Duke and, as he walked into his office, said in gravely voice, "Leave your badge on the counter and go." Hollis then slammed the door.

Teresa had already called EMS to get some medics over to see Hollis. She was talking on one phone and dialing with the other. Both she and Sam looked at Duke, who was now facing the closed door to the sheriff's office. He looked for a second like he was going to knock but didn't. His head was down and he put his hand over his eyes.

Teresa looked over at Sam, another phone was ringing, "Sam, will you get that?"

"Sure." Sam grabbed the phone, "Polk County Sheriff's Office. Yeah, he's still here. No, no charges have been filed . . ."

Sam took a call from another reporter as Teresa managed her phones. They both were on the phone, watching Duke standing by the door. He stood there quietly for the longest time, and then he unpinned his badge and walked over and laid it on the counter. Teresa looked up at him; she saw his face and the deep expression of remorse. Duke then took off his belt and without saying another word, laid it on the counter and turned and walked out the door.

After a few minutes, the sheriff came back out. He looked at the mess in the hall. It was a blood bath, his blood. He had put some gauze over the wounds in his neck and looked neat in his freshly ironed shirt. Hollis walked over to Sam and looked at the crowd outside that was now pressing to the other side of the street. He could see the news crew and was surprised they hadn't left. Hollis poured himself a cup of water from the dispenser and tossed the cup in the trash. "Let Harley out, will ya? And have him come down here."

Sam hung up the phone. "Sure, be glad to," he smiled.

"Sam."

"Yeah?"

The sheriff pointed to his nose, "You got some blood right here."

Sam rubbed his finger across his nose and looked at the blood on his knuckles, "Darn, you're right." Sam grabbed a tissue off his desk and rubbed his nose.

"Sam."

"Yeah?"

"Thanks."

"I didn't do anything, Hollis."

"Yes, you did. You stood up for me."

"My pleasure." Sam threw the tissue into the wastebasket and walked down the hall. Teresa was on the squawk box, calling in the other units. "Return to 81, return to 81. Code Red. Code Red."

Sam unlocked the interrogation room. "Come on," he said to Harley.

They walked down the hall. Both had to step over the blood to get to the sheriff's office. When they entered, Hollis had just unlocked the rifle case where he kept the shotguns. He pulled two out of the case and shut the door.

"Have a seat."

Harley looked at the sheriff with the gauze taped to the side of his neck. He smiled, "Whatcha doing, Sheriff? Is this where you start deputizing everybody?"

Hollis loaded the shotgun and set it on his desk. Then he loaded the other. "No, this is where I start loading shotguns."

"What're they for?"

"Well, Harley, they're for killing." He handed a shotgun to Sam, "You know how to use this don'tcha, Sam?"

Sam adjusted his bent frames and looked down the barrel, "Yeah, I know how. it's been a few years, but I know how."

"Good, because I'm going out to talk to that crowd. And if Rip Taylor decides he's gonna come back while I'm out there, I don't want you to ask any questions. You just aim and fire. Got that?"

Sam and Harley looked at each other, "You think he's coming back after you knocked him down?"

Hollis shook his head and kind of laughed, "You guys don't know Rip like I do. He's coming back, all right. I don't know when, but I know he's coming. And he wasn't lying, all hell's gonna break loose when he does."

Sheriff Brown handed Sam the other shotgun, "Remember, don't ask questions, just aim and shoot."

Harley looked at Sam and then at the sheriff, "But what about me?"

"Pray."

"Medics are here," Teresa said, poking her head into the office.

Hollis went to the doorway and looked down the hall. "Hey fellas, I already took care of it. Ya'll can go back now. I'm all right."

Both of the medics looked around at all the blood which was now beginning to dry. "We need to take a look at you, Hollis. You probably shouldn't be standing up. You should be sitting down."

Teresa laughed, "Yeah, right. You know Hollis. He dowsed it with some hydrogen peroxide, the same funky bottle he rinses his mouth out with. Ask him, he'll tell ya."

Hollis straightened up his shirt and tucked it in. "Cures everything."

The medics tried without success to get him to sit down and let them take a look at it, but Hollis would have none of it. Injuries, pain, and stuff like that healed best when not tampered with. Hollis had a "don't fester, don't bother" policy when it came to personal injuries.

After a few minutes of bickering and agitating, they left with medic bags in hand. Hollis looked at his watch; it was getting late, "Any word on the state police?"

"Haven't heard anything yet, but I'm trying."

Hollis looked at Harley, "You need to keep a low profile, son. You should either be in my office where they can't see you or back over there behind that dispatcher's desk. You don't need to be seen walking up and down these halls. Someone may take a shot at you through the window. And, Sam, I want you to sit right behind the front desk with a shotgun in your lap and the other on the counter, but not where it can be seen."

Sam twitched his mustache and picked up the weapons, "I'll do it. I'll sit there till you come back, but what if I see Rip outside? Do you . . . a . . . um want me to . . ."

"Don't leave the building. No matter what happens outside, don't go out there. Stay right here."

"But what if he . . ."

Hollis put his arm on Sam's shoulder and leaned over, looking down into his eyes, "No matter what, don't come outside."

Sam nodded, "Okay, I've got it."

"Promise me you won't go outside."

"I promise."

Teresa looked worried, "Hollis, why don't you just stay here? The backup units will be here in awhile. You don't need to go out there right now."

"They aren't going to do anything to me. They need to go home. I've got to get them out of here." Hollis grabbed his hat and checked himself in the mirror then started for the door, "Ah, Teresa, will you call Barbara and check on her for me real quick?"

"Sure, but what if she asks about what's going on?"

He turned around, walked back to the counter, and picked up a set of keys, "For God's sake, don't tell her anything. Just see how she's doing."

Sheriff Brown walked down the hall towards the door. He knew that Lucian was probably already out there, stirring up the crowd some more, and there was no telling what the people were hearing. He thought about what Teresa had said. Maybe he should wait for the deputies to get there. But it was already after six o'clock, and he didn't want to wait any longer. The last thing he wanted was for that crowd to be there when the sun went down. A mob at day is one thing; a mob at night is trouble.

With Lucian fanning the flames of lies, the whole town could become a raging fire. He had to put it out. He had to tell them the truth.

Hollis stopped at the door. The sun was blinding in the west. He could see people lined up for two blocks down the street. Some were carrying signs and banners. He thought to himself, *My God!* There were twice as many people here as he'd seen for the Fourth of July parade. He took a deep breath and paused, trying to think of what he was going to say. He looked back down the hall at Sam and Teresa. And it suddenly struck him that Sam with his wire-rimmed frames and shotgun looked like pictures he'd seen of Wyatt Earp. Hollis shook his head and wondered to himself at how quickly the day had changed everything. The town he loved had turned against him. His deputies had deserted him. His life had been threatened, and he had been humiliated and beaten in his own jail. A quiet, little town was now a city of chaos.

He thought, *All this for just one man.* "Sam?"

Sam looked down the hall at the sheriff still standing at the door. "Yeah, Hollis?"

Hollis held up the keys and then stuck them in the door, "Come lock the door behind me. Don't unlock if for anybody till I come back."

Chapter Fifteen

The heat from the sun smacked him in the face as soon as he stepped outside; it must have been a hundred degrees in the shade. The hottest hours in Arkansas in the summer are in the late afternoon. If there was a breeze at all during the day, it comes to an abrupt stop by dusk. That's when the humidity becomes unbearable. It feels as if the oxygen has been drained from the sky, and breathing is not refreshing anymore; suffocating, as if you are being strangled by warm, steamy hands.

Hollis walked through the crowded sidewalk and headed to the front of the courthouse. He looked across the lawn, and every face he had known his entire life was looking at him. Half of the people were fanning their faces, and the people standing next to those were leaning over, trying to get some of the circulation. They surrounded the courthouse and filled the street all the way past City Hall and the Mena Star Newspaper.

Immediately, people started yelling, "Sheriff, Sheriff!"

"Here comes the sheriff!"

"The sheriff is here!"

A reporter ran up to him with his cameraman in tow, "Sheriff Brown, are you going to be making a statement?"

"Yes, I am."

"Has Harley Wright been charged with murder?"

"You're about to find out."

"But can you tell me . . ."

The sheriff stopped and turned to the reporter, "Hey, listen to me and listen good. I'm gonna tell them, and you'll find out when I tell them and not before, understand?"

Hollis looked around and saw some handmade signs in the crowd. "We hang criminals," one declared. Another said, "Harley will hang."

A slight sigh of relief came over the sheriff as he walked down the sidewalk. There was only one sign that said, "Sheriff Brown, get out of town," and at least it didn't call for his hanging.

Maybe they won't be all that bad, Hollis thought to himself. He walked around the courthouse and made his way through the crowd to the top of the courthouse steps. Huge eaves protruded above the arched doorway, and the steps leading up to the entrance gave Hollis a perfect place to speak to the crowd. They were tugging on him as he made his way to the top, and he was glad that there were a couple of big oak trees across the street that were providing some shade from the afternoon sun. Hollis cleared his throat, and a boy handed him a cup of lemonade.

"Thanks, son." Hollis took a sip and looked out across the crowd. He recognized most the faces. Ole Tom Miller stood in the middle of the street. Gip Blankenship sat in the back of his pickup and waved. It reminded Hollis of the crowd at the old drive-in theater when the last premier hit town. Hollis took another sip and smiled at the boy, "Sure is good, son, your mamma make that?"

The freckled face boy grinned, "My grandma just brought us some, we've been waiting all day to find out whatcha gonna do. Is he going to prison? Did he do it? Is he going to the chair?"

The kid smiled, and his mamma pulled him to her side, "Shh. Let the sheriff speak; he's got something important to say."

The sheriff looked over at Timmy, the mayor's son, holding up one of the signs. He and his buddies looked like the cast from *Happy Days*. Not one of them had probably done an honest day's work in his whole life. "Will you put those signs down?"

"Huh?"

"Put 'em down. I don't want to see them anymore, and get that darn rope out of that tree."

"But what about our freedom of speech?"

Hollis didn't like his smart-alecky reply, "You can talk all you want from the back of my jail, if you'd like."

The boys put their signs down by a big trash can, pulled the rope out of the tree, and dropped it on the ground. Hollis waited until they were done and then held up his hand and gestured for everyone to get still. A few people shouted something from the crowd that Hollis chose to ignore, but most everyone started saying, "Shh, shh," and a wave of quiet went like that all the way down the street.

He looked around at the faces of the people on the steps. They were all people he had lived with or known: old school mates, friends, and neighbors. He knew every one by their first name and had at one time or another helped nearly all of them. He noticed that some were staring at his neck and realized that blood was seeping through the bandage he had taped to his throat. It must have looked pretty bad, based on their expressions. It did hurt, it stung, especially as beads of sweat were beginning to roll down from his face and drip onto the wound. Hollis wiped the sweat off his brow with his short-sleeve shirt. The crowd was almost silent now. Across the street, he spotted Lucian's truck, but he didn't see him in the crowd, nor was there any sign of Rip. He had halfway expected that one or the other might come up and start a scene, but there wasn't a sign of either anywhere.

Hollis cleared his throat, "Ahem, a terrible tragedy has occurred in 'Y' City as everyone knows."

People on the edge of the courthouse lawn started yelling, "Speak up! Speak up!"

"Shh. Shh," swept through the crowd. People turned their heads around to see who was talking.

Hollis started again, this time louder. His voice was hoarse. "A terrible tragedy has happened here in our community as everyone knows. And I have been questioning people for three days and gathering all the evidence I can."

A murmuring could be heard in the crowd. The reporters edged closer with their microphones practically pushed in his face.

"I realize that many of you are upset because we have lost someone we all knew, but the investigation is still going on."

The crowd murmured some more, and Hollis wiped his brow, "But I do have an announcement to make. The evidence that we have at this time eliminates Harley Wright as a suspect."

"What?"

"I knew it!"

"They're lettin' a murderer go free!"

Sheriff Brown raised his hands. "Shh!"

They could tell he wasn't happy with them. He looked downright pissed off. "Ya'll settle down! I cannot go into all the details now, but I will when the time is right. I have heard there is a lot of gossip going on concerning Mrs. Taylor, but out of respect for her, I am not going to divulge anything."

Jess Meyers, the car salesman (and local pornographer) stood up on a park bench and yelled out, "You can't do this! Tell us what went on!"

Another person yelled out from the crowd, "We want Leah Taylor's killer!" And person after person piped up behind her.

Sheriff Brown raised his voice, "Shh. Listen up!" Hollis looked like he was going to come down those steps and punch Jess out. Someone else yelled something at him, and then others in the crowd turned around and told him to be quiet.

"Shh. Let the sheriff speak."

"Everybody be quiet!"

Hollis began again, "Every time ya'll open your mouths, you are hurting the reputation of a very good woman. Leah Taylor was as fine of a person as anyone I have ever known. I know this, she never had an unkind word to say about any of you. Not a single one of you. She was generous, as many of you know. She never asked for anything in return, but I am going to ask something for her today. Go on home. We are conducting an inquiry here. The official cause of death has not even been determined. You will be notified when it has."

"We want to know what happened," someone yelled from the crowd.

"We know Harley did it."

"There is a cover-up!"

Hollis looked at them and shook his head, "What if it was your wife? What if was your sister? What if it was you? Would you want the whole town talking about you?"

Some of the women looked away, and some just lowered their heads. They looked at each other from behind their sunglasses and under the brims of their hats. "If ya'll cared so much about her, your chance to help her is over now. You should have cared half as much about her when she was alive."

"We want to see justice," someone yelled.

Hollis waved for the crowd to be quiet again, "Do you really want to see justice? Are you sure? All these men who want to see Harley get the chair, do you know what he has done? If he is to get the chair for what he's done, then at least half of you should get the chair for the same thing. And the other half of you would've done what Harley did if you had the chance."

The crowd got real quiet. Wives started giving their husbands suspicious glares. A man yelled from across the street, "The papers said he might be a serial killer!"

"Hogwash. Thurman, you know better."

A local reverend stepped up through the crowd with a couple of his deacons. He said, "This town needs to be cleaned up. We need to start hanging scumbags like him."

Hollis took a deep breath and looked at the reverend, "I feel sorry for you, Bearden. Someday, you are going to be judged like you've judged him. You've condemned him, so what chance have you got? But you're right about one thing, this town does need to be cleaned up, because there are a whole lot of scumbags out there."

Hollis looked at all the faces he recognized, folks he'd known his whole life, people he would have called his friends. People were started to look around at each other, and a few then started to leave.

Hollis cleared his throat and spoke up so that everyone could hear him, "Let me tell you something else." He looked the reverend in the eye. "Be very careful of what you say. Be very careful what you believe and hear, for I'll tell you this, there will be many men who think they are righteous who will enter the gates of hell."

The righteous reverend Bearden looked stunned. An expression of guilt quickly consumed his face, and he looked down and away. Many others were shaken as well. Women tugged on their husbands' shirts, and Hollis could hear them telling them to leave.

Hollis squinted his eyes in the setting sun and started back down the steps. The crowd was starting to disperse. The two deacons standing beside the reverend left. The freckle-faced boy held out another glass of lemonade, and Hollis patted him on the shoulder, "Thanks, son."

The reporters were hurling questions at him, to which Hollis kept saying, "No comment." He held up his hands and waved them on, "Ya'll go on home now."

The people were walking back to their cars, and Hollis felt greatly relieved that they were finally going to be gone. He hadn't really cared what they might have said about him. He was just glad that the trouble they had caused was over. He could get back to business without having to deal with them anymore.

The reporters followed right behind him as he headed back over to the jail, "When are you going to announce the official cause of death?"

Sheriff Brown stopped and turned around, "When the state crime lab has completed their report, which they haven't finished yet."

Another reporter interrupted, "We have heard you have fired some of your deputies. One has claimed you beat him. Can you speak on that? Was this as a result of the investigation?"

"I don't speak publicly regarding dismissals or terminations. It is an internal affairs issue, and I can't say anymore about that."

The pretty reporter from Channel 5 in Fort Smith spoke up, "Okay, one more question. Was there an altercation with the deceased's husband?"

"No comment."

"Did Rip Taylor do that to your neck?"

"No comment. I'm through answering your questions."

Hollis walked down the sidewalk and through the crowd. Some people who still standing around thanked him for coming out, a few others gave him looks of disgust. They didn't like the way things turned out. They had expected a different outcome. Just as Hollis was about to enter the jail, someone came running up to him, "Sheriff, Sheriff, wait up a minute."

The sheriff stopped. It was David Smith, another preacher. "I don't really have time to talk right now."

"I know you're busy, but please, just give me a minute."

Hollis bent his wrist around and pointed to his wristwatch, "One minute, that's all."

"I just wanted you to know that not everyone feels the same way about what's happened around here. We were here today because this community needs healing."

Hollis lifted his chin up and pulled back his neck for David to see, "You're telling me about healing?" Hollis lifted the corner of his bandage. "This is what needs healing."

"I'm sorry to hear about what happened to you, and we aren't having any part of those petitions. We support you all the way."

Hollis grinned. He looked down the street at all the cars backing out and people scurrying across the intersection. The sun was in his eyes as he looked at the handsome preacher. He had heard from various folks that he was a good man and very involved in the community. "Well, that's nice to hear. It is good to know that somebody out there thinks I'm doing a good job."

"We'd like to invite you to our services. We'd love to have you attend."

"Well, I appreciate that, I really do, and I don't mean to hurt your feelings or nothing, but I'm not the one you need inviting. You need to invite the people I see. I've got about twenty-something here on a regular basis, men and women."

"Well, yeah, them too, but can you let them out?"

"That's where we have a slight problem, you see. You hafta come here for them."

David hesitated. He was caught a little off guard. He wasn't expecting to be invited into the jail. "Well, let me think. I could probably get some men from my church to . . ."

"I've got all the people the churches don't want. I've got the wife beaters, the drunks, the thieves. I've had a mother in here who sticks syringes in her arm while her kids run around on the floor, unwashed and unfed. You really want her? Because before she came here, she was out there, and there weren't any personal invitations to any of these churches."

"If we would have known we coulda gone to see her."

Hollis folded his arms and looked at the man, "Oh, really? Because I've been here for twenty-two years, and I don't think I've seen four preachers in all that time, and those was just courtesy visits when one of their own got caught doing something they shouldn't."

The preacher looked very uncomfortable and tried to be somewhat apologetic, "Hey, if I would have known."

Hollis seemed amused by the young preacher, "If you would have known? What do you think this place is?" Hollis pointed to the jail, "These aren't choir boys in here, in case you're wondering, but if you want, I can take you back there and introduce you to some of them right now."

David looked at his watch, "Well, I'd like to, but we have a building committee meeting this evening, and I hafta . . ."

Hollis shook his head. "I don't mean to embarrass you, Reverend, but I want you to ask yourself this question, 'What would Jesus do?' Think about it. You don't hafta give me an answer, but what do you really think he would do?"

A car drove by, honking and a family waved at them as they drove off down the street. Hollis and David smiled and waved back. The sweat was beading on Hollis's forehead, and he looked at his watch, "Minute's up." Hollis stuck out his hand. "Well, thanks for the invite." He smiled, "Good to know I'm still wanted somewhere, huh?"

David started to say something, but Hollis turned and walked back up to the jail. The sun was behind the trees; it would soon be nightfall. What he didn't want the preacher to know, or anyone else for that matter, was that he was worried. It was going to be dark soon, and he was going to have to guard the whole jail by himself. Hollis knew something else; Rip Taylor would not rest until the score was settled.

Chapter Sixteen

Hollis knew he had missed a golden opportunity to ask for help when he was addressing the crowd. He let them walk away when he had an audience of four or five thousand people, which probably consisted of a thousand able-bodied men. But Hollis couldn't bring himself to ask for their help. He had the same flaws that so many men have, pride and stubbornness. He wasn't about to let them know how badly he needed them, not after the way they had acted.

He couldn't for the life of him ask those same people who had signed petitions to help him out. He wouldn't give them the satisfaction of knowing that he couldn't do his job without their help. Hollis Brown was human after all, and he had some very weak traits and one of them was ego. It had on several occasions gotten the best of him, but he would of course deny it. And there was something else he wouldn't admit; he didn't want anyone to know he was scared.

It was the hardest thing that he had ever had to do in his life, and it tore at his soul that he ever did it, but Hollis had gone to Rip the year before to ask him for money to pay for Barbara's medical bills. The medical coverage he had as sheriff was woefully inadequate for covering all her costs. Her treatments were going to stop if he didn't come up with more money. To pay for her chemo therapy the first time she had cancer, he had taken out a second mortgage on his home. When she relapsed, he had no reserves and his savings were gone. Rip did Hollis the biggest favor of his life and gave him the money. Hollis was desperate and felt like he was taking money from the devil, but he would do that if it meant saving his wife. And Hollis was no fool; he knew that when you take something from the devil, one day you are going to have to pay him back. He just couldn't do it with Harley's life.

Harley would never know just how done he was. Hollis was ready to charge him the minute he stepped out of that Texas Ranger squad car. The interrogation was just a formality. In fact, Hollis hadn't even planned on it lasting an hour. Everything was all planned, he had told Rip in advance that he would be charged, he had even told the governor, but then something happened. He heard the truth.

When he looked into Harleys eyes, he saw innocence. It's not what he wanted to see; he wanted to see guilt. But the truth ruined his plans. He knew Harley didn't do it.

Hollis tapped on the door and Sam came down the hall with the keys. Hollis sniffed the air when he walked in, "What is that?"

"Pizza. They ordered some before you left."

"How did that get in here? You weren't supposed to unlock the door, remember?"

"What was I supposed to do, Hollis? Have him shove it through an air duct?"

Hollis took the keys out of Sam's hands and locked it behind him, "You didn't know what was going to happen out there. Rip could have been right around the corner. Keep it locked."

Sam shrugged his shoulders, "Gosh, Hollis, I was just trying to help. What did Barbara feed you this morning, a bowl of pessimism?"

Hollis grumbled some more as he walked down the hall. The pizza sure did smell good though. Harley was kicked back behind the front desk with his foot up. He held some cards in one hand and a slice of pizza in the other. "Howdy, Sheriff." Harley threw a spade down and picked up the trick. "Gotcha."

"He's good, Hollis." Teresa smiled and took a bite of pizza. "You oughta play a hand with us."

Hollis put his hands on his hips and looked around the room in disbelief, "Do ya'll not know what just happened? I just ordered half the county to go home. Did ya'll not get that? And you're sittin' 'round playing cards in here while I'm out there. I mean . . ."

Harley took another bite of pizza, "Yeah, good job." He tossed down a queen of diamonds, "Nobody touch my lady."

Sam tossed down a king from his hand, "Sorry, Harley. I had to do it."

"You sure ain't no ladies' man, Sam."

Hollis looked into two different pizza boxes. They were both empty.

Harley grinned, "Get you some of that meat lover's pizza. Man, that's good."

Hollis opened up the last box, there was only one thin slice of pepperoni left. He picked it up, "Is this it?"

Harley looked over at the boxes. "Nah, there were three large pizzas there."

"There are three empty boxes."

Harley smiled, "Uh oh." He held out the crust from his piece, "You can have this."

Hollis ate the last slice and asked, "Did ya'll not even think about me?"

They all nodded without looking at him. Sam threw down an ace of diamonds.

Teresa threw down a spade. "Sorry, Sam."

They were obviously engrossed in the game and not him.

Harley smiled and threw down a low card, allowing Teresa to take the trick.

"Harley, you're so sweet.".

Harley finished off the crust and smiled, "Only for you."

Hollis ate the measly slice of pizza in one bite and poured himself a cup of coffee. "She's pregnant, Harley, and married."

Teresa waved the sheriff off, "Oh, he knows that. Hollis, Harley and I go way back. He used to flirt with me way back in . . ."

Hollis shook his head and tossed the pizza boxes in the trash, "I really don't want to hear it, not now, not ever. I'm just really touched by ya'll's gratitude."

They kept playing cards and laughing, even Sam wasn't listening. Hollis Brown couldn't believe he was being totally ignored by the three of them; they didn't look like they had a worry in the world. He had expected some sort of congratulations on how he handled the crowd, but he realized that all the time he was out there, they were in the jail eating and laughing it up. He looked at Harley with his long legs spread out halfway across the room, smiling from ear to ear, and joking with Sam and Teresa—he didn't seem to realize that the sheriff had just put his whole career on the line for him. He hadn't even gotten a "thanks." Sam was laughing more than he had in twenty years, and Teresa looked like she didn't have a care in the world. She wasn't really acting like she was married either, which created a twinge of jealousy in Hollis. He had been her hero since she was a little kid, and now here she was, totally ignoring him when he needed her most. He had expected something different from them. He wanted some praise, but instead he was ignored. Hollis wondered, *Is there something not right about this picture, or is there something not right about me?* He couldn't put his finger on it.

Hollis looked up to the sound of banging. It was his two other deputies knocking on the plate glass front door. Hollis looked at the three playing cards, "Oh, don't worry. Don't let me interrupt your game. I'll get it."

Hollis walked down the hall grumbling and unlocked the door. They walked in and looked at the mess still in the hallway, "Man, what happened here?"

"I had an altercation with Rip, and I had to fire Lucian and Duke."

"Fired? You fired them both?"

Teresa spoke up, "They stood by while the sheriff was nearly killed." She tossed another card down, "Take this!"

The officers immediately noticed Harley sitting down by the dispatcher's desk, "What's he doing out?"

"He's been questioned and I'm going to release him."

One of the officers threw his hat on the desk, "Aw shit! So that's why Rip blew up. You're letting scumbag here go?"

Hollis didn't like the comment. He pulled out a smoke and lit it and sat down on top of the desk. "Look, I've already gone one round with him. I'm not going to sit here and explain anything to you. Understand?" Hollis then reached over and pulled the work schedule down from the wall; he wrote something down and hung it back up, "We're going to a twelve-and-twelve schedule until further notice."

Crandle, "Nightstand," objected, "Hey, I've go three days off starting tomorrow."

Hollis tossed his glasses onto the desk, "You *were* going to get three days off, but things have changed. Both of ya'll be back here in the morning at seven. You'll have a seven-to-seven day shift everyday till I tell you otherwise."

"Hollis, you can't do that."

"I think I just did."

Teresa interjected, "Hollis, we've still got two coming from the state police, remember?" Teresa then pushed herself back from the table as if she was done with the game.

Hollis took a deep drag on his cigarette and flipped the ashes towards the trash can. He missed. "Yeah, but they aren't authorized to guard our jail. They are only authorized to patrol our highways."

"Why can't we have them come and guard our jail if we're short on men?"

"Because if they are going to guard it, then they are going to run it, and nobody but me is going to run my jail. You hear?"

Crandle was clearly not happy with losing his days off. He threw his ticket book across the front of the desk in the direction of Hollis. Hollis put his cigarette on the edge of the desk with the ashes hanging off. He walked around to where Crandle was standing. "You got a problem?"

"Well, I don't like losing my days off, and I . . ."

"Listen, I don't like having my head nearly ripped off my shoulders by a maniac either, but I don't go around crying about it because I have a duty. Do you understand? You have that same duty, and that duty is to protect the people. It comes before your holidays, time off, vacations, and everything else, and if you aren't going to live up to that duty, take your badge off now and don't come back. Do you understand?" Hollis stood there with his palm out, ready for Crandle's badge.

Crandle looked around the room and then nodded, "I understand."

"Good. I'll se ya at seven."

"Who's going to cover the jail tonight?"

"I am."

"All night? By yourself?"

"Yeah, me and maybe Sam."

Sam leaned back in his chair smiling. He still had the shotgun in his lap, "Yep, as long as I can play cards here, you can count on my professional services."

"I need ya."

"There is something I need to talk to you about though, real quick."

"What is it?"

Sam whispered something to the sheriff, and he turned around to his deputies, "Don't go yet, I may have something I want ya'll to do before you leave."

They both nodded, "Sure, Sheriff, whatever you say."

Hollis and Sam went into his office and shut the door. Harley was wheeling his chair across the room as adroitly as a kid on skateboard. The two officers weren't very impressed. Harley smiled, "Hot day out there, was it?"

"What do you think? It's June."

"I know it's tough." Harley spun around in his chair doing circles. "I appreciate all the hard work ya'll are doing."

"Gee, thanks, Harley, it makes our job so much easier knowing you care."

"I want ya'll ta know I think you guys deserve some time off. I think ya'll should go ahead and take it . . . and as far as I'm concerned, it's okay if ya'll don't come back at seven." He smiled.

"Trying to get us fired?"

"No, no, I just think yer doin' such a great job, that's all."

"Aren't you supposed to be locked up?"

"No, I'm free to go."

"So what are ya doin' here? I'll escort ya to the door."

"No thanks, fellas. Ya'll are supposed to protect me." Harley smiled smugly and then he snickered, "Say, Nightstand, I've been meaning to ask you something. When someone spills a drink on your head, does it just roll off the back or does it seep down your face?"

"That's it, punk. I'm gonna . . ."

Harley laughed and spun around in his chair, "Just askin', lots a folks 've been wondering."

Just then the sheriff and Sam cam back out and saw Jefferson restraining Crandle by the collar. "What's going on here?"

"Harley just gave us a demonstration of why everyone hates him."

Sheriff Brown raised his eyebrow, "He's being a smart-ass?"

Crandle shrugged his shoulder away from Jefferson, "Just give me five minutes with him. Just five minutes."

Sheriff Brown walked over to Harley, grabbed him by the collar, and pulled him out of his chair, "Son, you need to change and change quick. Lock him up."

"Come on, Sheriff, I was just playing with him. Don't lock me up. I've been locked up all day."

"You'd better understand something, Harley. These guys may have to put their lives on the line for you. And I ain't gonna have you bad-mouthing them or giving them crap."

"I didn't mean nothin'. I was just jokin'."

"It ain't no joke to them. They're having to work on their days off and adjust their whole lives for you right now. The least you can do is give them respect, or you can walk out those doors right now. I doubt you'd make it a mile from here before someone put a bullet in you. So make your choice, either I lock you up or I let you go."

Harley walked over to the big, steel door going to the jail cells, leaned against the wall with his arms folded, and shrugged, "Some choice."

"That's the best decision he's made in awhile. Lock him up."

Sam grabbed his hat and looked at his watch, "We don't have much time. Who's going with me?"

"Both of them are."

Crandle looked at Sam with surprise and then looked at Hollis, "Where?"

"On an errand."

"Fine, but where?"

To Sam's house."

"Why?"

"He's got some papers that I need to see." The sheriff yelled back at Jefferson, who was locking Harley up, "Hey, while you're at it, let the trustee out. I need him to clean up this mess out here."

"Lewis?"

"Yeah, Lewis." Hollis could see that the little deputy looked worried, "What's the problem?"

"I was just wondering why Sam needs an escort, that's all."

"Maybe he doesn't, but I'm not taking chances till this thing blows over."

"Where's Rip? You think Rip's pissed off at Sam too?"

"You ask too many questions, Crandle."

"Where is he?"

"I dunno."

Teresa, who had been on the phone, leaned around the corner and said, "I got word he is over at the funeral home."

Jefferson locked Harley up in a cell by himself and brought Lewis out. Sam left quickly with the two deputies and was told to hurry back before dark. As soon as they left, Hollis pulled out a bucket and mop and handed them to Lewis, "Get to work."

"Yes, Sheriff."

"Lewis?"

"Yes sir."

Hollis walked down the hallway and looked around outside, "You may have another job as soon as you get finished cleaning up."

"What's that?"

"Keeping me awake all night."

Hollis went back to the booking area and plopped down on the same rolling chair that Harley had played on. He looked at the video monitor of the cells in back. Harley was already stretched out on a bunk; he looked like he had fallen asleep. Hollis thought to himself, *He's sleepy, all right. I would be too after eating all that pizza.* The monitor alternated with shots from different cells every few seconds. Most of the inmates were playing cards or reading. Hollis looked at the monitors and rubbed his eyes. He tossed his boots up on the table and leaned back, "Man, I'm tired."

Teresa smiled, "You want me to rub your shoulders?"

"I should be rubbing yours, hon."

Her hands squeezed the muscles in his shoulders, "I'm fine, Hollis. By the way, I called home and let my husband know I'm going to be late."

Hollis felt the tension release as her hands squeezed the muscles in his back, "Oh, that's right — you should have left at six. Why didn't you go?'

"Why didn't I go? You didn't have any one here, remember?"

"But you get off at six. What time is it anyway?"

"Seven thirty."

"You'd better go; you've got kids at home."

She pressed her fingers deep into the muscles between his shoulder blades, "Here they are. Here's where all your tension is." Teresa rolled her fingers back and forth over the muscles in his shoulders. "Don't worry about me, Hollis. I've got a good husband at home. He can take care of them. I need to take care of you."

Hollis's head dropped down to his chest. He let out a long exhale. Teresa rubbed his neck and shoulders and felt the tension ease, and after a few moments, she realized he had gone to sleep.

She tiptoed past Lewis mopping the hall and locked the front door. It surprised her how much blood there was in the bucket, way too much for a man to lose. She watched Lewis scrub down the wall, and it seemed as if it took forever to get it off. The clock ticked slowly; everything was mysteriously quiet. When Lewis finished, he positioned himself as a lookout in a chair by the front door as the sun disappeared in the red, glowing western sky. Teresa flipped through a magazine, nervously watching the clock. Thirty minutes passed, then almost an hour. Sam and the deputies should have been back, and her occasional calls for them on the radio went unanswered. There was nothing, just silence. She thought about waking Hollis, but she didn't want to; he was so tired. Still, she knew something was wrong.

Hollis grumbled and rubbed his eyes. "What time is it?"

"8:24. You hungry? You should be. You didn't have much dinner."

Still rubbing his eyes, he said, "Yeah, come to think of it, I'm starving."

Teresa dialed the Snack Attack and, patting Hollis on the head, said to him in baby talk, "Well, you won't have to worry about getting food this time. Harley's all locked up."

Hollis stood up and stretched. He looked down the hall and saw that it was cleaned up. Lewis was sitting in a chair at the front door, looking out. "Whatcha doing, Lewis?"

"Looking. Somebody sure left a lot of trash out there today."

"Didn't take it with them, did they?"

"No sir."

Hollis pulled out a smoke and lit it, "Want some pizza? Teresa's calling."

"You know better to ask that, Sheriff."

Hollis motioned to Lewis, "Get him one too." He then looked at his watch and doubled-checked the time with the wall clock, "Is Sam not back yet?"

Teresa shook her head, "And they are beyond my signal. Something's wrong. They should have been back thirty minutes ago, I would think." The phone rang and Teresa answered, "Yes, yes . . . uh oh, what? He did what? How long ago? Oh my God! You are kidding. Oh no!"

Hollis could see the concern on her face. "What is it?"

"Rip's been to the funeral home. He's torn the place up."

"Tell them I'll be right there."

Teresa was still on the phone, "They said he has already left. Left about five minutes ago."

"What did he do?"

"He told them he wasn't paying for 'no F-ing funeral.' He said they could just 'throw the tramp' in the dumpster cuz he wasn't paying one red dime."

Hollis couldn't believe it, "He did what?"

"They thought he was gonna pick the casket up and throw her out onto the floor."

Hollis paced back and forth smoking his cigarette. He knew he couldn't leave until they got back. "Any word on Crandle and Jefferson? For God's sake, where are they?"

Teresa was on the phone with the funeral home, and she had the mic in her other hand, "I dunno, Hollis. I can't get any reception. It's like they disappeared. I don't know what's happened."

"Sheriff?"

"Yes, Lewis."

"I see a green car parked down at the end of the street. It's been sitting there a long time. Someone's in it, but I can't see who." Lewis squinted his eyes, "I think it's a Honda, possibly an '86."

"Keep your eye on it." Hollis looked at Teresa, "What else can go wrong?"

Teresa hung up the phone and called the unit again. "I don't like this, Hollis. This is getting awfully weird. I'm getting really worried, and it's almost dark."

Hollis walked into his office and pulled out his holster with his gun, a .38 Special. He hadn't worn it in probably six or seven years. He loaded the chamber with bullets and blew the dust out of the barrel. He walked back out, puffing on his cigarette, "Still no word?"

Teresa shook her head, "Nothing. And you know what else he said? He said they should burn her."

"As in cremate?"

"I think the exact words he used were, 'They should burn the bitch.'"

"Teresa."

"I'm telling you, he is hot. Joel is scared to death."

Hollis looked out the window into the street. It was almost dark now. The streetlights were coming on. He could see the lights on in the apartment building across the street. The far western sky was just a red glow as the sun disappeared. It wouldn't be long now till nighttime. His deputies were missing and so was Sam. Rip was on a rampage, and Hollis had a feeling it was just the beginning. His dispatcher had to go home, and the only help he had now was a skinny trustee at the end of the hall.

Hollis finished his cigarette and snuffed it out, tossing it into the trash. His hand rested on the handle of his gun, and his fingers rubbed over the contours of steel. It had been a long time since he had even touched it. He felt the safety button on the side and checked to make sure it was on. Hollis pulled it out and slipped it back in the holster. As the street turned dark, he knew only one thing: the day had been bad, but the night would be worse.

Chapter Seventeen

For a man like Hollis, not knowing is always worse than knowing. He liked to face his problems head-on; that's the way he was. Uncertainty, like the uncertainty of Barbara's cancer, took more out of him than it had his wife.

Teresa knew this better than anyone else, maybe even Barbara. Barbara was calm, but Teresa was there with him in the line of fire. She was on the battlefront, and she had to deal with that dreadful, awful, irritable side of Hollis Brown. She knew to just give him space, let him vent. She also knew that long ago, way back in his early years as a cop, Hollis didn't cope too well. He soaked his fears and anxieties in the bottle. He sought relief in a lot of wrong places. Very few people knew about his year of "personal torture," as he called it. He rarely ever talked about it because Barbara almost left him. He came to his senses and came out of it, and from then on he faced every problem head-on. He was a different man. Teresa knew that space and some levity were the antidotes to Hollis's irritable nature. She knew never to argue, that only made things worse.

Teresa called again on the radio, "Unit 312, this is 81.Come in, over." Hollis paced back and forth. There was no reply, the silence was stunning.

He looked up at the big map on the wall of Polk County and ran his fingers up highway 375 towards Shady where Sam lived. Half of the county was forest owned by the federal government, and some communities were entirely surrounded by national forest. Shady was one of those places. It had become a community of recluses. Thirteen miles from Mena, it was located on some of the most gorgeous peaks in the state. Sam's house hung out over a cliff. Hollis had been there before, but not for a number of years, and he couldn't remember whether he'd lost signal.

He stood there with his back towards Teresa, studying the map. "We should have a signal in Shady, shouldn't we?"

"Not always, Hollis. It gets bad there, just like it does on the other side of Rich Mountain."

Just then Lewis yelled out from the end of the hall, "Hey, the green car left. It took off down DeQueen Street . . . and, here they are. They're back!"

Hollis grabbed the keys and went down and let Sam in with the deputies. Sam looked scared to death. Hollis looked up and down the street as they entered, "Where in the world have ya'll been? You've been gone for over an hour."

Sam walked right by him and went down to the coke machine, "Man, I need a drink."

"Tell me what happened." Hollis looked back and forth between the deputies and Sam, "What is it? Tell me. What's going on?"

"They ransacked my house, that's what! And we stopped at my office, and it has been broken into, too."

"So, did you get the file?"

Sam pulled out a computer disk, "It's right here. I've got all of it. All my other files were destroyed."

"They did a number on his office," Jefferson shook his head, "and we found these." He handed Hollis some shell casings in a plastic bag. "I think these were a warning. They were laying on the floor."

Hollis took the bag and looked at the casings, "Nine millimeter, that'll do a job."

Sam popped open the can of coke and grabbed a Styrofoam cup. He pulled a flask out of his boot and poured himself a drink, "Hope you don't mind, but I need this. Taking a drink, he continued, "Hollis, I'm done. I'm through. I got the message loud and clear. My practice is over."

Jefferson and Crandle looked at the sheriff, "Do you need us to stay tonight?"

Hollis looked down the hall at Lewis. He looked at Sam, and then at the clock. "No, I think we'll be all right, but thanks for taking Sam out there. I appreciate that."

"One more thing, Hollis. Have you seen the funeral home?"

"No, why?"

"The windows to all the hearse are broken out. Every one of them."

Hollis just sighed and shook his head, "He's gone berserk."

Crandle sat down on the desk next to Teresa, "I think we really ought to stay here. You should get the state police in here too before anything else happens."

"I've got two who are already supposed to be here, but they haven't arrived. We can't get them on the radio."

Jefferson reached over to the dispatcher's desk and looked at the board. He picked up the mic and blew into it, "Testing, testing. Well, we couldn't get you either. You sure this is working?"

They all looked at the equipment and made sure that everything was connected the way it was supposed to be. It looked fine. Sam poured himself another drink.

"Hollis," Teresa suggested, "we haven't heard a call in over an hour. Don't you think that's strange?"

Teresa picked up the mic, "Firehouse One, Firehouse One, this is 81, over." There was only silence. Teresa repeated, "Firehouse One, do you copy? Over." Teresa looked at her boss, "There's no signal. We aren't getting out or receiving."

Everyone wondered how a radio system could go completely out. Then Lewis thought of something, "Sheriff Brown, remember the green car down the street? What if they disconnected our antenna?"

It made sense. Hollis sent Jefferson to check it out, and he found the source of the problem. Someone had cut a three foot section out of the coax cable from the antenna leading into the side of the building so it couldn't be spliced back together. Hollis didn't take the news well. With communication to the outside world cut off, he wouldn't be able to respond to emergencies or call the fire department or emergency personnel. There would be no communication with any police cars. Polk County Jail only had a phone, that was it.

Sam poured himself another drink and burped, "Well, that darn thing made too much noise anyway. Who needs it?"

Hollis took the drink out of Sam's hand. "Why don't you hold off for awhile?"

"But . . ."

"I'll make a fresh pot of coffee." Teresa walked over to the coffee maker and started another pot, "Sam, this is what you need."

Sam had a pleasant smile on his face. He looked at Teresa and grinned, "I'd tell you what I need right now, but you're already married. I need . . ."

"Some coffee." Teresa took the cup from Hollis and poured it down the drain. She looked at Hollis, "And I don't want you looking at this either."

Hollis and the deputies discussed what they should do while Sam vainly attempted to flirt with Teresa. Radio Shack was the only place that carried that kind of cable, and they were closed.

Finally, Lewis suggested they call Harley. "He can repair anything," he said.

Jefferson and Crandle were given the unpleasant chore of going and getting him out of his cell. Harley wasn't too happy about being awakened. He rubbed his eyes and mumbled. Teresa put a fresh cup of coffee in his hands, "Drink this."

Harley squinted, "What's going on. Why can't I sleep? I wasn't hurtin' no one."

"We've got a problem." Hollis explained the situation to Harley while he sipped on his coffee. Harley leaned back against the wall and eyed Crandle.

He rubbed his chin for a second, "I think I have the answer. You have antennas on all your squad cars, right? Just cut the cable off of one you're not using. Should be about three feet, and I can splice it together."

"Think that will work?"

"Sure it will work, just get me some duct tape and a knife."

Hollis and Jefferson took Harley out to the street where he proceeded to quickly cut the coax cable off Unit 4, Lucian's unit. Together the three of them went around to the back of the building where Harley carefully spliced the cable together as Hollis and Jefferson shined their flashlights for Harley to do his work. They stood in the shadow of the building, and Hollis was a little on edge being back there. He knew that anyone could be across the street in the dark with a gun and get off a couple of shots. They were open targets. Hollis kept the light trained on the cable while simultaneously watching the street. Hollis studied Harley as he twisted the ends of the cable wires together and then cut the tape into neat strips and wrapped them around the cable. He was impressed at how meticulous Harley was. He definitely had a talent. Hollis never had the talent to do anything like that, and Harley was clearly a pro.

"There, that should do it."

The three went back into the building, and they could hear Teresa on the radio as soon as they walked in. She gave them a thumbs-up.

"It's perfect."

Sam stood there kind of weaving a bit behind Teresa, "Why did you hafta go and do that? Now I gotta listen to that noise all night."

Hollis took Sam by the elbow and walked him into his office, "Why don't you lay down in here for a little while?" He took the CD-ROM out of Sam's coat pocket and put it on the desk. Sam didn't resist. He wobbled over to the couch and laid down. Hollis was relieved Sam didn't put up an argument. He just stretched out, tipped his hat over his eyes, and folded his arms across his chest. Hollis thought to himself, For an Auburn man, Sam sure was a lightweight. Hollis slipped the boots off the little man and set them by the couch. Sam's little half-pint, silver flask shined in the boot. Hollis picked it up and looked at it. For some reason he wanted to smell it. He hadn't wanted to do that for over twenty years, but for some strange reason, he wanted to then. Instead, he turned out the light and closed the door, walking back over to where Teresa was. He handed it to her, and said, "Get rid of this, will ya?"

She could tell he was a little on edge. He paced back and forth and lit up another cigarette. He was mumbling to himself as they all talked about Sam's place and the antenna being cut. Hollis was deep in thought and seemed distracted. He looked at his two deputies and seemed apologetic, "Ah, can I ask ya'll just one more favor?"

Hollis said he needed to go and see Joel down at the funeral home. It was a few minutes before nine. He said he wouldn't take long, because he wanted them to get home and get some rest before they had to show back up in the morning.

Lewis let him out and watched the sheriff walk down the street into the night. The funeral home was one block down. Hollis could hear the traffic up on Highway 71 going through town. It sounded like the usual Saturday night. On many nights like this, he would be cruising around through the drive-ins, keeping an eye on things and talking to the kids and the owners. He always enjoyed it; he liked keeping the town orderly. But on this night, he felt so inadequate. He wouldn't be there to watch things, and he felt so alone. The one time he needed them, they turned away.

Hollis stopped at the hearse in front of the building. He inspected the windows to see if they were shot out or if they'd been clubbed. They were shot out. Hollis thought to himself, *I bet they were shot with a nine millimeter.*

He stood there under the streetlights, looking down DeQueen Street to the old train station. It was noisy on the highway, but not bad because the train station kind of shielded the noise from the traffic. He shined his light underneath the cars, looking for shells. He didn't see any. He walked back over to the other side of the street, where Lewis had said the green car was, and shined his light around, and there they were, two shell casings. He found another that had rolled up to the curb.

Using a pen, Hollis picked them up and put them into his front pocket. He figured when they were tested, they would match the ones found at Sam's house. He also figured that a silencer was used. Someone would have reported three shots. There was an apartment building within a hundred and fifty feet and a row of houses on the next block.

Hollis looked around, trying to simulate what happened. He figured there were at least two people involved. One must have parked the car and cased the jail, while the other went up the next block and came up behind the jailhouse to cut the antennae wire. They left in a hurry, so either the driver went around to pick up the person, or the person must have returned quickly.. He figured the driver shot out the hearse's windows as he was leaving, because he certainly wouldn't shoot them out and then sit across the street.

A car turned the corner down the block, squealing its wheels and barreled up the block. Hollis realized he was in the open; he had no cover as the car raced toward him. He reached his hand down, yanked off the trigger strap, and grabbed the handle of his gun. The car raced for him, and Hollis knelt in the squatting position but didn't pull his gun out. He could hear music blaring, rap music. The car flew up to him and then passed him and came to a screeching halt at the stop sign. He could hear kids laughing, and then the car took a hard left and barreled up to the next block.

His heart felt as if it was trying to leap through his throat. He could hear the rhythm of his own pulse beating between his ears like it was a drum. Breathing rapidly, he tried to slow it down. He couldn't believe just how close he had come to drawing his gun, and it scared him. It was just a car of kids. His hands were shaking.

Hollis thought to himself, *This is insane; I need to get off the street before someone gets hurt.*

Hollis went to the back of the funeral home and rang the buzzer for Joel. Joel was the most genuine undertaker Hollis had ever known. He was a third generation undertaker. His grandfather had started the business back when they had only two choices, pine or cedar.

In police work, funeral directors and cops see a lot of each other, and over the years, Hollis had developed a lot of respect for Joel because, professionally, both men had to be there for families during the most traumatic times in their lives. It was often a thankless job, but Joel did his well.

Hollis pushed the intercom button beside the back door, "Joel, it's me Hollis. Let me in."

Joel buzzed him in, and Hollis saw the look of worry on Joel as soon as he walked in.

"How're ya holding up?"

"Hollis, this is the worst. I think he's gone mad. Did Teresa tell ya what all he did?" Joel didn't look like he was a funeral director. He looked like a baseball player, not huge but well-built and muscular. He wasn't pale either; his complexion was slightly tanned and not what you'd normally expect for someone in his occupation.

"Yeah, she told me. Show me what he's done." They walked from the back up to the viewing room where Leah lay. The place was dark and quiet as Hollis approached her casket. It was a rather simple, cherry casket, and it was open. The lights were dim and soft. Hollis was tentative about going over to it. He walked slowly across the carpet as Joel told him how Rip had stormed in, demanding to see her. She hadn't been back from the coroner's in Little Rock more than a few hours, and they had just finished their preparations when he arrived.

"The first thing he said after he got here was, 'To hell with the funeral, just burn her.'"

Hollis looked around, "Who was here?"

"Just me and the staff. The Kesterson family had just left after viewing Fred in the other room."

"Was Rip alone? Was Dallas here?"

Joel shook his head, "Nope, just him. He was so mad, he tore up all the flower arrangements and kicked her casket." Joel pointed to the side where the wood had splintered. "See here? Then he slammed the lid down and picked up the casket about two feet off the table, like he was going to topple it over. I swear I thought he was going to toss her out on to the floor and start kicking her."

"Every other word was a cuss word, but mainly he was calling her a 'two-timing bitch.' He said awful stuff about her, called her 'white trash' and a 'rotten whore,' and it just went on and on."

Hollis walked over and straightened up some flowers that were mangled and placed them at the foot of the casket. He was surprised there weren't more. "He tore up a few that we had to get rid of. What you see is what we salvaged."

Hollis placed his hand on the casket and put a flower on top, "Yeah, I'm kinda surprised she didn't have more."

Joel straightened up the flowers a little more and left the room. Hollis's eyes examined the wood and then glanced into the silk-cushioned casket. She was wearing a white dress with long, silk gloves. She was beautiful. Hollis had expected to see the pale face with bluish lips that Harley had described, but she was anything but that woman Harley had last seen. Her face was as he had always known her. She didn't look sad, nor was there a placid smile on her lips. Surprisingly, she didn't look dead either. Leah just looked as though she was thinking with her eyes closed. Joel couldn't have done a better job.

Next to her, snuggled on the side, was her Bible, and on the other side was her book of poetry. Hollis hesitated and then he picked them up. He thumbed through the pages of the Bible, it was well worn and written in. He came to a part she had bookmarked with a tassel and read quietly to himself. Hollis then held her leather-bound poetry book in his hand. He flipped over a poem or two; they were as beautiful as Leah.

"She would have wanted them, don't you think?"

Hollis turned around; it was Joel, "Where did you get these?"

"Out of her truck." Joel hesitated, "They didn't bring us a dress or anything of hers. Most families do. So we went out there, and I was given permission to pick something out of her closet. I looked for her picture to put on her casket. There were none in the house, at least, none that I would use. And as I was leaving, I saw her old truck and found these on the front seat. I took them because I think she would not have wanted me to leave them there."

Hollis nodded, "Look at this." He opened the Bible, "Will you make sure this is read at her funeral? It's Isaiah 43. She had it marked, and she wrote it out here like a poem."

"Sure." Joel took the Bible and read what she had written aloud.

"Fear not, for I am with you.
I have called you by your name;
You are mine.
When you go through troubled waters,
I will be with you.
When you wade rivers of difficulty,
You will not drown.
And when you go through the fires

Of persecution,
You will not be burned,
It will not consume you.
For I am the Lord your God,
You are precious in my sight.
You have been honored,
For I have loved you."

Hollis turned away from her, "She made it, Joel. She made it through all that."

"I think she'd like you to keep those."

Hollis was a little surprised, "Both?"

Joel nodded, "Her family's not going to miss them."

Hollis was kind of shocked. He was flattered that Joel offered them to him. Hollis suddenly had a tranquil, pleasing expression on his face. He was so glad he had taken a moment to come and see her. As they walked back out together, Hollis raised a question he had long wondered. "How do you do it? How do you deal with this all the time?"

"I wonder the same thing about you, Sheriff, and if you want to know the truth, I hate it. But I don't do it for the deceased; I do it for the living. Sometimes it's the last chance they have to get someone's attention."

Hollis thanked Joel again for letting him see her and for giving him the books she loved. He left feeling like a different man; he left revived. For some reason, just seeing her gave him peace. Leah had escaped all the chaos that had gone on that day, all the problems and hatred and anger. She could be hurt by it no more.

She had made it. She had finally escaped and left it all behind. There would be no more tomorrows that she had to run from today. Hollis, in a peculiar sort of way, envied her. She was finally at total peace, and for that he was glad, but he knew he would miss her.

Chapter Eighteen

They say you never know who your friends are till the chips are down. And in certain situations, if they aren't your friends, they might as well be the enemy. It also has been said that all it takes for evil to triumph is for good men to do nothing.

Hollis Brown was of the opinion that if a man does nothing when something needs to be done, then he is no good, he is not a friend and he never was; he was the enemy all along, conveniently disguised until he could betray you.

As Hollis walked back up the dark street towards the jail, he knew he was basically alone in this fight. But for some reason he didn't care, and he found it odd that he really wasn't worried as much as he thought he would be. You see, for Hollis, knowing was always better than not knowing, and he knew that he was going to find out exactly who was against him and who was for him. There was no middle ground, no fence, no room for vacillation.

Something happened to him when he went and saw Leah; a force was energized within him.

The night air had just begun to cool. Hollis stopped in the middle of the road; the streetlight on the corner illuminated the entire intersection. It was quiet and calm around the jail, totally unlike it had been all day. He looked down the street towards downtown. He could hear the traffic, mainly kids racing up and down the highway, and in the distance, a train whistled from the outskirts of town. He looked at his watch, it was 9:22. By midnight, the town would be so quiet, you'd be able to hear a cat meow from a block away.

Hollis relished the quiet, he always had. He never liked noise; he liked peace and quiet so he could think. And as he thought, standing there in the street alone, there was something he just couldn't forget. Leah's killer was still out there, enjoying this night. He was going to get her killer one way or another. It wasn't in Leah's nature to avenge anything, but Hollis would. Leah was a light, a torch for so many people, and someone had snuffed that light out. Heaven would be one light brighter because of her, but the world, for those who loved her, would be a much darker place.

He just couldn't accept the thought that her killer might be smiling or laughing. There was business to take care of, and he had the gumption to do it. It was at that very moment that every fear he had vanished from him. The people, their petitions, Rip, the deputies who deserted him, none of it mattered, Hollis wasn't going to cower down. They could sabotage his jail and try anything they wanted, but he wasn't going to give in. Whoever had killed her was going to pay, there were some scores to settle. There was going to be a fight, and it was going to be bad, but Hollis didn't fear the outcome. Those words that Joel had read kept going through Hollis's mind, and he had no fear anymore. He was ready to walk through fire and not be burned. He had faith in God that his life was in His hands and nothing could consume him.

Though the hour was late, Hollis felt revived. When he got back, he sent the deputies home and thanked them for staying over awhile longer. There was a lot to be done and not much time to do it. He got

Harley and Lewis to erect a barricade of sorts at the end of the hall and positioned Lewis behind the table laid on its side. The barricade wouldn't stop much, but after seeing the shell casings in the street, Hollis figured they should be prepared in case sometime that night there was a drive-by. He hoped the desk might serve as a deterrent, if nothing else.

Next, they completely sealed the other door on the side of the jail. It had been chained earlier, but he wasn't worried about someone breaking in now. He was worried about shots from outside, so they covered the windows on the side door with aluminum foil and tape that they found in the break room. Then they covered the front door in the same way, leaving perhaps a twelve-by-twenty-four-inch section to see out into the street. Then they positioned another table upright against the side door. It was thick enough to stop about any caliber bullet. The problem, Hollis realized, was that by barricading the side door, he had left only one exit, the front. There would be only one way in and one way out. But that was a risk he had to take because he couldn't be afford to be blindsided. In military terms, he wasn't going to leave his flank exposed.

The thing that Hollis worried about the most was a fire, especially with only one exit. He had twenty men on his hands, and some of them were dangerous. If a fire broke out, he'd have to get them out of the building, and he knew he didn't have enough handcuffs. His choice would be to pick the worst out of the lot and chain them together, and then chain them outside to a lamppost. He might be able to lock some others in the back seat of a squad car, and the rest he'd have to just keep under guard.

Teresa helped Hollis with his checklist, and Lewis and Harley helped with the details. Sam was still asleep on the couch. He was in la-la land. The few shots of bourbon and a dozen slices of pizza had done him in. Hollis looked at the clock. It was 9:45; it still wasn't too late to make some phone calls. Hollis walked into his office and turned on the light.

Sam grumbled from the couch, "What did you do that for?" He pulled his hat back down over his face, "Can'tcha leave me alone?"

"Got work to do, Sam. I've got to make some calls."

Sam wiggled his mustache around on his grumpy face. "Ah, let it be, Hollis, let it be. I was sleeping so good."

"This won't take long, and I'll be done." Hollis picked up the phonebook and started looking up the numbers of a few old friends. Teresa brought in a whole box of pizza. It was still warm.

"They came when you were over with Joel."

Hollis opened the box, tentatively looking inside, "I'm surprised there is any left."

"I hid it from Harley."

Hollis munched one slice and flipped through the phonebook, writing down some numbers. Then he began calling. All he got was one excuse after another. Every man he talked to, every so-called friend he had, could not come and help out. Not a one would leave his house and come down to the jail for even an hour. They were too tired; had been to their son's baseball games; had church the next morning; Billy Davis said he had an "important bible lesson" he had to work on for Sunday school; and Ross Cummings said he wasn't feeling well, he had "allergies." A few were honest enough to say they didn't want to get involved, "people might get the wrong idea" and think they were helping Harley, and it could hurt their businesses.

Twig Cummings was at least honest enough to admit that he feared retaliation from Rip. All the rest just gave lame excuses. Teresa could hear Hollis lambasting them. He let each one know what he thought of them and then hung up the phone.

Sam, still reclined on the couch, turned away from Hollis and pulled his hat back down over his face. Slightly slurring his words, he said, "You tell 'em, Hollis. Tell 'em they're a bunch of sissies."

Hollis slammed down the phone and picked up another piece of pizza.

Of all the men in town, all he had ready to help defend the jail was a little attorney (and drunk one at that). Every other friendship he had was laid to waste. Hollis so much as told them not to show their faces around him again. He knew that they would now get together and seek his removal for sure. It was imminent. He had called each and every one of them exactly what they were—cowards.

Teresa stepped around the corner and stood in his doorway. She looked at him with those big, soft, brown eyes and shook her head. "Well, boss, you've done it now," she said with a smile. "Whatcha gonna do in your next job?"

Hollis didn't look amused. She chided him with a giggle and a laugh, "Public relations just never has been your strong suit, has it?"

"I hate them."

"Well now, that's a good start, come on, let your feelings out. Don't stay bottled up. Take deep breaths and let it go."

"What are you trying to do to me?"

She grinned, "Make you smile."

"I'm not real happy right now."

"Then rise above it, and do it with a laugh. You're a better man than they are, so show them."

"Think so?"

"I know so. You're the best man in this town. The fact is, Hollis Brown, you've been doing it all these years without their help, and you can do it without them now." She stared at him and folded her arms, "Look at me. You . . . don't . . . need . . . them."

Sam grumbled from underneath his hat, "They're pissants. Sissy pissants who can't even . . ." his speech was garbled and trailed off, but he came back with a resounding, "tell them all off, why don'tcha?"

Hollis smiled, "I think he said it very well, don't you, Trese?"

"Yeah, shoulda had Sam talk to them for you."

"What's Harley doing?"

"Ah, he and Lewis are playing cards at the end of the hall. It's been pretty quiet. "I'm thinking about going home, but Tom might be able to come up here for a little while."

"Hey, hon, I never expected you to stay this long." Hollis chewed on another piece of pizza, "Let me make just one more phone call."

He called his preacher. It was more of the same story he had heard from everyone else he had called that evening.

Teresa heard him slam down the phone, and she got her purse. "I'm tired, Hollis, can you walk me to my car?"

Teresa gave Sam a hug then she gave Harley one as they started to leave. Harley and Lewis pulled the table back and unlocked the door. "Harley, who would have thought in high school that one day we'd see each other like this?"

Harley stood there, tall and handsome. She had never told him that she had a crush on him way back when. He was too young for her and way too reckless. Harley smiled, "It was good to see ya, Trese."

Hollis took her by the elbow, "Come on, let's go. Ya'll can talk later."

Teresa touched Harley on the chin, "You keep your head low tonight."

Hollis tugged on her arm and got her out the door, and Lewis locked it behind them. Teresa's car was parked around back, so Hollis walked her to the car. It was something he had always done. He had always treated her like a lady.

Hollis helped her into the car and made sure she put on her seatbelt. He squatted by the car next to her window, "I could never have made it through today without you. You know that, don't you?"

Smiling, she answered, "I could never have made it all these years without you, Hollis Brown. You've always been there for me."

She paused and bit her lip. He could see it quivering. "If you get fired, I'm going to quit."

"I'm not going to get fired."

"But if you do, I want you to know I'm leaving too. I couldn't work here if it wasn't for you. It just wouldn't be the same."

"What would you do?"

She patted her stomach, "Oh, I'll have plenty of work to do. I'm thinking of just taking care of my kids and maybe writing a book."

"A book, what about?"

Just then Hollis saw a green car coming down the block behind the jail. It was driving really slowly. They were in the shadows of the building where it was dark, but Hollis whispered, "Shh, put your head down."

"What is it?"

"Shh. Be still." Hollis reached his hand through her window and covered her head, pushing it down. "Be still," he repeated.

His eyes tried to adjust to the dark. He tried to get a look at the driver, but he couldn't see him or her. The car eased down the street and stopped. He reached his hand down to his gun again and unfastened the safety strap. His hand slid over the grip of the gun. He wanted to approach the car and find out who it was, but the one thing he kept thinking about was Teresa. She was there in the car with her baby. Hollis decided to run over behind a big oak tree for cover and approach the car from behind. Just as he was starting to run, a truck turned the corner and roared down the street behind the jail, and the green car took off.

"Damn!" They both were gone; all Hollis could see were their taillights heading off in the distance.

Teresa sat up, "Was that the car?"

"Yeah, same one. It had to be."

"What's it doing? What's going on?"

"You just get home and call me when you get there."

Teresa started her car, and Hollis watched her back out, following her with his eyes as she turned the block and headed toward her house. He walked around the courthouse and jail, just checking things out, to see if anything looked suspicious. He didn't see anything, everything appeared normal. There was a lot of trash and debris that people had left, and tomorrow he'd get the trustees to do cleanup, that is, if there was a tomorrow. In many respects, he was glad Teresa was gone. He didn't want her there if trouble happened. He would never forgive himself if she got hurt. It's why he didn't want her husband Tom to come down. He wouldn't want to put her husband in harm's way either.

Hollis walked all the way around the jail and started back up the sidewalk. He could see Lewis's head through the small section they had left open. It impressed him that the aluminum foil blocked out everything else; he couldn't see any movement behind it, nor could a shooter. Still, Hollis had an awful foreboding about the night. It was now around ten thirty. Within a couple of hours, the town would be as still as a sleeping mouse. *No one is out after midnight in this town,* he thought, *unless they are looking for trouble.*

Hollis reached the entrance to the brick building. He walked up the few concrete steps that were lit by the round "JAIL" light hanging above the door. Flying insects, mainly moths and June bugs, swarmed around the light. They were so thick that the address on the wall, 304 Mena Street, was almost obscured. The sheriff then noticed all the streets lamps on the corners all the way down to the train station. Each one had swarms of bugs flying incessantly around the lights. He looked at them and wondered why they all flew in the same circular motion. There were so many they looked like a collective cloud spinning underneath the lights. It fascinated him. He watched as a few bats dipped down from the darkness into the glow, devouring hordes of bugs. He stood there mesmerized by it.

As he reached for the door, something else caught his eye. Hollis glanced to his right as a green car quietly crossed the intersection two blocks down past the funeral home. And right behind it was a red sports car. He knew of only one like it in Polk County.

Chapter Nineteen

When Hollis came back in he sat down at the computer and put in the CD that Sam retrieved from his home. The story was there. Hollis studied the data; it was financial data on Rip's operations. Sam had reason to be scared, a lot of reasons.

Old Sam was in the same boat as Harley now, and the sheriff figured he was in the boat with them both. Hollis now knew why Sam was so upset when he got back; the little attorney knew way too much. He understood why Sam needed a drink the moment he got back and why he was so eager to stay around and help out at the jail. Sam was no fool; his life was a whole lot safer there at that jail than on the streets or at home.

Hollis scanned through the records — call it bribes or payoffs or whatever. There were a whole lot of people's names there; some were pretty famous. His name was there too, along with the amount Rip had paid for Barbara's doctors.

Hollis made a copy and put it in the safe. He slipped the original CD into Sam's coat pocket. He was still asleep.

Hollis nudged him. "Sam, wake up. I'm going out for awhile."

It was eleven thirty, and Hollis decided that he would go ahead and patrol the town since things were quiet down at the station. He always drove by his house to check on Barbara when he patrolled, and tonight, the urge to check out the house was even greater. As soon as Hollis pulled into the driveway, he smelt the sweet scent of the honeysuckle vines that grew along the side of his house. A mature, green leaf magnolia tree covered much of the front of the house, and the white blossoms released their fragrance into the night air. His house was dark, though. Every light had been turned off. The streetlight on the corner of the church illuminated much of the street but only part of his front yard. He couldn't see well in the dark, and the hedge around his house cast a long shadow across his yard.

Hollis always felt a peace in his home. It wasn't huge; it could be aptly described as modestly comfortable. It was a vintage-Dutch design with a high-pitched, sloping roof and ivy trellis sprawled halfway up the side of limestone rock.

They moved there from the ranch that he dearly loved. The ranch wasn't large, just forty-four acres, but when Barbara got sick, it became more than he could handle. Besides, he wanted to be closer to his wife, and when they bought the home just a few blocks from his office, he could run by and see her during the day, and he liked that. Having the home in town enabled him to relax more; he didn't have to bail hay and fix fences when he got off work. Instead, he could drop by and see his wife during lunch, sip some of her homemade lemonade, and relax under a shade tree while she cooked up a pot of beans to serve with fresh-baked cornbread and a plate of sliced, vine-ripened tomatoes.

He figured Barbara was asleep, and he didn't want to wake her or cause her alarm. Hollis carefully walked up the stone steps hewed by Dutch masons nearly eighty years before. Each stone was so meticulously cut that there was hardly a need for mortar. The steps were aligned with three-foot-high rock walls and stone flower pots filled with zinnias and tidal waves of petunias that Barbara had planted. Hollis noticed her gloves and spade lying on the porch as he reached for the front door. The screen was unlatched, but the front door was locked. The deadbolt was enough to satisfy him, so he went around to the rear of the house with his flashlight in hand to check the back door. The backyard was a gardener's dream. He walked through an atrium of crape myrtle trees along a stone pathway that Barbara had laid herself. There were an assortment of perfectly arranged bushes and trees throughout the backyard. A large mimosa provided shade for much of the backyard, and on the other side of their house was the largest weeping willow that Hollis could ever remember seeing. It towered twenty feet higher than the roof, and at night, it looked like an eerie, shaggy monster with long hair hanging all the way down to the ground. Hollis shined his light around the yard and saw nothing but a young cottontail scamper off through the fence. Hollis figured it was probably what had been raiding the okra patch and nibbling on their cabbage.

Hollis opened the screen door to their back porch. He felt a twinge of guilt because he had been promising to rebuild it. It was old, and the wooden slats in the floor had weathered and the screens were discolored. Ironically, though the back porch was the ugliest part of the house, it was their favorite because it was so peaceful and quiet. Hollis shined his light on the doorknob and twisted it. It was locked. He looked inside and could see nothing but the light Barbara always kept lit in the Vent-A-Hood above the stove.

Satisfied, Hollis got back in his cruiser and backed out of the driveway. They lived only one block from Janssen Park, and as was his custom, Hollis drove around the perimeter checking it out. Aside from the train station, the park was the focal point of the city and rarely, if ever, was there any mischief. There were no gangs or graffiti, usually no more than just a couple of local kids hanging out; sometimes lovers found a secluded spot to make out.

There were pavilions and picnic tables under the shade of hundred-year-old oak trees. The most notable attractions were probably the two ponds with the fountains spewing in the center. They ran night and day and were connected by an arched bridge, and in the still of the night, the fountains were just about the only thing that could be heard. Walkways meandered through the park, and several cannons and monuments stood erect, paying tribute to those who served and died in wars for the sake of others. Nine-foot-high, cast iron lamps were positioned every so often along the paths, providing just enough light to make people feel comfortable.

On foggier nights, the park resembled a scene you might expect in London as a fog rose from the ponds and spread like a blanket in every direction. But tonight it was clear; scarcely a cloud was in the sky, and the church steeple cast its long shadow across the park in the silhouette of the full moon's light. The temperature was more comfortable now that it had dropped down into the lower 80s, and by morning, it would be closer to seventy. The cicadas had not begun their nightly chant, but they would, and by three o'clock they would shatter the silence with their unified chatter. But for now, it was quiet and the air was still.

Hollis cruised around the park. He spotted a car and a truck parked in the corner of the parking lot. He figured they were just kids, but he decided to check it out just in case. Hollis turned into the drive and recognized the white car, he knew the plates. It was a couple of high school girls talking with some of the local boys. They were all good kids, came from good homes. He pulled up behind them and leaned out of his window.

They could see the smoke from his cigarette curl around his fingers. "Hey, Hollis, you're working late," one of the boys said.

"Goes with the territory. What are ya'll doing?"

He heard the girls in their car giggling and wondered what they were confabulating about. Mitzy Roberts stuck her head out of her window and smiled, and he could hear the other girl whisper, "Shh! Don't you dare."

Hollis looked at the guys in the truck in bewilderment, "What's goin' on?"

They smiled, "Girls. That's it."

He could hear them giggling and laughing in the car, saying, "Ask him. Go ahead and ask him."

Hollis took a long drag off his cigarette and grinned, "You boys be careful tonight." He drove off hearing the girls still clamoring. He didn't know what was so dang funny, but they were girls; they always acted like that.

As he drove off, he heard sirens take off from the fire station just a few blocks away. The horns wailed as the trucks sped through the streets and crossed the tracks, turning right and heading south down Highway 71. He thought about following them but glanced at his watch; it was almost midnight. He noticed the gas gauge was down to a quarter of a tank so he pulled into the station across the street to fill up before they closed. As he pulled into the station, a few truckers rolled into town, squealing their breaks at the light. From what Hollis could tell, traffic looked pretty light. It was already quiet, and most of the kids had gone home.

Ricky Myers was on duty; he'd been clean for about two years now. His hair was a little scraggly and his arms were tattooed, but he was on the straight and narrow and never got into trouble anymore. "Whatcha doin' out this late, Sheriff?"

Hollis milled around the store while the pump was filling up his car. "Oh, I'm getting in a little overtime, just like you."

"Overtime?"

"Yeah, Ricky, I'm gonna need every penny if I get fired." Hollis could see the petition on a clipboard behind the counter. "Can I see that?"

Ricky handed it to him, "They ain't gonna do that, Sheriff. Ain't nobody gonna replace you."

"Think?"

"Know so. I sure didn't sign it." He rang up the gas, "That's $40.49, anything else?"

Hollis looked at the names on the clipboard. There were twenty-five spaces on each page for signatures and it was a good sign that only twelve people had put their names down. He handed it back to Ricky along with a credit card, "What if I want to leave?"

Ricky shook his head, "Don't even want to think about it. People around here just want you to catch that robber that's been hittin' up places around here for a while now; that's all I hear them complain about."

Hollis grabbed a Snickers bar and tossed a waded dollar on the counter, "Say, have you seen an older-looking, green Honda driving around tonight?"

"Yep, sure have. It was here earlier."

Hollis was surprised, "It was? Who was driving?"

"You want to see for yourself? I'll just show you. We got cameras." Hollis pealed back the wrapper and took a bite out of his Snickers as Ricky pointed to the monitor behind the counter. He pushed some buttons and Hollis watched anxiously as Ricky rewound the digital images of cars coming and going. "Here it is! Time 10:20."

Hollis watched the green car pull into the station. The driver got out wearing a baseball cap. The bill of the cap was pulled down to just above his eyes, but the bright station lights still showed his face clearly. The sheriff watched as he spit on the pavement and then scratched his crotch. He knew who it was.

"Who did you think it was?" Ricky asked.

"It's who I thought, but I was hoping my suspicions were wrong." Hollis took another bite of his Snickers, "Say, can you make a copy of that?"

"No problemo. I can make you a copy right now, Sheriff."

"No, I don't want it now. Can you do me a favor? I want you make a copy to take home with you and bring it to my office Monday . . . and if something has happened to me before then, I want you to give that to the state police investigator."

"Be glad to, Sheriff."

Hollis got back into his car as Ricky turned out the station's lights. He drove down a relatively quiet Highway 71 toward Restaurant Row. All the restaurants were closed now, though a few employees were still cleaning up and taking out the trash here and there. Hollis noticed that the parking lot at Wal-Mart still had patrons walking to and from their cars, but the other stores across the road at the strip mall had been shut down for hours. Such was life in a small town. He turned left at the last light in town and drove up past the hospital, circling around through the Rich Mountain College campus. A million things raced through his mind. He reflected back over just the last couple of hours which seemed like years. Seeing that video at the gas station bothered him, and he couldn't shake it from his mind.

As Hollis drove back by the hospital again he started thinking about all the times he had been there, all the families he had consoled while doctors tried to resuscitate their loved ones in the emergency room. He remembered the clipboard he saw at the store that night. Some of those very same people had signed petitions to have him removed, and it angered him. Hollis recounted a time when he roared up to the emergency room with a pregnant woman in labor in the back seat. He remembered how he rushed her through the doors in a wheelchair as fast as he could, wheeling her all the way down to the delivery room. Her husband was one of the men he'd called that night for help, but he said he didn't want to get involved.

Looking at the hospital reminded him of all those times he had been there for others. It reminded him of all the things he had done. He wondered where all his buddies were now — his fishing buddies, hunting buddies, friends from church. They had deserted him, they were at home in bed or asleep in their recliners, clutching their remotes in the fat palms of their hands. Seeing the hospital depressed him, so he punched the accelerator and sped away, crossing to the other side of the highway and down a back alley behind the strip mall.

He came to a halt, and his car idled with the headlights beaming down the long drive behind the stores. He knew that if the burglar had any sense at all, he would be aware that there was no police force patrolling the streets. It would be the perfect night for another robbery. Hollis decided to have a quick look around in case he was able to spot the bandit at work.

He crept along the back of the stores, looking to see if any thing had been tampered with. Two of the stores had been hit within the last year. The thief had been pretty smart. There had been nineteen burglaries in the last two years with hardly a trace of evidence. He had taken some valuable merchandise: lots of computers and high-tech equipment, a cache of guns and collectibles. They had the thief on videotape wearing a ski mask at several stores, but he always cut the power to the buildings, disabling the alarm and surveillance. They weren't just hit-and-run operations either; he cleaned house.

All the stores looked secure, so Hollis turned off his spotlight and cruised down some back streets, coming out at the train station where he figured he could keep an eye out for any cars passing through town, like a green Honda.

Those burglaries really bothered him. He kept thinking about what Ricky Meyers had said. That was really the major beef that people had in town. It was really the only stain that he had on his record. He didn't like the idea that someone was smarter than him, that a criminal could get away with all that. He had to admit he had been fooled; all of his investigating had come up empty.

Every pawn shop within a hundred miles had been checked, and not one iota of merchandise had shown up. Teresa figured he either had a good out-of-state fence or he was unloading the stuff on the Internet. As Hollis sat in the squad car across from the station, he realized that his stubbornness may have been his downfall. He had burnt a few too many bridges in the police community. For six months now he had the number of the state police high-tech investigator on his desk, but pride prevented him from calling. He didn't want some techie solving the crimes and getting the glory.

If he solved those crimes, everything would probably be all right. From what Ricky said, that was the major gripe, and he would know; a convenience store clerk hears all the scuttlebutt in town. The word "incompetent" was being used with more regularity, and Hollis had to accept the responsibility for that.

Just then Sam's voice squawked over the radio, "Fire! Out on Fairgrounds Road!"

Hollis didn't understand what the big deal was; he had seen the fire trucks leaving long ago, "So?"

"It's Harley's house."

Hollis's shoulders drooped "Give me Harley."

A dejected, solemn voice came on the radio, "Yeah?"

"I'm sorry, Harley."

There was silence. Harley finally came back on. "It's not your fault, over."

Without saying another word, Hollis hung up the mic. He turned on his blue lights and pulled out on to the highway and sped down to Fairgounds Roads. He could see the black plume streaking across the night sky from where the fire was raging about a mile up ahead. Hollis raced past an old chicken house and a couple of dairy farms and then he pulled onto the street where Harley had lived. It was an eerie-looking scene. He drove past a propane tank lying in the street. There was debris all over, glass and wood and shingles. He saw a screen door hanging off a tree limb in a neighbor's yard. He knew immediately this was not just a fire. It was an explosion.

Hollis pulled his car over, making sure there was plenty of room for vehicles to pass. He got out and surveyed the damage. The street was lined with fire trucks and pickup trucks. Men were running back and forth everywhere. There must have been ten vehicles when he got there. Hollis walked slowly down towards the fire, watching the men running around. Hollis listened to the pumper truck still spraying the house down — a remnant really — there wasn't much left but the foundation and a couple of walls that hadn't totally collapsed. They were already rolling up some of the hoses on a few of the units and beginning to wrap it up.

There were only a couple of houses on the dead-end street. The house closest to Harley's had a swing set in the front yard. The house wasn't more than seventy-five feet from Harley's place, and it was a miracle it hadn't been destroyed too. The propane tank, or at least half of it lay in the street; Hollis saw the other half just beyond the driveway of the neighbor.

Close call, the sheriff thought as he looked around observing the damage. Had it come down through the roof, the fiery projectile would surely have taken some lives, most likely kids'. Hollis walked over and inspected the tank. It wasn't burned on the outside, which, he knew from experience, meant the tank had blown from the inside out. He had seen it before; sometimes they are just accidents, usually it's arson.

Hollis watched the action for a bit. There were a few guys still putting out spot fires in the woods behind the house, but for the most part it had been contained. With all the trucks and people running around, he knew it would be useless trying to get tire tracks now. He had been to a zillion fires in his lifetime, and like most firefighters can tell you, they just have a sense for whether or not it was arson just by the way the scene felt. This was arson.

Hollis stood in the middle of the street, probably two hundred feet away from the house. Gray and black smoke billowed into the air, and water hissed from the burning rumble. Lights spun around on top of the fire trucks, pulsating like strobe lights, and the headlights of the trucks lit up the smoldering rubble like spotlights.

Except for a couple of torched walls, the only thing still standing was an old fireplace. With the fire burning beneath it, and the smoke ascending in the air against a moonlit sky, it rendered the night an eerie, sadistic feel. It offered a surreal picture of hell. Hollis walked down the street towards the fire and then leaned against one of the fire trucks, pulling out a smoke. He knew the routine; he'd have to wait. When they were done putting out the fire, he could inspect the damage and make out a report. Usually he just got a report from the fire chief, but when it was arson or suspected foul play, Hollis was more involved.

Hollis lit his smoke and propped his foot up against the truck. A familiar face emerged from the fire; it was Lester Paul, the fire chief. Lester had his boots and gear on, and as he got closer to Hollis, the sheriff could see that his face was covered with black soot and sweat was pouring down his cheeks. He looked hot and ragged.

Hollis took a long drag off his cigarette, "Arson?"

"I need some water," Lester responded. He flung open the door of the truck and grabbed a half liter bottle of water and began gulping it down. Lester finished it and tossed the bottle back into the truck. He was exhausted, "Gimme one of those."

Hollis tapped a cigarette from his pack, handed it to Lester, and lit it. Lester took a quick puff, and then coughed, "Yeah, it was arson. They knew what they were doing too."

"Professional?"

Lester shrugged, "Hard to say. But they knew what they were doing." Lester took another drag, "They cut the propane line going into the heater in the bedroom, but the explosion happened in the kitchen, so I figure they must've lit a candle and put it on the kitchen table, then cut the line and left."

"How long do you figure it'd take after they left?"

"A couple of minutes max, then the house is like a bomb." Les flicked his ashes to the pavement. "Harley's house, wasn't it?"

"That's right."

Les shook his head, "Just tell him it could have been worse. What if he'd been here?" He reopened the door to the truck and reached in for another bottle. He poured some down over his head and then took a few more sips. Tossing the bottle back in the truck, he said, "I'll have a report in a couple of days."

Hollis always appreciated Les. They had always gotten along well. Both men were a lot alike, they didn't say much, they just did their jobs and kept to themselves.

Hollis thanked Lester for the input, and Les thanked Hollis for the smoke. Les looked back toward his crew. Steam was rising from the charred ashes. He turned around and looked at Hollis, "Say, when we got here," Les pointed to the neighbor's house, "he was standing out in the front yard. He might have seen something."

"Didn't talk to him?"

Les shook his head, "Nah, went straight to the fire, Hollis. Geez, those flames were nipping at all these trees around here. We were lucky we could contain it. As dry as this town is right now, we could have lost half the city." Lester tossed his cigarette to the ground and stomped it out. "Something else, there was someone back in those woods. I caught a glimpse of him in our headlights when we turned down the street, but he took off before we could get a close look at him."

Confused, Hollis asked, "Think he was the arsonist? Why would he be hanging around?"

Lester wiped the sweat from his face. His skin was red and black. He looked like he had gotten too close to the flames and suffered heat burns. He shook his head, "Doesn't make sense for him to stick around unless we've got a pyro on our hands, but most arsonists don't go running through the woods with a gun, if you know what I mean."

Surprised, Hollis said, "A gun?"

"A rifle. And who would be poaching?"

Lester pointed to the spot in the woods where his men saw the man and pointed in the direction he took off. He said they heard a car squeal from the next block over so they figured he had a car over there. Lester and Hollis were still discussing it when a late-model SUV turned onto the street and drove up slowly to where they were standing. Neither man recognized the car, but Lester squinted his eyes, trying to see the driver,

"I think that's the preacher—David something or other."

Sure enough it was. He parked across the street from the sheriff's squad car and strolled over to where they were standing. David looked at the fire. "Geez, it looks like Bagdad. What happened?"

The sheriff didn't look too pleased to see him, "What the hell are you doing here? Past your bedtime ain't it?"

David was wearing some jogging shorts and a T-shirt. He looked like he was going to a pick-up basketball game. He even had his baseball hat turned around backwards on his head. "Heard the call on the radio, and I thought you might need some help."

Hollis took a drag off his cigarette, chiding the young preacher, "Figured you'd be asleep, plumb worn out." There was a sarcastic growl in his voice, "Tough job writing those sermons."

"You finished or do you want to ridicule me some more?" David stuck out his hand towards the fire chief and they shook hands. He didn't bother doing the same with Hollis.

The sheriff looked him up and down, "Nah, I'm done. You can go on back home. I know you must have a real big day tomorrow with your preaching. Besides, this is men's work."

Dave looked down at the fire and then back at Hollis, "Man's work? Really? Looks to me like the men are over there putting out a fire, while you're standing around here smoking cigarettes and bellyaching about how tough you've got it."

Lester shrugged his shoulders, "Hey, I'm outta here. Call me if you need me."

"Will do," Hollis said.

The two men watched the chief go back to his men, and Hollis turned to the preacher once again, "So what are you here for, really? This gonna be part of your sermon, how one day in your life you finally showed up to help out?"

David was not happy with the sheriff's cynical response. He had halfway told himself just to stay home, and now he wished he hadn't bothered leaving his house. "I couldn't understand before why you couldn't get any help, but I'm beginning to understand now. You've probably run off every good man who worked for you."

Squinting his eyes, Hollis smirked, "Not every man has what it takes."

"What does it take, Sheriff? You think assholism is the number one ingredient to make a good sheriff?"

Hollis was a little surprised that the preacher cussed. All the preachers he had known were so careful to guard their words. He looked at Dave and decided to ignore the comment, "You know, I ain't even thinking about being a good cop anymore. I'm just wanting to make it till daybreak alive, that's all. Then I can quit."

"That's your business, but I'm here to help, and I really don't want to waste my time pulling you around in your little pity-party wagon, so if you need me, fine. If not, I'm going back home."

Hollis cocked his head to the side and looked at the preacher. For the first time, he looked at him like he was a man instead of a voice box. Hollis hadn't had much respect for preachers in the past, and he hadn't thought Dave was any different, but he was beginning to change his mind, "Hum, well . . . ah, I could use another man to watch the jail."

Dave nodded affirmatively, "I can do that. I can also shoot a gun if I have too."

Hollis spit on the ground and crossed his arms, "Let's not even talk about that. I'm hoping we'll still have a nice quiet night."

Hollis pointed to the small frame house next to Harley's, "Come on, I gotta check this out." They stood on the front porch and knocked on the door. The lights were out. Hollis wondered how anyone could go back to sleep with all the noise going on outside.

Hollis rang the doorbell, and a young man finally came to the door. He was in his mid-twenties. The sheriff had seen him before but didn't know his name. He could hear kids crying in the back room as the man stepped out on the front porch, "Hello, Sheriff."

"What's your name?"

"Billy Ray Johnson." The young man stood their in his white boxers scratching himself. He was still half asleep. Rubbing his eyes, he looked at Dave and the sheriff. They could tell he had probably just gone back to sleep when they rang the doorbell.

"Billy Ray, I ain't gonna keep ya long. I know you've got to get back to your kids. Did you know Harley?"

"Yeah, I know Harley. He's a good neighbor."

"Fire chief said you mighta seen something. Can you tell me what you saw?"

"Before the blast I heard music, but it wasn't real loud. I was lying there asleep, when all of sudden I heard some country music. So, I was lying there, hoping it would go off when my little girl started crying. I got up and started to go in her room. Then I figure I'd find out who in the heck was out there at this time of night, ya know, playing that stuff, so I figured I would run them off and go back to sleep. I open the door and looked up and down the street, but I didn't see nothing."

"You look over at Harley's?"

"Yeah, but he's got all those trees over there between us, so I couldn't see beyond them, but there weren't no lights over there, and I didn't hear any music anymore, so I figured whoever it was had gone. I've got real good hearing, so it might have been up the block."

"Then what happened?"

"I went back to bed and was just starting to go back to sleep when a car went racing down the street. It was hauling ass."

Hollis pointed to the end of the block where the stop sign was, "It was going that way?"

Billy Ray nodded and scratched his Jockeys, "It's a wonder it didn't wreck 'cause it was revved to about eight thousand RPMs. She was hauling."

"She? Did you see the driver?"

"Never saw her at all. I just know the car. There is only one car like that around here. It was a BMW."

Hollis and Dave looked at each other and were thinking the same thing. "How do you know it was a BMW if you never saw it?"

"I'm a mechanic, Sheriff. All I do six days a week is listen to cars. I can tell you a Ford from a Chevy and a Chevy from a Dodge. I can tell you what's wrong with your car before I ever pop the hood. That car was a BMW, and I've heard it race down my block before."

"So whose BMW do you think it was?"

"Dallas Taylor's."

"You're sure?"

"She's raced that car down my block before, plenty of times late at night."

Hollis scratched his chin and looked at Dave; he couldn't believe the wealth of information he was getting. He hadn't considered Dallas at all. He figured if Billy Ray had seen or heard anything, it would have been a green car, a Honda. "What happened next, after the car left?"

"About a minute later, there was a huge explosion. I could feel it. I heard stuff falling through the trees in back, and I looked out and saw one big fire raging up into the sky."

"So what did you do then?"

"I called the fire department."

Hollis took a deep breath and looked around. He looked back to where Harley's house was and down toward the end of the block.

"Billy Ray, I want you to do me a favor."

"Yes sir."

"I don't want you to tell anyone, no one, not even your wife what you heard."

Billy Ray smiled, "Don't hafta worry about that, I ain't got no wife no more."

"Sorry."

"I've gone on." He pointed back over his shoulder, "I've got what is really important. That's all that matters, but I promise I want say nothing to nobody."

The sheriff cautioned him, "Billy Ray, I just want you to know something about how serious this is. If word gets out that you saw or heard something, your house could be next."

Billy Ray nodded, "Got it. Say, how's Harley?"

"He's a mess."

"Tell him I said hello."

Dave and Hollis walked back to their cars, and some of the fire department trucks were starting to leave. Hollis was puzzled about something: if it was Dallas who had been at Harley's house, then who was in the woods with a gun? And why? The thought suddenly came to Hollis that it was a good thing that he had not gotten there sooner. If he had, he might not be alive. One thing for sure, Hollis was glad he finally had some help, even it was a just a preacher. There was now a glimmer of hope that he had not had before. It felt good that someone else cared. It felt good that he was not just standing in the street alone anymore, that someone had stopped by to help. Hollis had run off a lot of people, and yet he didn't like being an island or a solitary rock. Hollis thought to himself as he looked at Dave, *Man, am I ever glad you're here.*

Chapter Twenty

Dave followed Hollis back to the station. When they arrived, Hollis locked the car door, which was something he never did, and walked across the street to the jail where he saw Lewis peeking out of the window holding a .30-30.

Hollis grinned at Dave, "Welcome to Fort Knox."

Dave walked by Lewis and wondered if the sheriff let all the prisoners carry guns but thought it best not to ask. As soon as they walked in, everyone started talking at once.

Harley was clearly upset, "Is there anything left? Do they know who did it? Can I go see it? Can you take me out there? Come on, Sheriff, I've got to see it. I can't believe it. All my stuff—it's gone! All of it!"

Sam shook his head, "He's been like that ever since he found out. Can you make him shut up?"

The sheriff held up his hands, "Sh! I'll tell you all about it. Just shut the crap up!" He pointed to David, "Dave here is gonna help us out tonight."

Harley smirked sarcastically. "First time he's helped out anyone around here."

Hollis put down his flashlight and hung the keys up on the wall, "That's enough, Harley."

Dave gave the group a "howdy" wave. He realized instantly that this wasn't the warmest welcome he had ever had. Normally he would have tried to console someone who had just lost his home, but with Harley he didn't even bother trying. Not now.

Hollis looked at Harley rather sternly. He proceeded to tell him what the fire chief had said but omitted the neighbor's statement about the BMW, though he told Harley his neighbor had said hello. Harley wasn't on the verge of tears, but he was dazed, and everyone there could understand why. He had lost everything. Harley's head drooped down, and he started to mumble to himself.

Sam leaned over and patted Harley's back sympathetically. "We can't hear you. What are you saying?"

Harley shook his head, mumbling, "I can't friggin' take it. They burn my house down. Try to charge me for murder. The only person I cared about is gone." His voice was almost a whisper, "I've got nothing left, not a damn thing."

"It will get better." As soon as Dave said the words, he wished he had kept his mouth shut. They sounded so trite, so hollow – the standard, empty conciliatory response.

Harley looked up at him. He was angry. "It will get better? Really? Think so? Ever had a couple of thousand people surround you, wanting to see you hanged? Huh? Ever had a prosecutor tell you he's gonna fry your ass and charge you for a murder you didn't commit?" Harley stood up and walked over to where the preacher was, "You gonna tell me it's gonna get better? How about this; even if I do walk out of here, I've got the meanest, baddest son-of-a-bitch in the whole state who will do everything he can to make sure I'm dead. You still want to tell me it's going to get better?"

Harley stuck his finger in David's chest, "You don't know what it's like, and it's been that way all my life."

"That's enough, Harley. I don't want to hear any more about it," Hollis said. "At least he showed up out there at your house. Your friends didn't, and they didn't show up here either, so give him a break."

Harley grumbled and walked around the preacher, "I thought he mighta just showed up so he could shake us down for an offering."

Sam cast the preacher a suspicious eye and raised his eyebrow, "Or to enlighten us on the wretched vicissitudes caused by intemperance and indulgence?"

"Ya'll knock it off. David has come here to help not preach."

Harley scoffed, "That's a new one."

Dave looked around the room. He looked at Harley and Sam. "Ya'll just tell me what you'd like me to do."

"Despite what these knuckleheads are saying, just you being here helps out a lot. I was expecting to have no one to help me, and now I have three men, maybe four if you count Harley."

Harley held up his hand and flipped the sheriff off. Hollis smiled, "See what I mean? Three men and a child. Anyways, I've got enough men to guard the jail now, so don't run off."

Sam quipped, "Yeah, and I could use someone intelligent to talk to."

Harley flicked his middle finger towards the little attorney and yawned.

Pointing to his office, Hollis said, "Good, now that that's all settled, let's go into my office and figure out what we are going to do from here." The sheriff glanced up at the clock, "Still got a long ways to go tonight, fellas."

"Hey, can I get something to eat?"

Hollis pulled out his wallet and handed five bucks to Harley and told him to make sure he got something for Lewis too. After they went in and sat down, they could hear Harley pulling the levers on the snack machine in the lobby. Hollis kicked off his boots and rubbed his feet.

Dave and Sam sat on the couch. It was the first time Dave had been in the sheriff's office. One wall was covered in barn wood, which gave the office a warm, relaxed atmosphere. It was rugged and yet comfortable. Dave sank into the worn leather couch and admired some of the artifacts that were on the wall. There were lots of old maps, pictures of the Wild West days, and turn of the century photographs of Indians and loggers.

"Where did you get all this stuff?"

Sam snickered, "Didn't you know the sheriff here is a relic?"

Hollis rubbed his feet, "I wouldn't be talking if I was you. That seersucker suit of yours went out of style about eighty years ago."

Dave looked around at the walls. It looked like a museum. On one wall there were pictures of singers, some old, some new. He recognized a few like Patsy Cline and Mick Jagger. There was a portrait of B.B. King. Dave got up to inspect it and turned to Hollis somewhat astonished, "You paint?"

"Used to. Use to do a lot of stuff, but I don't have time now."

On the wall in a glass case were two guitars. One was a black acoustic and the other was electric. "Those there are my pride and joy. That acoustic belonged to Johnny Cash and the other to Robert Hill."

"Robert Hill?"

"Heckuva guitar player. Born and raised in Arkansas, like Cash."

"The sheriff is not your regular badge and boots. He's an anomaly, a closet eccentric," Sam said.

"Well, I'm not your average preacher either. I didn't grow up sitting on the front pew, not that anything is wrong with that."

Hollis rubbed his feet and moved his toes back and forth. Sam and Dave both noticed the sizeable hole in his sock where his big toe was protruding. "Tell me later. We need to formulate some kind of game plan."

The three of them began to discuss a strategy. Sam and Dave thought they should just hole up until the morning, but Hollis thought they were sitting ducks. He was worried about another fire. The antennae wire cut earlier in the evening proved his point, "Someone could just as easily set the building on fire as cut the antennae."

The sheriff said he thought it would be best if he remained on patrol most of the night. He reasoned that they would be less likely to try something if they knew he could drive up on them at any second. What he didn't tell Sam and David was that his biggest fear was that if another fire was set, the gunman from the woods behind Harley's house would be positioned across the street somewhere behind some bushes. The fire would set the stage for an ambush. Hollis had reasoned that was what was going on at Harley's house. They were hoping to kill two birds with one stone—taking revenge on Harley and capping the sheriff.

They discussed the different scenarios they could face. Dave suggested that he might be used as a decoy. He could dress up in Harley's clothes, and Hollis could call in the state police to escort him to Hot Springs. They could announce the move to Garland County over the radio. Hollis liked the idea, but he didn't like the fact that it would place David and the troopers in jeopardy.

 "What's the point?" asked Hollis, "We are just shifting risk from Harley, to you. Either way, both of you are safer here behind these walls."

The sheriff was right, but his plan wasn't that great either. They all knew that when the sheriff went on patrol, he was putting his life on the line. But as Hollis explained, "Every time a cop goes on patrol, he puts his life on the line. Tonight it's just a little riskier." And that was true.

"Let me go with you then."

Hollis looked at the young man. He knew he would feel a lot more comfortable with someone riding shotgun, but the truth was, he needed him more at the jail. The sheriff didn't want to hurt Sam's feelings, but if something happened at the jail he didn't think his friend would be up to the challenge. He had heart but not necessarily the instincts. And Lewis, well he was good enough guy, but he wasn't a decision maker, and Harley, well, Harley was just Harley. The sheriff gave it careful thought, and the more he considered his options, the more sure he was that Dave needed to stay there.

"Sam, I need you at the dispatcher's desk. You know what to do. You know all the procedures."

Hollis put back on his boots and grabbed another bottle of water from the fridge. When they walked into the dispatcher's room, Harley was leaning back in a chair with his feet up on the console. Two empty bags of chips lay on the floor beside him, and the wrapper of cheese crackers was crumpled in his hands. His eyes were shut and his mouth was open. Hollis muttered, "Sam, look at this."

Sam shook his head, "What on earth did the women ever see?"

Hollis chuckled, "Life is a mystery, isn't it?"

The sheriff went to the john and splashed some water on his face, freshening up before he walked back out into the night. He glanced at his watch; it was 2:33. Another three hours and it would be almost daylight. *Just three hours,* Hollis thought, *three hours and it would almost be over. Three hours is not that long.*

Just then Lewis yelled, "Green car!"

"Where?"

"Just turned the corner, Sheriff!"

Hollis looked around and grabbed his hat. He searched around the desk and felt his pockets, "Keys. Keys. Where are my keys?"

Sam grabbed them off the wall and tossed them to him, "For crying out loud, Hollis, can't you remember anything?"

The sheriff ran down the hall where Lewis had already opened the door, "Ya'll stay put. I'll call you on the radio."

Sheriff Brown jumped in his car and raced toward the end of the block. No car. He drove a few more blocks down to the train station.

All was quiet. He eased his patrol car around the train station and over the tracks to the highway. A couple of eighteen-wheelers went by, and Hollis took off down the highway to the north end of town, past a row of banks and shopping centers. Everything was closed and not a car was in sight, so he whipped his patrol car in between two fast-food joints and turned off the lights. He left the car running and picked up the mic, "81, see anything? Over."

"This is 81. Identify yourself, over."

"Sam, it's me."

"This is 81, I repeat, identify . . ."

"Sam, cut the crap, it's me. I lost him. Ya'll see anything? Over."

"No, Hollis. It's all clear, over."

"I'm heading out to the airport. I'll let you know if I see anything, over."

"Roger, out."

He knew that they were probably listening on a police scanner, and he wanted to see if the green car would come back through town if they thought he'd be heading to the airport. Hollis waited and waited. A steady stream of night haulers barreled through town, but there was hardly anything other movement. Occasionally he saw a vehicle he recognized, but most he didn't know. The few cars he did see were out-of-towners, travelers, families doing all-nighters heading to the coast. Hollis's eyes flashed back and forth, and he constantly checked his rearview mirror to see if anyone might try to creep up behind him.

There had been many a time over the years that he had to pull over a local joe. Hollis had an unwritten policy that if a local drove home across town and had been drinking, he didn't give him a ticket. But if caught him on the highway, he'd lock him up, no breaks. Mena was a small town with only a couple of stoplights, so he'd usually give someone a lift to his house or escort him to his front door if he was really drunk. If he arrested everyone who drove themselves home drunk, Hollis figured he'd probably only get one vote during the election: Barbara's.

Just then, he recognized a chamber-member's car slowly careen down the road. Hollis figured he probably had been drinking out at the country club. Hollis studied the car, and it stayed in the lane. He was relieved. He really didn't want to have to deal with a drunk tonight. After a few more minutes of waiting and watching traffic, he lit a smoke and flicked the ashes out the window.

Hollis hoped the green car had gone home. He hoped it was over, because he was exhausted. He'd been up for nearly twenty-three hours and was running on potato chips, pizza, popcorn, and stale coffee. His feet hurt, his back hurt, his head was bruised, and the back of his skull had been slammed into a concrete wall, not to mentioned being nearly strangled to death by a maniac. Hollis wanted it over. He wanted to just close his eyes and let the problems melt away. He wanted rest. He looked down the street on that hot summer night and closed his eyes. The eyelids coming down across his eyes felt soothing. He felt as relaxed as if he had his feet in a pan of nice, warm water. Hollis gently rotated his fingers over his eyelids, massaging them. His body sunk in the seat of his car, and his neck relaxed against the headrest. He could hear the trucks cruising through town, and his brain went into autopilot.

Hollis was almost asleep when he heard the squeal of tires. His eyes opened and a green streak raced down the street before him. "That's it!"

He punched the accelerator and turned his wheel, and his car ignited down the highway. The buildings flashed by his window and, at about eighty miles an hour. He hit 10th street, yanking the wheel for a hard left and burning rubber around the corner. His car popped a hubcap that went sailing across a parking lot. The street went up a steep hill then down to a dead end at Dallas Avenue. Hollis hit the brakes just as soon as he crested 10th, skidding to a stop at the intersection. His knuckles were bone-white. He looked down Dallas Avenue and saw no sign of the green car, but then he saw its lights in his rearview mirror heading west back toward the highway.

"Damn!" Hollis hit his blues and cranked the wheel all the way around, burning a complete 360 in the street and flooring it all the way down Dallas and back onto 71. He grabbed the mic, "81, 81, in pursuit of green car going westbound on 71. Do you copy? Over!"

Sam was excited, "We've got you loud and clear, over."

The car was now only about an eighth of a mile ahead of Hollis and wasn't going that fast. Hollis hit his siren and came right up on the car. The car slowed down, and he could see two heads in the front seat. The first thought that came to his mind was trouble.

The car didn't immediately pull over. It passed a few businesses and then finally eased into the parking lot of the Outback Barn, a local lumberyard. There wasn't any traffic anywhere; the whole town seemed deserted. The parking lot was dark; there wasn't a single light on, and so Hollis pulled in behind them. He kept his car about forty feet away, not too close. He carefully loosened the strap on his gun without ever taking his eyes off the two people in the front seat. Hollis watched intensely for any quick movement. He could see the two people talking, and he reached for his patrolman's log on his dashboard and wrote down the license plate number.

"81, give me a run on Arkansas tag DMY 648, over."

"Roger . . . be careful."

"Hurry."

Hollis got out of the car, slipping his fingers over the side of his gun and eased off the safety.

"Unit 1, this is 81, over."

"Go ahead, 81."

"I don't know how to look it up, over."

"Shit!" Hollis realized he hadn't told Sam how to research the database. There had been just too many things on his mind. He couldn't think of everything. Hollis wondered if he could tell Sam over the radio how to perform a search but decided it would take too long. He had a suspect in an arson case in the car in front of him, and he might have a rifle in the car with him. Hollis couldn't wait.

"81, this is unit 1. Forget it, over. I have suspect at the Outback Barn, am approaching suspect now."

Sam came back on the radio and told Hollis not to approach the car, but it was too late. Hollis hung the mic up on the dash and stepped out. In his left hand he held the flashlight and shined it into the back window of the car. If he saw any movement in the car at all, he would drop down to one knee and raise his revolver in a firing stance.

Hollis listened; the car's engine was still running, which was never a good sign. His boots crunched the gravel as he walked up to the driver's side of the car. The night was still muggy, and sweat dripped down from his brow. Then the driver's side window began to roll down. Hollis slid his fingers down over the handle of his revolver.

"What did we do? We weren't speeding, were we?"

A young boy stuck his head out of the window, and he squinted into the light. It was Zack Thorton, son of the local tire dealer. Hollis grabbed the door handle of the car, yanking it wide open. He snatched the wide-eyed youngster by the shirt, jerking him out of the vehicle. He slapped the boy on the top of his head and yanked him around by the collar, ripping his shirt. The sheriff shoved him against the side of the car. Hollis screamed at him, "What in the hell are you doing out at this time at night? You're gonna get your ass killed!"

Stunned, the lanky boy muttered, "Just . . . just driving, Hollis. We're just hanging out."

Hollis held Zack with his right hand and flashed his light into the car. It was another local boy, a bad seed. He had been busted before and was known for not being much good. Hollis looked him over closely and then gritting his teeth, he snarled, "Get . . . your . . . hands on top of your head . . . NOW!" The boy raised both his hands slowly and stepped out.

"Turn around."

The boy turned around, and Hollis snarled again, "Don't move."

Zack didn't move a muscle either. He stood there against the car, eyeballing his ripped shirt without so much as moving an inch. Hollis stood there next to him and shined his light in his eyes, "Son, what are you doing hanging out with him? Does your Dad know who you're riding around with? Does he know you're out this late?"

"No sir."

Hollis yelled over at the other kid, "What's yer name, boy?"

The kid's eyes were glazed over, and Hollis could barely see his face with his long, grungy hair hanging down. He shook his head like all the dopers do and swung his hair out of his eyes, "Ah, like, they call me Roller."

Hollis shined his light into Zack's eyes again, "What are you doing hanging out with him, huh?" Hollis pushed Zack tightly up against the car and ran his hand down the side of his legs. "Stay here." He leaned into the car and sniffed the air, "Jesus Christ! How much have ya'll been smoking tonight?"

"Not much."

"Shut up, I don't want to listen to your bull. I know better." The sheriff then walked around the car to where Roller was and spun him around. He shoved him up against the car and kicked his legs apart. He patted him down while his eyes stayed on Zack. "Give it to me. I want it all now!"

He pointed to the dash, "It's under there, ain't much."

Hollis felt around under the dash. He pulled out about small packet, opened, and smelt it. "Who did you get this from?"

"Some guy passing through, don't know his name."

Hollis looked at Roller. He wasn't but nineteen; he had no hope and no future. "Don't you move, you dope smokin' ass, you hear?"

The sheriff went around to the other side of the car where Zack was still standing. He took Zack's wallet and thumbed through it. He removed the driver's license and tossed the wallet into the front seat, "Got any more dope, Zack, or is this it?" Hollis held up the bag.

"That's it."

Hollis then stepped in front of their car and poured the pot on the ground. "Watch this." He pulled out his lighter and lit it. "Evidence gone."

Groaning, Roller said, "Oh mannnn."

Hollis glanced over at Roller and mimicked him, "'Oh, mannnn.' I just did you the biggest favor you've ever had, son. Especially you, Zack."

"Yes sir."

"Don't you have a baseball scholarship to the U of A? Huh?"

Zack nodded, "Yes sir."

"Get back in the car, both of you." The two boys got into the car immediately, and Hollis lit a smoke. He walked around to where Roller was sitting and leaned his forearm on the window.

"Gimme your wallet." Roller leaned to the side and handed it to the sheriff, "You'll get this back when you come into my office and see me with your mom."

"What?"

"You want to drive around for the rest of your life in someone else's car, bumming off them? Or do you want to end up in my jail getting smack around by guys a lot meaner and tougher than you are?"

He shrugged his shoulders, "Well, no . . . not really."

"Then you better get your shit together, both of you, because you just got the one break that I'll ever give you. You won't have another. You boys understand?"

Just then car lights flashed into the parking lot. An SUV drove in; it was Dave. "You all right, Hollis? Everything okay?"

Hollis patted the car on the hood, "You boys get home." The green car pulled slowly out of the parking lot, and the sheriff walked over to Dave's car, shaking his head. Hollis took a drag off his cigarette and mumbled to himself.

"What?" Dave asked.

"I'm losing it," Hollis said. He fastened the strap back down on his revolver. "Those boys don't know how close they came to being shot tonight. I just knew that was him."

"It was a green car, a Honda."

Hollis sighed, "Yep, and that means the other one is still out there." He looked at his watch, it was 3:02. "And they ain't done yet."

Dave looked at the tired sheriff, he looked beat down. Large sweat rings were under his arms, and the back of his shirt stuck to him like it was just another layer of loose skin. The sheriff didn't look well; his countenance was drained. He leaned against his patrol car, and they talked for a few minutes. Both of them stared off down the highway and at the tracks heading out of town.

Dave hesitated and then pointed to Hollis's cigarette, "You know you're killing yourself? You afraid you'll still be here after Barbara's gone?"

"Kinda. Don't want to hang around and be alone."

"She might not either. What if you die from smoking and she lives, ever think of that?"

Hollis tossed down his smoke and stomped it out, "Guess you're right. Well, if I don't make it through the night, tell her I quit, why don'tcha?"

Chapter
Twenty-One

Natives of Arkansas are accustomed to radical changes in nature. Most lifelong residents have all experienced "the hush," a deceptive lull before the storm. For that brief time, nature seems to hold her breath, nothing moves. The wind stops blowing; there's not a rustle of leaves. What lurks is not tranquility or peace. Slow-passing, dark clouds roll spectacularly overhead and begin a methodical rotation in the sky. The birds cease their chirping. The cicadas cling desperately to the trees, their chattering wings tightly held. Everything but the sky stands still. The footsteps of danger are often not loud, rather, they quietly encircle those who are about to be destroyed. Fortunately, some men possess the instincts to know it's coming, and they seek safety before the storm.

As David followed the sheriff back to the jail that night, Hollis noticed the eerie quietness in the street. He had never seen the town so deserted. Nothing moved. It was strange for him not to hear some annoying, barking dog in an alley or see a cat prowling down the sidewalk.

Lewis removed the barricade at the end of the hall and had the door opened when Dave and the sheriff hustled up the steps.

"Lock it tight." Hollis's expression was rather grim.

"Who was it?" Lewis asked. "We was worried when didn't get no word back."

Hollis walked down to the coffeepot and poured himself a cup, "Hold it. Hold it, fellas. Nothing happened; it was Zack Thorton. Ya'll settle down."

"Zack? What's Zack got to do with this? How's he involved?" Sam asked.

Hollis looked at Sam and Lewis and mumbled some unflattering words about himself and then growled, "Forget it, just forget it."

Dave poured the old coffee into the sink and started a fresh pot. "He was just in the wrong place at the wrong time."

". . . and doing the wrong thing," Hollis added, noticing that Harley was still asleep at the dispatcher's desk. His mouth lay open, and his arms hung down by his sides. He was slightly snoring. He certainly didn't look like any Romeo. Hollis sat down next to him and plopped his feet up on the counter, "Has ole Goober here been passed out since I left?"

"Sleeping like a baby," Sam replied.

Lewis laughed, "And he snores like a chainsaw."

"81, this is 411, over." It was one of the state troopers.

Hollis reached behind him and picked up the mic, "This is 81. Go ahead, over."

They could hear the roar of the engine when he came on, "Got a possible DUI going northbound on 71. Do you want me to pursue, over?"

Hollis looked up on the map and bit his lip thinking. "411, is he swerving? Has he crossed the center line, over?"

"Affirmative, he's crossing it right now."

"411, go ahead. Pursue suspect. Apprehend if necessary, over."

"Roger, 81. Over and out."

Hollis put up the mic. He looked at the clock a bit worried. He didn't like the sound of the call.

"What's the matter?"

Hollis shook his head and got up and looked at the map. "We don't usually have drunks leaving Mena this late at night, they are usually coming in from Oklahoma or Hot Springs."

"He'll be all right."

"Yeah, Hollis, it's been a long night. You've done all you can. Sit down."

Harley sat up rubbing his eyes and looked around, "What's going on? What ya'll talkin' about?"

"Nothing. Go back to sleep."

"Can't. Ya'll keep interrupting the best part." Harley stood up and stretched his long arms up to the ceiling and yawned, "But it did feel good." He smiled, "She was fine."

"That's nice to know," Hollis said.

Sam scrunched up his face, "Man, and I ain't had any since . . ."

A frantic voice came over the radio; they could hear the sound of his engine racing, "81, in pursuit of suspect. In high-speed chase."

Hollis grabbed the mic, "Where are you?"

"I passed Acorn, turned westbound on 270, over."

Hollis looked at the map, "If he goes much further he's gonna lose signal." He clicked the mic, "411, this is 81. Cease pursuit, I said cease pursuit, over."

When the trooper responded, the signal was already breaking up, "81, I am gaining on him, looks like . . . slowing down."

"Where are you now? Over."

"81, this is 411, I am almost on him. Looks like he's pulling over."

Hollis didn't like him being out there alone. He was ten miles from town at least, and there was no backup. Hollis didn't think the trooper was hearing his signal anymore. "411, this is 81. Turn around, over."

"This is . . . can you repeat . . . can't copy, over."

A look of worry came over Hollis's face, "He's outta range!" Hollis keyed the mic, "411, TURN AROUND, OVER!"

". . . pulling over . . ."

"411, DO YOU COPY? Over." Hollis repeated, "411, are you there?"

All the men in the room listened to the radio. Nothing. Only the sound of empty static could be heard. Hollis reached into his pocket for his keys. They weren't there. He walked around the room mumbling.

"What are you doing?" Sam asked.

"I'm going out there." Hollis grabbed his hat, "Ya'll help me find my keys!"

Dave stood up, "Here are mine. Take my car. Come on, we'll both go."

"You stay here. You ain't going out there."

Harley grabbed the keys from Dave, "Hell, I'll go." He yelled down the hall, "Lewis. Unlock the door!"

They all shouted at Harley, "YOU?"

"Yeah, me. Come on, let's go."

The sheriff looked disgusted, "I ain't going anywhere with you."

Harley dangled the keys, "You're wasting time. Let's go! Come on!"

Sam pointed to the door, "Get. Both of you."

Hollis grabbed a scanner, "Alright, we've got radio. Let's go!"

The two men ran down the hall and out the door. Harley burnt a stretch of rubber all the way around the courthouse and took off down Mena Street. He blew through the light at the train tracks and floored it. Hollis buckled up.

He yelled, "Where in the heck did you learn to drive?"

"Getting chased by cops!" Harley smiled, "I outrun ya'll every time!"

They flew by all the businesses and ran through every light until the town was out of sight. Harley punched the accelerator to the floor as the hit the long, straight stretch to Acorn. The speedometer topped ninety, then a hundred, then a hundred and ten. Every muscle in Hollis's arms was clenched as he held on securely to the handle of his door.

"Harley, slow it down."

"We're here, whatcha worried about?" Harley slowed the car down to about sixty to take the hard left onto Highway 270, and just as soon as the vehicle rounded the turn, he stepped on the accelerator again. He motioned to the scanner in Hollis's hand, "See if you can get him."

"411, this Unit 1. Can you read me?"

They heard nothing. Their car sped down the highway into the empty night. Not a thing was on the desolate road. Up ahead they saw the train tracks where the highway and the tracks intersected. "Slow it down, Harley. You're going to wreck us, for Christ's sake!"

Hollis looked up the valley to see if a train was coming, but the horizon was clear. The moon's light lit up the whole valley, and they could see the metal tracks shimmering far around the bend.

Harley let off the accelerator some, and the car slowed down to about eighty miles per hour. As they approached the crossing, Harley punched it as they sailed up the ramp to the tracks. "Hold on!" he said.

The car went airborne way over the tracks, flying for thirty or forty feet before they came smashing down on the asphalt highway and fishtailed down the road. Hollis was scared to death of Harley's driving, but he had to admit to himself that his driver had supreme control over the car. He was good, far better than Hollis. Hollis keyed his mic again but there was still no response, and the two of them went speeding down the barren two-lane highway. About two miles past the tracks, they approached the Narrows, a dangerous series of S curves through the canyon. On one side was mountain, on the other side a river at the bottom of steep, rocky ravine.

Hollis yelled, "Dead Man's Curve, SLOW IT DOWN!"

Harley let off the accelerator, and they rounded the curves with the tires squealing around every turn. The car rocked and bounced around the corners, and Hollis looked out of his window, frightened, to the river below. He could see the moonlight reflecting in the cascading water and glimpsed their car's shadow skimming along the rocks. Hollis just gripped the door and clutched his seat and didn't say another word until they made it through the Narrows and the road straightened out for another long stretch.

Up ahead, they saw a car. It was coming toward them from the opposite direction.

The two cars converged, both traveling at incredibly high rates of speed. Hollis glanced over at Harley; his driver looked like a man possessed. "Harley, slow it down."

"I can't."

They watched the car approaching, and in a matter of seconds it flashed by them going just as fast as they were going. Hollis jerked his head around, "Did you see that? Did you see what kind of car that was?"

The sheriff looked over his shoulder as the car's taillights disappeared around the bend. The car was gone in a flash. He turned back around and looked down the highway. He knew that a car speeding away from where a state trooper had been meant trouble. Under any other circumstances he would have turned around in an instant and given chase, but there was no way he could now, not with a trooper not responding to calls.

Both men looked intensely up ahead for any sign of the trooper. Hollis looked down every side road they passed. The sheriff feared he might have careened off the road and down an embankment. He could be lying in a heap of burning rubble, smashed at the bottom of a riverbed, but Hollis didn't think so. He remembered that the last thing he heard from the trooper was that he was pulling over.

Suddenly they saw something up ahead reflect their lights. It was a car with baby blues on top. "There he is. He's up there, on the right. See, Hollis?"

The trooper's lights were off, which was not a good sign, and his door was wide open. As they got near, Hollis could see his hat on the ground outside the car. "Oh my God."

Harley skidded to an abrupt, dusty stop behind the state trooper's car, and both men jumped out. Harley probably saw it before the sheriff—there was a bullet hole through the windshield. He saw a shell casing lying up ahead on the road.

"Stay back." Hollis shined his flashlight around the car. He held his other hand on his holstered gun and cautiously approached the vehicle, training his light in the back seat and then the front. Then he saw the trooper slumped over, crumpled in his seat. He looked dead.

"Officer down!" Hollis grabbed the passenger door and flung it open, inspecting the bleeding man. He had taken a single gunshot to the chest. Blood and flesh where splattered everywhere, dripping from the ceiling and dashboard. Blood was running from the side of his mouth. His eyes were shut and there was no sign of breathing. Hollis instinctively rolled the man over flat on his back and ripped open his shirt, exposing a single gunshot wound to the upper left side, just above the heart. At that moment, the trooper moaned.

Hollis couldn't believe it. He was still alive. He had lost so much blood; it kept oozing out of his chest, draining down his side in streams of red, matted liquid. His eyes rolled around in his head, and Hollis knew he didn't have long to live.

"Open up the back door!" Hollis commanded.

Harley opened up the door to the SUV and together they lifted him into the back, trying to be both gentle and expedient. He groaned, and Hollis told himself, *Don't stop, don't give up.*

As soon as they moved him over into the car, they jumped in the front seat and Harley whipped the car around in the middle of the road.

"Stop!" Hollis shouted.

Harley brought the car to screeching halt, "What is it?" He revved the car's engine. "What?"

Hollis jumped out and ran back over to the state police car and flashed his light around. On the dash he saw the ticket book and notepad. Harley looked over and saw the shell casing in the road. He threw the car in park and ran to get it.

Hollis was right behind him. "Hit it," he said.

Harley punched the accelerator, and they shot off like a rocket down the narrow, two-lane highway into the night. Hollis glanced through the notepad. He looked at the last entry, "Green Honda, CDX 549." But he had known already who it was.

Hollis tossed the pad on the dash, leaned over into the back seat, and tied the seat buckle around the trooper. He took off the officer's boots and positioned them behind his head, trying to elevate him some. He knew that there would probably be no chance they could make it, not the way he was bleeding.

And as fast as Harley was driving, Hollis doubted any of them would make it. He was going so fast it sounded like the car's engine would just explode. "Damn it, Harley, slow this thing down. You'll kill us all."

"I know what I'm doing."

Up ahead they saw lights, car lights. They were coming straight for them. The two cars sped down the moonlit highway, racing towards one another at unbelievable speeds. The engine was whining at full throttle, and the headlights glared so brightly they couldn't see. Hollis held his hand in front of his face, trying to shield them from the light, and then suddenly the other car pulled over and they shot by it like a rocket. Harley never took his eyes off the road; he didn't flinch a muscle.

Hollis looked back over his shoulder and saw the other car turned around. "Oh, shit."

"Is he coming?"

"Yeah. Haul ass."

Harley floored it, but he couldn't go any faster. The engine was maxed out, and up ahead was Dead Man's Curve again. Their tires squealed around the first cliffs, and the car leaned into each succession of quick, sharp turns. They swerved across lanes and cut the corners of each bend, but no matter how fast Harley drove, the other car was steadily making up ground behind them. Hollis held on for dear life.

When they came through curves and hit the long, flat stretch, the other car was almost on them. Just then, way ahead, coming through the valley, they saw the train. The locomotive's lights raced across the terrain. They could hear the whistle and see it coming. It was roaring full speed ahead.

Both men looked down the road in desperation at the train up ahead and considered the alternative — a maniac killer behind them. He was getting closer; his bright beams were blinding as he raced up behind them, closing the gap. They had maybe a mile to go before they reached the track.

Hollis yelled, "Go. Go!"

Harley punched it, "I don't think I can make it!"

The trooper in the back moaned again. He was still alive.

The train's whistle sounded again. It was racing north full speed. Hollis looked back over his seat, and the car was now almost on them. He pulled out his gun and started to aim across the back seat, but they rounded a curve, and he was tossed hard against his door. The speedometer kept rising: 110, 120, 125. The faster they went, the quicker the other car approached, until then it smashed into the back of the SUV and lifted them up. They began swerving, and Harley tried desperately to keep control. Rocks were flying as they fishtailed along the shoulder of the road, and Hollis dropped his gun. The train-crossing lights were flashing, and the barrier arms on both sides of the track were lowered across the road. They were only a hundred yards from the crossing.

Hollis yelled, "We aren't going to make it! Stop!"

"Yes we are."

Harley then hit his brakes, and immediately the other car smashed them from behind, jarring them with the impact. The train's horn blared. It had almost reached the crossing, and Harley punched the accelerator again. They were seventy yards from the crossing, sixty, fifty . . . twenty. The other car was right behind them.

"GET DOWN!" Harley shouted.

They smashed through the barrier and soared up the ramp, going airborne again. Hollis could almost reach out of his window and touch the screaming locomotive, and then . . .

KABOOM!

They landed, bouncing and skidding down the highway with the front windshield smashed. Finally, they came to a screeching halt. Both men looked back at the fireball blazing from the front of the train going down the track. Flames torched the night sky, and they listened to the horribly deafening sound of grinding metal. Hollis grabbed his heart as if to slow down the pounding in his chest. It was the most frightening scene either man had ever witnessed — the burning, twisted wreckage trailing off into the night. Hollis knew from experience that it would be almost a mile before the train could come to a complete stop.

Charred glass was shattered over the front seat and on both men. Harley was bleeding, blood dripped down from his scalp. They looked at each other, panting, their bodies soaked in sweat, and their eyes wide with shock.

Hollis looked back at the trooper, who moaned again. He would make it, now.

They listened to the long scream from the wreckage still going down the track. Harley gulped. His mouth was parched and dry. "What now?"

Hollis couldn't say a word. He just looked straight ahead and pointed.

Chapter
Twenty-Two

The town woke up. Sirens howled. Fire trucks wailed through the streets of Mena as Hollis and Harley roared back to town.

Residents in Acorn called when they heard the big boom. Nobody had any idea what had happened. They just knew there was an explosion, a fire, and surely a fatality. There had to be.

Whenever something like that happens, there is always confusion and a lot of conflicting stories. No one knew what happened yet, not even anyone back at the jail. In route to the hospital, Hollis did manage to radio Sam on the scanner, giving him brief details, but they didn't know much. There was an officer down and a train wreck, the rest were sketchy details.

The emergency room personnel heard the report, and when the men came barreling into the drive, the medics were ready with a gurney outside. The wrecked SUV screeched to a halt. It looked as though it had been through a war zone. The front grill was smashed, one light was out. The cab and roof were bent, the windshield was obliterated, and Hollis looked like he had been through hell and back.

They started to put Hollis on the stretcher, but he jerked his arm away and pointed to the back seat, "Not me! Him!"

Within seconds they wheeled the officer through the doors and were running down the hall pushing the gurney into the operating room. Hollis painfully limped inside. He had been injured but didn't know it; his hand was cut, and his knee had suffered some abrasions from the impact.

The two of them received medical attention while the young trooper was fighting for his life. Hollis wondered if he'd suffered a concussion; the events were still scrambled in his mind. He could still hear the train's horn blaring in his right ear. He still saw the train's light glaring in his face whenever he closed his eyes. It took a few minutes for everything that happened to reassemble in his head; meanwhile, Harley chatted calmly with the staff of nurses.

One of the nurses asked him, "Let me see if I have this right, you drove the sheriff out there to rescue the officer, you saved his life driving him back here, and only yesterday you were going to be charged for capital murder?"

"Something like that." Harley yawned, "Say, ya'll got some doughnuts around here?"

At about that time, Dave rushed through the big metal doors. Hollis would have preferred not to see him. He instantly worried about Sam being back at the jail alone with Lewis. It was then that he realized that no one at the jail was in danger. He had been the target all along; that's why trooper Stephens was shot; that's why he was lured out there away from the city. Hollis had been lead into a deadly trap.

Dave was stunned. He looked at the two men getting bandaged up and stammered, "Wha . . . wha . . . what happened? Who was in the wreck?"

Harley got off the table and grinned, "Sorry about your car."

Hollis stood up and limped over to the door, "Yeah, sorry. Did you bring my car down here?" He was purposely avoiding all of Dave's questions. The sheriff motioned to the waiting room, "We can discuss it out here."

Hollis then told him, in confidence, what had happened with the green Honda and the chase. They wouldn't know for sure until they could ID the body, but he was sure it was Lucian. Lucian was the one he had seen on the video at the gas station earlier that night, and he suspected he had been the one in the woods with a rifle at the fire. Hollis figured that Lucian was doubling back and was going to set up on the ridge in Dead Man's Curve. Hollis would have been an easy mark. Even if he didn't get a direct hit—which he probably would have, considering how good a marksman he was—any shot through the windshield would probably send Hollis over the edge of the cliff.

The young minister looked confused and asked the obvious question, "But why? Why would he shoot another officer?"

"I honestly don't know. I can understand why he might want to kill me, but there has got to be something else."

"You think he was just obeying orders?"

Hollis was positive he was. Lucian had been a pawn; somebody else was making the decisions. He was expendable. Hollis looked at the clock on the wall. He was tired and just wanted to go home, but it was still dark. Dave got the sheriff a fresh cup of coffee from the machine and told him to sit down. The two of them talked in the lobby for a long time while Harley was in the other room chatting with the staff. They could hear him describing the chase.

It was just all too much for Hollis. His hands were jumpy, his nerves were frayed. He was tired and wanted a smoke—actually, he wanted a drink. He thought about asking for a sedative to calm his nerves, but the rational side of him reminded him that it was not over yet, as much as he wanted it to be. He wasn't through. He was already formulating the charges that would be forthcoming. He was sure he would be charging Dallas. He dreaded having to do it; he dreaded the reaction from the town, but on the other hand, Hollis lamented to Dave that he didn't care anymore.

The young, handsome preacher was shocked. He sat there next to Hollis on the cushioned seats in the brightly lit lobby and listened to the sheriff vent his troubling thoughts. Hollis exhaled his worries like smoke. His words came from deep inside as if he had been holding them back forever. Dave took it all in and said very little. Hollis conveyed to him some of the details, and Dave was quite astonished at what the sheriff had discovered.

Despite it all, it sickened Hollis to have to charge Dallas for the murder of her mother. One event, one stupid event, set into motion a whole series of dominoes tumbling into one another. The two women had argued as mothers and daughters often do. Leah might have been pushed and hit her head, or maybe she was struck. That wasn't murder though. Murder didn't happen till she was put in her car; that's when it became deliberate murder. That's when everything crossed the line.

Finally, Dave asked, "What are you going to do?"

Hollis rubbed his head and tossed the empty coffee cup into the trash. "I'm going back to get the warrant drawn up. I'll call the judge and get his signature. I've got no choice but to arrest her. If nothing else, I can hold her on the arson."

"What do you want me to do?"

"Stay here." Hollis pointed to the room where Harley was, "He's still in danger, and it might be best if he was here right now. We can get these doors locked, I'm sure, just to keep out trouble."

"Hollis?"

"Yeah."

Dave looked ashamed, "If I would have known the whole story, I would have been there along time ago. I'm sorry I didn't try to help out sooner."

Hollis didn't say anything; he looked too tired to speak, so he just nodded. The two went down the hall and stood outside the operating room, looking at trooper Stephens with the swarm of medical staff around him. A nurse came out and gave a pretty positive report.

It looked as though he might make it. The bullet had shattered his ribs, and his ribs punctured his left lung, but it missed his heart completely. No nerve damage was detected either, so it looked as though, when he recovered, he would get full mobility back. That was the early prognosis anyway. It couldn't have been better news. The one phone call he never wanted to make was to tell an officer's wife that she just lost her husband.

Hollis thanked the nurse and went back down the hall to where Harley was. He told him to stay put, explaining that he'd be gone for awhile. Hollis wanted to tell the young man something. He looked at the tall, tanned young man smiling and joking with the nurses and realized there had been a strange twist of fate. If it had not been for Harley Wright, Hollis knew he would be a dead man. It was Harley's driving that saved his life. He would never have made it back across the tracks. He would probably have been gunned down out there on that road, or maybe he'd have been shot driving through Dead Man's Curve, bursting into a pile of burning rubble at the bottom of the cliff. If not for Harley, he would have perished on that road and not Lucian.

Harley looked at the sheriff, puzzled, "What is it? You're lookin' kinda pukey, Hollis."

He tried to say something to him; he wanted to tell Harley thanks, but he couldn't get out the words. Instead, Hollis put back on his sheriff's face and told Harley, "Hang here, we're gonna lock this place down."

He took the keys from Dave, and Dave asked him again if there was anything he could do. Hollis simply told him he could use some help at the jail. He asked him to get on the phone and start calling people ASAP. He didn't know how the town would react when the news came out. Another mob could form, and there could be big trouble. One thing he knew for sure was he didn't expect Rip to just sit around.

Dave watched the sheriff go out and get in his squad car. It would be just a short drive back to the jail. Hollis looked at his watch. It was just after five o'clock. It was pitch black, but the sun would be up in another thirty minutes.

Hollis could hear Sam on the radio. He was shouting, his gravely voice blurred through the speakers. Hollis rushed to the squad car, unable to understand. The only word he heard for sure sounded like "Barbara."

"Oh God," Hollis thought, "please not Barbara."

He picked up the mic, "81, 81, this is unit 1, over."

Sam shouted over the mic, "Unit 1, I've been trying to reach you. Barbara called! Someone is trying to break in!"

Hollis keyed the mic. "WHAT?"

Sam voice boomed across the radio speaker, "Get there, now! She just called a minute ago!"

"I'm going, Sam. Tell her I'm coming. Tell her to load the gun and I'll be right there."

"Hollis!"

"WHAT?"

"The phone is dead."

Chapter Twenty-Three

Hollis started the car and took off out of the hospital parking lot, squealing his tires. He hit the accelerator halfway through the turn and floored it across town, running red lights and stop signs alike. His heart pounded in his ears. He couldn't get there quickly enough.

Hollis came to the corner of Janssen Park. His house was only three blocks away. He could see the church steeple far in the distance, but the park was dark except for the opalescent light of the century-old street lamps along the pathways. The fountains were flowing, and the sound of water rushed into his ears. Hollis sped by them, then by the picnic tables and benches.

Up ahead he could see his house in the shadow of the steeple tower of the cathedral. His house was dark, and the streetlight on the corner had been shot out. He threw his weight down on the brakes, bringing the car to a screaming halt halfway into his yard. He jumped out and bounded up the rock-hewn steps to his front porch. Hollis grabbed the doorknob. It was locked. Hollis shook it, but it didn't turn. The door was deadbolted from the other side. Hollis then pushed the doorbell and could hear the electronic buzzer inside. Hollis could see the kitchen light turn on and off every time he hit the buzzer.

"Barbara?" Hollis looked back over his shoulder. He felt the presence of someone there. Hollis shook the door again. "Barbara, it's me."

There was no answer. Just silence.

Hollis tried to look in the windows, but the curtains were all drawn. He rattled the door again and then stepped back and raised his leg, ready to kick it in, when he heard the shatter of glass in the back of the house.

Hollis ran over to the edge of the porch and leaned across the railing, peering around the side of the house. It was nearly pitch black; he couldn't see anything. He leaped off the porch and landed in the soft grass by the azalea bushes. Hollis reached for his gun, but it was gone. It fell on the floor during the chase, and he forgot to pick it back up. He looked around the side of the house for something to use as a weapon—a shovel or hoe, anything. But there was nothing there but bushes, long-stemmed gardenias, and a water hose. With every step, he listened, gradually approaching the back of the house. The big, screened-in porch was so dark that he could barely see inside. He had to feel his way towards the door. His heart still pounded in his chest. His nose twitched in the air; there was a strong smell of mimosa blossoms and magnolias. He sniffed again and could smell the honeysuckle.

His boot crunched some broken glass right in front of the screen door, it wasn't a window that he heard break; it was a jar, one of Barbara's canning jars for peach preserves. Hollis reached down and picked up a piece of the shattered glass that lay on the concrete steps going up to the porch. The moon tucked away behind the clouds and oak trees. Hollis reached out his hand, feeling for the door handle and awkwardly stumbling on the step.

Inside the porch, he found the kitchen door, but it was locked too. Hollis rattled the door handle—nothing. His hands shook. He turned the doorknob again—still nothing. He squinted his eyes and looked in the kitchen window for anything that moved. He could make out the refrigerator and stove, the back-and-white checkered linoleum, and the soft glow of a nightlight that was plugged into the wall. Still, there was no movement whatsoever.

"Barbara," he called, rattling the door, but Hollis knew that he had to be very careful or he might get shot by Barbara. He had always told Barbara to aim and shoot if anyone ever broke in. And if she was watching the back door when he came through, it was so dark she probably wouldn't see it was him. And, of course, she couldn't hear him either.

Hollis turned around. He could see the shimmering, broken glass behind him as just a bit of the moon came out. Someone had knocked it over or dropped it. Someone had just been there. He stepped back from the door and scanned the yard, looking through the maze of trees and shadows. A fragmented cloud passed over head. The moon appeared and disappeared, playing games in the sky.

Hollis twitched his nose, he could smell something. It wasn't gardenias or roses. It wasn't honeysuckle or magnolias. It was a musk, a cologne. He twitched his nose again, trying to figure out where it came from. He could smell it; he definitely could smell it.

Quietly, he eased off the porch and shut the screen door and stepped around the row of bushes next to the house. His left hand felt along the side of the house where their bedroom window was. He came to the bedroom window. The screen had been removed. Hollis's heart throbbed with anxiety for Barbara again. He tried to look in, but the curtains were closed, and he smelt the fragrance of musk more strongly now. Hollis turned around slowly and scanned the yard, but he couldn't see anything. He tried to jimmy the window, but it was locked. Whoever had been there had not gotten in.

Hollis decided to try the front door again, but he could barely see the front yard for the big weeping willow tree. It blocked his view of everything. The huge tree drooped over one whole half of the yard. It stood towering above the roof with its long, vine-like branches hanging like a canopy over the yard. As Hollis started for the front yard, something grazed his head. He jumped back quickly and swung. His fist swiped through the air, connecting with nothing but a wire, the telephone wire, hanging from the soffit and dangling in the air. It had been cut. Just then, Hollis thought he could see something in the shadows of the willow tree. He heard a twig snap. Someone was there.

Hollis didn't take his eyes off the impervious figure standing in the shadow of the tree. It didn't move. He wondered if his eyes were deceiving him. Was it an illusion? He felt the presence of a foreboding spirit, like the carnation of evil lurking right before him. Hollis wiped the sweat from his face. Then it was gone. It vanished, disappeared.

He rubbed his eyes, perhaps it had been his imagination. He swept his arms through the branches of the willow, but nothing was there. He sniffed again, the musky scent was unmistakable, but he also detected the scent of whiskey. Hollis felt through the tree. Thousands of leafy branches brushed across his shoulders and arms as he tried to find whoever was there.

Just then, he heard another twig snap. It was right behind him. Hollis spun around in the direction of the sound, but he might as well have been a blind man, because he could see absolutely nothing under the covering of the tree. He moved stealthily through the thick darkness, trying to find his way out. He heard something again, and he turned back around just as a heavy, metal object caught him on the side of the face. He stumbled backwards and fell on his back to the ground.

Hollis quickly rolled over to his knees, frantically searching with his hands on the ground. He couldn't see anything at all now; he had been temporarily blinded by the blow. He tried to gain his balance but tumbled over on his side. Then he heard a snarling growl above him. A husky voice growled like a seething, chained dog.

Hollis held up his hand defensively, "Rip."

His hand felt around in the darkness trying to get a hold of something, anything. Suddenly there was a flash of light, a glimpse of metal flying in his face. A steel-toe boot sent him flying backwards again to the ground. It felt s though an axe had split his head wide open. Hollis rolled over again and pushed himself up on his knees; blood streamed down his face. He looked up blinded. He could hear heavy footsteps circling him and harsh, snorting breathing.

Hollis listened to the coarse sound above him, and the smell of whiskey was now thick in the air. There was a loud, barbaric grunt, and he was kicked again. It felt like a bayonet was thrust into his side, cracking his ribs and sending him sprawling on the ground. Hollis retched in pain, and the taste of blood filled his mouth. He stretched out his hand, trying to find anything he might use to defend himself; there was nothing but grass and twigs at hand. Hollis looked up helplessly into the darkness and called out again, "Rip, don't. Don't do this."

There was no response. Hollis only heard the deep, gruff sound of breathing. It came near him and circled again. His vision was coming back, blurred and fuzzy. Hollis stretched out his hand and felt a rock in the grass. He clutched his fingers around it, but just as he grabbed it, the heel of a boot came smashing down on his fingers crushing them to the bone. Hollis rolled over in agony and let go, and just as did, he was kicked in the side and then kicked again. Hollis tried desperately to crawl away. He felt around, but he didn't know where to go. He looked up and could barely make out an eerie silhouette standing above him. It was a grotesque sight; he could see Rip moving for him through the weeping willow vines. The moon lit up his face, and his scowl was highlighted by the shadows. His eyes were deep, dark sockets, empty, bottomless holes in his face. His teeth snarled, and he grunted with each breath.

Hollis held up his arm, trying to shield himself, but his feeble efforts were in vain. Rip's boot smashed into the side of his head, just above the ear, knocking Hollis nearly unconscious. Hollis reeled across the grass, landing in dirt, and out of instinct rolled over trying to cover his skull from the blows that he knew were coming. He had seen it before. He knew the savagery of the man. He felt the kicks to his legs, the boot heel smashed into his back. It was just beginning, and it wouldn't end until almost every bone was broken and his body was ragged with gashes and holes.

Rip's powerful legs lifted Hollis's body off the ground with each kick. Hollis called out over and over again for him to stop, but Rip said nothing. He just growled and snorted like an animal. Finally, Hollis lay flat on his back. He couldn't move anymore, and Rip stood over him. He raised his boot high in the air and stomped Hollis's jaw with his heel. The blow cracked his jaw, and pain shot through Hollis's face. He rolled over. His face was in the dirt; he couldn't move.

The sheriff lay there; lucidity was slipping away. Rip rolled him over and pulled out a long, sharp, wide blade. The thick, curved knife flashed in his hand as he rotated it tauntingly back and forth. Hollis could feel his breath. He looked up into a menacing scowl, those evil eyes, and the stringy, sweaty red hair drooping over Rip's face.

Rip grabbed Hollis by his hair and pulled the knife back, "I'm gonna butcher you like a pig."

Hollis looked up into the face of death and accepted that he was going to die, when suddenly someone came from behind, twisted the knife from Rip's hand, and then knocked him backwards. Hollis looked up with one blurred eye and watched the man pick Rip up and throw him down hard on the ground.

Hollis struggled to see, and then Rip cursed his rescuer's name: "Duke!"

Rip lunged for the big man and caught him with a blow to the side of his head, but Duke punched back. His huge fist cracked the sides of Rip's face like he was swinging a baseball bat. The two men went toe to toe, swinging at one another through the willow tree. Hollis could barely make out what was going on. He managed to roll over on his elbow and tried to push himself off the ground. He could see that Duke was able get his huge arm underneath Rip, and he hoisted him in the air and smashed him face-first down into the ground.

Rip rolled over almost to where Hollis was lying and picked the knife up again. In a second he was back on his feet. He circled around Duke with the knife in his hand. Rip lunged for him and missed. He cussed him and taunted him. Then he charged, swinging the blade through the air, slicing through the willows, but somehow the big man escaped. Duke dodged the knife, moving side to side, and then Rip caught him with his boot. Rip kicked Duke's legs again and again with his steel–toe boots. One final blow took him down and Rip charged at Duke. In an instant, Rip was on top of him.

Hollis was able to get up on his knees. He tried to stand and get back in the fight, but he had no strength. He collapsed helplessly on the ground and could only watch as Rip had the deputy down and his blade drawn over him pushing it closer and closer to his chest.

Duke's massive hands gripped Rip's wrist. He began turning the knife away from him and towards Rip. The two of them struggled, and Hollis could see the knife's tip was almost turned to Rip's chest when Duke let out a horrific scream and heaved the blade up into his stomach, slicing it wide open.

Rip leaned back on his knees; his hands still gripped the handle. They shook violently, and blood rolled out of the side of his mouth. Duke looked up into his eyes, still keeping his grip on the knife. Rip stared down in disbelief, gurgling. His voice slithered some incoherent, garbled, snakelike words. His muscular body rocked back and forth and he cast one eye towards Hollis. He opened his mouth like he was going to say something, but it was filled with blood, and then he closed his eyes like a window shade drawn down at night. His head fell against his chest, and like a tree falling, his whole body toppled over, landing with a heavy thud.

Rip Taylor was dead.

Hollis and Duke stared at each other, both mortified in shock. The porch light turned on, and Barbara came running across the yard. She was in her nightgown and sobbing at the sight of her husband. Barbara fell on the ground beside him, crying and hugging him tightly. She softly touched his face and kissed him, and Hollis put his arm around her squeezing her tightly to him. He looked over at Duke and nodded. He silently mouthed the words "thank you" to Duke and then kissed his wife.

They heard sirens in the distance; police cars were coming their way. Hollis figured someone had finally gotten a hold of the state police. It's about time, he thought, they always were late. Duke and Barbara both helped him to his feet, and the old sheriff put his arm around each one of them as they lifted him up. He stood up straight, though he was still a little faint. His clothes were torn, his face was covered in blood, his jaw was swollen on one side, and stubbornly as always, he said in a raspy, defiant voice, "I'm all right. I can walk. I'll be just fine." Then Hollis glanced at Duke and smiled, "I guess this means you want your job back?"

The first light of dawn peeked over the little houses. A glow shone on the horizon, and for the first time, Hollis could see Duke's face clearly. The big man smiled.

Barbara and Duke held his arms, steadying him as he limped across the yard towards the porch. Hollis was weak, and he knew that he did need to sit down, at least for a little bit. They police sirens were closer now, maybe no more than two blocks away, and Hollis could hear their engines revving down the neighboring streets.

There was a distinct ringing coming from somewhere in the yard.

Hollis turned around and looked at Rip. For the first time, he could see him as he actually was. The knife was plunged deep into his gut, and his hands were still gripping the handle. His eyes were open; a cold, dead look was petrified on his face. But there was something else, something that he had never seen on Rip before, something no one had ever seen. He had the look of fear.

The phone continued to ring.

Hollis hobbled over to Rip's body and unclipped the phone from his belt. He looked at the number of the caller and answered.

"Hello."

"Is he dead? Did you kill him?" It was a voice that he immediately recognized. He was surprised even when she said those words how soft and seductive she made them sound.

Hollis looked at the phone, not sure of exactly what to say, and then he answered solemnly, "Yes, he's dead."

There was a long silence on the other end, and then very hesitantly she asked, "Who is this? Is this you, Daddy?"

"No, Dallas, this is Hollis Brown. Your Daddy is dead."

With a click, she hung up the phone.

Chapter
Twenty-Four

News never travels faster than when a tragedy occurs, especially in a small town. It has something to do with our morbid curiosity as human beings. Perhaps it is our love for fascination, or maybe it's an innate character defect. But within moments it seemed as if the whole town knew that Rip Taylor was dead, and rumors were running rampant.

As the sun began to rise that morning, Barbara tenderly washed and cleaned the wounds of her husband. She, Duke, and Hollis sat together around the kitchen table while the state police cordoned off the yard with crime scene tape. Other investigators arrived later and took pictures, a nd they removed the body before the searing heat contaminated the evidence.

As Barbara bandaged her husband, Hollis wondered what prompted Duke to finally show up. "How did you know where to go?" he asked.

"It was Dave." Duke said. He hadn't slept that whole night, and then the preacher called; he was already on his way to the jail when he heard Sam on the radio calling the sheriff about Barbara.

Hollis changed into a new set of clothes by the kitchen sink and sipped his coffee out of the side of his mouth. His face was more numb than anything else, and he mused that it was nothing to worry about; he had had worse at the dentist. They listened to the cicadas and watched the cottontail raid Barbara's cabbage patch.

The state police investigator knocked on the door and asked some preliminary, routine questions. Hollis obliged him, but added that he'd give them a full report later; he had pressing business to take care of down at the station. He put his arms around his wife and Duke, and the state police left.

There were people gathered all the way down the block, and when they arrived at the jail a crowd was gathering, it was not as large as the day before, but it was a start. When they pulled up in Duke's car and got out, Hollis looked around surprised. They were all smiling faces, and a whole lot of them he didn't recognize. Many of them were Mexican. He recognized Santana and Carlos but really none of the others.

There were a lot of other people too—teenagers, farmers, and elderly residents—some of which he knew well, some he hadn't seen in years. Waiting for him at the top of the steps were Harley and Dave. Hollis looked at the preacher curiously, "What's with this?"

"You said to call people."

Dave had started calling, and each person he called he asked that they call another. He pointed to the crowd, "They came down here to defend you; they are all ready to defend the town."

Hollis couldn't believe it. He called everybody he could think of and nobody showed up, but within an hour, Dave was able to get hundreds there. He had a better way with people than Hollis, and while Dave was calling the townsfolk, Sam was calling the state police who started sending units from all over—Texarkana, Hot Springs, and Fort Smith. Hollis saw a unit positioned on every corner around the square. He was impressed by all the people who showed up, who cared. He was moved. The sheriff walked through the crowd with the aid of Duke holding him up by his arm, and at the top of the steps stood Harley, smiling.

It seemed out of place to see him out front on the street. "What are you doing?"

Harley grinned real wide, "Oh, I don't know there, Hollis. I just thought I'd see if you wanted to go for a ride later."

Everyone started laughing, and Hollis broke into a smile, "Not for awhile. I think I'll pass." He looked nervously around and then looked back at Harley and cautioned, "You know, it still might not be safe for you out here."

Harley didn't want to hear it. "Will you quit mothering me? You think I care? Do you remember where I was yesterday at this time? I'm a free man."

Hollis thought about that; Harley was so right. Just twenty-four hours before, Harley was rolling into town in the back of a Texas Ranger squad car. He was shackled in chains. His life for all practical purposes was over. He hadn't had a prayer, and now not a happier man could be found.

Hollis limped up the steps and through the doors. The barricade had been moved, everything was back in order. Sam was on the phone, ordering things around like a little general, and Lewis was manning the dispatcher's desk.

Several state troopers were there standing guard, and Sam hung up the phone. He hadn't seen Hollis since before the wreck, since he charged out the door in the middle of the night with Harley. Many times that night Sam figured he'd never see his friend alive again. The only thing that Sam could say was, "Why in tarnation aren't you at the hospital?"

Hollis sneered and limped down the hall, "I heard you were screwing everything up down here. I had to come down here to fix your mess."

Sam gave him a beady squint in the eye, "Don't you get me started, Hollis Brown. You ungrateful, stubborn, obstinate, ornery . . ."

"Stop. Just kidding ya, Sam. Yer doing good."

Sam twitched his mustache and bowed his shoulders back, "You better be grateful, that's all I got to say."

Hollis noticed that both he and Lewis had on deputy shirts. Sam's shirt bulged out and was obviously about two sizes too large. "What's with the shirts?"

"Trying to look professional, that's all." Sam pointed his finger at the sheriff, "And don't you say anything either."

Hollis agreed and thanked him and Lewis for holding down the fort. He then got down to business. Within a few moments, Hollis came out of his office with the prepared warrant for Dallas's arrest. The list of charges was long. It read: "WARRANT FOR THE APREHENSION OF OLIVIA DALLAS TAYLOR." And the charges were as follows: Capital First-Degree Murder. Attempted Murder. Conspiracy to Commit Murder. Arson One and Two. Attempted Murder of a Police Officer. Conspiracy to Commit Murder of a Police Officer. And several other minor offenses.

Hollis didn't go with the state police that morning out to "Y" City to the Heaven Falls Ranch when they arrested Dallas. He didn't want to see her. Later he was told that they met her coming down the drive with her BMW packed. Apparently Dallas was planning on leaving for quite a long time. No one knew where she was headed, but it didn't matter. They handcuffed her on the spot. She wasn't brought back to Mena; the town had had enough. She was transported directly to Fort Smith and booked.

One of the biggest surprises of the day occurred a few hours later when they searched Lucian Cogburn's farm. What they found shocked everybody, especially Hollis. They discovered, hidden away in his barn and shop, computers and appliances, televisions and stereos. They found tens of thousands of dollars in electronic equipment, along with a shipping room where he had been boxing up stolen merchandise and selling it over the Internet. At long last, the thief of Polk County had been discovered

His deputy had been a crooked cop all along. He would do anything to cover his trail, even murder. Lucian must have figured that if Hollis was out of the way and he became sheriff, he could steal the whole county blind and no one could stop him It took eight hours and two moving truck to haul off all the merchandise that he had stolen, and then it was returned to the rightful owners.

When the warrants went out that Sunday morning, the brash prosecutor's career was over instantaneously. They issued a warrant for Rick Snively for obstruction of justice and withholding evidence in a criminal investigation. He had sent many men to prison for far lesser crimes than he committed. His was a very serious offense. Lots of men are tempted by money or power or even by beauty, and maybe he had been seduced by all three. But even when he had fallen prey to Dallas's seductive charms, providing inside information to a murder suspect is like giving them a license to kill. Rick Snively had told Dallas that Saturday afternoon that Hollis had retrieved her cell phone with Leah's blood on it, and that information almost cost Hollis his life. It was the catalyst that set into motion a dangerous chain of events. Rip might not have gone to the great extremes that he did just for the sake of getting Harley. But when he found out that his own daughter was the suspect in her mother's murder, he surmised that he had only one choice: to eliminate Hollis at all costs.

And so it was a day of reckoning. It was a day that the folks around here will never forget. And, as expected, the press did arrive to get the story. They got some good photographs of Dallas in the back of a state trooper car. The burned Honda being hauled away provided some exciting pictures for the paper, as did the officers loading up all the stolen loot at Lucian's farm. They also got a few shots of Harley and Hollis, though Hollis never did like to have his picture taken. Sam posed with Dave and Lewis, and then they took a photo of Duke and Hollis together. I don't know if any of them ever made the paper, although the ones of Dallas did.

Hollis finished the last of his duties and shut the door to his office. A reporter asked, "So you're quitting, just like that?"

Hollis looked around the headquarters where he had spent the last twenty-something years, "Yeah, I think I'm done here."

The reporters clustered around the cramped dispatcher's office, "Is it true that you are going to reinstate Theodore McCully as deputy?"

"You mean Duke?" Hollis stood by Duke, "No, I am not going to reinstate him as my deputy."

Duke looked surprised. You could tell his feelings were hurt.

Hollis then unpinned the badge from his shirt. He stood in front of the big man and smiled, "I want him to be my sheriff." His grin was wider than the moon. They snapped some shots of the two men as Hollis handed him the keys, "It's all yours."

He grabbed his hat and headed for the door. Lewis was on the phone. Hollis stopped and nodded at his trustee. Then he pointed to the phone, "Put it down."

Lewis looked nervously at the sheriff, "Ah, I've got to go. Sheriff wants me." Lewis hung up the phone, "Yes sir. Did I do something wrong?"

Hollis moved a couple of the reporters out of the way and walked over to the filing cabinets. He opened the drawer and pulled out a file and laid it on the desk. He then fumbled around looking for something and found it. It was a big stamp with an ink pad.

He ordered Lewis, "Come here."

Lewis walked over to the sheriff apprehensively. Hollis didn't smile. He had a dead serious look on his face.

"I want you to see something." Hollis pulled out the papers in the file and laid them on the desk and began stamping them one by one. In big, red letters every charge was stamped "CHARGES DISMISSED."

"You're free to go, Lewis."

The skinny trustee with shaggy hair was stunned. "Are you serious? I can go, just like that?"

"Yep, and one of the deputies is going to drive you." Hollis pointed to Jefferson, "Can you give him a ride home in a little bit?"

"Sheriff, how can I thank you?" Lewis asked.

Hollis put the file back in a different cabinet and slammed the door, "Get out of here. Don't come back."

Hollis looked around at everybody in the room. People had filled up the hallway, and cars were parked all the way around the block. He put his arm around Barbara and headed for the door, and there was Harley.

"You're free to go, Harley. You want someone to take you somewhere?"

Harley held up his hands, "I don't have anywhere to go."

Hollis had almost forgotten. The young man had lost everything, everything he owned and loved in the whole world, and yet despite it all, he managed never to lose that smile. "I'm homeless. I ain't got nothing."

Barbara tugged on Hollis's arm, but Hollis didn't say anything.

Harley looked at Hollis, "Can I go with you?"

"Get your gear, Harley. We've got a bed."

Harley grabbed a little satchel of belongings, and the three of them left. They were driven back to the house, past the park and Sunday-morning strollers. The sun was already heating up the lawns and lakes; another scorcher was on the way. Hollis showed Harley his room, and Barbara cooked the two men a huge breakfast with a skillet full of eggs and a plate piled high with pancakes made from scratch.

Barbara was every bit the cook that Hollis had said, and she was the most gracious host. Harley felt good sitting there with the two of them eating a home-cooked meal. It was a feeling he hadn't experienced since he was a kid. Seeing Barbara work in the kitchen reminded him of how it use to be long ago when he was kid before everything in his life went so wrong. He did feel at home, finally.

When they were almost done, Teresa called. She wanted to bring the kids by and wanted her husband Tom to meet Harley. The sheriff rolled his eyes, "Can't this wait?" Hollis reminded her, "I've been up for two days, hon."

They watched Hollis's expression as he listened to Teresa. His words were few, "Oh, crap, that's not good." Then he hung up the phone.

Harley reached for some more pancakes and piled on the syrup. He licked his fingers and glanced at the sheriff, "Something wrong?"

"That was Teresa. She said it's on the news, Dallas has already got herself a high-priced attorney. He's flying in for a press conference. Says she's innocent."

Harley smacked his lips and took a bite, "That ain't good. Ain't good at all. She can't get off, can she?"

Hollis sighed, "I don't even want to think about it. There is gonna be a price to pay for us all if she ever does." He walked over to his wife, "Hon, I'm going to take a nap."

Barbara hugged her husband. It wasn't a small hug either. She put her arms around him and squeezed him tightly for the longest time. Her fingers clutched his shirt, and a tear rolled down the side of her cheek.

Hollis kissed his wife again and then pointed around the kitchen, "You want something, Harley, help yourself. What's mine is yours. I'm getting a little shut-eye."

"Hollis?"

"Yeah?"

"You forgot something."

"What?"

"It's in here." Harley motioned for Hollis to go with him. They went back to the bedroom where Harley had tossed his satchel of clothes. He reached inside the bag and pulled out Leah's journal and Bible. "You forgot these. They were on your desk."

Hollis and Harley looked at each other. "But I would like to read them too, if that's okay."

Hollis held her Bible. His hand felt the soft, leather cover. It was well worn and read. "You want me to have this?"

"It's what she would like, don't you think?"

Hollis thanked Harley and taking her Bible, went to his room. The air-conditioning filtered cool air through the room, and he never felt so comfortable in his life. It was his custom to get down on his knees and say a prayer before going to sleep, to thank God for making it through another day. And so he did.

After Hollis climbed into his bed, he held Leah's Bible in his hand and flipped through the pages. She had written notes on nearly every page. Her bookmark was nearly in the middle, and he turned to the page. She had a passage rewritten in her own hand, and again he read quietly to himself the words of Isaiah 43.

"Fear not, for I am with you.
I have called you by your name;
You are mine.
When you go through troubled waters,
I will be with you.
When you wade rivers of difficulties,
You will not drown.
And when you go through fires
Of persecution,
You will not be burned,
It will not consume you.
For I am the Lord your God,
You are precious in my sight.
You have been honored
For I have loved you."

Hollis closed her Bible and very slowly drifted off to sleep. He felt comfort and peace. He felt his body moving through a fog. He was driving a car. The highway was before him, patches of clouds passed over his windshield, and then he heard the sound of running water—a river. He found himself standing on a bank's edge above a river he had seen many times before, and standing on the other shore was a beautiful young woman. He heard laughter and saw children with her, and he saw other people too, but he couldn't quite make out their faces. He believed it was her family. She swept her foot into the shallow current then splashed the water into the sky. And he heard her laugh.

From across the shore she smiled at him. It was a beautiful smile, full of such happiness and peace, and she waved. And then, into the fog she turned and slowly disappeared.

About the Author

Wade Rivers was born in Oklahoma but grew up in North Little Rock, Arkansas. He was once the consumer advocate for the state, became an investment banker and realtor, and now resides on a ranch in the Ouachita Mountains with his family. Today he enjoys the passions of his life: the rivers, God, his children, and writing. "Y" City is the first publication of many works he has written.